Praise for *A Trace of Smoke*

Winner of the Bruce Alexander and Macavity Awards for
Best Historical Mystery

"Vivid and dramatic descriptions allow readers to easily conjure up the
imagery as if you were watching a great old black-and-white film on
the big screen."   —*RT Book Reviews* (4½ stars, Top Pick!)

"*A Trace of Smoke* is compulsive reading with all the juiciness of the
tawdry world of *Cabaret* but told with keen insight to the historical
criminality taking place."
          —Sara Colleton, executive producer of *Dexter* and *The Painted Veil*

"Moving through the Berlin of 1931, with the monstrosity of the
next decade stirring beneath the streets, Rebecca Cantrell's characters illustrate the very human desire to cling to innocence and joy, to
do right no matter the cost, to shelter light amid growing darkness.
Both personal and historical, *A Trace of Smoke* clings to the mind."
          —Laurie R. King, *New York Times* bestselling author of *The Game*

"Cantrell nails both the 'life is a cabaret' atmosphere and the desperation floating inside the champagne bubbles. A promising debut."
                                                           —*Booklist*

"Cantrell delivers a historical mystery that works on every level. It's a
riveting page-turner. It's an insightful study of a young woman in peril.
It's an unerringly accurate vision of a society slipping steadily toward
madness. And it's written with a sense of clarity, pace, and attention

to detail that tells you this author is going to be writing terrific stories for a long time. So don't miss her debut."

—William Martin, *New York Times* bestselling author of
The Lost Constitution

"[A] haunting debut novel . . . evocative, compassionate, and compelling." —*Kirkus Reviews* (starred review)

"Evocative and hauntingly crafted, *A Trace of Smoke* is a treasure of suspense, romance, and murder. Cantrell's ability to spin history into a visceral reality is done with the artistry of a master storyteller."

—James Rollins, *New York Times* bestselling author of *The Judas Strain*

"Set in 1931 Berlin, Cantrell's scrupulously researched debut tolls a somber dirge for Weimar Germany in its last days. This unforgettable novel, which can be as painful to read as the history it foreshadows, builds to an appropriately bittersweet ending."

—*Publishers Weekly* (starred review)

"Rebecca Cantrell spins an engrossing, poignant tale in *A Trace of Smoke*. Her tightly crafted debut grips one in the secrets, among the shadows, and in a redolent decadence that will linger with you."

—Cara Black, bestselling author of *Murder in the Rue de Paradis*

"A likable and captivating protagonist, both vulnerable and strong. As Cantrell's debut finishes with a flourish, Hannah Vogel lives on in the imagination, and one might hope—in a future installment."

—*The Honolulu Advertiser*

"An absorbing plot, sharply drawn characters, and a fascinating re-creation of the turbulent days in Berlin just prior to the Nazis' rise to power make *A Trace of Smoke* a first-rate first novel."

—Bill Pronzini, 2008 MWA Grand Master

"A gritty, realistic portrayal of 1930s Berlin. Keeping the suspense high, Cantrell does an excellent job of projecting the fear of the time through her characters. Strongly recommended."

—*Library Journal* (starred review)

"A beautifully written novel . . . [Cantrell] fills our real-world shadows with dread, and she does it with such style that we look forward to each terrifying turn of events. Her sense of the rich, electric period that she has chosen to write about is spot-on, her characters consistently compelling, her dialogue as natural as—well, war."

—Loren D. Estleman, award-winning author of *Gas City*

"A very impressive debut. The flavor of the times is captured wonderfully."

—*Deadly Pleasures*

"Hannah's quest takes the reader on a tour of the dark side of German society at a critical moment. It's immersive and compelling."

—*Mystery Scene*

"It's dark, it's dangerous, it's bittersweet, and while I was reading it, I couldn't put it down. . . . A heroine to respect and one I enjoyed meeting."

—*Dear Author*

ALSO BY REBECCA CANTRELL

A Trace of Smoke

REBECCA CANTRELL

A Night of
Long Knives

A TOM DOHERTY ASSOCIATES BOOK
NEW YORK

A NIGHT OF LONG KNIVES

Copyright © 2010 by Rebecca Cantrell

A Forge Book
Published by Tom Doherty Associates, LLC
175 Fifth Avenue
New York, NY 10010

www.tor-forge.com

Forge® is a registered trademark of Tom Doherty Associates, LLC.

The Library of Congress has cataloged the hardcover edition as follows:

Cantrell, Rebecca.
    A night of long knives / Rebecca Cantrell. — 1st ed.
        p. cm.
    "A Tom Doherty Associates book."
    ISBN 978-0-7653-2045-2
  1. Women journalists—Fiction.   2. Röhm, Ernst, 1887–1934—Fiction.
  3. Germany—History—Night of the Long Knives, 1934—Fiction.   I. Title.
    PS3603.A599N54 2010
    813'.6—dc22

                                                    2010019443

ISBN 978-0-7653-2822-9 (trade paperback)

First Hardcover Edition: June 2010
First Trade Paperback Edition: April 2011

Printed in the United States of America

0 9 8 7 6 5 4 3 2 1

To my mother, my mother-in-law, and my son

Acknowledgments

I'd like to thank my meticulous and charming editor, Kristin Sevick, and my enthusiastic and supportive agent at Reece Halsey New York, Elizabeth Evans, for your help through the editing process and the publishing world.

Thanks to the writers and historians who helped ground me in the worlds of fiction and 1934 Berlin: Kelli Stanley, Amy Coulter, Mysti Rubert Berry, Mischa Livingstone, Richard Gorey, Kim Howe, Richard Friedman, Chris Keane, John McCormick, Brigitte Goldstein, Harold Marcuse, Klaus von Lampe, and Mirna Stefanovic Derfel. The writers of Kona Ink continue to astonish me with their insight, brilliance, and sheer pigheadedness. Thank you, Kathryn Wadsworth, Karen Hollinger, Judith Heath, and David Deardorff.

A special thanks to my family. Thanks to my son for thinking of the Rottweilers and the wonderful line about the sausage. You think like a writer too, my scientist child. Thanks to my husband, Toby, for providing unending support, even while running his own business and training for (and finishing in great shape!) the Kona Ironman World Championships. Thank you also to my mother and my mother-in law for all the listening and caretaking. You are the reason that books get written, the world keeps spinning, and mothers are the heroes in this book.

1

Wind rustled in grass browned by the drought plaguing Europe. Unseasonable heat and a parched smell invaded the gondola. The *Graf Zeppelin*'s massive shadow stole over tidy Swiss houses, streets, and fields. I wiped my palms on my thin cotton dress, sweating as much from fear as from heat. I had not been so near Germany since I fled three years before, after kidnapping the purported only son of Ernst Röhm.

Röhm was chief of staff of the storm troopers and commanded thirty times more men than Hindenburg, the president of Germany. Yet reports of homosexuality dogged him. Doubts that the small boy squirming in front of me could quash. Anton provided final proof of Röhm's virility.

"Good day, Frau Zinsli," said Señor Santana. Like everyone else in the past three years, he used the name on my forged Swiss passport. I had left my real name, Hannah Vogel, behind. Except for brief visits to London to meet my lover, Boris, I had not had a true conversation with an adult I trusted in more than one thousand days.

"Good day." I looked out the window again. We were nearing a large lake. The zeppelin was scheduled to land in Zürich, Switzerland, but I remembered no lakes near Zürich.

"How is the young man of the house?" Señor Santana nodded to Anton and snapped his fingers for Dieter, the waiter. Twice. "Bring me a cup of that excellent coffee!"

"Yes, sir." Dieter's gray eyes searched in vain for the beautiful Señora Santana.

"Have I told you that my plantation supplies the coffee for the zeppelin line?" asked Señor Santana.

"You have." Several times.

"Wonderful harvest this year." Señor Santana produced two sheets of stationery from the pocket of his cream-colored linen suit. Even at its hottest, Europe was no match for South America in temperature, and he always looked crisp and fresh.

"Will you show me a new plane?" Anton asked. "Please? Please?"

"Do not beg." I tousled his short blond hair. Without turning, he removed my hand. Too old for that, at nine?

"My husband loves being begged for his silly planes." Señora Santana, a former flamenco dancer, made her entrance. She paused at the edge of the viewing area, as if expecting applause, patted her sleek black hair, and dropped gracefully into a chair. Spicy perfume drifted over me, and I coughed.

Anton ran to her, hand out.

"That counts as begging." We had left Pernambuco, Brazil, five days ago and his manners had already deteriorated.

Señora Santana laughed and dropped a chocolate-covered ball of shredded coconut into his palm.

"Gracias," he said around the sweet.

"Thank you," I said as well. The Santanas seemed harmless. They were traveling to Hamburg to visit his warehouses. Fashion interested her more than politics, he spoke only of the coffee business, and neither was outwardly pro-Nazi.

I turned to the window just as we floated north over the midnight-blue mass of the lake. Cool air dried the sweat on my arms and raised goose bumps. The only lake this large in Swizterland was Lake Constance. Its depths were frigid in both winter and summer. But on the northern edge of Lake Constance lay Germany.

Dieter set Señor Santana's drink next to him and he took a large sip. He handed a sheet of paper to Anton with trembling fingers. Nervous energy, or too much of his own product?

"A drink, Frau Santana?" Dieter was besotted with the glamorous Bolivian and rarely let her out of sight. His fingers fidgeted with brass buttons on his jacket.

"Please." Her accent lent the German words an alluring lilt. "A cold lemonade."

I rubbed my palms along my cold arms, fighting to stay calm while we flew north. It was probably a sightseeing diversion. No need to worry.

Anton drew a feather, his Indian symbol, and scribbled his first name inside it. He loved Karl May's popular Westerns and wanted to become an Apache brave like Winnetou. He had invented an Indian communication system, complete with symbols, twigs, and smoke signals.

"Can you show me a new design?" Anton asked. "A plane I never saw before?"

Señor Santana tapped the sheet with his bitten fingernails. "Perhaps you have seen them all."

He and his wife exchanged a smile as Anton looked stricken. Watching him squirm was part of their game.

The northern edge of the lake came into view. Fishing boats dotted the beach, and dark pines surrounded a German lakeside town. I stared down, heart racing.

"Maybe one more." I barely heard his words, but I knew that behind me Señor Santana folded a new plane, fingers quick and dexterous, and Anton copied each movement, tongue peeking out of the corner of his mouth as he concentrated.

"Always straight creases," he said, before Señor Santana could remind him. I nodded in agreement without moving from the window.

The pines were beneath us now. We were in German air space. I inhaled sharply.

"What's wrong?" Anton's voice sounded worried.

"I do not know yet." I never lied to him, although it would be easier. "But we are off course."

"Probably nothing." Señor Santana patted my arm. "A course correction. No danger. Zeppelins are very safe."

"Indeed." Did he know how easily the zeppelin's hydrogen-filled envelope could ignite? We might as well be riding a bomb. Into Germany. But at least we were not descending. Yet.

Señora Santana fanned herself with a painted black fan, nails flashing crimson. "Where is that boy with my lemonade?"

"A side trip could be an interesting diversion, don't you think?" Señor Santana set his airplane next to his empty coffee cup.

"I have an important appointment in Switzerland. Not Germany."

"Germany!" Anton gave me a worried look before tossing his new airplane out the viewing window. The greetings he sent to each country we visited spiraled down toward our homeland.

After we lost sight of the plane's white form, he waved to people below, as he always did. When we flew low over South America, everyone waved back: men waved tanned arms, housewives waved aprons, children waved handkerchiefs or leaves, babies waved sticky fists.

But in Germany only children waved. Adults scuttled into houses or under trees.

In spite of Hitler's rhetoric, Germany was at peace with her neighbors. What had its citizens to fear from the sky? I had more to fear from the land now that Nazis ruled it. If I landed in Germany, Röhm's men would kill me and snatch Anton.

I cursed the day I had accepted the assignment, of chronicling the zeppelin's voyage, from the Swiss magazine where I worked, under a pseudonym, as a travel writer. I had almost turned it down. But I longed to return to Europe. I wanted to see Boris. I missed him. I missed the feel of his body next to mine, his smell, the sound of his laugh, his tenderness with Anton, and his solidity. He was the only tie to my old self, and the one person I dared to trust. On the sultry streets of Rio de Janeiro, the danger of Germany had seemed very far away. Like a fool, I had agreed to go.

"We're docking!" Anton shouted.

The zeppelin's motors had changed pitch. He was correct.

"Could you please keep an eye on him?" I asked the Santanas. "I must fetch my hat."

"But of course." Señora Santana laid her arm possessively across Anton's shoulders. "The boys will make more airplanes."

"Wait here, Anton. Until I come for you."

He nodded, and a grim look that should have belonged to an adult crossed his face. I trusted him to stay, brave but worried, until I returned. He caught my eye and winked. I touched my left eyebrow, our secret farewell gesture.

I walked out of the viewing room at a measured pace, but as soon as I was out of sight, I sprinted down the opulent corridor to our cabin. The carpeted floor swayed beneath me and I staggered.

When I opened our door, the scent of Argentinian roses enveloped me. Every day the steward replaced the bouquet. Just the kind of lovely and extravagant gesture my flamboyant brother had adored in the years before his murder. He had been dead for three years; I grieved still.

The cabin looked in order: beds folded flush to the wall, neatly packed suitcases lined up by the door, camp stool covered with my contraband newspapers. Since suspending freedom of the press, along with most other freedoms, a prison sentence awaited anyone bringing foreign newspapers into Germany.

I glanced at the *Berliner Illustrierte Zeitung* from the twenty-fourth of June 1934. The Führer and Il Duce shook gloved hands. Mussolini wore a black hat set straight across his head, a well-tailored uniform, and the air of confidence that befits the fascist dictator of an entire country. Hitler carried his homburg half crumpled in his hand. He wore a baggy raincoat belted too high and an aggrieved expression. Someday, Hitler's insecure smile seemed to say, I too will sweep away the last vestiges of freedom and own my land as you do yours; remember that when you deal with me. Mussolini smiled back, unimpressed.

What had really happened at that meeting? The world might never know, with most of the once-powerful political journalists dead, in concentration camps, or in hiding. If I had not fled Germany, I would be among their ranks and, while I was grateful for my freedom and the time with Anton, I felt guilty for not exposing Germany's sad and dangerous story to the world.

On top of the newspaper rested a twig with one bend in it, a secret Indian message that Anton had last stood here alone. One bend, one person. I slipped the twig into my dress pocket.

I scooped up the newspapers and dumped them on the floor at the end of the corridor. No point in going to prison for those, assuming I evaded prison for kidnapping. I grabbed our suitcases and hurried to the control room.

Captain Schmelling stood in front of the spoked wheel, gauges ranged on both sides. Struts angled off either end of the dash. Anton adored the captain and had spent every moment that he could in the control room, the top of his head barely level with the chrome compass. He even flew the zeppelin for a moment. After deeming the quietly anti-Nazi captain unlikely to have connections to Röhm's SA, I had felt safe enough to let Anton enjoy his time in the male world of zeppelin officers. I regretted it. Who had alerted Röhm?

Although it was strictly forbidden, I turned the round doorknob and entered. Captain Schmelling spared me a quick look. "Women are not permitted on the bridge." He gestured to his first mate.

"Why are we landing in Germany?" I sidestepped the mate.

"Engine trouble." Captain Schmelling looked straight ahead. "We must make minor repairs at the main hangar in Friedrichshafen. All passengers are to disembark."

He nodded again to his first mate, who grabbed my arm and propelled me out of the control room.

"Have a cool drink at the lounge. The delay is regrettable, but unavoidable." The mate noticed my suitcases. "You won't need those."

I pulled my elbow out of his grip and ran back to Anton. Engine trouble. I could not make myself believe it. In our lives, nothing was accidental.

What would Röhm expect? For us to assume that we had landed in Switzerland and walk off with the other passengers? He would station men by the ladder. Hide? He would ransack the zeppelin.

That left running. And he was a canny old soldier. He would position men at the exits.

A hot breeze from the land streamed through the gondola windows and against my face, replacing the cool breezes from the lake. All around the gondola, windows stood open to keep the passengers cool. He might not have foreseen that. What if we climbed out a window at the rear of the zeppelin and exited out the back of the hangar? At 236 meters, the zeppelin was big enough to hide the Reichstag building. More than big enough to conceal us while we made our escape.

I hoped.

The landing looked typical. Men raced across the withered field to catch ropes dropped from the sides of the zeppelin. No sign of brown-shirted storm troopers.

I placed our suitcases outside the viewing area so that the other passengers would not see them. Anton stood between the Santanas, his arm pointing out the window.

"Anton." I touched his bony shoulder. "You did not pack your bag. Come."

He raised his delicate eyebrows in surprise, as he always packed his bag perfectly, but he said nothing. He knew that I would not tell a lie about his bags without a good reason. I longed to tousle his hair, grateful for the trust between us. It had kept us alive so far.

"Excuse us," I said to the Santanas.

"You must do your chores properly," Señor Santana said. "Especially since you are the man of the house and must take care of your mother."

"I will always take care of her."

"Such a serious boy!" Señora Santana fanned herself again. "He needs more fun in his life."

"He is a little man," her husband argued. "Fun is only for small boys."

"Fun is for everyone." I wished that Anton had more of it.

He followed me to the hall.

"We are not going out the front," I said when we were alone.

"Why?" His voice dropped to a whisper.

Our lives together had been too filled with secrets. "I think there are men here for us."

During the voyage I had scouted the passages and rooms. We made a detour to a supply closet to snag a coil of rope I had seen there. After I draped the heavy rope over my shoulder, we hurried toward the rear. The interior grew more and more utilitarian until we teetered along a metal catwalk.

The floor jerked, and I stumbled. They had tied off to the mooring mast. Next we would be towed backward into the massive hangar. That meant we had only minutes until the passengers climbed down the long wooden ladder to the ground.

Together we ran to the back window. I measured with my hands. Barely large enough. My size did not help in a fight, but it was an asset while running. I glanced at the concrete floor, four meters below, then tied the rope to the frame that separated two windows. I yanked. The frame held firm. Good German engineering.

Anton's eyes shone. He loved adventure, and it had been so long since we had been in immediate danger that he had almost forgotten it was no game. That was just as well. It would do no good to have him too terrified to think. When danger threatened, let him keep his head clear and be strong like Winnetou.

"As soon as we stop," I said, "I will throw our bags out the window, then drop the rope. On my signal, climb down as fast as you can. Run to the wall and wait."

If we hurried, we might get out of the hangar and around to the front of the airport before the storm troopers noticed that we were not among the other passengers.

The zeppelin slipped inside the hangar. Everything darkened. He clutched my hand. A brave nine-year-old, but he still had limits.

The zeppelin stopped. We bobbed in place. I dropped the suitcases and rope to the hangar floor. A gray comma of rope curled on the far-away concrete.

I hoisted him out the window. Rope burned against my palms as I slid down after. The hard floor jolted my ankles, but I snatched up the suitcases and sprinted toward the back wall. His white singlet flitted ahead of me like a moth.

At the start of the trip, the captain had informed us that the hangar was so immense that it had its own weather patterns. Sometimes clouds and rain formed inside. Right now it was clear and too hot, the same as outside. I hefted the suitcases and sprinted, winded. The singlet stopped. He had reached the wall.

"Come along," I whispered. Vast emptiness swallowed my voice. I peeked over my shoulder at the rippling silver surface of the zeppelin. My gaze rose to the huge swastikas painted on the tail fins. How had this happened to my country, the land of Goethe and Schiller?

Anton grabbed the handle of his suitcase, and we skirted the wall, heading for the back exit. The sunset outlined the front of the hangar in orange, but little light penetrated this far.

My ragged breathing pricked my nerves. Stealth and speed were our only weapons.

An arm encircled my neck. A hard muscle pressed against my throat. Anton cried out, but I could not see him.

"Shut your trap," breathed a squeaky voice in my ear. A cold blade pressed against my ribs. "I can let some air into you. We only need the boy."

I nodded my chin against his arm. The knife retreated, but the man held my neck fast. His sweat smelled of vinegar.

"Put her out," said a voice with a Swiss accent.

The honey odor of chloroform suffused the air. I held my breath. Too late. My captor gripped me so tightly, I did not fall.

2

I drifted awake, slung over the back of a storm trooper who smelled as if he had not bathed since before the zeppelin left South America. To my left, Anton lay as lifeless as a rag doll in the arms of another massive storm trooper. Was Anton still breathing? I struggled into wakefulness. I could not move toward him.

"You give him too much, Mouse?" asked the man on my right. He spoke like a man in command. He had excellent diction and a light Swiss accent, like the actor Emil Jannings.

Mouse bent his head to Anton's chest, and I flopped around on his shoulder. "He's breathing good." I recognized the squeak. The man who had held the knife to my ribs. And, from the sound of his accent, he was from Berlin. A traitorous voice from home.

Grass crackled underfoot when we marched onto the field. The first passengers milled out of the hangar, silhouetted against the sunset. I thought I recognized Señor and Señora Santana at the front of the pack. They always rushed onto the field.

Because explosive hydrogen filled the zeppelin, smoking was forbidden there and in the hangar. They spent the entire trip snapping chewing gum and dashing off every time we docked to grab a quick smoke. Twin matches flared and illuminated their faces. Surely they must see us. Red embers glowed at the tips of their cigarettes, and the smell of cigarette smoke wafted across the field.

I opened my mouth to call out, but instead I floated away again.

This time I came to in the backseat of an automobile, jammed between Mouse and the storm trooper who had carried Anton. I assumed that Jannings must be the driver but would not know unless he talked.

Anton lay across my lap. I breathed to clear my aching head. He twitched and I squeezed his hand.

The automobile shot forward through the twilight. We must still be near Friedrichshafen, where the zeppelin had docked. Not far from Switzerland.

Flight was our best alternative.

I shifted so that my shoes rested against the floor. When we jumped I would need to push against something solid. Anton tensed. The men on either side of us seemed not to notice.

I counted a few breaths, then cautiously cracked open an eye. Dark trees flashed by the window, illuminated by the last gray light of evening. We traveled about forty kilometers an hour, so perhaps we were in a town with a tree-lined street, full of friendly houses. Did such a thing exist in Germany anymore? I must hope so. It was unlikely that this would work, but we had to escape as soon as we could.

I grasped Anton's hand. Be ready, I thought. One, two, three.

I lunged to the left, swinging my elbow at Mouse's trachea. Unfortunately, his muscle-bound shoulders surrounded his neck, so the target was small. I missed, but scrabbled for the door lever anyway, right hand clasped in Anton's.

Mouse grabbed my arms and tossed me back against the seat. For good measure, he slammed his elbow into my left side. My breath whooshed out. The man on the right yanked Anton across the seat.

Jannings's hands stayed relaxed on the steering wheel. "Keep her quiet, but don't—"

Mouse grabbed the back of my head and slammed my face into the front seat. My nose struck the wooden top. Blood dripped onto the black leather upholstery.

Anton struggled in the other man's arms. He boxed Anton's ear.

Mouse yanked me upright. Springs squeaked in protest. I struggled to inhale. Blood ran from my nose.

"Mind her face, you stupid bastard," said Jannings. "We're not to damage it."

Mouse grimaced, obviously used to causing pain, but unused to keeping faces pristine while doing it.

He drew his palm across the blood from my nose and wiped it on the automobile seat, leaving a dark streak on the leather. My eyes watered.

"It ain't broken." He released me and I slumped against the seat.

Air returned to my lungs in painful, shuddering breaths. Each one sent a dagger of fire down my side, but my body craved oxygen.

Anton bit his assailant on the thumb. He grabbed Anton by the scruff of the neck and squeezed. I could not speak to tell Anton to let go, that they would hurt him. Mouse wrenched Anton off the other man's hand. Beads of scarlet blood dotted his thumb. With an ease born of long practice, Mouse twisted Anton's arms behind his back. He yelped.

"Easy on the little one," said Jannings. "He's not to be harmed."

"He bites." Mouse did not let go of his arms.

"He's a child," said Jannings. "Should I hold him while you drive? We could switch, if you're not up to the task."

Mouse swore under his breath, and Anton swore back at him. I looked at him, shocked. I had not heard such language from him in years. But he remembered everything, even the vocabulary of his early years being raised by a prostitute.

I gritted my teeth and drew in a long breath. "Where," I gasped, "are you taking us?"

"Where we're told," said Jannings. "And no harm will come to you unless you fight us."

"We will comply. Release the boy."

"Do it," Jannings said.

Mouse let go of Anton's arms. Anton rubbed his wrists and glared.

"Respect your Uncle Mouse."

"You're not my uncle." Anton looked ready to attack. "I don't have any uncles."

I studied Anton. His emphasis on the word *uncle* gave me pause. Before I took him in, an uncle in his world was a pimp. Was Mouse a pimp? Did Anton recognize him? I held his hands to calm him down.

"Winnetou stalks the deer." I hoped that he would know what I meant. Winnetou knew that stalking meant waiting for your moment, quietly. Anton nodded and some tension drained out of his shoulders.

I turned toward Jannings. "We are Adelheid and Anton Zinsli. Swiss citizens. I demand to be brought to our embassy." I said it more because it was what a Swiss citizen would say than because I expected results.

"I'm sure it will get sorted out." Jannings's eyes met mine in the rearview mirror. "Fräulein Hannah Vogel."

Anton gasped, and I cursed inwardly. "I have no idea to whom you are referring."

"You will," Jannings answered. "In good time."

Anton fumed next to me. Bruises bloomed on the pale skin of his arms. I fought down a rush of blind rage at Mouse. He would pay for hurting Anton.

After the anger subsided and my nose stopped bleeding, I had time to become afraid.

We drove north and east, probably toward Munich. But Röhm should be in Berlin. Or Venice. I thought of the pictures of Hitler and Mussolini in the newspaper. Röhm absent from them. Since we left Germany in 1931 he had stood on Hitler's right in almost every photograph I had seen. His absence was unexpected. I hated the unexpected.

"He'll be glad it went off so well," said Anton's assailant. I named him Santer, after the villain in the Winnetou books. His breath reeked so strongly of beer that I smelled it even through the metallic scent of blood in my nose.

"It's not over yet." Mouse ran a scarred hand through his greasy blond hair, revealing gray streaks at his temples. His pale blue eyes had more cunning than I expected.

"Will be soon." Santer flexed his fist. "They won't give us any more trouble."

Santer in the books died most painfully, I reminded myself. I fingered my side. It hurt every time I inhaled. I breathed shallowly to lessen the pain. Every so often I endured a deep breath to keep from getting dizzy.

"How's your side?" Mouse asked. "I don't reckon I cracked more than one rib. Just enough to keep you quiet."

No accident then. He had known just what he was doing. Breaking ribs was probably his trademark.

"Thank you for your restraint." Sarcasm dripped from my words, and he smiled.

"Feisty one, ain't you?" He wound a strand of my hair, the same shade of blond as his own, around his index finger.

I yanked my head away.

"None of that." Jannings watched in the rearview mirror. "The boss has his own plans for her."

Mouse shrugged. "Maybe after."

I sucked in a deep breath and winced. Anton shot Mouse a murderous look. I grabbed Anton's arm.

"Cracked rib," I told him, thinking back to my nursing training during the Great War. "Nothing serious." I did not add that it might be serious and was always painful. Instead I smiled, but he looked unconvinced.

"Where are we going?" I asked again.

No one bothered to answer. Mouse tipped his uniform hat over his eyes and started to snore.

Santer reached across me. I gasped when he pressed on my rib. He thumped Mouse on the chest. Mouse snorted and turned to the side.

Silence reigned.

Even with the windows down, it was too hot jammed between Mouse and Santer. I hugged Anton's small form. Under normal circumstances he never would have allowed it, but he was as frightened as I.

We looked out the window. Dark fields streamed by. If houses existed out there, all were unlit.

"This is Germany," Anton whispered. "My homeland."

"You were born here." I wished he had not used the word *home-land*.

I ran my fingers along the bridge of my nose. It did not feel broken. "It was a different country then." I did not try to keep anger and bitter-ness from my voice.

"It's a better country now," Jannings said. "Stronger."

"Stronger does not always mean better," I answered.

"It does." Jannings kept his eyes on the road. "You'd do well to remember that."

Santer fell asleep. I thought of attempting another escape, but the automobile traveled at least eighty kilometers per hour. Even if we landed uninjured, we had nowhere to hide. I twisted around. The round hump of the trunk was where we might end up if we tried to flee again.

Anton sat as alert as an Indian scout, waiting for his chance. I was proud of him, but furious with myself. How could I have accepted the zeppelin assignment? Switzerland was too close to Germany.

We approached the outskirts of a large city; Jannings slowed. House windows glowed yellow on either side of the road. Perhaps someone would hide us, or come to our defense.

"Almost there." Jannings handed Mouse a brown bottle. He with-drew the glass stopper. The odor of chloroform filled the car. I kicked at his hand. If the bottle broke, everyone might go down. But Mouse was too strong and had no qualms about leaning on my rib.

Anton struggled against Santer, cursing.

Mouse smashed a damp cloth against my throbbing nose. A sticky sweetness filled my mouth. Air shimmered, moved, and then it was dark.

I woke stretched flat on a bed, my clothing stuck to me. How long had I been unconscious? My head pounded, my nose ached, and my side burned. Moaning, I rolled onto my injured rib. We told our patients to lie so, to let them inflate the uninjured lung fully. Now that it was my own rib, I regretted how blithely I gave that instruction to wounded soldiers almost twenty years ago, surprised none had taken me to task for dispensing such painful and probably useless information. I lay still, breathing shallowly, afraid to open my eyes. Was I in a concentration camp?

I forced open my eyelids. Dark wainscoting clad the walls to waist height, flocked yellow wallpaper above. My suitcase rested next to a waxed, pine Biedermeier wardrobe, near the front door, as if deposited by a friendly bellhop. Heavy curtains covered the windows, blocking out all light. A green-shaded lamp shone on the night table next to my bed. Next to the table stood a solid wooden chair.

Seated in the chair was Ernst Röhm.

He had caught me. Despite my fear, an unexpected feeling of relief washed over me. At least my running was over.

He wore cream-colored pajamas and a dark brown dressing gown. Ankle crossed over his knee, he read as if he were a husband at his wife's bedside. His face was more tan than I remembered, except for a pale stripe across the top of his forehead where his uniform cap rested.

"The princess awakes." He rolled the *r* in his Bavarian throat.

"Good evening, Herr Röhm." I avoided his military title, an insult he would recognize. I dared not start this encounter from a point of weakness.

"Chief of Staff Röhm or Minister Röhm," he corrected, running a hand along his black hair, shaved bristle-short on the sides and a fraction longer on top.

I thought of pointing out that, although a member of the Cabinet, he had no official department. It must rankle him to be the only Cabinet member without a portfolio, but he spoke before I had a chance to needle him.

"You've been a naughty girl and caused me a great deal of trouble." He shook his fat finger at me as at an errant child.

"I did not publish the letters." I wished that three years ago I had used those sexually explicit letters to destroy his career. Instead

I had chosen to flee from Röhm and his scheme that required me to marry him and raise Anton as a Nazi.

He smiled, pushing up the pink scars that ran across his cheeks and nose. "But you did not come back as you promised, did you? You left me at the altar."

"Poor dear." Wincing, I hauled myself into a sitting position. I had to be cool and fearless, as my brother Ernst would have been. "Let it out, Old Bird," he used to say. "Stop worrying about what's proper and start thinking about what's funny."

Röhm uncrossed his legs. "I wanted you in the dress my mother wore to her wedding, a kiss at the altar, and photographers to capture it. That June."

"You would have made a lovely June bride," I said, "with flowers in your hair."

He chuckled. "Your sharp tongue is so like your brother's."

Knowing it was useless, I pulled out the weak bargaining chip I had, the one I used to buy time to escape before. "The letters—"

"Your blackmail letters don't concern me." He waved his pudgy hand impatiently. "You follow the news. The *Munich Post* published similar letters in 1932. Those charges were dismissed. At that time I commanded thousands of men. Now I command millions."

He stared into the middle distance. "And I have my son. Anton will prove useful to me. You . . ." He smiled. I almost flinched. "You are an unexpected conquest. I did not expect my men to take you alive. Either they are very skilled, or you were deliberately careless. Perhaps you wanted me to catch you?"

"What do you wish from me?" He wanted something or his men would have had no scruples against disfiguring my face.

"Same as before."

I swallowed a wave of nausea. "If you command millions of men, surely you can find one woman to command as well."

"But as you well know, women do not interest me. In the absence of such . . . interest, I am forced to pretend." He rose from his chair and approached the bed. Every hair on my arms stood on end. How had my brother loved such a man?

His gaze traveled from my hair to my eyes before settling on my mouth. I drew back as far as the bed would allow, every inch of my back pressing against the cold headboard.

"You see, Hannah"—his voice was low and husky—"I'm no longer young. My imagination's not as vivid as it would need to be to marry an ordinary woman." He sat on the edge of the bed, trapping me farther within the bed's tight sheets. He stared into my eyes and I wondered if he noticed that they were blue or whether for him they would always be brown, like my brother's. His hand rose and hovered over the crown of my head, as though about to stroke my hair.

"What do you want from me?" My voice came out sharp and feminine, very different from my brother's.

The sound startled him. His hand froze, withdrew. Quietly, but forcefully, he whispered, "Your face. The face of your brother. The boy I loved."

I shuddered, knowing how dangerous Röhm could be, especially to those he loved. "No."

He chuckled again, then rose and returned to his chair. "You are the one for me, Hannah. Or at least your brother was. Our marriage will make the party happy. When we have another child, it will finally put to rest enough doubts that I can concentrate on my real duties."

"I must see Anton."

"It's difficult, isn't it?" He leaned back in his chair. "When a parent is separated from his child."

I ground my teeth. Even if he was Anton's father, a fact I doubted, he had spent only days with him. He let a drug-addicted prostitute raise Anton until his existence proved politically convenient. He had not missed him out of paternal affection. He was paying me back for the kidnapping. One part of me did not blame him. The other was ready to kill him to get to my son—more mine than his anyway.

The door was behind Röhm. He leaned close, musky cologne and horse sweat smell reminding me of my father. Officers started the day by riding. I swallowed another wave of nausea.

"Even if you escape this room, pigeon, how will you find him?" He raised one black eyebrow.

"The police—"

He threw back his head and laughed, long and hard. "I own the police. I own the party. Soon I will own the military."

"Hitler allows this?"

"The Corporal does as he's told," he answered, heat in his voice.

I sagged against the carved wooden headboard and sucked in a long, painful breath.

"Cracked rib?" he asked, without a trace of sympathy. "My soldiers and I can do as we please with you, as long as you can stand at the altar."

I had seen enough accounts, always in non-German papers, of the torture of the party's enemies to know what he could do to me. I had heard of a body recovered with fist-sized hunks of flesh missing. The death certificate listed the cause of death as dysentery.

A concentration camp had opened at Dachau, just outside of Munich, little more than a year ago. The Nazis had filled it with Socialists, Communists, journalists, and anyone else they disliked. For all I knew, I was there now.

But this room felt like a hotel. And Theodor Eicke of Himmler's SS ran Dachau. Röhm would not stay somewhere that Himmler ruled. They were locked in an ongoing rivalry for Hitler's favor. Röhm had Hitler's affection, force, and millions of brown-shirted SA men at his disposal. Himmler had a knack for treachery, his highly disciplined SS blackshirts, and the top generals in the German army on his side.

I bet on Himmler to win in the end. Hitler needed those generals more than he needed his old friend. Röhm would prevail only if he tread lightly. I almost smiled. He never bothered to tread lightly. Still, he had come far, and it would not do for anyone to underestimate him. Look where that had landed me.

His hard blue eyes appraised me. I lifted my chin and gave him the most nonchalant look I could muster.

"You will be assigned a detail of men. To watch you when I'm not enjoying the pleasure of your company."

"And Anton?"

"If you wish to live, this afternoon you and I will be married. White dress, photographers, press, and party dignitaries. After a few weeks, if you behave, you shall return to Switzerland. I'll say you're ill and need a special cure available there. I don't need a wife at my side constantly. But you will have watchers, always, in case I need you to come back."

I stifled a shudder. "Will Anton attend our wedding?"

"Anton will attend the National Political Institute for Education in Potsdam. He can come to me in Berlin on weekends." His voice was confident and sure, the voice that convinced soldiers to leap out of trenches and be cut down like wheat. "They will mold him into a proper soldier for the National Socialist movement."

"He is only nine." My heart thumped against my ribs. Those schools taught brutality. They admitted only children of Nazi-approved racial background, and with perfect hearing and vision. After that at least one fifth of the children either washed out or went home too badly injured to continue. "He cannot board until eleven."

"I spoke to the headmaster." He smiled as if we were having a pleasant morning's conversation.

"You have been thorough." I swung my legs over the side of the bed. My head spun. Effects of chloroform or hopelessness? I closed my eyes.

"As is my wont." The chair creaked as he stood. "You will find that I am effective. But not a brute."

I raised my head to look at him, skeptical.

"I reward loyalty and obedience." He pushed me down on the bed with one hand, palm flat against my breastbone. "The reverse is also true."

Pain stabbed from my rib. I could not breathe. Flashes of light dazzled my eyes. I struggled to inhale, but more than that, I struggled to keep fear from my eyes. Never show a dog fear, my father always said. Darkness closed in around the sides of my vision.

3

Röhm lifted his hand, and I sucked in a lungful of air, unable to keep from crying out when my lungs pressed against the rib. I bit back a second cry. Let him kill me then, but I would not buckle. As soon as I could lift my head, I glared at him.

"We'll get on well, pigeon," he said.

I will stab you in your sleep, I thought. "I suppose I must hope that we do," I answered aloud.

He gestured to a door set against the wall. "Bathe yourself. Change your clothes. I've laid out a dress on the sink and drawn you a bath."

"How thoughtful."

"I've also removed the lock and handle."

I rose shakily and stumbled to the bathroom. The floor pitched and moved, like the zeppelin's.

I hooked my finger through the hole that had recently held the door handle and lock and opened the bathroom door. Knowing that it would not keep him out should he want to come in, I closed the door and collapsed with my back against the wood, floor tiles cold against the backs of my legs.

I caught my breath. Röhm felt certain he had me trapped. But there must be a way out. There was always a way out. I turned on the light. The only exit from the bathroom was the door, and a window too tiny for a towel to fit through. Early morning light shone through. I had been unconscious for hours, for the entire night. Anton might be any-where. I clenched my hands. I would not give in to worry.

Blood stained the front of my cotton dress. I considered washing it, but did not. Instead I stripped it off, cursing Mouse each time I moved. Remembering Anton's twig, I searched my pockets. Like Anton, the little twig was gone.

I folded the dress and placed it on the counter, avoiding the mirror. I could not see myself this way.

Röhm had arrayed his toiletries with military precision on a table near the sink. I rummaged through his shaving kit, but it contained only a shaving brush and soap. He had secured the razor, to keep me from harming myself, or him. Thorough indeed.

The water in the massive tub was barely lukewarm. I thought of heating it, but I would not give him the satisfaction of knowing it both-ered me. I scrubbed dried blood from my face and hands, and washed my hair. Imprinted in the soap was HANSELBAUER SPA. Bavarian?

Large and luxurious towels hung by the bathtub. A spa. Was he here for a cure? I hoped his illness was fatal.

Cleaned up, I took stock of myself in the mirror over the large sink. My nose looked fine. A purple bruise the size and shape of Mouse's elbow rested below my left breast. I slid my fingers across the bruise to press on each rib. Only one rib cracked, just as he had predicted. He knew his business.

I ran Röhm's hairbrush through my wet bobbed hair. Worried lines on my gaunt face marked me as a reluctant bride-to-be. Tears welled up, and I forced them down. The way through this was to remain calm and cool. I would escape and break Anton out of that Nazi boarding school.

My father would have been proud. I was about to marry a highly decorated officer. Iron Cross First Class, wounded thrice, and an Army captain. The leader of millions of brawling street thugs.

My father would have been unhappy that Röhm was a known ho-mosexual, more so if he discovered he loved my brother. But as my mother always said, "A perfect man is one you don't know very well."

I drew on the clothes he had laid out. A full complement of under-garments, including stockings and garters, topped by a light summer dress with red flowers. The dress fell modestly to my calves. I bought it in Rio de Janeiro for my much-anticipated reunion with Boris in Switzerland. Instead I would wear it for Ernst Röhm. Unwilling to ask for help no matter how much it hurt, I struggled to button the back.

After a long drink of tepid water from the tap, I smoothed my dress and opened the bathroom door.

"I took the liberty of ordering breakfast," Röhm called.

"You excel at taking liberties." I reentered the bedroom.

"That dress becomes you, pigeon. You look like your brother." He leered.

I swept past him without comment. I stuffed my bloodstained dress and underthings into my suitcase, my fingers feeling the zeppelin tickets for the return trip to South America and our fake Swiss passports. Röhm knew those identities. I did not see how we could use them or how I could escape to obtain others. But we had more than a week before the zeppelin's scheduled return to South America. Perhaps something would change the odds in my favor.

Unsure what to do, I crossed to the window and drew open the curtains. Sun shone on a silver lake surrounded by pines. It was a beautiful Saturday morning, somewhere. "Where are we?"

"Your honeymoon chalet." He moved to stand behind me. He wrapped his arms around my waist. "If we're lucky, this is where you will conceive another son for me."

I froze. His arms tightened against my hips.

A gunshot echoed nearby. I jumped.

"Only one of the boys hunting. Potting little brown rabbits before breakfast."

It sounded too close to be rabbits. He leaned down, and his breath flowed across the side of my neck. His moustache grazed my skin. I fought a wave of nausea. Another gunshot cracked.

A knock on the door brought him up short. "Room service with our breakfast. Retire to the bathroom until the server is gone. No need risking your reputation by having you spotted in my bedroom before the ceremony."

Or having me try to run past the waiter.

As I walked toward the bathroom, he reached out and patted my bottom. I gritted my teeth. As soon as I could arrange it, his day of reckoning would come.

After he closed the bathroom door, I switched off the light, then knelt to look through the hole that had contained the doorknob. He fussily straightened his bathrobe and patted his hair into place. I wondered if he expected the room service waiter to be attractive.

"Come in. It's unlocked."

The door slammed against the wall. Attractive or not, the waiter would get no tip. I stifled a smile. Röhm drew an angry breath and turned.

A short man wearing a riding outfit complete with tall boots stormed in, back ramrod straight. Long dark hair flopped across his brow.

The smile froze on my face. My mouth dropped open, as did Röhm's. The man was Adolf Hitler.

He strode across the soft carpet brandishing a riding crop. Röhm raised his arm to fend off a blow. I held my breath. The whip did not fall.

"Röhm!" Fury blazed in Hitler's red face, but his whip hand trembled. Did even Hitler fear Röhm?

Röhm dropped his arm and stood at attention. Always the officer. He snapped his right arm into the Hitler salute. "Heil Hitler!"

"Röhm." Hitler's harsh Austrian voice filled the room. "You are under arrest." He used the familiar *you*, as if they were intimate friends. I had heard he used it with no one else.

"On what charge?" Röhm loomed over Hitler.

"High treason," Hitler said, and I knew that Röhm was lost. "As you well know."

I trembled. The punishment for treason was death. And I knelt in the traitor's bathroom.

Two men in black SS uniforms marched in, guns drawn. They

glanced wildly around, plainly as terrified as I. The sight of Röhm and Hitler standing nose to nose focused them.

Those shots had nothing to do with killing brown rabbits, and everything to do with killing brownshirts. The blackshirts must be killing the brown. If Röhm was being arrested, it meant that Himmler had won Hilter's loyalty, and Röhm had lost.

Cold sweat ran down my back. Was Anton stashed in the hotel? Did he hear the same gunshots as I, wondering if they came for him? Did they?

"Dress yourself." Hitler's pale blue eyes clashed with Röhm's.

He gave Hitler the look that he must have used when he famously marched those sixty-five French prisoners across the front lines with a half-empty revolver and a lung pierced by shrapnel. Hitler faltered. Then an SS man scooped Röhm's clothes off the stand near the bed and threw them at him.

He let them fall to the floor. "You have made an error, old friend," he said quietly to Hitler, using the familiar form of *you* as well. Their familiarity made the whole scene feel like a lovers' quarrel. The most dangerous kind.

"Would that—" Hitler seemed on the verge of saying something else.

A man and woman, both in silk dressing gowns, burst through the door behind the SS men.

"I am the doctor for Chief of Staff Röhm," said the man. "What is happening here?"

Hitler turned to the doctor, who gasped and gave a crisp Hitler salute. "Heil Hitler!"

His companion followed suit, pale arm trembling.

"This is not a pleasant place for you to be today." Hitler ran the back of his index finger across his stunted moustache. "I suggest you and your wife leave at once."

The doctor shot Röhm a look. He closed his eyes and nodded once. The doctor hustled his wife out.

Hitler shook his head sadly, then followed. The leather of Hitler's tall boots squeaked as he stepped into the hall.

The SS boys stood pat, pistols trained on Röhm.

"May I dress in private?"

"Plenty of men have seen you naked." The shorter one sniggered. "Dress here."

"When this is over, you will regret those words."

The short officer retreated a pace. He glanced at his fellow. They looked like young boys caught smoking in the alley. Then they tightened their grips on their guns and straightened their spines. Neither looked Röhm in the eye again.

He dressed with the quick efficiency of a man used to changing while under fire in a trench. Never once did his eyes stray to the bathroom. I prayed that they would not. I must stay well away from these events. Closer, another gunshot cracked. Röhm glanced in the direction of the sound, but other than that he gave no sign.

Röhm pulled on his polished black boots and stood straight to attention. "I am ready, children."

4

The SS men ignored the insult and gestured uneasily with their pistols toward the door. Regal in his rumpled uniform, Röhm marched out with the calm, measured tread I had watched so often in newsreels. His armed guards followed uncertainly. The shorter one jerked the door shut behind them.

I tiptoed out of the bathroom and back toward the bed, knees shaking. I had to get away before anyone came back. Röhm had lined up his slippers on the right side of the bed, as if he would return by bedtime. I thought of what might have happened in that bed if Hitler had not arrested him. I had been rescued by Hitler himself. Perhaps his only good deed.

On the night table, in the cut-glass ashtray, rested a set of Mercedes keys. I grabbed them. His automobile would undoubtedly be too flashy a method of escape, but it would be faster than walking.

My suitcase stood, still closed, next to the wardrobe. My hands shook so much that I dropped the keys twice before managing to put them into the suitcase. I lifted it, gasping at the pain in my side. If I slipped out unnoticed, perhaps no one would link me to Röhm. Hannah Vogel and Anton Röhm were certainly in danger, but if Röhm had not publicized our false names, who would care about Adelheid Zinsli, widowed Swiss reporter, and her son?

Dizziness threatened to overwhelm me. You can do this, I ordered myself. You must do this. For Anton.

I swung the door open and poked my head out. Wooden doors lined the walls; burgundy carpeting ran down the empty hall. When I stepped out, the now-dressed doctor and his wife came out of their room next door. Both looked as shocked to see a woman sneaking out of Röhm's room as they had been to see Hitler. A morning of surprises for everyone. I cursed inwardly. They could link my face to Röhm.

I gestured for them to walk in front of me and followed down the hall. Hopefully they knew the way out.

The doctor and his wife headed to the lobby and past the cold fireplace. Heads of dead elk and deer adorned the walls. Under each hung a polished silver plaque listing the hunter and date and location the animal had been killed. I wondered where the SS would display the trophies they bagged today. From far off in the hotel, doors slammed, and another gunshot echoed.

I had to find Anton.

I approached the front desk. "Excuse me," I said. "I have become separated from my son."

The concierge looked at me with wide eyes. "Pardon?"

"My son. His name is Anton. We came here to . . . meet a friend for breakfast."

"We do not serve breakfast so early." His corpulent form turned toward an SS officer standing to my left.

I held back my impatience and fear. "He is wearing a white singlet and short gray pants." Another gunshot echoed down the hall, and I flinched. "Have you seen him?"

"I have seen no children today."

"Last night?"

The SS man on my left cleared his throat.

"I thought you said that you came for breakfast," the concierge said. At any other time he would probably have been more suspicious, but the black-uniformed men racing to and fro were enough to distract anyone.

"Did you see a boy last night?"

"I have not seen a boy at this hotel for days, Frau . . ." He paused, waiting for my last name.

I did not give it. "Whom else may I ask?"

He gestured toward a swinging door that I suspected led to the kitchen. I picked up the suitcase and hurried in.

A girl in her late teens made coffee with shaking hands. She spilled dark grounds on the counter, the homey smell out of place in this nightmare.

"They want coffee. And rolls." She pushed her long blond braids behind broad shoulders. "Hard for the SS to shoot people on an empty stomach."

"Have you seen a small boy?" I heard panic in my voice and brought it under control. "My son is nine years old. He has blond hair and is wearing short gray pants and a white singlet. His name is Anton."

"There are no children that young at the Hanselbauer. We cleared the place for the SA. Chief of Staff Röhm is taking a cure."

"May I leave my suitcase here?" I could move faster, although I hated to be parted from it, even for a moment.

She shrugged. I tucked the suitcase into the corner next to the warm stove.

I thanked her and hastened out of the kitchen and down the hall. Most doors in the hallway stood open, rooms empty. The brown-shirted SA men who had not been summarily executed huddled in a mass in the laundry room, guarded by black-uniformed SS officers. None were the men who had kidnapped us. All too young.

"Excuse me," I said to the grizzled SS officer in charge. "Has anyone seen a small boy?"

"We have found no children." His voice was cultured and smooth. He pointed his pistol at the group of SA soldiers, standing in various states of dress next to piles of unwashed sheets. "Have any of you seen a small boy?"

They shook their heads dejectedly.

"I hope you find him," said the old officer. "The hotel is a dangerous place for a boy today."

I thanked him, glancing at the despondent boys he held at gunpoint. A dangerous place indeed.

With mounting dread I returned to the lobby. In the dining room Röhm sat at a corner table with a cup of coffee. Two men loomed near him, guns drawn. Röhm stared into empty air, so lost and childlike that, for a brief instant, I pitied him. Then I remembered all that he was responsible for and the pity faded. I started toward his table. He must tell me where Anton was.

An SS officer with a straggle of white blond hairs on his upper lip, probably his first moustache, put his hand on my arm. "No one is allowed in there, Fräulein. Hitler's orders."

I pulled away, speechless.

I hurried back toward the kitchen, past the sunny breakfast room. On the tables white sheets covered half a dozen bodies. No one stood guard over them. I stepped through the archway.

Steeling myself, I lifted the first sheet with trembling fingers. Santer had kidnapped his last child. I rushed from body to body. The bodies looked too big to belong to Anton, but I checked each anyway. The final sheet concealed Jannings. Only Röhm and Mouse knew where Anton might be. But where was Mouse?

I stole back into the kitchen. The waitress slumped on a round stool in the corner, weeping into a napkin.

"Trade clothes with me," I said.

She stared at me with wide uncomprehending eyes. I had no time to explain. Instead, I reached into my suitcase and extracted twenty Swiss francs. "Give me your dress, and your apron. Then leave the hotel."

Her gaze locked on the money. That penetrated her fear.

"Before they start doing what soldiers do," I told her, although the group seemed far too focused and disciplined to break down into rape.

She twitched on her stool. "What soldiers do."

"Take the money."

She set the money on the table. I turned my back to her. As she undid my buttons, I regretted that it was not Boris taking off this dress, as I had imagined in the shop in Rio de Janiero. She stripped off her own, and we exchanged.

As I slipped her dress over my head I smelled her perfume. Violets.

Round in all the feminine places, her flesh bulged as I buttoned the back for her. Her dress hung on me like a sack.

"Good luck." She pocketed the money. "I hope that you find your boy."

"Thank you."

I turned toward the door. She stood motionless.

"What do I do?" she asked, fear plain in her voice.

I placed a hand on her shoulder. "Walk out the front door. As soon as you are out of sight, hide behind the trees and head for the first house that belongs to someone you can trust. Stay there."

She nodded and embraced me, trembling. I bit my lip against the pain in my rib. "You can do this. Think of tomorrow, or of yesterday, just not today. And keep walking."

When the kitchen door swung closed behind her, I realized that Boris would never see that dress.

Enough of that. I wrapped a kerchief around my too-short hair, tied on a clean white apron, and grabbed the coffeepot.

As I had hoped, the guard at the entrance to the dining room let me pass unquestioned with the coffeepot and apron. For the National Socialists it is always about the uniform.

I walked as quickly as I dared to Röhm's table.

"More coffee?"

He shook his head without glancing up.

"Where is Anton?"

Röhm looked at me, hard blue eyes unfocused. For the first time since I met him, he seemed unsure of himself.

"It's over," he said. "Haven't you heard them shooting the boys?"

"I can get Anton away from this."

"It was Himmler. You saw his SS men arrest me. He poured poison in Hitler's ear."

"Anton." I longed to slap him, but knew that would attract too much attention. Pity, as I owed him one. "Let me save him."

He shook his head, and intelligence returned to his eyes. "You kidnapped him and kept him from me. He is safer where he is."

I gestured toward the breakfast room with the coffeepot. He must have seen them bring bodies in there. "Do you think that anyone you know is safe where they are, now?"

Before he answered, four guards stormed across the room.

"Time to go." They hoisted him to his feet. He shook off their arms and marched out the door, as calm as if he were leading them on a parade ground.

I stumbled out of the dining room alone, blinded by tears. How could I find Anton? Anyone close to Röhm was in horrible danger, and that included us.

I tripped, and the coffeepot crashed on the broad pine planks. Hot coffee seared my ankles.

"Elsa!" roared the concierge.

I dropped to my knees to hide my face and picked up shards.

A leg encased in black SS trousers and a boot stopped in front of me. "Let me help you, Fräulein."

A blond head popped into view, and strong fingers picked up pieces with me. He had the ingrained politeness of a good German boy, yet minutes ago he might well have been shooting another good German boy.

When I stole a quick glance at his face, I dropped the corners of my soiled apron and pieces of the coffeepot clattered to the floor. "Wilhelm?" I gasped.

"Hannah?" He scowled. "Why are you in Germany?"

I had neither seen nor heard from him since he helped Anton and me escape, although I had known Wilhelm since he was a boy. His infatuation with my brother had led to hours spent in my shabby kitchen in Berlin, spinning fantasies of what they would become in their grown-up lives. My brother became a celebrated cabaret singer, but was murdered in his early twenties. And Wilhelm had grown into a

Nazi, by the looks of his uniform one of the most extreme Nazis, a member of the SS. Above his black uniform collar his pale face had thinned from a boy's face to a man's.

"Röhm took Anton. I must find him." I wondered if I could trust him, but at this point I had nothing to lose. I jerked my hand back to keep another man's shiny SS boot from treading on it. The shard I had been about to pick up crunched, but he did not look down.

"Can't you keep track of one little boy?" His long fingers gathered pieces of porcelain and dumped them into my apron, warm hands lingering on mine.

"Have you seen him?" I squeezed his hands gratefully.

He shook his head. In a low voice he said, "I checked the rooms. To make sure that no one was hiding. If he'd been here, I would have found him."

Yet he had not found me. If Anton fled quickly and quietly, Wilhelm might have missed him, too. We both gathered the broken pieces while men tramped past us, boots heavy on the wooden floor.

"I thought you were through with the Nazis." I struggled to keep an accusatory tone out of my voice.

"I was through with the SA. The discipline of the SS suits me better."

I bit back a retort. "What will happen to Röhm?"

He checked around the room. Everyone appeared too busy to notice our conversation. "Firing squad, I imagine." He smiled. "Finally."

He had reason to hate Röhm, but I still did not like his look of smug satisfaction. Before he joined the Nazis, he had been a gentle boy.

"Just Röhm?"

"There is a long list of names. The Reich List of Unwanted Persons." His voice was matter of fact, as if he did not realize or care that each name belonged to a person with family and friends. "They are to be killed. Röhm's name is on the top."

"Why Röhm?" The broken pieces were all in my apron, but we remained kneeling.

"He planned a putsch." He dusted his pale hands. "He planned to use the SA to start a second revolution."

"I see." I did not see. Nothing I had heard indicated that Röhm was disloyal to Hitler, although remembering his tone when he said the Corporal would do as he was told, perhaps I had been wrong. "Where will they execute him?"

Wilhelm paused until a flaxen-haired SS man passed us by.

"This group is being transported to Stadelheim Prison in Munich," he said. Both Röhm and Hitler had been incarcerated in Stadelheim Prison after Hitler's failed 1923 Beer Hall Putsch. Now Röhm would serve time there without his old friend.

Wilhelm rose and extended a hand to me. I grabbed his calloused palm to pull myself up, holding my apron closed with my free hand, careful to keep my fingers away from the sharp edges of broken crockery. "Get out of Germany, Hannah. It's not a safe place for someone like you."

"Someone like me?" Anger showed in my voice, but I did not care.

"A Jew-lover."

The words rolled around in his mouth like candy. I stared at him, shocked. Where was the young man who helped me escape with Anton only three years before? Wilhelm was queer, also a forbidden group in the Third Reich. How could he be a fervent Nazi, knowing that they loathed him and everyone like him?

He wiped his hands on his black uniform trousers. "And a Socialist."

"And a German," I reminded him. "This is as much my country as yours." I gestured to the brownshirts being marched under guard through the lobby and out the door. "Or theirs."

He shook his head, blue eyes on the door, probably watching for his commanding officer.

I stepped closer. "Is it a safe place for one with your . . . habits?"

"My youthful indiscretions are behind me," he said quietly. "I don't make those kinds of mistakes anymore."

"That does seem to be the expedient course." As much as I tried, sarcasm spilled into the words.

"It is the only course. Paragraph 175 offenders are sent to the camps."

I gulped, thinking of Oliver, Frances, Lola, and the other men I had met at El Dorado, the queer club where my brother used to sing. Some had helped me to investigate his murder, and at least one I had trusted with my life. "Who is in the camps?"

"Oliver," he murmured. "Among others. Everyone else is deep underground. Some have married."

I wondered what my brother would have done, had he been alive. He would not have arranged a show marriage, and he would not have been able to be one iota less flamboyant. He would have been among the first rounded up. Killed because of whom he was fated to love. "Be careful," I whispered.

"If I find Anton," he said, "I will bring him to your friend Bettina's in Berlin. If I can."

"Thank you." I knew what that might cost him. And I knew that he spoke the truth. He would help me if he could. The kind warrior child who had followed my brother home from school still lived inside his black SS uniform.

"If you need me, come by the El Dorado. I'm there until four most days."

"El Dorado is still open?"

"Not in the same form." He smiled wryly. "But you will still find me there."

He clicked his heels together and bowed, then marched out the front door with his familiar loping stride. Would I ever see him again?

I carried the shattered coffeepot back to the kitchen and changed out of my coffee-stained uniform into a clean dress from my suitcase. I wiped a wet rag over the coffee on my ankles and snagged a roll from the counter. Who knew when I would get another chance to eat.

Nibbling the roll, I folded Elsa's dress and hung it over the sink. She would need it when she came back to work. For her, tomorrow would be another ordinary day. Not for me or the men covered in sheets in the breakfast room.

I slipped out the front door and stood on the covered porch, morning sun in my eyes, the scent of pine in my nostrils. Men swarmed into cars. The sun reflected off the brim of Hitler's cap as he leaned over to tap his chauffeur lightly on the shoulder with the handle of his riding crop. The chauffeur nodded and drove the open-topped Mercedes through the pillars. They crunched down the gravel driveway, others close behind.

I scanned the cars parked in front of the hotel. At least ten black Mercedes ringed the parking lot. Any might match my stolen keys. I did not have time to check each.

Then I spotted the largest Mercedes. It spanned two parking spaces. Chrome headlights had been polished to a high shine, the curving black hood reflected the single white cloud in the sky, and the convertible top gleamed. Long front fenders swooped back to wide running boards. The perfect place for an escort to stand to flank some notable occupant. A red flag with a swastika fluttered from a pole near one black rear fender. The staff car. It shouted out the pomp and importance of its owner. Röhm's. Who else would have gall to use that monster?

I hurried over and peered into the backseat. An old-fashioned ivory-colored silk wedding dress lay across the black leather. The wedding dress that had been meant for me. It looked costly. I would have to find a way to return it to Röhm's mother. If I was correct about what was to happen, she would have lost enough already. My brother had taught me that a parent cannot determine the fate of their child, and I could not blame her for his politics.

I ripped the wooden flagpole off the fender and tossed the Nazi banner on the dirt. Behind me someone gasped. I did not turn to see who. If they had not seen my face already, I had no intention of showing it. A foolish act, but it was too revolting to drive with a Nazi flag flapping behind me. Bad enough to be in a Nazi staff car.

When I opened the door, the smell of leather, musky cologne, and horse sweat filled my nostrils. Gritting my teeth, I reached inside and turned the key.

The engine roared to life. I tossed my suitcase in the front seat, wincing at the pain in my rib, and sped after Hitler, tires spewing gravel.

The automobile accelerated, and wind from the open windows tore at my hair. I drove recklessly and was soon close enough to see the convoy. Hitler's black staff car, twin to the one I drove, led the way. A few cars followed, then a truck with the sides covered. Where was Röhm?

Wilhelm had said they were taking him to Stadelheim Prison. If he was correct, that meant death by firing squad. I stayed as far back as possible. Even without its red flag, the massive automobile was ridiculously obtrusive. Why had Röhm chosen such an outrageous automobile? I shook my head. Everything about him was exaggerated, why should his car be different?

With one eye on the road, I checked the front seat. The leather shone. Every surface gleamed, not easy when it had been parked at the end of a dusty gravel road. Röhm's chauffeur paid close attention to details. I wondered if he too was dead.

I popped open the glove box. Inside rested a leather portfolio and a Luger. Sunlight glinted off its barrel.

The chauffeur did think of everything. I set the pistol on the seat next to me. Things might have turned out differently if Röhm had kept it in his bedroom, instead of his glove box.

An SA convoy heading toward the Hanselbauer Spa blocked our path. I wondered if they had come to rescue Röhm, if they had time to hear what had happened. I smiled bitterly. Perhaps they were wedding guests.

Hitler's convoy halted. I slammed on the brakes and parked behind a screen of pines, hoping to avoid explaining to a battalion of SA men and Hitler why I stole Röhm's staff car. I checked the clip, grateful that my soldier father trained us how to use guns. Loaded.

I slid a pair of field glasses out of my suitcase and looped the strap over my neck. Anton had loved using them on the zeppelin. I remembered how he had propped tanned elbows on the sill of the viewing window, how his red tongue poked out of the corner of his mouth as he twiddled with the focusing knob. He once saw a party of vaqueros herding cattle and whooped so loudly that they looked up and waved. We waved back, both delighted. I ran my index finger along the strap. Anton would be safe to wave and whoop again. I would not let the Nazis grind him up in their machine. I would find him.

Taking the Luger but leaving the wedding dress, I climbed out. Afraid to make a sound, I left the door ajar and crept along a carpet of pine needles. I lay on my belly behind a tree and peeked out, the glasses only centimeters from the ground. Hopefully I was impossible to spot from the road. The dust from the convoy blew over me, and I suppressed a sneeze.

Hitler stormed out of his staff car and stalked toward the lead SA truck. Riding crop tucked under his arm, he shouted at the brown-shirted driver. I could not make out what he said, but he used his familiar angry tone. The driver quailed predictably under the abuse.

I trained the field glasses on each automobile, but did not find Röhm's close-cropped dark head. Had he been shot inside a truck? I found myself in the bizarre position of praying to find Röhm alive and unharmed. Only he and Mouse knew Anton's whereabouts.

Silence. Hitler had stopped shouting. He spun and marched back to his staff car. The SA man turned his truck around and led the way. The rest of the convoy followed. Would they end up in Stadelheim as well? These young men might be driving themselves to their own executions. Already Hitler had such power over them. I did not understand how he did it, but I could not deny that he inspired blind devotion in his followers. I shuddered to think how many other young men he might send to their deaths, or of those they might kill on the way.

Clutching the pistol, I crept back to the staff car and followed the convoy toward the prison, perhaps also to my death, an irony not lost on me. Hitler's web had snared me as surely as it had those young men.

5

In the two-hour drive to the prison, I had plenty of time to formulate a plan, but I came up with nothing. I had to see Röhm or find Mouse, assuming that either was still alive. If not, well, I did not let myself think about that. There would be plenty of time to fall into despair later.

I pulled off the road and rolled to a stop far from the convoy and safely behind a stand of trees. A strip of parched grass separated me from the prison. The cars in the Nazi convoy had halted at the gate. I climbed out to see better, then took out the field glasses. Black-uniformed SS men unloaded the SA brownshirts. Slouched down so that only the field glasses stuck above the doorframe, I recognized Röhm marching, strong and fast, leading his boys to their fate. SS jeers drifted toward me, but the SA paid them no mind.

It would take hours to process them. I only hoped that the Nazis would be thorough enough to give Röhm a few more hours to live, assuming they did not inconvenience themselves with the details of a trial. That could drag out for weeks. Remembering the men on the tables in the breakfast room, I suspected that they would not bother with a trial.

I slipped behind a tree when Hitler's staff car roared past and away from the prison. He had not gone inside. Röhm had probably seen his old friend for the last time.

I shook my head. The politics, however fascinating, did not concern me. I had not come to save or bury Röhm, only to get Anton back. And for that I needed to know what tools I had.

When I opened Röhm's portfolio, the rich smell of expensive leather wafted out. On top lay paperwork for a marriage license for Ernst Röhm and Hannah Vogel filled out and ready to sign. Underneath that was the paperwork to change my name to Hannah Röhm after the wedding. I put those papers on the seat and looked in the portfolio again. It also contained three passports, all newly issued. One for Hannah Vogel, one for Anton Röhm, one for Ernst Röhm. Thorough. Maybe if he had spent more time placating Hitler and less time making my life difficult, he would not be in prison.

I kept out the Hannah Vogel passport for access to the prison. I did not want my Swiss identity to be linked to Röhm's. I locked the paperwork and other passports in the glove box with the Luger. It would not do to be found with Röhm's passport or a gun if I was searched in prison. They would have to stay here while I went inside, hopefully to see Röhm.

I checked every centimeter of the automobile, from the trunk to the front seat, finding only a bundle of tools, the wedding dress, and a packet of hard candies embossed with swastikas. I pictured Anton popping them into his mouth, sucking on the Nazi symbol encased in sugar. Repulsed, I dropped the candies onto the floor.

Before moving my suitcase to the trunk, I removed my satchel from it, then applied lipstick and combed my hair. From my days as a crime reporter in Berlin, I knew that it always helped to look attractive when visiting prison. I locked the doors and tucked the keys into my satchel with my Hannah Vogel passport.

Now that I had a real identity, all that remained was concocting a good story. Before his death, my brother and I had loved spinning wild tales to embarrass our sister, but back then only he had the nerve to put our stories into action. I had been forced to acquire a great deal more nerve since his death. I hoped it would be enough to bluff my way into prison. And back out.

My shoes wobbled on the gravel. The sun was high in the sky, and heat shimmered off the pavement near the prison. Another scalding day.

I followed the SS men's route to the guardroom. Gulping a deep breath of outside air, in spite of the twinge from my rib, I opened the wooden door.

"Papers," a prison guard said gruffly. His gray uniform marked him as a longtime guard, instead of an SS man.

I handed him my Hannah Vogel passport. "Hannah Vogel." It was the first time I had used my real name in three years, and it felt as false as my other identities. "Here to see Ernst Röhm."

The guard blinked, looking surprised. Röhm had been delivered only minutes before. The guard must wonder how I knew he was at Stadelheim.

"I heard that he is here, along with a number of his men." I gave up no details, but made it harder for him to deny it. It would be easier for him to confirm something he thought I already knew than make up a lie. I hoped.

"He's not allowed visitors. None of them are." I put his age at sixty, old enough to be the father, or the grandfather, of many of those arrested. How did he feel about this?

A quick volley of shots cut through the air. We both jumped. They had already reached the firing squad stage. My mouth went dry. "How often?"

"Executions are staged every twenty minutes," he said slowly, as if uncertain whether he was allowed to tell me, but used to answering direct questions. "You should leave."

"I am here on behalf of his mother, Em-Emilie Röhm," I stuttered, glad that I had researched Röhm enough to know. "She wishes me to pass on her love before it is too late."

Emotions ran across his face. He probably had children of his own, and he must have once had a mother.

"No visitors. Not yet."

"Will he be alive later?" I twisted my hands, desperate to question

Röhm before he was executed. "Or should I tell his mother that she will never have a chance to say good-bye? Wouldn't your own mother want to tell you that she loved you one last time?"

Who could deny a mother her last wishes?

Not the guard. His face sagged, and I could tell he was thinking of his own mother, or his own children.

"I'll call someone." He leaned his head through the inner door and yelled. Minutes later a younger guard appeared. "Take over for a few," my guard said. "Visitor."

The young guard raised his eyebrows. I had to be the first visitor here for these prisoners.

"Follow me," the old guard said. "I can give you fifteen minutes."

"Frau Röhm will thank you."

He grunted. He knew as well as I that no mother would thank a man implicated in the death of her son.

We shuffled down the long corridor, walls painted gunmetal gray for a little more than a meter and a half, about as high as the top of my head. Beyond that they were a lighter gray. Humid air pressed in, rank with the smell of unwashed bodies and fear. I breathed through my mouth.

We passed a courtyard in the middle. The view through the barred window showed beaten earth. A line of eight bloody streaks against one wall showed where the last round of men had been executed. My guard strode by without looking. Nauseated, I hurried along on his heels.

When we reached a room near the courtyard, he said, "You have five minutes."

"You said fifteen."

"It took us over five minutes to walk here." He held up five fingers swollen with arthritis. "Plus five to walk back. I must be back at my post on time."

I read the number painted over Röhm's door. Cell 474.

"Do you need an escort?" he asked, worried for my safety or perhaps about his rules, here in the prison where they had just illegally executed eight men. I shook my head.

The giant metal key screeched in the lock as he opened the door. I stepped into a wall of oven-hot air. The door clanged shut behind me.

Röhm stopped pacing midstep. Even in this heat, every button on his tunic remained closed. He would not shed his uniform for reasons of personal comfort.

"Ready for me?" he snarled, turning toward me, face pink from the heat.

I held up my hands. "It is I. Hannah."

He nodded and stepped back, shoulders relaxing. "How many of my men have they executed?"

I did not lie to spare him. "I heard one set of shots. Eight men per round, I think."

He winced. "It's over then."

"Tell me where Anton is. Or do you think they won't kill your son?"

"What could you do?"

"Get him to safety."

"And then? Raise him as an enemy of the Fatherland?"

"Are you less of an enemy?"

He hung his head over his barrel chest. When he raised it again, his eyes shone with unfamiliar tears.

"They are loyal to Hitler, you know," he said in a quiet voice. "As am I."

"I believe you. But we have little time."

"How did you get in here?" Sweat dribbled down his face.

"I said I represented your mother." I saw no reason to lie.

"You will tell her that I love her. That my last thoughts were for her. And return the dress."

"Is Anton with her?"

The door swung open, and in walked Hans Frank, Minister of Justice for Bavaria and Hitler's personal lawyer. I recognized him from newspaper photographs. He was the oily man who helped to finance the Nazi party in the early days through lawsuits against their opponents. Dark hair was slicked back from his receding hairline, and his soft chin quivered in surprise at seeing me. I was no more happy to see him.

Röhm stepped forward and shook his hand. Military manners ever present, he introduced me to Frank. "This is Fräulein Vogel, my fiancée. Fräulein Vogel, Minister Frank."

Hans Frank captured my hand in his own clammy one. "Delighted to meet you," he mumbled, without meeting my eyes. "It is late for that kind of charade, Captain Röhm."

He used Röhm's military rank from the army, not the one assigned by the Nazis.

My guard peeked in behind Frank's shoulder and beckoned. I ignored him.

"Ernst." I used his first name for the first time ever. It was my brother's name, and it bothered me to use it for this ruthless Nazi. "Tell me what I need, and I will go. You will rest easier."

Röhm laughed. "Should I tell you then that I love you? Isn't that what women wish to hear on their last visit?"

What a lovely game he played, still hoping to cast doubt on his homosexuality, something Hitler was certain to use as a justification for killing him. But a dangerous game for me. "I—"

My guard stormed into the room and grabbed my arm tightly enough to leave bruises. "Please." I was on the verge of tears and did not care who knew.

"Give my love to my mother," Röhm said. "She will be grateful, and perhaps you will be as well."

"But—" I glanced at Minister Frank. I could not finish my sentence in front of him. My eyes went back to Röhm.

He held my gaze for a second and gave a small nod. It was all the confirmation I would receive. The guard yanked me out of the cell.

I stumbled down the corridor. We stopped next to a group of eight brown-shirted young men looking into the courtyard where the firing squads had shot the last group. My guard said something in a low voice to one of the two men guarding them.

"Take off your shirts!" the first guard bellowed.

The eight young men unbuttoned their shirts and removed them. Most folded them and hung them over their forearms, as if at a tailor's fitting. The first guard gathered them up. The boys would not be wearing them again.

The second guard leaned across and used a charcoal pencil to sketch a black circle around the left nipple of the first young man. He proceeded down the line, circling each one's left breast to mark the heart. Unable to stop myself, I put my palms to my cheeks. Targets. He was drawing targets on them for the firing squad.

One boy sobbed off to the side, praying. The others stared straight ahead—terrified, but trying to be brave. They looked about the same age my brother Ernst had been when he died by violence at the hands of a Nazi. Twenty.

I stared at their pale young bodies. Most were too young to have chest hair. A few did not need to shave. They folded their arms across their chests self-consciously. For some I might have been the first woman to see them half-naked since they were children.

My guard remembered me and dragged me away.

We reached the guardroom door when another volley of shots sounded. I dropped to my knees and vomited.

They were only boys.

Still on my knees, I rested my head against the cold stone wall. My empty stomach heaved. Pain from my rib was so excruciating, I thought I would lose consciousness and collapse on the floor in my own mess.

The guard hauled me up with one hand.

"I'll clean it up," he said. "Get the hell out of here."

He thrust me through the door and into the hot sun. I sat on the front steps and sobbed. It did no good to remind myself that these boys had helped bring Hitler to power. That they were part of a group that savagely beat Communists and Jews in the street. Eight boys, gone. Eight mothers to weep.

I wiped my mouth with a handkerchief and took a shuddering breath.

Hans Frank appeared behind me. He stopped on the first step and put on his hat.

I jumped to my feet and tripped, barely catching myself with a hand against the wall.

"Be more careful, Fräulein Vogel," Hans Frank said. Lovely. He remembered my name. I wondered what else Röhm had said about me after I left the cell.

"Good advice in these times, Minister." I studied his face, but he gave nothing away.

"Good advice in any times."

"Did he have other messages for me?"

He drew a handkerchief from his pocket and patted his brow. "He said that all revolutions devour their own children."

6

I needed to find Röhm's mother. Besides Mouse, she was my only link to Anton. And who knew where Mouse was, if he even lived.

Afternoon sun beat down as I hurried across the parking lot and behind the trees to Röhm's Mercedes. He would not ride in it again. One never knows what will outlast one in life.

I glanced around the empty parking lot before opening the door. No one seemed to be watching as I slid onto the hot leather seat. When I started the engine, I winced at the noise. Like everything about Röhm, it would not be quiet and demure, no matter the consequences. Driving as slowly and quietly as I could manage, I pulled onto the street.

The steering wheel burned my palm so I drove with the tips of my fingers, wishing that the chauffeur had left a pair of driving gloves. Had he been killed? Likely. The SS were killing everyone close to Röhm. Was his mother safe? Was I? Was Anton? I stepped on the accelerator.

If my brother had managed to avoid being sent to a camp, his relationship with Röhm would probably have put him in front of a firing squad with those other young men. There were many reasons to be murdered in the Third Reich.

Near the prison I had to stop at a fuel depot. When I pulled to the pump, a young man ran out.

"Petrol?" He almost fell in his haste. About twenty, the same age as the boys executed. "Fräulein?"

"I am sorry. My mind was elsewhere." At Stadelheim Prison.

"Do you need petrol?" he asked again, looking worried.

"Petrol and a map of Munich."

"Of course." He pumped the petrol, running his fingers along the fender as if it belonged to a beautiful girl he could only dream of touching. "You have a swell car. It's a government car, isn't it? I've never seen one here without a chauffeur. You are lucky to get to drive it. Those cars cost more than I make in five years. How does it accelerate?"

I hesitated. It was difficult to talk about something as trivial as an automobile. "The handling is impeccable."

"I bet you must be married to a famous party leader."

I jerked my head to indicate the wedding dress on the backseat. "Almost married."

His eyes widened, and his freckled face broke into a gap-toothed grin. "Are you going to your wedding in this car? I could wash it for you. It's a little dusty. Party leaders take great care of their cars. They are always so clean, and you don't want to be in a dirty car on your wedding day."

"Just petrol and the map. The wedding has been postponed." Indefinitely.

He filled my tank and brought out a map. "This one comes from the petrol company. It has most streets, but I can help you too if you give me a street name. I'm pretty familiar with Munich. My father drives a taxi. Where are you going?"

"I can sort it out." I had no intention of telling anyone my destination.

"Whatever you say, Fräulein." He turned away so quickly that I almost missed the hurt in his eyes. No one could help me without putting us both into danger, even someone as innocent-seeming as a fuel depot attendant who loved cars. If the Nazis were feeling thorough, they would wipe out everyone linked to Röhm, most especially his purported fiancée. I had to be careful about whom I trusted. Bad enough that I drove his Mercedes. I did not need to tell my destination.

While the attendant washed my windows and checked the oil and fluids, I studied my new map. I knew someone who might help me find Röhm's mother's address, if he still lived.

"You're all full up on everything. Usually something is low, but your chauffeur must be the careful type."

"He was." I regretted the use of past tense. Perhaps he was still alive. If he had aligned himself with the forces who killed Röhm, he could be driving this automobile as soon as someone recaptured it from me. Who knew where anyone's loyalty lay?

"Drive safe." The attendant waved.

I waved back, checked the map one more time, and pulled into the street, repeating the directions in my head, anxious not to become lost in Munich, the cradle of National Socialism, in the staff car of one of the most prominent and, by now, newly murdered National Socialists.

As I cruised through the broad streets, I rolled down the windows so that the breeze cooled my face. Heads turned to follow my progress, eyes full of fear. Even though I had removed the swastika banner, everyone recognized it as a Nazi staff car. Mercedes made only a handful of this model. I must get rid of it soon, but for now I needed to move around as quickly as possible.

Tall white university buildings with red-tiled roofs came into view. Archways invited me to slip into its cool halls and mingle with the students. Girls with hair shorter than what was fashionable in South America hugged books to their chests. Their skirts fluttered innocently in the breeze. But many boys walking next to them wore the brown uniforms of the Hitler Youth. I drove on.

The only person I knew in Munich, Ulrich Herzog, used to live near the university. He claimed that the apartments were cheaper, but I think he liked to ogle the young girls. Ulli worked as a journalist for the *Munich Post* before the storm troopers shut it down in 1933. I had read that, finally taking revenge for the *Munich Post*'s fierce anti-Nazi stance, Röhm's men had pillaged the place, destroying files and beating anyone foolish enough to be at work that day. Hopefully Ulli had stayed home.

Trying to remember his house number, I crept down the street. I had been to his apartment only once before, many years ago and while not entirely sober. I hoped he still lived there. We had been part of a closely knit pack of political and crime reporters who met more and more often as the political and crime beats began to overlap during the Weimar Republic. We were anti-Nazi, mostly left wing, and not as frightened as we should have been. I shuddered to think of the fates of my old friends. But perhaps Ulli had been spared.

When the Nazis ransacked the newspaper offices, he would have been high on their list of most-hated reporters; he had succeeded where I had failed. In 1932 he published explicit letters a street hustler stole from Röhm. Although not as explicit as the letters Röhm wrote my brother, the letters Ulli published were later used as the basis for a charge of offenses against Paragraph 175: homosexual activity; charges were eventually dismissed, but not before humiliating Röhm and the Nazi leadership.

If I had published my letters, he never would have had to publish his. I hoped I did not have Ulli on my conscience.

The black monster and I cruised down a wide avenue shaded by chestnut trees, leaves singed brown by heat and dryness. Still, a cooler breeze drifted in my windows than when I had sat behind the bare parking lot at Stadelheim.

I passed Ulli's apartment building, unwilling to park directly in front in case someone noticed the staff car and alerted the Nazis. I did not wish to call down their wrath anywhere near Ulli. Farther down the street the parking places were occupied. I parked half on the sidewalk and half in the street. What policeman would challenge the driver of a Nazi staff car? Especially today.

I moved the Luger, passports, and portfolio from the glove box to my suitcase. I could leave nothing valuable, in case someone recognized the automobile. If the Nazis, or the police, arrived, I would have to abandon it. But I left the wedding dress on the backseat so I would not have to explain it to Ulli. I had enough to explain.

A male chaffinch flew by, trilling his high-pitched song. I followed his slate-blue cap as his tiny figure flitted and ducked between chestnut leaves. As a child, my brother kept a pet chaffinch for a week. Ernst set it free because he loved its song too much to keep it imprisoned. Our father beat him black and blue for releasing the bird, but Ernst stoutly maintained that it was worth it. I had not heard a chaffinch in years. They do not live in South America.

Cheered to have seen the bird, I turned back to the apartment building. At least I was in my home country. I spoke the language. I knew the customs. But over the last hours I had come to realize that I did not know the people anymore.

I lugged my suitcase up the steps. The house-proud landlady had been at her work early. The front steps shone from a morning washing, the newly polished buttons and silver nameplates unsullied by a single fingerprint. I shuddered, reminded of the silver plaques beneath the animal trophies at the Hanselbauer, and pressed my thumb on the button under the nameplate for Herzog.

No answer. I rang it again and stepped back off the stoop so that Ulli could see me from his front window. If he had heard about the events of today, he would be cautious, especially if he saw the staff car drive by.

His window, if I remembered correctly, protruded from the second floor. I edged into the empty cobblestone street and looked up, to show him my face. I waved. His lace curtain twitched, almost imperceptibly. No one in the other five floors showed interest in my presence, which was just as well. I returned to the stoop.

The door opened, and a hand pulled me into a dark foyer that smelled of disinfectant and brass polish.

In front of me stood a once-dapper, now harried-looking man. He was about 1.8 meters tall. His wavy blond hair, once the envy of the girls in the newsroom, stood up in all directions as if a chaffinch nested there. Dark circles smudged under his violet-blue eyes.

"Hannah!" He enveloped me in a bear hug.

"Careful, Ulli," I gasped. "I have a cracked rib."

He held me at arm's length. His gaze lingered on my pale face and tired eyes. "You look terrible. What are you doing here?"

"I came for the flattery." I hoisted my suitcase and grimaced. "Can we get upstairs?"

He lifted my suitcase and led the way to the second floor without a word, slippered feet silent on the stairs. I followed, clinging to the polished metal railing, dizzy. When had I eaten? The stolen roll in the kitchen of the Hanselbauer, hours before. And I had thrown that up after the executions.

Ulli's front door stood open, and we hurried inside. He dumped my bag next to a coat stand so covered in coats, hats, and umbrellas that it looked ready to collapse. I stepped past a pile of boxes in his entryway. He pushed the door closed with his boot, then turned to lock it.

Only after he finished did I speak. "Things are bad, Ulli."

"Let me get you coffee. And bread with liverwurst. We can talk while you eat. You look dead on your feet."

I let myself be led back into his apartment. Dust coated the old-fashioned living room furniture. Only one chair was clear enough to sit on. But the brass clock on the mantel was clean and had the correct time. At least he remembered to wind it.

In the kitchen, books and papers covered the round wooden table. Here too the chairs were full. A stack of clean but dusty yellow plates balanced next to the sink. Sheer lace curtains with daisies loomed into the design rippled in front of the open double-hung window. My mother would have liked them, as I suspected his mother had. I imagined him picking out curtains and smiled. He would do it only if the woman shopping with him was very attractive.

He dropped a stack of books onto the tile floor with a thump and dusted off a chair for me. He pushed papers aside on the table. I put my elbows in the scrap of cleared oak while he bustled around pulling bread and a small cutting board out of his cupboards. He wiped a knife on his pants and used it to cut a thick slice of rye bread. Even as I wondered what had been on that knife or how many days he had worn the trousers, my mouth watered.

"Hitler's men are taking revenge today," I said.

"I've heard rumors." He set dark rye bread spread thick with liverwurst in front of me. "But till I feed you, right and wrong can wait."

I smiled, recognizing the quote from Brecht's *Threepenny Opera*. A group of us had attended the opening in Berlin in 1928, during a brief period when we all had money, or expense accounts, and time. The golden years after the brutal inflation and before the worldwide depression when it looked like we might be able to play and dance and forget the war, the flu, and our own near starvation. Those lovely brief years of denial. I bit into the bread and nodded with my mouth full. After I swallowed the bread, I said, "They are purging the SA. Röhm is in Stadelheim."

He turned back to his stove and poured a cup of coffee. "Are you certain?"

I drank the coffee. Lukewarm, but strong. "Dead certain."

"What a story." His lovely blue eyes shone, earlier tiredness gone. I could tell he thought of the piece he would have written. I had missed other reporters more than I realized. "Makes me wish the *Post* were still running real news."

"The Nazis might come for you too. Have you anywhere to go?"

"I should be their best friend. I published the Röhm letters in 1932, attacked their boy before they could do it themselves." He poured himself a cup of coffee and sat next to me.

"I heard." I ate more. The salty liverwurst tasted smooth on my tongue and I enjoyed it silently. I did not know when I might eat again.

"Hannah?" Ulli said. "Stop eating and talk to me."

"What happened to right and wrong can wait until you feed me?" I smiled, but quickly turned serious again. "You must leave at once. They have a list, and they are killing everyone on it. Who knows how far back their memories reach?"

He crossed his legs, revealing an ink stain on his dark trousers. As hard as it was to believe after seeing his apartment, he had once been a meticulous dresser. For the first time, I wondered what he had been doing in the year since the paper had been closed.

"How have you been holding up since the *Post*?"

"Better than you by the looks of it." He flashed his trademark charming smile, the one he used to melt the resistance of his sources.

I smiled back, charmed in spite of myself. "Flatterer."

"My ribs are intact and I had a good breakfast. I can't complain."

I washed down my bread with the coffee. "Do you have Röhm's mother's address?"

"Do you think she's in danger?" His fingers twitched as if he longed to write this down. "Are they killing family members?"

I winced. I hoped not. "You cannot cover this story. At least not here."

"Perhaps I could get it published in Switzerland." His fingers reached for his pen and ratty notebook. "How do you know Röhm's in Stadelheim?"

"I spoke to him. And to Minister Hans Frank."

"He's in jail too?" His eyebrows shot up.

I shook my head. "Visiting Röhm."

"How big is it?"

"They are doing mass executions. Eight every twenty minutes." My voice shook as I thought of the young boys I had seen moments before their death. "Without trials."

He stopped writing and dropped his hand over mine. We sat silently.

"What were you doing in the prison?"

"I have no time to explain, and you must leave here before they come for you." I brought the plate to the sink.

"I'm not that important." He scribbled notes without looking up.

"You hope not." I rinsed the plate and cup, knowing that he might not get back to clean them for a long time. "Once I have that address I am on my way too. It is not safe here."

"I saved most of my files before the savages started burning them." He hurried into his cluttered front room and rooted through boxes of papers. Dust filled the air and I coughed, once, painfully.

"How'd you get the rib?"

Instead of answering that question, I filled him in on Hitler's arrest of Röhm at the Hanselbauer and the convoy he met on the way back. Ulli deserved to know that, after what he had endured at the hands of the Nazis.

"Were you there?" He pulled out an old folder and blew dust off it. He flipped it open and thumbed through the papers. "On the road?"

"Leave out my name. But I followed them."

He pulled out a slip of paper with an address written on it in his speedy scrawl. "You were in that Nazi Mercedes that cruised by before you knocked?"

"Röhm's. But he is not using it."

He copied the address into his notebook, tore out the page, and handed it to me. "You stole the staff car of the chief of staff of the SA?"

"He owes me a favor. More than one."

He whistled softly. "Remind me not to owe you favors."

Pain from my rib stopped my laugh. "I owe you one." I folded the scrap of paper and stuffed it into my satchel.

"Perhaps," he said. "I don't know if that address is still accurate. She's an old bird, in her late seventies. She might be dead."

"Her son thinks she is still alive. His information might be more up to date than yours."

He ran his fingers through his thick hair, and it fell into place as perfectly it had in the old days, although a few gray strands lurked there now. "Perhaps you should have asked him for the address."

"I did, but the Minister of Justice for Bavaria interrupted us."

"Like any man would turn down a chance to talk to you for a conversation with Hans Frank."

I laughed in spite of the twinge of pain. "Röhm's tastes run differently than yours."

"More for me, I always say."

"As if you do not have enough already."

He blushed, and it took years off his face. He looked once again like the dashing but determined reporter so many had once admired.

"You will leave right away?" I put my hand on his arm. "You have somewhere to go?"

"I could go to—"

I put up a hand to silence him. "I do not want to know."

He stopped, face grave.

"It is that bad, Ulli. Trust me."

He nodded, finally seeming to feel the weight of my fear for him.

"I must go," I said.

He helped me carry my suitcase back to the front door, pressing a wrapped liverwurst sandwich and an apple into my hands. "I don't know what the hell you're doing, Hannah, but be careful."

"I have no time to be careful," I said. "Perhaps not even time to be reckless."

7

Dust rose off the front seat when I dropped my suitcase on it. The chauffeur certainly would not have driven around with it in such condition. I imagined how mortified he would be if he had heard the attendant suggest washing it.

I climbed in and closed the door. Chestnut leaves rustled. Another chaffinch called, farther away, but the bright notes of his song carried perfectly. Life went on, for almost everyone.

Poring over the street listings on the map, I found the address Ulli had written. Frau Röhm lived in the northern part of Munich, in a more posh neighborhood than Ulli's. I sped to what I hoped was her house. Though Röhm said that she was still alive, he had not disclosed her whereabouts.

The wattle-and-daub-style house was smaller than I expected. Dark timbers framed its whitewashed spaces. Red geraniums grew in window boxes, blossoms wilting in the heat. I parked in front. A Nazi staff car here would not be unexpected.

Satchel in hand, I walked up the stone path. I left the suitcase and wedding dress. I did not want Röhm's mother to see the dress. I did not want to remind her of the wedding her son might have had on a day when he might be executed instead. Was she responsible for turning him into the brawling thug he became, or had that happened

in defiance of her best efforts? My parents had little control over
Ernst's personality, in the end.

When I knocked on the massive front door, deep barking resounded
inside the house. A large dog, or two, by the sound of it. Someone
heard me.

My chest ached with each breath. The blazing sun licked at my eyes.
I'd had no real sleep the night before, only short chloroform dreams,
and I dozed standing there listening to the bees and the muffled
barking.

"Quiet!" shouted a female voice. The dogs stopped instantly, as if
she had flipped a switch. The dogs knew their place.

A burly maid answered the door, looking worried but composed.
She looked more suited to field work than serving in a house. Her
cobblestone-gray eyes flicked past me to Röhm's Mercedes, and her
powerful shoulders drooped to see it empty. Perhaps she hoped that he
would be sitting there, come to pick his mother up for the wedding.

"I am here to see Frau Röhm," I said. "I carry a message from her
son."

"Your name?" Her large hands gripped the doorframe.

"Hannah Vogel."

Surprise flickered across her eyes. She knew something about me.
She ushered me inside, past a pair of Rottweilers sitting motionless
on either side of the door. Muscles bunched under their coats. They
growled menacingly, displaying strong teeth, making certain I knew
how dangerous they were.

"Good dogs." I did not believe it. Nor did they.

Both muzzles swiveled to the maid, waiting for a signal. She shook
her head, and the dogs stopped growling. They did not soften their vigilant stances and regarded me with distrustful chestnut-brown stares.

Her meaty hand took my satchel and set it next to an old-fashioned
umbrella stand that looked as if it were made from the leg of an elephant. For the sake of the elephant, I hoped not. Two pairs of women's
shoes were lined up neatly next to the door. No children's shoes. I
glanced around for signs of Anton. Nothing.

The maid showed me to the parlor and brought a cup of tea. It was nearly teatime. The parlor was done up in traditional style, heavy furniture filling the space. Chocolate-brown curtains covered the windows. They were probably rarely opened, to keep sunlight from fading the furniture.

Atop the carved mantelpiece rested a silver-framed picture of Frau Röhm on her wedding day, wearing the dress her son had expected me to wear, the dress that lay spread across the dusty backseat. She looked young but stern. Her grip on her new husband's arm was firm, her chin set, her smile forced. Everyone leaned toward her, as if anxious to please. I sipped my strong hot tea. I needed the energy.

Next to the picture stood a humidor. Did she smoke cigars? Although tempted to peek inside, I wanted to be on my best behavior so I remained sitting upright, like a proper lady, in a round-backed chair that creaked when I moved.

The piano in the corner shone from vigilant dusting. I imagined a young Ernst Röhm playing there, pudgy legs dangling above the floor, a stern teacher cracking the boy on his knuckles with a ruler. I was about to tell this woman that the son who sat there long ago was soon to be executed, if not already dead. I drained my cup and wished for something stronger.

Atop the polished piano sat a picture of Röhm as a young soldier. I crossed the thick red rug to look at it. He had been handsome then, slim and elegant in a gray tunic, holding his rapier rigid. In the picture he sported an oversized nose. The boy before the Great War stole his face. Next to it rested a picture of a baby in lace sitting on a serious woman's lap. He had her deep-set eyes. He had siblings, but I saw no pictures of them. Was he the favored son? That would make the blow worse.

Behind the picture rested a twig. Heart pounding, I drew it out. A message from Anton. It had four bends in it. He had been here with three people. Frau Röhm, probably the maid, and someone else. Perhaps Mouse?

I tucked the twig in my pocket and hurried across the parlor. I eased open the parlor door, but before I could step through a growl stopped me. The Rottweilers glared at me. I stepped a foot over the threshold and they stood in unison.

I eased the door closed, wishing I still had my satchel and the Luger inside. But I did not. I would have to talk my way through this without alerting Frau Röhm. I was no match for the dogs or Mouse unarmed, as the pain in my ribs reminded me.

I paced back to my chair and sat, taking the saucer and empty teacup into my lap.

The door opened and I stood, trying to decide how to tell her what I knew of her son, and mine. Much depended on what she already knew of his fate.

A fragile-looking elderly woman preceded the maid into the parlor. Wispy hair floated around her head like dandelion fluff. Despite her age, she carried herself as erectly as her son. Fortunately, the dogs remained outside.

"Frau Röhm." I curtseyed automatically, my mother's training. I spoke loudly, in case Anton might hear me. "I am sorry to disturb you today."

"I've received disturbing calls from others as well." Her voice quavered with age, but her tone was clear and determined, her accent pure Bavaria, just like her son. "And you do not need to raise your voice. I am not yet deaf."

After the maid seated her on an uncomfortable-looking horsehair chair, Frau Röhm waved her away. She settled in like a crow into its nest, turning and fidgeting before sitting still. She did not invite me to sit. "You have news of him?"

"I do." What could I tell her? "I just left him at Stadelheim."

"You are the Vogel girl." She smoothed her palm across her old-fashioned lace dress. "The one who kidnapped my grandson, Anton."

I set my cup and saucer on the table with a quiet clink. The maid poured me more tea. "I am not entirely certain that Anton is—"

"Yet he was going to marry you today," she talked over me. "Or so I heard. I've never known a woman to have that kind of influence over him."

She cocked her head, assessing me as a potential daughter-in-law, perhaps questioning my breeding qualities. I stared straight into her eyes. She was so much like her son that I detested her already. "I would not say that I have influence."

"He never brought a girl home before. You must have something, although I cannot quite see it myself." She sipped her tea.

I sipped my own tea and waited for her to have something polite to say. The maid stood with her gaze aimed at the floor, waiting too.

"Was he well when you left him?" Done castigating me, she wanted information.

I did not dare anger her until I found out Anton's whereabouts. "Quite well, Frau Röhm. He wished me to convey his love to you."

"Did he?" she asked with a little girl smile. "It is kind that he remembers me at such a time."

"And he also wished for me to pick up the boy, Anton," I lied, giving it a try. "He said that you—"

"He said no such thing, of course." She shook her gnarled finger at me as her son had done in the hotel room, chastising a naughty child. "Think me not a fool because I am old, Fräulein Vogel."

She would have made a terrible mother-in-law. I tried not to imagine how my life would have gone if I had been forced to marry Röhm.

"Are those ungrateful worms going to murder him?" She leaned forward on the chair, clear blue eyes drilling into mine.

I bowed my head, unwilling to meet those eyes, so like her son's. I did not want her to see my anger and the part of me that pitied her. She was still a mother, with a son soon to be killed, even if she had been responsible for raising him to ally himself with monsters. "I believe so."

"Do you know how many times he was wounded defending this country?" She picked up an embroidery hoop and stitched a piece of yellow linen. She hardly glanced down as the red thread wove in and out, the needle guided by fingers that quivered, either with age or emotion.

"Three," I answered without thinking.

The needle pierced the fabric again and again. "Once he came back here, barely off crutches. He'd been hit by fourteen pieces of shrapnel.

He lost his nose. I nursed him to health and sent him back into the war."

Her eyes strayed to the picture of the young Röhm on the piano, and her fingers stopped stitching. "No matter what they did, he always went back. Until now."

"I am very sorry—"

She cut me off again. Just as well, as I did not feel sorry. "He went to prison for them. Stadelheim. That's where he is?"

"Cell 474."

"And they will shoot him like a dog. Hitler, who ate at my table many times, will have him killed."

"We do not know . . ." My voice trailed off. That too was a lie. We did know. I stood like a chastened schoolgirl, sweaty hands clasped in front of me.

"I gave my son to the Fatherland. He spent his life in its service. They bloodied him, almost killed him."

You should never have given him up, I longed to say, but I kept silent. He was her son, and he would be taken from her because of the weight of his decisions. It was not my place to criticize her. I had to appease her until I found Anton. Was he here? How could I get past the dogs to search?

"When he tried to restore Germany's greatness in the putsch, they arrested him." She shook her head in disbelief. "But he stood firm through it all. He will stand firm through this too."

I picked up my cup, the china hot against my fingers, unsure what to say. He might stand firm, but I did not think he would live. I sipped bitter tea.

"They will lie about him too. To conceal their own treachery." She returned to her embroidery as if alone.

I listened for other sounds. Nothing. Even the dogs were silent.

"I want to bury his body in our family plot." Her voice was as calm as if she ordered meat from the butcher. "I am his mother. That is my right. A mother should be able to bury her son with honor."

"A mother should never have to bury her son."

"Get his body for me." She ignored what I had said, as she had for the entire conversation.

"I am uncertain if I can."

"Give me my son, and I will give you yours."

My heart leaped. She had Anton, or she knew where he was. If she had him, then he must be safe. She would take good care of her grandson. I hoped.

"Give me mine first." I struggled to keep my voice calm. I did not want to reveal how desperate I was to get him back. But she was a mother too—she knew. "Then I will get you yours. I give you my word."

She shook her head, white hair flying. "My son trusted you to keep your word three years ago. I won't make that same mistake."

I bit back my anger. Her words held truth, but I did not want to hear it. I wanted Anton. I finished my tea and set down the cup. I must at least pretend to agree to her terms, but I would not capitulate too easily. "They will not release his body to me. I am not next of kin."

"I shall write a letter. Saying that you act in my name." She waved a hand toward the desk. "Fetch paper and pen."

The maid hurried to do so, pulling thick writing paper and an elegant black fountain pen out of cubbyholes in the desk. She carried them across the room to Frau Röhm, along with a heavy book on which to rest the paper.

Frau Röhm put down her embroidery and picked up the glossy pen.

"Even with such a letter, I have no guarantee of success."

"I hope for your sake that you do." Her veined hand traced spindly letters, the only sound the scratch of nib on paper.

I thought of Anton, perhaps somewhere in this very house. I pictured him listening at a keyhole and remembered how he had hid in the wardrobe long ago to eavesdrop on my conversation with his father shortly before we fled Germany. Anton was resourceful; he would do better than most children in such a situation. Still, he was only nine years old.

Frau Röhm finished and waved the letter to dry it, handing the pen and remaining paper to the maid. The letter she held out to me. "Take this with you."

I hesitated, then took it, the paper heavy in my hand. "I must see Anton first."

She picked up her embroidery hoop and went back to work. I stood in front of her, holding the letter.

"Good luck, Fräulein Vogel." Her tone made it clear that our interview was over.

"The day that you receive your son, I receive mine." I tried to sound as tough as she. But I had little to bargain with, and we both knew it.

"I keep my word," she said. "Which is more than can be said of you."

"That remains to be seen."

She gestured to the maid to show me out. "If you see my son alive—" Her voice broke, but she steadied it. "Tell him that his mother is proud of him. He has lived his life by the warrior code. None of those political monsters has a tenth his courage. And they know it."

I nodded, but she bent over her embroidery. Her hands shook, and I sensed that she was near tears. She cleared her rheumy throat. "Do you have my wedding dress?" she asked, eyes still on the cloth.

"I do."

"I want it back."

At least I had one thing that she wanted. "The moment I have Anton, you may have it."

"Fair enough."

The maid beckoned. I followed. I had nothing more to say, and she looked quite capable of throwing me out of the house. Her arms were more muscular than Boris's. I must contact him soon so that he would not go to Switzerland and worry when I did not arrive as scheduled.

The dogs growled when I walked down the stuffy hall. When the maid chirped at them, they fell silent. Like everyone in that household, they were well trained.

The maid followed me to the front door, probably to ensure that I left. At the door she handed me my satchel.

I hurried down the path to the staff car. Was Anton still here? If not, Frau Röhm must know where he was. I folded her letter and tucked it into my satchel. Where was Mouse?

Light-headed, I took a deep breath. A familiar pain from my rib stabbed into me, and for the first time I smiled at the pain. Perhaps it *was* Mouse's calling card. I fingered the bruise. If damaged ribs really were his calling card, then that was a lead to track him down, especially if I was correct about Anton's hint and he was a pimp. I knew just the person to ask. But for that I needed to go to Berlin, and if she kept to the schedule she had used for all the years I had known her, she would not be available until Tuesday afternoon. Until then I would play along with Frau Röhm.

I opened the car door, but did not climb in. I wanted to be visible to anyone in the house. I reached my arm in and leaned on the horn, blowing it over and over while watching the house's windows. Curtains twitched in the parlor, and a veined hand rested on the windowsill. Nothing else moved. If Anton was there, peeping through the curtains without moving them, he would know that I was here. I pointed to the walkway. If he could escape, he would come there. But nothing indicated that anyone was in the house besides Frau Röhm and the maid.

The heavy door swung open, but I did not stop sounding the horn. The maid stormed down the walkway. Only after she grabbed the car door did I stop blowing the horn. Frenzied barking cut through the air.

"What do you wish?" she said. "This is not a racetrack."

I smiled politely. "I need your telephone number."

"You did not need to make such a fuss."

I tore a page out of my notebook and handed it to her, along with my pen. Still muttering, she scrawled numbers across the page.

"I do apologize," I said, and she snorted, probably well aware of my insincerity.

I drove around the block and parked next to a stranger's driveway. Unless they were out of touch or completely blameless, they were in for a shock when they returned home to a Nazi staff car. Still it could not be helped.

Carrying my satchel, suitcase, and the unused wedding dress, I headed back toward the Röhm house. No point in returning to Stadelheim today. If they had already executed Röhm, it would be a day before they released bodies. And I had more to do here.

I walked to the house across the street from Frau Röhm's. It had looked empty when I first drove up and no one came out when I honked the horn moments before. I hurried along the path, hoping no one in the Röhm household noticed me. This house was larger than the Röhms'. Three stories and built of stone. A matching stone wall shielded the walkway from the street.

Surveying the yard for signs of inhabitants, I knocked on the front door. The golden-brown grass meant that the owners had stopped watering. I stood in the shadows by the front door and rapped again more loudly, listening for footsteps inside. If anyone answered, I would pretend to be selling the wedding dress, a common thing to do in these times of high unemployment.

No one came to the door. I stood on tiptoe to peek in the front windows. For the first time that day my heart lightened. White sheets draped the furniture. The owners were away, and for an extended time. What a piece of luck! I circled the house.

In the back, as I had hoped, was a solarium, glass panes glinting in the sun. Inside, an empty table waited for its next breakfast. Faded lithographs of citrus fruit lined the walls, and an old yellow rug covered the tile floor. A wonderful place to sit on a summer morning and read the paper while one lingered over coffee. I pictured Anton and Boris sitting in those chairs, Anton drinking milk, Boris coffee. We could trade sections from the newspaper and decide what to do the next weekend. A wonderful, ordinary, and completely impossible life.

I stopped imagining and searched the flower bed for a large rock. I brushed its smooth warm surface clean of dirt. Hoping to muffle the sound, I wrapped the wedding dress around the rock. I swung it against the glass pane near the door handle. Glass tinkled to the floor inside. In another yard, a dog barked twice.

I reached through the broken pane and unlocked the door, careful not to cut my arm on the shards of glass still embedded in the frame. Hefting my suitcase and the wedding dress, I hurried inside and closed the door. I hated to damage the home of a stranger who had never harmed me, but it was the only way to do what I must.

In the main house, I hurried past a draped harpsichord and the oil-painted faces of stern dead ancestors. My footsteps echoed through the rooms.

I found stairs and climbed to the attic. Books lined the walls. On another day I would have stopped and looked through them, curious what Röhm's neighbors read, what they thought about. But today I kept walking.

The long day's heat filled the attic. I began to sweat at once. Surprisingly empty, the attic contained only an old table, two mismatched chairs, and dusty steamer trunks. Groaning at the pain in my rib, I dragged a chair and the table to the front window and brought out my field glasses.

As I had hoped, I had an unobstructed view of Frau Röhm's house. I rested my elbows on the table to steady the glasses and checked each curtained window. No sign of Anton. But I would watch all day to catch sight of him, alive and well. I loved him. He was as surely my son as if I had carried him in my womb. The men whom I had loved, I loved because of *who* they were, but Anton, and my brother Ernst, I loved simply *because* they were. They did not need to have a collection of appealing traits. They simply needed to be.

I wrestled open the reluctant window to better hear the sounds of the street and let in fresh air. I remembered my days at the newspaper, where I always opened the windows to let out the cigarette smoke. Back when I wrote about murderers but did not have to run from them.

Soon the broad-shouldered maid left to walk the dogs. The dogs trotted along, obedient. What would I do about them? Perhaps I might find tinned meat and sleeping powder. But the dogs seemed too well-trained to eat food from a stranger. I worried for a full half hour, pacing in front of the window, until she returned without the dogs. Then I worried what she had done with them.

Through the long thirsty afternoon and evening I watched, sweat running down my body. But I stayed at my post. What if I missed a glimpse of him, if Frau Röhm sent him outside to play in the late afternoon sunshine? He might be only meters away. I dared not take the chance of her moving him without my knowledge. If he was there and safe, I would break him free.

I read her letter, making certain that it did not contain orders to have me executed when I presented it. I did not trust her.

After the maid returned, no one came to the house, and no one left. No one opened the curtains or so much as peeked out. If I had not known that people lived there, I would have assumed the Röhm house was as deserted as the one in which I currently sat.

I pulled my reporter's notebook and my old jade-green fountain pen out of my satchel. Like Ulli, I needed to write things down to make sense of them. Glancing every few seconds at the house across the street, I passed the time by writing everything I had seen or heard since Röhm's arrest. The kind of thing my mother always warned me against. Trouble would likely come of it, but someone must bear witness, describe the last moments of those eight boys, and the hundreds of other boys I had not seen. I wrote until my hand cramped, shook out the cramps, and wrote more.

When night fell, a light appeared in the parlor where we had tea. The light moved upstairs. To a bedroom? Soon after that the light extinguished. Presumably she was in bed. But what about the maid? Did Frau Röhm have other servants? Was Mouse still there?

The maid opened a small door on the side of the house. I focused the field glasses on her as she hauled out a garbage can, visible in the light from the streetlamp. She wiped her palms on her apron and went back inside.

Minutes later the maid emerged from the front door. She turned and stood with her back to me, probably locking the door. Her ample figure trotted to the streetcar stop. After she caught her streetcar I closed the attic window and hurried downstairs.

I washed dust from my hands and face by moonlight and dried off with one of my unsuspecting host's opulent towels. What a terrible houseguest I was. I broke the glass in the solarium door, and I dirtied the towels. I certainly would not be invited back.

I ran a glass of lukewarm water and stationed myself near the front window. Standing, I ate the food that Ulli had packed for me, grateful for his thoughtfulness. I had to wait until everyone across the street slept soundly.

When I was full, and the borrowed house restored to order as much as possible, I crept out the broken back door and circled round to the front yard. Dried grass crackled under my suitcase when I set it behind a stone pillar near the street. I laid the wedding dress atop the suitcase to keep the silk clean. I drew the Luger out of my satchel. If Mouse was in there, I would need it.

I crept across the street carrying the gun and a damp towel I had borrowed. Hoping that no one watched, I hurried to the side of the Röhm house.

Folly to try to break through the thick front door, but the servant's entrance where the maid had put out the garbage might have possibilities. I tried the side door, hopeful. Locked. I expected that. But it did have a window. I wrapped the towel around the gun's stock and used it to break the glass. I reached through the window frame and unlocked the door. Amazing that more people were not burglars. It was ridiculously easy. Then I remembered the dogs, grateful that they had been taken away.

Once inside I swept up glass with the towel. Perhaps no one would notice. I smiled at my own naïveté. The maid would know when she came back to get the garbage cans in the morning. But by then I hoped to be long gone.

Luger held in both hands, I crept down the hall and into the kitchen, dark shapes of the worktable and sink reassuring in the moonlight. Everything put away, surfaces wiped. Certain that no stray shards of broken glass flew this far, I took off my shoes and carried them in my left hand, the pistol in the other.

My stocking feet pattered through the kitchen and into the dining room. The table was set for breakfast. One place, not two. If Anton was here, he was not expected to breakfast with his grandmother. And no place was set for Mouse either.

I searched the front room, the bathroom, and the foyer. No sign of Anton.

I walked up the stairs, back against the wall, each footfall careful and light. Still, a step squeaked. I froze, every muscle taut. No other sounds disturbed the night. Heart pounding, I skulked up the rest of the stairs.

Three bedrooms and a bathroom, and none contained Anton. The room with a closed door I assumed must belong to Frau Röhm. I would check that last.

I tiptoed up the narrow stairs to the attic. It contained a jumble of furniture, coatracks, steamer trunks, and a stuffed elk head, but no small boy was buried in the drifts of dust.

I sneaked back downstairs. I had nowhere else to search. I set my shoes next to the door. I tightened my grip on the Luger and pressed down the door handle, slow and steady. A soft click told me when the catch released, and I pushed open the door. Frau Röhm lay on the bed, snoring, a white cap on her head, sweating in the heat.

She was alone.

My heart fell. Anton was not in the house, and I had seen no evidence that he ever had been, except for the twig. Mouse must have stashed him elsewhere.

I backed out of the room and bent to pick up my shoes. The snoring stopped. I hurried down the stairs hugging the wall opposite the creaky step. Hard footsteps crossed the floor above.

Caught.

I tightened my sweaty fingers around the Luger. Was she armed too?

8

Frau Röhm's quavery voice floated down. "I assume it is you, Fräulein Vogel. As your thorough search has revealed, he is not here. I cannot keep him in the house until this political situation is resolved. But have no fear. He is with someone I trust."

Mouse?

"Be on your way, and do not come back without my son." She cleared her old throat. "I sent the dogs to a neighbor after you left today, because I need you uninjured. I expected you to search the house. Tomorrow I bring the dogs back. I hope you understand what that means for intruders." I thought of threatening her, but did not think she would tell me anything. She was every bit as tough as her son. If she told me anything under duress, I bet it would be lies. My best course was to stay on her good side. I thought of sneaking off without answering, but decided that only honesty would do.

"Thank you, Frau Röhm. I will return, through the front door, as soon as I can."

Burning with embarrassment, I let myself out the back door, glad that I had at least cleaned up the glass.

Refreshed after a good night's sleep and a pilfered breakfast in the abandoned house, I was relieved to find the staff car where I had left it the night before. I drove back to the prison. I thought of ditching the car, but so many threads linked me to Röhm as Hannah Vogel, what was one more?

I hoped to see Röhm before they executed him. I hoped to give him his mother's message of her pride in his courage, and her love for him. Perhaps he would relent and tell me Anton's location. Perhaps listening to the executions of his men had softened him up. If not, I had a plan for finding Mouse.

I parked at the far corner of the lot away from the other cars, so I would have a good view from the front stairs of anyone fussing around the staff car. Here many might recognize it as Röhm's, and I needed to make certain that no one watched when I returned.

For the second time, I crunched across gravel to the guardhouse. The guard stood behind the wooden counter, back to me. Papers littered the table in front of him. Execution orders? Were they so organized?

"Good morning, sir." When he turned, I recognized him as the old man who had cleaned up after me the previous afternoon. His eyes also flickered with recognition, and a trace of anger.

"I am here to see Ernst Röhm again." I pulled Frau Röhm's letter from my satchel. "I have additional messages from his mother. And she has authorized me to start the transfer of his body if he has been executed."

"He's still alive, I think. But no one is allowed to see him." The guard did not spare the letter a glance. "Orders."

"Has anyone visited him since I went in?" I rested my elbows on the counter and fanned myself with Frau Röhm's letter. At least the letter was good for that much.

He hesitated, then paged through a large black ledger. "Hans Frank."
I craned to read the entries, but he snapped the book closed.
"Am I in there?" I dearly hoped not.
"Your visit was unofficial."
My relief was short lived. If my visit was unofficial, then so might others have been. I might never know who else had visited Röhm. On the other hand, at least I was not listed in the book. A link between

Röhm and myself rendered invisible. "Did he have official visitors, besides Minister Frank?"

"I'm not supposed to be telling you that." His eyes slid left and right, probably to check that no one overheard our conversation.

"His mother wishes to know who has been with him. She wishes to know all she can of his last hours. Surely you can understand that."

He shuffled his feet, looking uncomfortable. At heart he was a good sort, and my conscience twinged, but the stakes were high. We stood in silence.

"No one else since I've been on duty," he answered finally.

"A priest?" Röhm might pass messages out with a priest.

"Not even a priest. That would be in the book."

I wondered how last night had been for Röhm, sitting alone in his cell listening to the executions, knowing that his turn would come soon enough. He was tough, but even he must have a breaking point. Another round of shots cracked through the air. The guard and I jumped.

I put the letter flat on the counter upside down, for him to read if he chose. He kept his gaze on me. "Is there a way I may see him unofficially? For her?"

"Not possible. I almost lost my post for letting you in before." He grimaced. "And it seems to me that you saw more than enough yesterday."

"I am sorry if I caused you trouble."

"I'll tell you when he's executed, Fräulein," he said in a soft voice. "I'm sorry, but I can do no more than that."

I picked up the letter and looked around for a chair to sit and wait. They had been removed. No one was to linger here. If anyone, like me, was foolish enough to come, they were to leave again as soon as possible. Relatives were not welcome.

I left the guardroom, feeling the heavy door pull itself closed behind me as I stepped into the hot clear air. Today promised to be hotter than yesterday, fine and beautiful. A day for sailing or walking in the park eating ices. A day that should have passed in simple frivolity for the young men in the prison. Instead it was their day to die.

I sat on the hot stairs in a wide-brimmed hat I had brought from South America. Every twenty minutes a set of rifles popped, killing eight more boys. Even though it was quieter here than in the guardhouse, I flinched each time. If Röhm still lived, how did he feel? He knew many of them by name, had slept with more than several if rumors were to be believed. He must be imagining them standing, and dying, because they had followed him. Their young talent and energy wasted. I dropped my head into my sweaty hands.

Throughout the long day I sat alone on the stairs. I stood when men came and went. Most dressed in SS-black, but a few wore civilian suits, looking as much like bankers as Boris. But they dealt in the figures of death, not the numbers of commerce. Most passed without notice, but a few looked surprised. None dared speak. Probably none wanted to know if they had murdered my husband, my brother, or my son.

I passed the time between volleys by trying to keep my mind blank. I forced myself not to think of the mothers, the boys now gone, and the lives they might have led. Far away in her dark parlor, curtains drawn, I knew that Röhm's mother sat his deathwatch with me, red thread flashing through yellow linen.

I thought of leaving for lunch, but had no appetite. For reasons that I could not articulate, it felt important to stay and wait. Someone must listen. Soon the Nazis would forbid even that.

A little after six a scattered volley of shots erupted from the part of the prison that housed Röhm. Unlike the firing squads, they were irregular. Two different weapons firing out of sequence, perhaps three. I counted nine rounds. It sounded as if at least two men had fired their guns empty. Something had not gone according to plan. I smiled bitterly. That sounded like Röhm.

Minutes later Theodor Eicke, familiar from newspaper photographs, walked out the front door in SS dress uniform, hat tucked under his arm, a pair of leather gloves held in his right hand. A wet fleck clung to the knife crease of his trousers, near the hem. Blood?

He inclined his barbered head toward me. His hair was parted on the left, temples a distinguished silver. With his square face and large eyes he looked like my old physics teacher, but his eyes were cold and dead. "Good evening." He bowed in my direction.

I shuddered and scrambled to my feet. This man had set up the concentration camp at Dachau, not far from here. More than anyone else, he bore responsibility for countless daily tortures and humiliations. In front of me stood the man who transferred soldiers out of his camps if they showed the slightest compassion for the prisoners. How could I make small talk with him? Yet I must.

"Good evening," I answered, mouth dry.

He pulled a cigarette out of a gold case embossed with a swastika. He offered it to me, and I shook my head. "Waiting for someone?"

"For news of someone." I cleared my throat.

He struck a match, and the smell of sulfur drifted over to me. I coughed.

Well bred, he blew the smoke away from me. "News of whom?"

"I am here representing Emilie Röhm, mother of Ernst Röhm." I kept silent on my own connections with Röhm. I did not want someone like Eicke to know about me. Only anonymity might keep me alive.

I held up Frau Röhm's letter, wilted from the damp heat. He stepped close and skimmed the spidery words. The acrid smell of gunpowder clung to him, an undertone to the more familiar odor of cigarette smoke.

"He died well. The Führer ordered that we send him in a pistol and let him do the honorable thing."

"Did he?" I asked. I had seen Röhm convince others to do the "honorable" thing, but I wagered his own survival instinct was too strong. I rather hoped he had used the revolver to take one of them with him. Someone should resist them.

"Said he wouldn't do Hitler the favor." Eicke picked a shred of tobacco off his tongue. "The old bull had balls, to the end."

I nodded, staring at his long fingers as he flicked ash onto the steps.

He smoked in silence, inhaling deeply before letting smoke trickle out of his mouth. I gave him a moment, then spoke. "Is there anything more I can tell his mother?" I stressed the word *mother*, to remind him that somewhere, someone mourned Röhm.

He paused, perhaps deciding what to divulge. "Tell his mother that when we came back he was stripped to the waist. He stood at attention and offered a final salute before he was shot. An officer to the end."

I pictured Röhm clicking his heels and saluting his executioners as he had saluted Hitler in the hotel room at the Hanselbauer. Before I was twenty, I had lost my first fiancé, my real one, in the Great War. If I counted Röhm as a second fiancé, I had been made a widow before I became a bride, twice. I had not thought I would grieve at Röhm's passing. Yet I did. He was human and, his faults notwithstanding, probably more humane than those who would replace him.

"How many times was he shot?"

"As many as necessary." Eicke straightened his collar, smoothing the silver oak leaf patch sewn there.

So, more than once. Nine, if I had counted correctly. I imagined Eicke and the other man dropping him with the first shot, then firing at him as he lay on the cement floor of his cell. I hoped that the first shot had killed him.

Eicke dropped his cigarette on the steps and ground it out with his toe. A motor started nearby. A black automobile, expensive but not as fine as Röhm's, pulled in front of us. A chauffeur with hair so blond that it looked white leaped out of the driver's seat and hurried to open the rear passenger door. When he stood at attention next to the door, Eicke nodded to him.

"How do you know these things?"

Eicke settled his officer's cap on his head, pulling the brim down with his thumb and forefinger. "Because I shot him myself."

9

Eicke walked to the automobile, stride calm and unhurried. Minutes ago he had murdered another human being, but he seemed unshaken. He pulled on his gloves and waved one black hand at me before climbing into the backseat. I was too stunned to wave back. The chauffeur closed the door with a solid thunk. Eicke looked straight ahead, done with his business at the prison. The chauffeur shot me a curious look before climbing into the front seat and driving away.

I watched until the automobile reached the trees and the sound of the engine died away. The gunpowder smell lingered. The smell of fireworks, picnics with my father, and death.

I swallowed and returned to the guard desk. The guard raised his head when I came in, his blue eyes faded and dull. No shots had sounded since Röhm's. Perhaps the Nazis were finished for the day.

He shuffled papers. "Fräulein, I've been informed that Ernst Röhm has been executed."

I nodded. I had been informed too. For three years fear of Röhm had ruled my life. And it was over. I was free. Hannah Vogel could do whatever she wished, go wherever she pleased. Yet I was not happy with how I had won my freedom. I would never be fully free of Röhm. I pictured him on the floor of his cell, Eicke standing over him, firing his pistol empty.

"You have my condolences." The guard stared at the wall behind my head. He had witnessed Röhm's performance, where he told me that he loved me. He had probably spun an elaborate story of my attachment to Röhm. Despite everything, the old guard felt sorry for me, the first human feeling I had seen that day. I gave him a tired smile.

"I wish to have his body released for burial in his family plot." I pulled out the letter.

This time he scanned the paper. "It looks in order. But I cannot help you."

"Cannot or will not?" Was he fishing for a bribe? Prison guards did not earn much salary, and I had bribed more than my share while working as crime reporter Peter Weill, but I was terrified to try it here, with Nazis all around.

"Cannot." He shook his head. "The bodies aren't being released. Yet."

Did they need to make the bodies presentable for viewing? I closed my eyes and tried not to picture how Röhm must look, with nine rounds in him. "So, he is in no condition for his mother to see." I was surprised that my voice sounded so calm.

The guard grimaced. "If he was shot in the courtyard . . ."

I shook my head. "He was shot in his cell. Nine times, I believe."

His eyes met mine for the first time. "It might be days before they release him."

"How do I claim his body?"

The guard shrugged. "I can't help you here. You must go to Berlin for official permission. There are signatures you will need."

I scribbled notes as he detailed the next steps. Berlin. I could be there in seven hours. It was my home, and Mouse's. If he was on the run from the Nazis, it might be where he would go to ground. If he was there, I would find him.

There had to be a train this evening. And even if I did not find Mouse, after I had the official signatures, I could trade them for Anton. If Frau Röhm kept her end of the bargain, we would be on our way back to Switzerland by Tuesday.

It was still light by the time I reached the Munich train station. I abandoned Röhm's staff car on the sidewalk, keys in the ignition. I hoped that the police would remove it before someone else stole it and got into trouble, although it would be better for me if it were moved elsewhere so that no one could trace me to the train station. I would have parked farther away, but I did not want to carry the suitcase and wedding dress any farther than I had to with my aching rib.

A vendor stood in front of a cart, white apron smeared with mustard. A lone wurst rested in a steel pan of water that no longer looked hot. Trying not to think about how long the wurst had been floating there, I bought it with a roll and a dollop of mustard. I wolfed them down where I stood. It was not warm enough, but my stomach did not care. I had not eaten since my stolen breakfast. Stadelheim had robbed me of my appetite.

I mounted the stairs into the giant monstrosity of the Munich Hauptbahnhof. The brickwork and soot stains reminded me of the Borsig factory in Berlin: utilitarianism dressed up to look grand. An architect had worked hard on the building, but I would have traded the columns and arches for larger signs directing travelers where they needed to go.

I wandered about, trying to get my bearings. In the busy station people spoke in the soft Bavarian accent that Ernst Röhm and his mother had used. I missed the clipped tones of Berlin.

I hunted up the ticket counter and purchased a fare on the night train to Berlin from an agent with his hat pulled so low over his face that I would not have recognized him if he had been my own brother.

Even though I dreaded it, I called Frau Röhm. The maid answered.

"Hannah." I did not want to use my last name on the telephone.

"I will fetch her."

I scooted a cigarette butt out of the telephone booth with the toe of my shoe, thinking of Eicke smoking on the prison steps. How would I tell her? What if she wanted details?

"Röhm." Her voice sounded old and tired.

"It is Hannah. It is with great regret—"

"Do not lie to me. Or give me stock phrases. You are a writer. You can do better."

I blinked. Straight facts then. "Your son—"

"Dead?"

"Yes. He died bravely, I heard."

"Of course he did." Her voice broke, and the maid came back on the line.

"Is there more?" the maid asked.

I told her that I must go to Berlin to complete the paperwork for his body to be released for burial. I did not tell her that he had been shot multiple times. Nor by whom.

Then I ended the call and found the platform for my train. First to board, I lugged my suitcase down the narrow corridor to my compartment, muttering with each stab in my side. I longed to find Mouse and break his rib. He should feel the same pain he inflicted.

I slid the steel door open with the hand that held the wedding dress, the other still curled around the handle of my suitcase. I checked the door lock before I went in. Not strong enough to withstand a couple of good kicks. Even if the door were sturdy, the conductor had a master key. No security here.

Sighing, I entered and examined the window. It tilted in at a forty-five-degree angle. No going out there. Even too small to toss out my suitcase.

Stop it, I admonished myself. No one but the prison guard and Frau Röhm know you might be here. This is how the train compartment is set up, and you cannot change it. Relax and sleep. Who would be following you? No one knows that you are linked to Röhm. Except for everyone invited to the wedding.

I laid the wedding dress across the seat and stowed my suitcase. It would not be a full train. A few mothers with children and a couple of businessmen milled about on the platform. No one seemed out of the ordinary, and I did not see a single Nazi uniform—neither the brown shirts of the SA, nor the black ones of the SS.

A businessman in a pin-striped suit kissed a young woman good-bye, hands buried in her luxuriant long hair. I imagined it was Boris seeing me off on a short trip, regretful but secure in the knowledge that we would be reunited soon. A simple pleasure, perhaps, but one that we had always been denied. After the couple separated, she touched his cheek once. Her lips mouthed a farewell. He kissed the top of her head and climbed onto the train.

The platform contained only those left behind, waving. I suppressed an urge to wave back. But of course I had no one to wave to. I was alone.

"All aboard!" The conductor slammed his door. With a lurch and a whistle, the train started. We trundled out of the station and through the yard. Soon we picked up speed. The buildings of Munich streamed by my window.

Two thumps startled me. "Tickets!" A deep voice rumbled through the door.

I unlocked the door and opened it to reveal a round conductor with a walrus moustache brandishing a ticket punch. I handed him my ticket. "The attendant will be around in ten minutes to unfold the bed. Make yourself comfortable."

I could not imagine what comfortable felt like anymore, so I sat with my hands folded in my lap and dozed.

The soft knock of the attendant woke me. I let him in. He wore a dark uniform and a different cap from the conductor. "Fräulein." He touched his cap. "I'm here about your bed."

He gestured with his silver master key. "Top or bottom?"

"Bottom." Easier to get out of in a hurry.

I stepped aside as he snicked his key into the silver slot. He folded my bed out of the wall, one hand under it as if he could stop it if it fell down too far. His efficient hands pulled the sheet and blanket free on the top corner and folded them back in a triangle. He smoothed his hand once over the bedding, straightening it. His actions reminded me of how the steward prepared our beds on the zeppelin. Only days ago I had slept on a bottom bunk, with Anton on the top as Indian lookout, complete with a bow and arrow we had fashioned in South America. I had put my foot down about putting curare on the arrow tips, although he had put up a spirited argument in favor of complete authenticity.

I locked my door and positioned my suitcase across the threshold. It would not slow anyone down much, but sometimes a second can make a difference. I slipped into a nightdress.

Where did Anton sleep tonight? Safe with a friend of Frau Röhm's? Or had the Nazis killed him to eliminate evidence that Röhm was not the moral degenerate they claimed? I forced my thoughts away from such morbid possibilities. Frau Röhm knew where he was, and he was safe. I only had to fulfill the terms of our agreement, and she would give him back. An old woman did not need the care and bother of a young boy she would not live long enough to see grow into a man.

I had to believe that. In the last three years Anton had become a part of me. Keeping him safe was more than a duty. Watching him grow up unfettered by the violence and anger that my brother had endured was a pleasure. His wonderful sense of humor and steadfast belief in right and wrong reminded me of my own as a child, values far too easy to lose track of on the journey to adulthood. I had never regretted my decision to walk away from my life to keep him safe, and I would sacrifice everything to get him back. The Nazis would not turn him into a mindless drone of the state while I still lived and breathed.

After the lights of Munich gave way to the darkness of the countryside, I carried his passport, the one that said Anton Röhm, into the bathroom. It was a death sentence. I cut out the picture with nail scissors. I might need it later. The rest I cut into tiny bits and slowly fed down the toilet and onto the tracks below. When I finished, the pieces were scattered over miles of Bavarian countryside.

I tucked the picture into my satchel, trying not to think that it might be the last one of Anton I might see. I climbed into the bottom bunk. Unable to sleep, I mulled over which identity papers to use in Berlin. Hannah Vogel; Frau Röhm knew her, and that identity was already linked to Röhm. I thought of the Swiss passport and ticket in my suitcase. Our Swiss identities as Adelheid and Anton Zinsli were compromised. Someone had informed Röhm that we traveled on the zeppelin. That was why he diverted it. I ran through the list of passengers and crewmen in my head. Who had it been? I came up with no answers, but decided to leave that identity in my suitcase. It might be useful to have in case Hannah Vogel got into trouble. Hannah Vogel was quite proficient at that.

The clack of the train and rocking of the car were hypnotic. The stress of the last day caught up to me, and when full darkness came around midnight, I sank into a troubled sleep, jerking awake often. When I gave up and rose, we were pulling through the flat outskirts of Berlin, sunrise gold on the horizon. The sun rose a little before five at this time of year. In South America, we lived near the equator and the days were almost the same length in summer and winter. I had missed Berlin's late summer nights, when twilight lingered until well after ten o'clock.

As dangerous as I knew the city was these days, my heart lightened. Even if the Nazis ruled from here, they never captured the majority of votes. Munich was the cradle of National Socialism, Berlin only accidentally its home because the capital was here. This city was where my friends lived, where I spent many happy years. I could not wait to walk the cobbled streets, hear the sarcastic jokes, drink the wonderful beer, and feel at home. I knew the people. I knew the places. After years on the run, I was home, even if only for a little while.

I washed and dressed quickly, eager to arrive at the station.

I packed everything into my suitcase and draped the wedding dress over my arm. I stood in front of the door as we pulled into Anhalter Bahnhof station. When we stopped, I pulled open the door and jumped to the platform, not waiting for the conductor to come along with his wooden steps.

Trains from all over Europe arrived around me, steam puffing into the sky. I inhaled the Berlin air, ignoring my rib. Nothing smelled like that air in all the world. The scent of cinders, manure, and automobile exhaust mingled with a thousand ladies' perfumes. Home. I had not realized how much I missed it, how out of place I felt everywhere else. For better or worse, this was where I belonged. Yet I knew I would have to leave it soon.

Still, my heart was light and I barely noticed the pain in my side as I tramped out to catch the subway. I had hours before the city offices opened, and I knew a place in Berlin where I would be taken in, fed, and helped to get well. A place, and a person, that made me feel safe waited.

10

I walked down the brick path, admiring the manicured lawn and the roses blooming by the front door. A red bush on the left, a white one on the right, like Rose-Red and Snow-White from the Grimm's fairy tale. At least the roses loved this heat.

Their scent hung on the still morning air. Whoever had chosen them had taken fragrance into account. I smiled and rang the doorbell. It was answered promptly, as it always would be, even so early.

"Are you selling something?" The woman at the door tilted her head back to peer down her nose at me. She stared at the wedding dress in my hand. "We have no interest."

She pushed the heavy door, but I maneuvered my suitcase between the door and the jamb.

"Why, Frau Inge. It is I. Fräulein Hannah. I am certain that Herr Krause will see me."

"I do not remember any Fräulein Hannah." It was plain from the way she pursed her lips when I said my name that she did. "And I cannot disturb Herr Krause at this time of day."

"Who is at the door?" A warm thrill ran through me at the sound of Boris's deep voice.

Frau Inge turned, no longer blocking my view. Boris walked into the front hall carrying a piece of toast. His dark hair made a nice contrast with his half-open white shirt. My breath caught in my throat. He was every bit as gorgeous as he had been six months ago, when we shared a week in London.

"Boris!" I pushed past Frau Inge into the foyer. I set my suitcase on the marble floor and let the wedding dress fall. I grinned at him. Emotional tears welled up in the corners of my eyes and I did not even care that I felt like a schoolgirl.

"Hannah?" He dropped his toast and crossed the hall in two quick steps. Out of the corner of my eye, I saw Frau Inge watch the toast hit the marble. "You are full of surprises!"

When he swept me into his arms, I cried out.

"What have you done to yourself?" He set me down gently. "Where is Anton?"

"I . . ." My voice trailed off, and I stared at him. His citrus-and-cedar scent enveloped me. I leaned into him. Everything would be fine.

Frau Inge stood by the open door, one hand resting on the door handle, as if ready to close it with me on the outside.

He looked at the silk dress pooled on the floor. "Is this a proposal?" He gave me an amused smile, and ran one hand through his thick brown hair. "I haven't a thing to wear."

I laughed, wincing at the pain in my side. "Perhaps I carry it as a hint."

"I have other questions for you," he said in a worried tone. He paused, looking at Frau Inge. "Frau Inge. Please take Fräulein Hannah's bag and dress to my bedroom."

She slammed the front door. She yanked my suitcase up with one hand and the dress with the other and stormed up the stairs. A few seconds later a crash echoed from the bedroom—the sound of my suitcase hitting the floor. Lucky I had nothing fragile in it.

His arms cupping my shoulders, Boris leaned down and kissed me. I slid my arms up his back and fit my body against his. A low moan escaped from deep in my throat. I wanted him right there on the marble floor.

He pulled back.

"She's right upstairs." His voice was husky.

I nodded, trying to catch my breath.

He led me to the kitchen and set me down at the table. It was littered with papers. Typical Boris, up early to work. He poured a cup of coffee and handed me the remains of an omelette, his own breakfast.

"I cannot eat your breakfast—"

"Of course you can. I'll have Frau Inge make me another."

"Good. She would poison mine." She had always treated me with disdain. Perhaps she hated me personally, or perhaps she hated anyone who upset her routine.

"That's my Hannah." He smiled. "Eat something, then tell me why you're here. And where is Anton? You're supposed to be in Switzerland."

"I could not keep away." I stared at him, so solid and real, drinking coffee in his sunny kitchen. My eyes lingered on the honey-brown skin at his hands and throat. He had been spending time on his sailboat.

"Eat. You'll want to keep your strength up." He tidied the papers into a folder.

I ate. She was a fine cook; I had to give her that, even as she stomped around upstairs, venting her displeasure. I savored the flavor of chives and cheese in the warm omelette.

"So why are you really here? It's not safe."

"The zeppelin was diverted to Friedrichshafen."

"Röhm?" He sipped his coffee.

"How is Trudi?" I could not tell him much with Frau Inge about to barge in.

He laughed. "Changing the subject?"

"And I want to know how Trudi is."

"Married to a Nazi officer."

I choked on the omelette. Trudi, his daughter, was only seventeen. "A Nazi?"

He fidgeted with the cream pitcher. The skin under his brown-gold eyes tightened. It always did when he suppressed his feelings. "They eloped two weeks ago. Apparently Frau Inge suspected something, but I had no idea. Trudi never brought him home to meet me. Doubt-less she knew I would not want her to marry a Nazi."

I should congratulate him on his daughter's marriage, but neither of us approved of the groom's politics. "Is she happy?" I asked instead, washing down the omelette with strong coffee.

He shrugged. "So far. He's a strapping man. Handsome and charm-ing. She thinks it's true love."

"That should last at least six months."

"Such confidence in the power of true love."

He reached over and stroked his fingertips along my cheek. My breath caught again. What I felt had less to do with true love and more to do with physical need, the same as the grown-up Trudi. Boris's full lips curved upward in one of his slow sexy smiles. "I'll give Frau Inge the day off."

I finished his breakfast, trying not to imagine the expression on her face when he sent her home. Somehow, I did not think she would be thrilled to have a holiday.

He returned, looking peeved.

"Is Frau Inge on her way?" Before he replied, a slam from the front door gave me my answer.

He led me up the marble staircase to the second floor.

His bedroom was as I remembered it. Morning light shone through an open casement window. His blue quilt sat square on the bed. The only thing out of place was my suitcase, on its side near the end of the bed, and the wedding dress hanging, not in the wardrobe, but on the back of the bedroom door, a calculated bit of insolence from Frau Inge. Other than that it was as if time had stopped in this room.

What if I had stayed here, eating Frau Inge's food and sharing Boris's bed, instead of kidnapping Anton and spending three years on the run, among strangers? Once I had Anton again, I could stay here still, perhaps. But what if I did not find him?

"What's wrong?" Boris stood in front of me, smelling of starch and cologne and himself. "We can go back downstairs if you're not ready. You can tell me what's going on. And where Anton is."

I shook my head. I did not want to talk about it, not yet. I wanted to forget everything but our bodies and this room, if only for a while. That would give me strength to do what must be done.

I pulled his face down to mine and kissed those full lips I had dreamt of. He tasted of coffee and sugar. He wrapped his arms around me, and I groaned in pain.

He released me at once.

"Cracked rib. Left side."

An annoyed expression crossed his face, but before he could say anything I stood on tiptoes and kissed him hard.

I undid the buttons of his shirt and pulled him close. I had no interest in talking. I longed to feel his skin against mine.

While he unbuttoned my dress I traced the muscles of his back, already damp with sweat.

He slid his hands down my body, and I shuddered.

He lowered us onto the bed, careful to keep his weight off my ribs. He drew back his head and looked at me, brown eyes dark. "I've missed you."

I smiled and ran my fingers through his hair, then pulled him down to me. We had spent only weeks together in the past three years, but our bodies fell into perfect rhythm.

Afterward he pulled the sheet over us, and we dozed. I never slept as well anywhere as I did in his arms.

When I awoke the angle of the sun shining through the window told me that over an hour had passed. I had to start the process for claiming Röhm's body. I slid my feet sideways across the fine linen sheets, trying to be quiet. His eyes opened lazily.

"Sneaking off?" He ran one hand along my hip in a way that made me want to stay right there forever. His perfectly barbered hair was disheveled, his eyelids still heavy with sleep.

"I need to . . ." I could not finish the sentence for staring at his relaxed dark eyes.

His hand traveled up to the bruise on my ribs and stopped. He leaned forward and kissed it. An electric shock ran down my body, and

I arched under his lips, hoping for another kiss. He traced the bruise with his index finger, feather light.

"How did this happen?" Anger ran across his face. Anger at me, or at what had happened to me?

"I must obtain official signatures before I can leave with Anton."

"Signatures for what?" He glanced at his bedside clock. "Nothing opens for at least an hour."

"I know, but—"

"Come now, Hannah. Tell me the whole truth. Let me help you."

I stared into his determined gold-flecked eyes. "You do not want to know."

"Let me decide." He smiled impishly. "I promise to forget whatever you say."

I longed to share my burden. Surely the danger was not so great? I had done nothing wrong, or illegal, had I? I looked into his eyes. Nothing but concern. He raised his eyebrows and tilted his head expectantly, fingertips absently gliding along my collarbone.

I held his hand so that I could concentrate. I could not think with his hands on me.

I described everything that had happened since Röhm diverted the zeppelin to Friedrichshafen: our kidnapping, his execution, and my agreement with his mother. I did not tell him that I intended to hunt for Mouse in Berlin. He would only try to stop me.

A muscle twitched in his jaw while I talked, but he did not interrupt.

"Do you think," he said in a controlled voice, "after we get Anton back, you can avoid antagonizing the Nazis, even for a little while?"

"It is not my fault." I stood and tugged the top sheet away, wrapping it around myself like a toga.

He lay calm and naked on the bed. His wry smile was adorable, but I tucked the sheet tightly around myself and looked at the floor, the wedding dress on the door, anywhere but at his relaxed body on the bed.

"You attract trouble." He sounded playful, but his brown eyes were serious.

"I don't try to." I sounded as old and reasonable as Anton.

"I know." His tone was conciliatory, but I was in no mood to agree with him. It did not help that he was correct. Trouble did find me. "But I worry."

I gazed at him, head propped against his pillow, a helpless expression on his handsome face. No one had ever worried about me like that. I had always imagined I would like it, but it chafed me, as if I owed him something I was unsure I wanted to pay. "Do not worry about me. I can take care of myself."

"And that is why both times we've made love in this room you've been wounded?" He referred to a gunshot wound I had the first time I visited his house. He was a patient man. But I could try the patience of a saint. "Always on the left side, and always the ribs."

"It certainly did not dissuade you." I knew better than to argue.

"It doesn't dissuade you either." He climbed out of bed and drew me gently into his arms.

I smiled at his chest. "Mostly not, no."

He tilted my face up to his. "I have no right to question you."

He was apologizing, but I knew that I was wrong. "I—"

He leaned down and kissed me. My eyes filled with tears. I pulled my lips from his and buried my face in his chest. I wept, each sob causing a fresh pain to lance from my rib. I could not stop. I cried for myself, for Anton, for those young boys executed at Stadelheim, and even for Röhm. Boris held me and told me that everything would be all right. I appreciated the gesture. But I did not believe him.

11

An hour later, I climbed out of Boris's front seat at the former Lichter-felde Cadet School. According to the Stadelheim guard, men had been executed here too. Now an SS barracks, someone could give me the official signature needed to release Röhm's body to his mother.

I waved good-bye, and he touched his hat like a chauffeur before pulling back into traffic. I was well fed and well rested, with Boris's house key secure in my satchel. I had a home minutes away by street-car. It felt so domestic, I almost laughed. For a second I let my mind dwell there. We could have had a happy life together, under normal cir-cumstances. He was a good, kind man, and a wonderful father. A blush traveled to my face when I thought of where else he excelled. Even though I knew we had only a few stolen days, I was grateful.

This morning I would get the forms stamped and sealed. Tomor-row I would follow my lead on Mouse. I would find Anton one way or the other.

I allowed myself a moment to relax and believe that everything would turn out well. Anton and I would flee to South America and never leave. He would grow fluent in Spanish and brown as a monkey. Perhaps we could even persuade Boris to join us.

Steeling myself to complete the one task necessary for that to hap-pen, I turned to face the stone sentries. At least three times as tall as I, they stood at attention with rifle butts between massive boots, faces

stern under stone helmets. These soldiers, and all that they represented, were at Hitler's disposal. A frightening thought. My father had
attended this school. How had he felt as he walked through these
gates—protected or at risk?

Eyes straight ahead I crossed the long courtyard. Black tiles formed
squares against lighter gray stone. I focused on the tall brick building
with its three Nazi banners that hung from the third floor to the
ground, the red bright in the morning sun, the white circles with their
swastikas larger than the windows. A statue of a massive dark eagle
perched atop the building. Subtlety was not in the vocabulary of Nazi
decorators.

A long line of women, some with small children, started at the front
door. The line stretched along the side of the building. I was not the
only one who had come here seeking answers. How many men had disappeared in the past days? I thought of the bodies under the sheets, and
of my own brother, who had almost vanished three years ago. Only
through chance had I found out about his death, and even now, he was
buried in an unmarked grave, a fate I suspected he shared with the men
sought by most of the women here.

I walked down the line. Most women cried, or their faces bore traces
of tears. I remembered my own tears, and how it had almost cost my
life to find my brother's killer, but I had succeeded. These women
would not even have that satisfaction. Most would never learn who had
killed their loved ones, and I feared that many more would die before
the Nazis received their reckoning. With a sinking heart, I positioned
myself at the end of the line.

"Sorry to see another woman here, and that's the truth," said the
woman in front of me. Her hair was pulled back into a braid that hung
to her waist.

"Why are you here?"

"Same as you, I imagine. Had a no-good husband who fell in love
with the SA. He spent a week's wages on one of those brown uniforms. Was out every weekend marching." In contrast to her rough
tone, her eyes brimmed with tears. "Wanted to belong to something

bigger than himself. The Fatherland." She snorted and stared at the long line of women in light summer dresses between her and the door.

I shrugged, uncertain what to say. I felt for her, but her husband might have been responsible for the deaths of other men, the grief of other wives. Too much blood had been spilled in Germany, and many had soiled their hands with it. Who could sort out anyone's personal responsibility? Those who ordered the purge were clearly responsible. But what of those forced to pull the triggers or be killed themselves? What of those who worked to put the Nazi edifice in place? Those who voted for it? Or those, like me, who ran away?

She held out a work-roughened hand. "Maude."

I shook it. "Hannah." Neither of us gave last names, already cautious of revealing more. "How many men are missing?"

She shook her head, brown braid swinging. "One for every woman here, I wager."

I stared at the line, shocked. At least one hundred women waited outside the door, and who knew how many were inside, how many were yet to come, and how many were too afraid to come at all. I had hoped that the ones I'd heard die at Stadelheim had been enough to placate most of the Nazis' fury, but these men must have been murdered elsewhere. Not a single woman had visited Stadelheim yesterday, so they would not know to come here to claim the bodies. Where had the men that these women searched for died? Just how many men had been killed along with Röhm?

Wind as hot as breath blew across the stone. Another woman walked between the sentries and limped across the courtyard, shoulders slumped, eyes downcast.

The women looked defeated, and I became angry. I would not let the Nazis win. They had killed these men, but they would not kill their stories. I would mark them, even if only in my own memory and my notebook. Unlike most of these women, I would soon be out of Germany and beyond the Nazis' reach. I would use my impending freedom to carry their stories with me.

I pulled out my notebook and fountain pen, careful not to let Maude see Röhm's Luger. I had tucked it into the bottom of my satchel that morning while Boris was in the bathroom, not wanting to start another discussion about the dangers I always found myself in. Besides, today promised to be simple and safe. I would be meeting bureaucrats and filling out forms. I would even be using my own name. Afterward I would return to the safety of Boris's arms and his luxurious house.

"May I write down your story? I promise to use only initials."

Maude stared at me, probably taking my measure. "Don't suppose I have much more to lose."

Her telling was spare and matter of fact. Her husband had not come home, and she had heard from another SA wife that he had been executed. Fearing that it was true, she had come here to find out. She hoped to recover a body to bury. Although she remained dry eyed, pain tinged every word.

"What will you do with that?" She gestured to my notes.

I tucked my bobbed hair behind my ear. "I want someone to know. Where it is safe."

"They might kill you for that," she said, as casually as if we discussed the price of butter.

I thought of the journalists in Dachau, or worse places, of Ulli in hiding. "Seems as if they might kill me for any number of things."

She snorted again. "Guess that's true for everyone now."

It would be dangerous keeping the notebook, but I would be out of Germany with it soon. The Nazis had no reason to suspect me of anything and read it. Or so I told myself.

The limping woman stopped behind me. She looked no older than I. She leaned her face against the rough brick wall and sobbed, still sobbing when she shuffled forward, dragging her forehead across the wall without seeming to feel it. Tiny smears of blood from her head marked the orange bricks. I thought of the bloody streaks on the wall at Stadelheim.

"You are bleeding." I tried to slide my hand between the woman's forehead and the bloody bricks. "On the wall."

She batted my hand away without moving her head. "My son," was all she said.

I stood in front of her, helpless. I had lost a fiancé, a father, a brother, and an enemy, but losing a son would be worst of all. The thought of losing Anton paralyzed me. Not a word of comfort came into my mind. There was no comfort for this, not for her and not for me. But my son was alive. He had to be.

"I am sorry," I whispered, knowing the inadequacy of the words, but having no others.

She kept her face to the wall.

"Leave her alone," Maude said. "If she wanted help, she'd let you help her."

I patted the woman on the shoulder, but she seemed not to notice, locked away in a world of pain no comfort could penetrate. Still I stayed next to her, hoping that knowing another human being stood beside her and cared might alleviate her suffering. In the end, it was all I could do.

Eventually I left to talk to other women, to smile at bewildered children who would grow up fatherless. They waited to learn the fate of their men: fathers, husbands, brothers, and sons. I wrote what I dared about the missing: first names, an initial for the last name; ages; and the reasons their children, wives, sisters, and mothers stood in hot sun, afraid of the answers they would find inside the walls, but waiting all the same. Knowing was better than not.

Mass killings had not been limited to Stadelheim. In Lichterfelde Nazi guns had been busy. Rumors were of over a thousand dead. Röhm, his top lieutenants, and various SA members. But also on the list were politicians, such as former Chancellor von Schleicher and his wife, shot down as they answered the door. One almost had to admire Hitler's audacity. For years he had kept careful lists. He had maneuvered himself into a position where he could finally kill all his enemies at once.

By lunchtime I was numb from stories, vanished men, and grieving women, but still I wrote even as the line grew behind me. I had brought no food. I had expected to finish within three hours. But Maude was barely halfway to the door. I returned to my place behind her.

She munched on a sandwich: black bread and butter. Likely she could not afford salami to put between the slices. Still, it smelled wonderful. My mouth watered.

"Nothing to eat in that satchel?"

"I thought to be finished before lunch." I shrugged, pretending that I was not hungry. "I did not grasp the scale of this until I arrived."

Maude nodded. She and most other women here had expected long lines and had brought lunch. Or did everyone in Germany today always carry food with them when they left the house, ready for the unexpected?

Anton always insisted on carrying food stores. If he still had his suitcase, he had jerky, dried fruits, and a handful of Brazil nuts. I remembered watching him roll it into a bundle, telling him that it would attract ants. I should have let him be.

Maude broke off half her sandwich and handed it to me. "How many you talk to?"

"Many." I held up my notebook for her to see, but I did not hand it to her. "Thank you for the bread."

"Your story in there?" She brushed crumbs off her faded work dress. She wrapped up the last bits of her sandwich and tucked them away, probably for dinner.

I shook my head, mouth full.

"Who are you here for?" Her brown eyes narrowed. "Or are you here only for the stories?"

I swallowed a mouthful of rich bread. "I came to honor a promise to a soldier's mother."

She shook her head and her braid swung again. "So you're the only one here not grieving."

I had not thought of it that way. "I am not grieving like most." A pang shot through my heart at the thought of waiting in such a line to learn news of my brother or Anton. I remembered those young men standing shirtless in Stadelheim, trying to be brave while being marked with a target for the firing squad. "But I do grieve for those who died."

"Not quite the same, is it? A little far away."

I held up my hands, palms out. She was correct, and I certainly did not intend to argue.

"Still," she said, "I wouldn't wish this on anybody, and that's a fact."

Throughout the long afternoon we crept toward the front doors. I had brought my wide-brimmed hat, but most had not, and crying and sunburn reddened their faces. Hot wind blew over us without offering any respite. Not Berlin weather. Where was the rain?

A woman who lived nearby fetched two milk jugs of lemonade. She passed down the line, filling a warm tin cup and handing it to us, one at a time. When my turn came I drank the lukewarm brew, grateful to have some liquid in me, trying not to think of how unsanitary the cup must be.

I pulled my sketchbook out of my satchel and sketched the women and the stone sentries guarding the gate. The women's slumped despair contrasted with the sentries' erect attention. With hearts of stone, they could not understand the posture of defeat and grief.

I drew portraits of women on the worst day of their lives, squinting against the light, sweat darkening the sides of their dresses, lips downturned with sorrow or clamped into hard lines. Almost impossible to watch without being overwhelmed by their grief and by my own worry. But I did. Someone had to bear witness.

Finally my turn came. I packed up my notebook and sketchpad before stepping into an office that I suspected was a converted closet, windowless and small and lit by a single bulb hanging from the ceiling. The stale air was hotter even than outside. Behind a gray metal table a thin middle-aged woman scratched on a form with an old pen.

"Frau Doppel." She introduced herself without looking up.

"Fräulein Vogel." I remained standing, waiting to be offered a chair as manners dictated. I rested my hands on the back of the chair. It teetered.

Frau Doppel raised her head and scowled at me. With her long pinched face, she looked uncannily similar to Frau Inge and just as cheerful. I named her Frau Doppelgänger in my head. She gestured to the chair.

I sat gingerly, expecting to crash onto the painted floor. The chair held.

"I was told at Stadelheim—" I reached into my satchel for Frau Röhm's letter.

"To come here," she finished for me. She thrust a sheaf of forms into my hand. "Fill these out. Come back tomorrow at the time on the card I gave you. If you are even one minute late, you forfeit your meeting time and must wait in line for another."

At least I would not have to stand in line tomorrow. "When can his body be released?"

"We can release the body in a few weeks," she answered in her monotone.

"Weeks?" I thought of being separated from Anton for weeks. My stomach clenched. I wiped sweaty palms on my dress. "I am claiming the body of Ernst Röhm. Surely—"

"Ernst Röhm?" For an instant she was shocked out of her routine. Her surprised eyes settled on me. I held my breath, worried about her reaction.

I had no choice but to soldier on. I set the forms on her desk and handed her the letter. "His mother authorized me to petition for the return of his remains."

She nodded and pulled the paper close to her face, squinting. "You are Hannah Vogel?"

I nodded and gave her my passport, hoping that Röhm had obtained it legally, or from a good forger. She examined it closely.

"It will still take a few weeks." She handed me my passport and returned to her writing.

The chair squeaked when I leaned forward. My rib hurt, and I shifted again. "Is there no way to expedite it, especially in view of Captain Röhm's position?"

She leaned forward and tapped a long fingernail on the top of my forms. "His position is dead. That pederast has been removed from authority. If he hadn't been so debauched, perhaps no moral cleansing would have been necessary."

So it had already come down to talk of a moral cleansing, and Röhm dead less than a day. I suppressed a sigh and wiped sweat from my forehead with the back of my hand.

"How many men were . . . cleansed?" I struggled to keep distaste out of my voice. She was a source, like any other source. I had interviewed murderers and rapists. I could keep calm.

"As many as needed to be."

"Were there trials?" There had been no time for trials, but someone should remind her how justice was usually done.

"The Führer doesn't need trials." Her eyes widened in shock that I had suggested such a thing. "He is the supreme judge."

Focus on what a great quote that is, I told myself. Not the content. "But whom will he judge next?"

"Only those who deserve it."

I bit my lower lip. I should not start a political argument with her. She worked for the SS. The least she would do was lose my form. I shuddered to think what she might do if I really provoked her. "I see." And I did. I tapped the papers on the desk to square the corners.

"Thank you for your assistance." I forced out a polite phrase. "I imagine you have had a trying day."

"I have. Some of these women are indescribably rude."

I bit my lip again. "Indeed," I said, although the effort to be polite cost me.

I tucked the forms into my satchel and left.

Cooler and fresher air greeted me in the corridor. Even though still in the SS building, I leaned my notebook against the wall and wrote every word she had said, hand shaking with anger.

The notebook was filling up fast. I slipped it into my satchel. Carrying the information with me was practically a suicide note. Yet keeping it in my head, unwritten, was unthinkable.

12

I hitched my satchel up on my shoulder and stepped out of the massive arched entrance into the late afternoon sun. The line of women still stretched off to my left. Nearly five. I suspected most would not have the pleasure of seeing Frau Doppelgänger today. They would have to return tomorrow and wait again.

I had just started down the stairs when someone touched my arm from behind. I whirled, reaching into my satchel for my notebook, making certain it was out of sight.

"Hannah?" said a surprised voice with a hint of a British accent.

"Sefton?" Relief flooded my voice. Sefton was a British correspondent. Tall but portly, he was not an attractive man, but what he did with the written word would leave any woman weak at the knees. He was a good man and a good reporter, honest and tough. We had all been part of the same crowd in the twenties, and I reminded myself to ask him how things had really been for Ulli since the *Post* closed.

"Hannah!" He pulled me into a bear hug. My cheek scraped against the wool of his tweed jacket. He smelled of pipe tobacco. Grateful to see someone from my old life, the life I had before I met Anton and lived on the run, I hugged him hard, ignoring the pain in my rib.

Stepping back, I looked him up and down. He had gained a few pounds, and a double chin rested under his once-square jaw. His cleft chin still looked strangely out of place, and pouches under his eyes testified to his habit of long nights, shortchanging himself on sleep. Still Sefton, though, and only a little the worse for wear. I grinned at him like an idiot.

"I thought it might be you. Some women in the queue said that a gorgeous blond reporter was asking questions, taking notes." He stepped back and wriggled his eyebrows, thick and bushy like Groucho Marx's. But Sefton was no funny man, and a bolt of panic shot down my spine.

"Nice line, but I doubt they would call me gorgeous," I answered, voice light. That he had wormed my description and activities out of the women in line so easily frightened me. If he could, so could others.

We strolled across the courtyard toward the sentinels and tall iron gates. "I quote 'em like I hear 'em, Gorgeous."

It had been too many years. "I thought you went to Paris."

"Back for the occasion." He waved his arms at the empty square. "*Daily Express* thinks all this worth covering."

And they probably had few reporters as fluent in German, or as knowledgeable about German politics, as Sefton.

"I wish we could cover it here." I thought of Ulli taking notes in his apartment, and of my own notes. Neither of those stories would see the light of day in Germany until after the Nazis lost power. I had a feeling that would be a long time.

"I asked around about you." He steered us past the giant stone sentries with their rifles pointing to the clear blue sky. "You've been a ghost for the past three years."

"I was fired as Peter Weill." I checked behind us, to see if we were being followed. No one that I could see. "I took another job."

"Where?" His eyes were curious. My disappearance had caused at least a ripple in the small world of the Berlin press.

"None of your business, you nosy bastard." I raised my voice over the rumble of passing cars.

"Fairly spoken." He draped a heavy arm over my shoulders. "Dinner, the Adlon? My treat."

"How extravagant." The Adlon was the most luxurious hotel in Berlin. The royalty of Europe had stayed there, even the kaiser and the tsar. Sefton had a deep expense account and a good salary, a popular combination in a reporter.

"Anything for a long-lost friend." He smiled the gracious smile that hid his innermost feelings.

"What I think you mean," I said, "is anything your expense account covers for a long-lost friend with a notebook full of potential source material."

"You wound me." With the ease of a member of the lower British aristocracy, he gestured to a waiting taxi and installed us in the back. I was grateful that I had worn a hat today. It would not do to show up at the Adlon with a sunburn.

The taxi drove through Lichterfelde and onto the wide streets of Unter den Linden. Only someone of Sefton's resources could afford such a long taxi ride. I took off my hat, leaned back, and let wind blow through my hair, comfortable for the first time since I said good-bye to Boris that morning.

Tall, leafy linden trees shaded broad sidewalks. This part of Berlin felt quite apart from Lichterfelde. The taxi slowed as we neared the tall columns of the grand city gate of Brandenburg. The bronze quadriga decorated the top again. Napoleon had looted it in 1806, stealing Berlin's winged Victory with her four horses and chariot. After his defeat, she returned with much pomp and an Iron Cross replaced her olive wreath, the symbol for peace changing to the one for war. I wondered what the Nazis would do to her.

Sefton paid the exorbitant fare, plus a generous tip. His prodigious tips often led him to stories, but I think he did it more out of a sense of noblesse oblige than out of expectation of return. Still, he received the best service of any newspaperman I knew.

"Why don't you have an automobile here?" He could probably buy one many times over with what he spent on taxi fare.

"At the shop. I love taxis. You never know what you will learn from the drivers. Do you drive?"

"A bit." I had learned to drive in South America and could not imagine doing without it.

He proffered his arm. "Into the breach, my dear?"

I wrapped my fingers around his arm, and we stepped onto the sidewalk near the hotel. The clean stone façade loomed six stories overhead, topped by a dusty-green copper roof.

A liveried doorman swept open the doors and ushered us into the lobby. The plastered ceiling swooped up in graceful curves, a church that worshipped sophisticated dining instead of God and sacrifice. Bright frescoes on the ceiling evoked the pastoral good life for which denizens of a giant city liked to cultivate nostalgia. The famous staircase beckoned one to climb to the rooms on the second floor, like a scene from the American movie *Grand Hotel*; not surprisingly, since the movie was based on Vicki Baum's book set here. A strong sense of unreality permeated the air. I stopped walking; I did not belong.

Sefton put his hand on the small of my back and steered me toward the dining room while I tried not to stare at the lavishly dressed and bejeweled women. I was underdressed and underlineaged. But the Adlon cared more about your pocketbook than about your history, and Sefton was paying.

Sefton knew his way around a menu, so I let him order for both of us. Just like old times, during the golden twenties. Life was quite civilized for almost five years after the Reichsmark was introduced and before the world economic collapse.

The food tasted excellent, and the wine lived up to the exceptional reputation of the renowned wine cellars, said to contain over a million bottles. The wine cellars were among the largest in Europe, and ended in a tunnel that led to a building across the street. Hotel guests had used it to escape after the gunfire started during the Spartacist uprising in 1919.

We did not talk about politics, or the contents of my notebook, while eating. Instead I caught up on what my colleagues had been doing for the past three years. Ulli had fallen mostly out of sight, although rumor had it that he had started to drink.

My friend Paul had been fired from the newspaper where we used to work together, the *Berliner Tageblatt,* in October 1933, when the Editor's Law decreed that no Jews could work for newspapers. Sefton did not know where he was. My nemesis Maria was still Peter Weill, although the Nazis only let her write about Jewish criminals. She probably took it in stride, although she had been dating Paul when I left Germany three years ago. But Maria was not one to let sentiment cloud her chances of advancement.

As at all major newspapers, a Nazi fact-checker had been installed at the *Tageblatt*. The Mosse family, the Jewish owners of the paper, fled to Britain after Hitler became chancellor. Surprisingly, my old editor, Herr Neumann, fought the Nazi fact-checker until he himself was let go. I had not expected that kind of backbone from him.

I drank too much wine during the long dinner. Intoxicating talking to a friend, someone who knew me by my true name and identity; knew my history, if not my present. It had been so many years, and I had resigned myself to never meeting anyone from my old life, except Boris. But he did not have the depth of mutual friendships and career that I shared with Sefton. The Adlon's dining room felt like a world out of time, where I could visit my old life.

"Now, my dear," he said when the plates were cleared away. "Tell me true how you've been amusing yourself since you cut out."

I sobered. As charming as he was, he was still a newspaperman. "This and that."

"Last I heard, you were wanted by the police for questioning about the murder of a Herr Lehmann and a Herr von Reiche." He swirled wine around in his glass, voice light but broad face serious. "And Ernst Röhm claims that you stole his son."

"Quite a list of allegations." Behind him a white-coated waiter cleared the neighboring table with the bounce of the truly young in his step. We had dawdled so long over our meal that we sat alone in the room. Even the idle rich had more interesting places to be.

"The latter was hushed up so quickly, I imagine it must have been true." Sefton sipped his wine, eyes never leaving mine. "Would be bad for Himmler and his SS men to have their moral outrage tempered by physical proof that Röhm slept with a woman, at least once. The boy would be a useful pawn for someone."

"Your sources are fascinating." I swallowed the water, chilled at the thought of someone using Anton as a pawn. "But are they accurate?"

He waited until the waiter carried away the empty wine bottle. "Why are you back now, when Röhm is supposedly dead?"

"Do you think I killed him?" I controlled my voice, careful not to give emotion away. I trusted Sefton to get the best story he could and publish it. It made him a wonderful reporter and a friend with whom one must be on guard.

His deep chuckle rolled across the table. "I don't think you killed him. But you know more than you are telling."

"I am a reporter." I smiled. "I always know more than I tell. As do you."

His gaze roved around the empty dining room before he spoke. "I could take a story out, if you gave me one."

We stared into each other's eyes. Fear was in his, and mine. I wanted the women's story to see the light of day, but the consequences if it were traced back to me were dire. I could do nothing until Anton and I were out of Germany. Too risky. I shook my head.

"Hannah?" He covered my hand with his. "You were the only one with the courage to talk to those women."

I pulled my hand back and sipped my wine. We both knew that he was correct. No German reporter would have risked it. And no foreign reporters either, until he arrived. I alone had recorded the women's stories. Why hadn't he?

The waiter came by our table. With his olive skin and dark eyes he looked Italian, as out of place here as I. "Will there be anything else?"

Sefton's face looked impassive, but I suspected he was angry at being interrupted. "Charge it to my room."

He signed the check without checking the amount. Even with the sale of my brother's jewelry, and the knowledge that I had two of his valuable rubies tucked away in Switzerland, I had never done that. Sefton, I must remember, was different from me. And always would be.

The waiter bowed and hurried across the room. He glimpsed the clock and smiled: a boy at the end of a school day. Free for an evening of fun. With the random violence of the Nazis, it could just as easily have been him in front of the firing squad, or me.

"Do you want their stories to die along with their men?" Sefton's voice was still low, as if the waiter were not the only one we needed to be careful around.

"No." I folded my hands in my lap, twisting my thick linen napkin. The young men deserved to have their story told. Bad enough that they had been killed, worse still to die unremarked and forgotten, like my brother, Ernst.

But the risk.

He leaned forward on his tweedy elbows, once handsome face intent. "It's bigger than a single one of us, you know. That's why I came back. The world needs to look at Berlin and see what's happening before it's too late."

"I know." I thought of Anton, one small boy, alone among strangers. "But I am in the middle of something personal."

"Who isn't?"

I shrugged. "I have certain . . . responsibilities, and I cannot take risks as if I did not."

I hated saying those words. We both knew that I wanted that story to get out, had wanted it from the moment I wrote my first note.

"I could make sure it couldn't be traced back to you. Which is better than what will happen if the SS get that notebook you were using back at Lichterfelde."

So he knew or surmised about the notebook. I clenched my hands under the table to keep calm. "You were thorough while talking to your sources."

He raised his thick eyebrows. "I am always thorough. It's why you can trust me."

Was it? Could I trust him? I thought of all I knew about him, the years we spent together hating the Nazis. I did trust him, and I hoped that I was not wrong.

We sat in silence. His sipped his wine with impeccable manners and grooming, at ease in his surroundings. He did not need to be here. He could be home in Britain, in some other luxurious hotel, sipping tea and wondering about cricket scores. But he had placed himself here on purpose, knowing the risk.

He pulled an artfully gnarled pipe out of his jacket pocket. A white dot shone on the side of the polished black stem. A Dunhill, expensive and British, of course. He tamped tobacco in it and lit up, forgetting to ask me if I minded, a rare oversight.

"And if you were caught, would you lead them back to me?"

"I would do my best not to, of course." He puffed to start his pipe drawing. The smell of high-quality tobacco wafted across the table. "But if they tortured me, I'd probably give in eventually. Stiff upper lip and all that, but a man's only human."

I laughed. He was honest.

"Come up to my room." He wriggled his eyebrows. "I have a type-writer."

"You old rake," I said, but I gathered up my satchel and followed him to the elevators.

He smoked silently as we waited for the elevator, as if afraid that a single word might change my mind. I stood next to him, mouth dry. I suppressed an urge to run out of the lobby and folded my sweaty hands. I would do this. The dead men and grieving women deserved it. I would not let the Nazis silence them.

"This is a one-time affair," I told Sefton, my voice high with nerv-ousness. "I cannot be involved again."

He put his hand on my arm, as if to keep me from bolting.

"I'll take a one-night stand over nothing at all." The elevator doors opened. The elevator operator suppressed a fleeting smile, and I shot Sefton a poisonous glance before stepping into the elevator cage.

Sefton shrugged in mock innocence and gave the operator his floor number.

A sumptuous hall led to his room. I tried not to be intimidated by the gorgeous rugs and elaborate sconces. It was just a hotel.

He unlocked his room with a giant metal key. Inside the room the ceiling practically disappeared overhead. A massive walnut bed with an elaborate headboard and a Battenberg lace coverlet looked like a handkerchief in the huge space. The desk alone cost more than all the furniture I had ever owned. The smell of beeswax furniture polish hung in the air.

"Not quite up to my standards," I said. "But I suppose it will do to type a story."

He looked around as if seeing the room for the first time. "It's a nice little room."

"Indeed."

He pulled a battered black Remington typewriter out of the wardrobe, where it had rested on the floor next to a pair of polished black dancing shoes. He set it on the desk, careful not to damage the finish.

"A portable?" I ran my fingers over the gracefully arched keys. "You actually lug that back and forth?"

"Perils of journalism. Makes me wish I had a valet."

He rolled in a sheet of paper and opened a tiny white box with a new ribbon. "I like it crisp." He changed the ribbon. "I have my standards."

I smiled as he pulled out his desk chair for me and bowed. Certainly a more pleasant place to write than the bullpen at the *Berliner Tageblatt*, but part of me missed the energy and the collegiality.

I stared at the blank page, gathering my thoughts. I pushed down on a round white key. It clacked against the paper, the action smooth and well-oiled. Easy typing. I made my first mistake and groaned.

"British key layout. Harder to type stories in German. So I grant you some mistakes. I'll clean it up later." He stared out his window at the street below. "Just get it down."

"Is anyone out there?"

"Should there be?"

"Not on my account. Not as far as I know."

"There is a man pacing across the street. He doesn't look like a Nazi. More like a businessman waiting for a rendezvous."

"Those naughty businessmen."

"Just type." He sat on a leather club chair and picked a newspaper off a giant stack. He was the only person I knew who read more newspapers every day than I.

I typed a full account of Röhm's arrest, the events at the Hanselbauer, and what I had seen at Stadelheim. Sefton read each page as I pulled it out of the typewriter. Occasionally he whistled, but he said not a word until I finished.

I slid my chair back, and he handed me a glass of water. I downed the water, then rotated my wrists around, tired.

"How do you know what Hitler said in Röhm's room?"

"Off the record?"

He nodded.

I hesitated. But I had trusted him this far, and he needed to know that the story was true. "I was in the bathroom, peeking out the door."

He froze, mouth open. I had never seen him look so comically surprised before. He needed a full minute to regain his composure. "What were you doing in Röhm's bathroom?"

"Taking notes." He was getting no more than that.

He chuckled and shook his head. "I see."

He stared at the page in his lap, then lit a fire in the grate and dropped the paper in. I snatched it out of the flames.

"Are you insane?" I blew out the fire. Ashes fell on the rug.

"I can't smuggle so many pages across the border. They'd be found."

I clutched the singed paper. "So, you memorized them? Stored them in that wine-soaked brain of yours?"

His gaze flicked to the typewriter. Next to it sat the tiny white box that had contained the new ribbon.

I looked at the box too, and smiled. "You old fox. Every character that I typed is on the ribbon. You carry out the typewriter with the ribbon in it. The story is all there."

"I must type my poor fingers to the bone transcribing it," he said in a mock-injured voice.

"That is my top story. Make no mistakes."

"I won't," he promised. "It's more dangerous than I thought. Like you."

"You confuse dangerous with being in danger."

"Sometimes." He dropped a sheet into the fireplace. "It's the same damn thing."

I crumpled a sheet and fed it to the flames.

"What about the women you met today? If it's a one-night stand, I want to get all I can."

"Such a gentleman."

He gestured to the typewriter. I leaned back, and my spine cracked. He called for tea from room service.

I used only the women's initials, but I typed up a full accounting of my morning. "You must shape it into a story. Or turn it over to your friends in intelligence."

"I have no friends in intelligence. Don't spread such rumors."

"You may have no friends *with* intelligence. But your *being* in intelligence is not a rumor."

"Did that come from Röhm?" He tapped his pipe against the grate.

I stopped typing, surprised. "You and Röhm were close?"

He shifted his eyes to the side.

"I showed you mine. You show me yours."

"We met," he said after a pause. "At various events. He once took me to that bar he fancied. The one with the transvestites and those Chinese gongs."

"El Dorado."

"That's the one. Anyway, he would try to get me sloshed and then plead for me to carry messages to the British government."

"And did you?"

"I told him that I didn't have that kind of influence."

"Did he believe you any more than I do?"

He shook his head. "Answer from the government was that we only deal with Hitler, and then only through the embassy. Shame, really. I think Röhm would have been more sane than Hitler. He wasn't as enamored with killing. Loved war, though. Liked the idea of soldiers fighting soldiers. Hitler's more enamored with soldiers killing civilians, I fancy."

"What is the take on this purge, overseas?"

"People say now that they are eating each other, it won't be long before the Nazis are out of power."

"Nonsense," I said. "This was a power consolidation. And a warning to his opponents. This is not over."

"A man who will kill his best friend will do anything."

Someone rapped on the door. I jumped. It reminded me of another hotel, another rap on the door.

Sefton carried the typewriter back to his wardrobe and set it next to his shoes with the current page still in it. He closed the wardrobe door while I tidied up the paper and ribbon box. When all traces of our activities were hidden, he opened the door to a white-jacketed waiter pushing a tea tray with a silver tea set and lovely china cups.

The waiter stared at the ashes, surprised to see anyone lighting a fire during the hottest summer month in Berlin in years. Sefton smiled, not bothering to explain, gave him a lavish tip, and ushered him out the door.

Light reflected off the silver surface as Sefton poured. "Why'd you look so dodgy when the waiter knocked?"

I picked up my cup with a hand that still trembled. "They came into Röhm's room that way. He expected room service with his breakfast." I sipped tea to steady myself. "But it was Hitler."

He eyed me over his teacup. "You were in Röhm's room, about to have breakfast?"

"You are not getting that story." The information I had given him so far could have come from the SS twins, or Hitler himself, but what happened in the room before they arrived could have only come from me.

I finished my tea and typed up the stories of the women at Lichterfelde. He burned each page after he read it. The smell of burnt paper filled the room.

"What about your notes? Shouldn't you burn those?"

"Not till I get word from you that the information is safely out."

"It's a huge risk, Hannah." His voice was deep and uncharacteristi-cally serious.

I eyed his innocent-looking typewriter. "A risk we both run."

Together we crushed the ashes with the fireplace poker and shovel.

The rays of the setting sun slanted through the window, and I real-ized with a start how late it must be, almost ten. Boris might be wor-ried. I was unused to anyone worrying about me.

"I must get home." I packed my notebook into my satchel.

"Where is home?"

I smiled. "Home is where they must take you in."

"I was thinking of a physical address. Where I could reach you."

"I will contact you. Care of the Hotel Adlon."

He embraced me, holding tight. I winced and he loosened his grip, but he did not let go. "Be careful, Hannah."

I looked up into his worried eyes. "You too Sefton. Trouble for you is trouble for me."

"You always seem to be in more trouble than I."

I stepped away and turned to go. No point in arguing with him when he was correct.

13

Sefton opened the door, and I stepped into the empty hall. The tea things tinkled as he wheeled the tea cart out behind me. Not wanting to face the elevator operator after Sefton's talk of one-night stands, I crept down the stairs to the lobby, each step jarring my rib.

By the row of wooden telephone booths on my way to the front door, I thought of Frau Röhm. I had not contacted her yet today. Even though it was late, I pushed open a door and stepped inside. It closed behind me, offering a feeling of privacy. Unlike public telephone booths, those at the Adlon smelled of beeswax wood polish, just like the rooms.

I fumbled through my satchel and pulled out the scrawled paper the maid had given me. I gave the number to the operator and she connected me.

The telephone rang in that closed-in house in Munich. I imagined the dogs looking at it curiously, then barking and waking the neighbors.

The telephone rang and rang. Frau Röhm, as I knew from embarrassing experience, was a light sleeper, so she would hear it even if she slept. How long would it take her to come down the stairs to answer? Terribly late to be calling. What would my mother have said?

"Röhm." The maid's voice was heavy with sleep.

So she slept there? Odd. She had not the night I broke in to search for Anton, but perhaps Frau Röhm gave her the night off, just as she sent away the dogs. "Hannah. I must speak to Frau Röhm."

"She is not taking calls." In faraway Munich, the maid yawned into the telephone.

"It is urgent."

"She instructed me that she is taking no calls, no matter how urgent." Her voice was firm. She followed orders.

"Please take down a message." I gave a brief account of my meeting at Lichterfelde and my appointment on the following day to finish filing the paperwork, then hung up and stepped out of the gleaming glass door. I still had not told her that the prison burned Röhm's body.

I hurried to the subway. Even so late, it felt humid and sticky inside the cars. I forced open a window, grateful for the breeze. The hot car reminded me of the zeppelin. After living so long in South America, Anton loved hot weather and could tolerate extreme heat far better than I.

I rode the rest of the way to Boris's trying not to think of Anton sleeping in the stifling heat, alone. Instead I wondered if I had done the right thing in giving Sefton the women's stories. We were both in danger, and who knew if it would help to bring down the Nazis? I resolved not to involve anyone else in our information-gathering scheme. I wanted no more blood on my hands than absolutely necessary.

I walked the last few blocks. The yellow glow of the streetlamps did not reach the sides of the grand houses. In a sumptuous neighborhood such as this, I would not ordinarily be afraid, but tonight every shadow seemed to hide an SS informer. Like everyone else in Germany these days, I had something to hide.

I hurried between Boris's pillars and up the stone path. Lights burned in his bedroom and in the kitchen. I smiled. How wonderful to have a home to come back to, especially after a day like today.

The stories of the women who had lost their men in the purge almost overwhelmed me, but being here protected me, let me stop worrying for a night about whether Sefton could get the stories out, or if the SS would come for me. I could sit in the parlor and drink wine and ask Boris about his day at the bank like a proper housewife with nothing to worry about.

Soon I would trade Röhm's body for Anton, and we could leave Germany under our own names. Perhaps Boris might be persuaded to go with us now that Trudi was married and on her own. How would we fare as a normal couple, able to spend days and weeks and months together? It sounded heavenly, but since I left my parents' house I had lived with no one but my brother and Anton. Perhaps we would tire of each other. Thinking of this morning, I smiled. I certainly would not mind spending so much time in Boris's bed that it became routine.

Grateful that Frau Inge must be long gone, and I would not face her hostility, I unlocked the front door. Finding the kitchen empty, I climbed the stairs to the bedroom. The door was closed.

I swung it open, but instead of Boris lying in bed, Frau Inge stood in front of the long mirror. She wore my wedding dress and her hair was loose around her shoulders. The dress, I noted, fit her perfectly. For the first time, I saw a beautiful, flirtatious girl in her. She must have been quite attractive when she was younger and more carefree.

Her eyes met my reflection, and we stared at each other, both shocked into silence. I dropped my satchel. The Luger inside clunked against the wood floor.

"I . . ." Her voice trailed off. That was a shame. I would have loved watching her try to explain.

"I believe you are wearing my dress." My voice dripped ice. Even then I saw the ridiculousness of the situation. It was not my dress. It belonged to Frau Röhm. And I had hoped never to wear it. I should not care if Frau Inge tried it on. But I did.

"Pardon me." She sounded uncontrite.

"I would appreciate it if you would leave my things alone."

"As you wish."

Her fingers fumbled with the long row of covered buttons that ran down the back. How long had she needed to do them up on her own? I let her struggle for a full minute.

"For heaven's sake." I finally crossed the room to undo them myself. She stood still. I pulled a long sleeve off her thin arm.

"Herr Krause is not with you?"

I shook my head.

"He has not been home since this morning. His dinner is warming on the stove," she said.

That explained what she was doing here so late.

"Thank you." I gave the appropriate response through gritted teeth. Where was he? Worry coursed through me, but I turned my mind from it. He was a grown man who could take care of himself. He worked in a bank. What could happen there?

She stepped out of the dress and handed it to me, fingers caressing the silk one final time. "It is lovely. I am certain that you and Herr Krause will be as happy as two maggots in bacon." I stifled a smile at the old expression. Trust Frau Inge to make happiness sound so unappealing.

"Will we?" I folded the dress over my arm, conscious of its weight.

She smoothed her slip and crossed the room to gather up her dress. "After your marriage."

"I see." He had never indicated that he expected marriage, but she must have drawn her own conclusions from the wedding dress.

"Herr Krause would make a fine husband, if he wanted to."

"Indeed."

"Kind and caring." She slid her dress over her head. Her voice was muffled. "And faithful."

She looked so triumphant as she spoke that I was confused. "He is all those things."

"Is he?" She stepped into her shoes and rolled her luxuriant hair into a bun, transforming back into a no-nonsense housekeeper.

The front door creaked open, and Boris's familiar steps entered the hall. Why was he home so late? It was almost eleven.

"I will not tell him that you were wearing my dress." I pitied her.

"You think you need to keep my secrets?" She turned and hurried down the marble stairs. I hung up the wedding dress and followed more slowly.

She was heaping boiled potatoes on his plate when I walked into the dining room. His face was flushed under his mussed hair. Had something happened? Perhaps to Trudi?

"The meat is drier than it should be," Frau Inge said. "It's been warming for hours."

"I am certain it will do nicely," he said, "and you well know that you did not need to wait."

"I see." She took in his rebuke without further comment. She looked at me as if to ask if I too wanted dinner, but instead clamped her mouth closed.

"Long day?" I dropped my hands to his tense shoulders. He jerked away.

"No longer than yours." He chewed his potatoes tiredly.

He turned to where Frau Inge stood in the doorway to the dining room, the pan that had held the potatoes gripped in her hand as if she was ready to brain me with it. "You may go home for the day, Frau Inge. We will clear."

She nodded once and headed through the door to the front hall.

"When will you get Anton back?"

I sighed. "I filed the paperwork today, but it may take a few weeks. I tried to talk to Frau Röhm about it, but she is not taking calls."

Muffled thumps told me that Frau Inge was still in the kitchen, probably putting away the pan. A moment later the front door closed quietly.

"At least she did not slam it," I said with a smile. "Such progress."

He set his fork down on the china plate with a chink and folded his arms across his chest.

"Did something happen to you today, Boris?"

"Did something happen to you?" A muscle twitched in his jaw.

"I am more concerned about you." I did not wish to talk about Sefton and the danger I had put myself in. "You seem—"

"No distractions," he snapped. He had never used such a tone with me before. "Tell me about the rest of your day."

I paused, shocked. "It was—"

"Why don't you tell me the highlights? Shall we pretend we're a normal couple? What did you do for dinner?" He spat out the word *dinner* and thrust his own nearly full plate away.

"I ran into a friend after I received the paperwork for Röhm's body, but—"

"A friend?" His emphasis was insulting.

I looked at him, puzzled. "Yes, an old friend. But I would rather talk about—"

"Of course you would." He poured himself a glass of wine. He did not offer me one. "But I want to talk about your old friend."

"Why?" I was exhausted, and nearing the end of my patience. Whatever upset him, he had no right yelling at me. I poured myself a glass of wine and glared at him.

"I had a late tea with a client at the Adlon today." He drained his glass.

We would have to have this out. But I could not tell him about Sefton. I trusted Boris with my life, but it was not my place to trust Sefton's life to anyone. I stalled for time. "Bankers know how to live."

"I saw you there, eating with another man." He refilled his glass.

"My old friend." Even though I understood why he was upset, and felt guilty, I was angry that he thought I was doing something as foolish as having an affair. I had enough to worry about without that.

"You drank three glasses of wine, then disappeared into the elevator that goes to the rooms with your old friend." He gulped another swallow of wine.

"You are wasted as a banker. You should be a private investigator." In the same situation I would have trusted him. Perhaps.

"You did not come back down for two hours." His tone was clipped. He finished his wine and poured a third glass. At this rate he would be drunk in no time. "I waited."

I remembered the businessman Sefton had mentioned. "I see."

"Is this man the reason you are in Berlin?" He lifted his chin, as if readying himself for a punch. "Explain yourself."

An order. But he knew that I did not follow orders. Ever. "I should not have to."

"Shouldn't have to?" He drained his glass again.

"My actions are my business. Not yours. Just this morning you said

that you had no right to question me. Even if you had, have we exchanged promises of fidelity?" Anger seeped into my voice. I could not
draw him into my dealings with Sefton. The less he knew, the better
things would be for him if any of us ended up in an interrogation cell,
a too-likely fate.

He slapped both palms flat on the table. It rang like a shot. I jumped,
and a sharp pain shot from my ribs. My eyes watered. That was enough.
I would not be afraid of him.

"Dallying in hotel rooms with other men is not my business?"

"Only if you are the one dallying." I regretted that as soon as I said it.

He stood and paced the room. Four steps, turn, four steps, turn.

"Boris, I am sorry, but I cannot tell you what I was doing." My
voice sounded placating, a tone with which I was unfamiliar. I did not
usually have to placate. And I did not like it.

"If you won't tell me what you were doing, tell me what you
weren't." His voice had a tone of angry command that reminded me
of my father.

"I assure you that I was not doing what you seem to think. I cannot
tell you more."

"Can't tell me or won't tell me?" He did not believe me.

"It amounts to the same thing in the end." I touched his warm fore-
arm. "Please, Boris, it is for your own good. You must trust me."

He froze and gave me the same cold stare I had seen in front of
Moabit courthouse, one of the first times that we had met. Just like then,
he looked at me as if I were a stranger, and a stranger he did not much
care for. "Must I?"

"No." I sighed. I was not the kind of person to salvage this relationship, beg for forgiveness, and tell him everything. Probably the reason I
was thirty-five and unmarried, as my mother would have pointed out. "I
suppose you do not have to trust me."

I stormed up the stairs. I did not want to be in the same house with
him for another minute. When I picked up my suitcase, my rib twinged
again, and I bit my lip.

He stopped me at the top of the stairs. "Where are you going?"

"Away."

"Do you have anywhere to go?"

"I can look after myself. I have managed for years without you. I can manage tonight."

And to think that I had been imagining a future with him on my way home.

He ran his hand through his thick hair. Dark shadows rested under his eyes.

"Stay," he said.

I fought back an overwhelming urge to flee. Part of me wanted to walk out the front door, and be on my own again. I knew how to walk that road.

He held out his hand. "Please."

I took the new road, the harder road. His hand felt colder than usual, but his grip was firm.

14

For the first time, we slept on opposite sides of the bed. Or perhaps he slept. I spent most of the night staring at the wall, angry that he did not trust me, but angrier at the circumstances. He had every right to be suspicious when he saw me go into another man's hotel room. I understood that he wanted to know the full truth of my life. But I had to protect him, and protect Sefton. I could not pull Boris into the dangerous morass of my life. But if my life was one giant morass, where was he to stand?

Early the next morning I rolled over to study him in the soft light. His measured breathing told me that he slept, although he was a light sleeper. The lines of anger on his face had relaxed. His jawline was still strong, but wrinkles around his eyes and mouth had deepened since I first met him, only three years before. What burdens did he carry? Did he have as many secrets locked away as I? Would I ever find out? Or were we incapable of spending more than a few nights together at a time, and doomed to keep the most important things hidden from each other?

What had happened with Trudi? He had only told me in barest outlines, but I knew it must have hurt him deeply when she left. Even if the groom had not been a Nazi, it would have been a blow. He had doubtless waited years to walk her down the aisle in a white dress and give her away to a man that he could trust. And he had been robbed of that. He had not lost her as completely as I had lost Anton, but he too had lost the future he had planned for himself and his child.

I longed to stroke his dark hair off his forehead, trace the lines around his eyes and mouth, but I did not want to wake him and start another fight. Instead I slipped out of bed, performed a hasty toilet, and left. Perhaps tonight we would be calmer, and I could explain.

To avoid Frau Inge, I waited until I heard her moving in the kitchen, then slipped out the front door without breakfast. I stopped at a tea shop on my way to Lichterfelde and my appointment with Frau Doppelgänger. She was not someone to face on an empty stomach. I filled out the forms carefully, knowing that a single misplaced word could cost me days. Frau Röhm had been thorough in her letter and provided the details I needed.

I nodded to the stone sentries and walked up to the imposing brick building. A breeze too warm for this early in the morning swept across the courtyard, promising a day as hot as the one before.

A line of women snaked out from the door, although not as long as yesterday's. I smiled apologetically as I moved past. I made my way down the battered halls of the former military school. What would my father say if he saw me in the halls of his old school, come to retrieve the body of a man shot for high treason?

What would have become of my brother had my father lived? Would he have been forced to tread these halls, to learn to kill? I missed him. Ernst would have had advice about Boris, certain that I could solve our problems with outré undergarments.

At quarter past nine I rapped on the wooden door to Frau Doppelgänger's office, feeling like a child sent to the headmaster.

"Come in!" Frau Doppelgänger's voice carried through the thick door. Had she been a man, she would have been a natural on the parade ground.

I entered the room and crossed to her desk, forms in hand. "The forms for Ernst Röhm."

She snatched them out of my hand and read, expression signaling her desire to find something wrong or missing. "These seem to be in order."

She stamped a form and handed it to me. A receipt. I stuck it into my satchel.

"When can I expect to have his remains?"

"Two weeks, at the earliest." She stamped the tops of each form. "Some of those cleansed have been buried at Perlacher Cemetery in Munich. If your Röhm is among them, you will not be able to retrieve him."

"Surely his body could be exhumed?" I said, through gritted teeth. I did not like her calling him my Röhm, and I did not like the thought that he might never be returned to his mother.

"You would have to petition the cemetery. But it would be highly unusual."

"I believe that the entire matter has been highly unusual."

She lowered plucked eyebrows. "Nevertheless, you must wait two weeks to find out his status. If necessary, you may file an exhumation form then."

She dropped my forms atop a mountainous pile. Dealing with Hitler's death machine had become a time-consuming job.

"Thank you for the information," I said, more to prevent my forms from disappearing into the pile, than because I was grateful.

She inclined her head in a tiny nod. "One more thing."

"Yes?" Perhaps she had found a way to expedite the release of Röhm's body. Perhaps a bribe would work. She did not seem the type, but perhaps she was new at it.

"This is highly irregular."

"Indeed?" Considering what passed for regular, irregular might be just the thing. What would be an appropriate amount?

"You should be grateful that I made the connection. It was only by the purest chance."

"Connection?" My stomach dropped. Any connection she made about me could not be good.

She retrieved a large set of keys from her pocket and unlocked her drawer. "At the cost, it must be urgent."

My heart pounded, but I feigned calm. "The cost?"

She withdrew a familiar yellow envelope. A telegram. I relaxed.

"This came to this office this morning, for a Hannah Vogel."

It must be from Röhm's mother. No one else knew I was here, except Boris and perhaps Sefton. Neither would send me a telegram. "Probably from Frau Röhm. About her son."

She pressed the yellow envelope into my palm. "We are not a telegram drop office. If another one comes, we will discard it."

"I apologize for the inconvenience." My fingers itched to open the envelope, but I had no intention of reading it in front of her.

She escorted me out of the office with such an air of indifference as to the contents of the telegram that I suspected she must have already opened and read it.

"*Auf wiedersehen*," I said before she closed the door. Another woman waited outside. Her red-rimmed eyes stared at me with a total lack of curiosity. She had time for no troubles but her own.

I slid the telegram into my satchel. It would be foolish to read it in a Nazi stronghold. I hurried down the long hallway.

I had almost reached the front door when a familiar high-pitched voice stopped me. "Fräulein Vogel," it said.

I froze.

I composed my face, grateful that he stood behind me and could not see my fear.

"Kommissar Lang." I turned to face a small thin man with perfect military bearing. He had not changed since he had interrogated me three years ago about the death of my brother, except that he wore an immaculate black SS uniform and his dark hair was cut shorter. His boot-black eyes were still bright. His square face looked relieved.

"Hauptsturmführer now. In the SS."

"Congratulations." I felt inane saying it, but it was protocol. He was such a proper man, it was hard not to respond in proper fashion, something he was certain to use to his advantage.

"Walk with me." He stepped forward and slipped my hand into the crook of his elbow. I almost flinched, but caught myself. I must be careful with him, as always. Should I run? I doubted that I could outrun him. As if he read my thoughts, his grip on my hand tightened.

"Of course," I said, as if it were an ordinary request, as if I always went for strolls with former police officers who had interrogated me until a doctor ordered them to stop because I was retching uncontrollably. Now that the Nazis held power, no doctor would intervene. I was in for a pleasant stroll.

We walked out the front door in step. I bet he was quite a marcher at rallies. The women in line looked at him with worry and hatred, but he seemed unaware. Probably inured to it.

"I have been searching for you for three years." We went down the front steps.

"And now you have found me." I was not happy to know that the SS had been searching for me for one minute, let alone years. No good could come of that.

"That is merely a fortuitous accident." He smiled. We crossed the stone tiles, navigating over dark lines onto lighter colored squares as if we crossed the playing field of a game. A dangerous game, and I did not know the rules.

"How did you know I would be here?" Suspicion rang in my voice.

He turned his head to face me without breaking step. "I asked to be notified if anyone came to claim Röhm's remains. I did not expect it to be you."

We strolled together past the sentries and into the street. My heart hammered in my chest. He had been notified by Frau Doppelgänger. Had she read the telegram? If so, had she told him the contents? I wished I had read it immediately so that he did not have that advantage over me. He had enough already.

If it contained news of Anton, Lang might know that Anton was Rohm's long-lost son. If the Nazis knew that living proof that Röhm had sired a child was in Germany, they would bury such an inconvenient fact to make it easier for them to pursue their crusade of having cleansed Röhm for homosexual debauchery. But surely if the telegram was from Frau Röhm she would be circumspect?

A horse clopped by on the street, an unfamiliar sight in a world that had changed over to automobiles. His glossy chestnut coat shone. Instead of a soldier, an SS man rode him. The rider caught sight of us and raised his arm in the Hitler salute. Lang released my arm and saluted back. "Heil Hitler!"

I used the opportunity to step away from him.

The horse cantered off, one rider as good as another. I thought of Anton. Because of his insistence on riding bareback, we had been through three riding instructors. I could think of no logical reason to force him to use a saddle, so I kept interviewing instructors until we found a retired vaquero who kept horses and agreed to give him bareback lessons if he used a saddle every other lesson. I liked how, to Anton, riding was about friendship between the rider and his horse, not a performance for court, a ritual of hunting, or a prelude to riding in military formation. I wanted him to be unlike his father, and unlike mine.

Lang gestured in front of him, and we walked again. He moved protectively so that he stood between me and the street. An old-fashioned gesture, the man walking on the street side to protect his companion from traffic or getting mud splashed on her skirts by a passing horse and carriage. Boris always did the same.

"What happened three years ago?" he asked, voice soft, quite different from his last interrogation. Perhaps he had learned skills in the SS. I shuddered to think what they might be.

I took a deep breath, trying not to let the pain it caused show on my face. I owed him no explanation, but treating him like an enemy, even though he was, was foolish. I could risk no foolish mistakes. "I apologize for the way I . . . left things three years ago." That was true. I regretted being on the run from the police on top of everything else. "I was frightened for my life, even in police custody."

"You left precipitously, which anyone can understand," he said with a smile intended to be soothing.

I tensed. He would only soothe me to lull me into something.

"Yet you did not return after Herr von Reiche was killed." He paused. "Why?"

I waited. I had nothing unincriminating to say. We strolled down the street in the warm sunshine, past the tea shop where I breakfasted earlier, thinking that Frau Doppelgänger was the only opponent I would face.

"Because, I believe, you were tied in with Röhm." His palm cupped my elbow, as if afraid I might bolt.

"Oh." I did not want to admit more links to Röhm. This was not the time to be in his circle of friends. What was in the telegram?

"At first I thought that you lied to me at the hospital and that you were, in fact, the mother of his child." He looked at me expectantly, as if he thought I would answer. We both moved aside to let a woman push a pram down the sunlit street.

"That would be a natural assumption." He had heard Anton call me Mother, and he knew that Anton was Röhm's son. I wanted to give nothing away. The woman pushed the pram into the tea shop, and I longed to follow.

"After I did a more thorough research of your background—" He tightened his grip on my elbow. "—I found no record of you ever being hospitalized for childbirth."

I imagined the hours he must have spent poring over hospital records. "Not all children are born in hospitals."

He inclined his head. "True, but Anton Röhm was. I uncovered a different birth certificate for him, one that did not list you as his mother. An Elise Karlson, who was admitted to Steglitz Hospital on the day Anton was born, was his true mother. As I'm certain you are aware, she was a prostitute and died of an overdose shortly before you fled Berlin."

"I see." I did not see. With his typical thoroughness, he had uncovered Anton's true birth certificate, not the fake one I had been presented with. He knew more about Anton than I. But why was he telling me?

"So the boy is merely your foster son. I believe that you and your brother were caring for the boy before Röhm took him."

"Your attention to detail in a three-year-old case is most impressive." We passed off the street into a leafy park. I kept pace, although I longed to stay where people could see us.

"It interested me. You interested me. A woman linked to Röhm."

"I am not linked to him." At least not once I gave Frau Röhm his remains. I hoped to never see another Röhm besides Anton after that.

Leaves rustled underfoot. Even here the drought changed the trees.

We stopped and faced each other on the dirt path. A squirrel scurried up a trunk behind Lang's left shoulder. It looked pastoral and soothing, but was not. "Yet you are claiming his remains, why is that?"

"As a courtesy to his mother."

"How are you acquainted with Frau Röhm?" He tilted his head, as if ready to take notes.

I had no good answer to this question, so I answered a different one. "She asked me to claim the body when I last saw her."

"You must realize that if you were to make allegations about yourself and Captain Röhm, it would be exceedingly dangerous for you?" He stepped close. His voice did not change, but a chill ran down my back in spite of the heat of the day.

"I am not a fool." I looked straight into his dark eyes, forcing myself not to step away. "And there are no allegations to be made."

He stepped back a pace. We walked deeper into the shade. The roar of automobiles faded. No one would hear me scream, if it came to that. I shivered.

"Yet I heard that you were betrothed."

I had to tell him part of the truth to get out of this. The only question was how much. How much did he already know? "Röhm's men found me a day before his arrest."

He folded his arms across his chest. I did not think I convinced him. "He intended to force me to marry him." I had to admit that a wedding had been planned, since he already knew that much, but best that he knew it was against my will and I had no love for Röhm. This was no time to be seen as a Röhm loyalist. "But circumstances conspired against him, and he was arrested before he could."

"And why did he wish to marry you?"

"Why not?" I had no wish to discuss Röhm's sexuality. I studied the well-tended path.

"Where is the boy?" He leaned his upper body forward, like a crow.

"Switzerland," I lied quickly. "Under an assumed name."

"Röhm did not kidnap him too? That seems most careless."

"Röhm did not find him," I lied again. He could not know that Anton was in Germany. For a fleeting second I was grateful that I did not know his location. "That was part of the incentive to make me marry him. Anton's freedom."

"You would have married a man such as Röhm to keep a boy safe with whom you have only an accidental relationship?" He sounded skeptical.

"Many relationships are accidental," I said, thinking of Boris.

"You are a curious woman, Hannah Vogel."

"Like the proverbial cat."

He looked as if he was about to say something personal. I did not want to hear his confidences. I said, "Why did you wish to know who claimed Röhm?"

"I am tasked with tying up loose ends from the Night of the Long Knives."

So, they had already named the purge, started the mythology before they even buried the bodies. Did Hitler take the name from a Nazi song, or was he harking back to the slaying of Vortigern's men during the time of King Arthur? Wherever it came from, that was how history would record it. "And?"

"Anyone with links to Röhm might be considered such a loose end. Such as yourself. And Anton Röhm."

"Oh."

"Keeping the boy in Germany is tantamount to suicide." He leaned close. "You must know that."

"He is not here." Did the telegram prove me a liar?

"I hope, for both your sakes, that is true. His claim to be Röhm's son would be of great interest to the party. They would deal most harshly with him, or anyone associated with him who tried to use him as a propaganda tool."

"He makes no claims that he is Röhm's son. Nor do I make them for him."

"I can't quite believe all that you have told me, Fräulein Vogel. But I do believe that you think you have valid reasons for lying."

"Have I?" I did not know what to say.

"That brings me to something else."

Always something else. "Oh?"

"Why were you interviewing the women in line at Lichterfelde yesterday?"

I stopped, shocked into silence. If he knew that, he had to arrest me. "I—I—"

What if I had also led him to Sefton? Anton, at least, was safer where he was than with me. Assuming that he still lived.

"You look quite faint." He patted a nearby iron bench. I sat before I fell, metal hard against the back of my legs.

"You must realize," he said, "that for such actions I must bring you in to the interrogation room."

15

I nodded, still speechless, and grabbed the front of the bench with both hands, trying to anchor myself. To pull myself together, I took a painful deep breath. I winced and looked at Lang. He had interrogated me once before, when he had less power, and it had not been a pleasant experience. I waited.

"I have no appetite for beating women." He lowered his eyes as if he knew to be ashamed of this admission. "It's rather old-fashioned of me, but there you have it."

Once a reporter went into an interrogation room, few returned. They were tortured, then either killed or sent to the camps for more torture and a slower death. What would he do?

He patted my knee with a sweaty hand. "You are caught up in something much larger than yourself, Fräulein Vogel, and I have sympathy for that."

What did he want? A bribe, or something worse? "Sympathy?" I croaked. SS Hauptsturmführers had sympathy only when it suited them. And whatever suited him did not suit me.

He moved his hand, leaving a damp spot on my knee. "This time, I'll close my eyes and not report you."

I stared at him, unable to believe it. What was his price?

"If it happens again, I will have no choice but to turn you over. And there are many men without my scruples. Men who enjoy beating information out of women." His dark eyes bored into mine. "Do you understand?"

I nodded.

He stood. "It has been an instructive morning, Fräulein Vogel."

"Thank you," I said, and I meant it. Whatever the price, he gave me my life back. I had to find Anton and leave Germany before the price came due. I did not think Lang believed in second chances.

He bowed, clicked his heels together, then turned and walked out of the park, erect bearing making it easy to follow his dark figure until it vanished from sight amid the brown trunks and green leaves. I glanced up and down the empty path. Was I alone? Had he assigned someone to watch me?

I sat so still that a gray squirrel stopped by my foot, sensing that I was a threat to no one. When I trusted my legs enough to stand up, I put a hand on the warm wrought iron armrest and pushed myself to my feet, dizzy. The startled squirrel darted up a tree and chattered.

My shoes stumbled along the hard-packed dirt pathway toward the sounds of automobiles and, eventually, voices. Death had stared me in the face and, inexplicably, it had passed me by.

But why? Why had he let me go? Did he expect me to lead him to someone else? All I had to offer was Anton, and I would die before I helped the Nazis take him.

I climbed onto the streetcar and sat in the corner, away from the other passengers. Few passengers rode in the car. Two workmen argued on a bench. One had an oversize moustache, the other peculiarly long fingers. I noted each face, each posture, in case one of my fellow passengers followed me. The car started with a familiar jerk, and I settled into my seat, glad that the streetcar's clacking kept me from hearing their conversation.

I examined the yellow envelope, careful to keep it low in my lap so no one would see. On the front was my name and the Lichterfelde SS address, typed by a machine with a new ribbon, each letter crisp and clear. I turned the envelope over, but the back held no clues. The flap looked sealed, but Doppelgänger or Lang might have steamed it open. I ran my fingertips along the edges. Dry.

I studied the envelope, tilting it back and forth. No signs of water-staining from steam. So either no one had opened it, or they had been careful.

I slid my fingernail under the flap. It came open easily.

1934 JUL 3, AM 07 00

S65 CABLE = MUNICH 118 15
LICHTERFELDE SCHUTZSTAFFEL HEADQUARTERS
HANNAH VOGEL, 0915 APPOINTMENT
M TOOK A STOP CALL IMMEDIATELY STOP
ER

My eyes teared, and I crumpled the paper in my left palm. The car jerked to a stop. A tall man entered. He sat at the bench across from mine, exuding the scent of cheap tobacco and sulfur. The smell carried me back to my meeting with Eicke. I studied this man out of the corner of my eye. Clean-shaven and nondescript. The kind of man I passed a hundred times without noticing. Until today.

I longed to move to another seat, but dared not risk calling attention to myself. Was he SS or was I going crazy, jumping at shadows? Whether he was SS or not, I needed to concentrate on the telegram. The sender was ER, and I knew it must be Emilie Röhm. Not wanting to hold it anymore, I dropped the balled-up telegram in my satchel. M I assumed to be Mouse. A was Anton. Mouse had taken Anton. That implied Anton had been with Frau Röhm, or she had known his location and it had not been with Mouse. Would Mouse bring Anton to me, now that I had filled out the paperwork for Röhm's body? Or had Mouse kidnapped Anton away from Frau Röhm, or perhaps double-crossed her? I remembered the easy way that Mouse had hit him. He might even now be beating Anton somewhere. I clenched my hands and told myself not to create monsters in my imagination. Germany had enough real monsters already.

What would Lang have made of the telegram, if he had read it? He would surmise that A was Anton and ER was Frau Röhm. But I did not see how he could know M's identity, and the telegram did not mention Anton's location, so it did not contradict my assertion that he was out of the country. Frau Röhm had been discreet enough. I hoped.

I left at the next station and paused at a kiosk selling newspapers. Pretending to read the headlines, I kept an eye on the three men with whom I had shared the car. The conductor announced the closing of the doors as I purchased a bar of chocolate. All three men stayed seated. While unwrapping the chocolate I watched the car pull away.

Relieved that they were not SS, I glanced around the street for a telephone booth. One crisis at a time. I ate the chocolate, found a booth, and called Frau Röhm's house in Munich.

The maid answered on the first ring. "Röhm." Her voice sounded clipped, afraid.

"Hannah here," I said, unwilling to give out my last name, wondering who might be listening to Frau Röhm's telephone line. Lang, tying up loose ends?

"Give me your number. She will call soon."

I read the number off the telephone, relieved that Frau Röhm behaved as if she suspected that her telephone was no longer secure. The less the Nazis knew about our movements, the better.

I hung up the receiver. People scurried past to a nearby café for lunch. Mouse had Anton. Was my boy eating lunch? I fingered my cracked rib. Was Anton hurt?

A man walked by carrying a wire cage containing a yellow canary. His tiny beak opened and closed, but inside the wooden-and-glass telephone booth I could not hear his song. The telephone rang. I picked it up before the end of the first ring, eyes on the canary.

"Hannah?" I recognized Frau Röhm's quavery voice.

"Speaking." The man with the canary crossed the street and disappeared into the crowd.

"I have no time for formalities. Mouse refuses to bring Anton back to me. The bastard says that we must buy him."

I bit back a cry. Frau Röhm did not control Mouse. Anything might happen to Anton. Anything at all. But surely Mouse would keep him safe if he thought him worth money?

"You are to meet him at nine tonight at Britz Mill. Do you know where that is?"

"I do." Years ago I read a newspaper article on it. A windmill in southern Berlin, far from public transit, and deserted at night. The perfect place to arrange a ransom. No one would see us, and he could shoot us both without attracting attention. I had to stop thinking that way.

"I cannot come." Frau Röhm sighed angrily. "I haven't the strength, even with the pills. Getting old is a curse."

Better than dying young. I held my tongue. "I understand." I did not want her there. One enemy was dangerous enough.

"If you do not pay the ransom—" A cough interrupted her. I waited for her to finish.

A middle-aged man tapped on the glass and pointed to his wrist-watch. Apparently he felt I had spent enough time using the telephone. I turned my back to him. "What happens?"

She cleared her throat. "Mouse will turn Anton over to the party. He has sources there who will pay for Anton's elimination."

I thought of Lang's assertion that the party would be happy to do away with Anton and anyone who held him and knew that Mouse could be telling the truth. The telephone booth spun, and I gripped the receiver hard.

"How much money?" I had little money with me. I would never get to Switzerland in time. But I trusted Boris to help us, argument or no.

"I've seen to that. One of the last men whom I trust has left a package for you at Hotel Adlon's front desk."

Hotel Adlon? Where Sefton was staying? A coincidence? Or did Frau Röhm know only one hotel in all of Berlin? The Adlon was famous even in Munich. Just the place where Ernst Röhm would have put up his mother.

"Hannah," she said sharply. "You can find that?"

I nodded, then realized that she could not see my nod over the telephone. "Yes."

"Do not fail." She broke the connection.

I hung the receiver on the cradle and dropped my head into my hands. I did not believe in ransoms. Only two years ago the Lindberghs paid double ransoms on a child who was probably dead before they received either ransom note. My best chance lay in my finding Anton before he arrived at the ransom location. Anton had not been safe with Frau Röhm, but with Mouse he was in worse danger. I checked my pocket watch. It was an old-fashioned gold timepiece my father had bequeathed to my brother. He rejected it as too masculine and passed it to me, claiming it was lucky. It had better bring me luck, as I had less than nine hours to find Anton.

The man rapped on the glass again. I opened the door. He looked frantic rather than angry. Who knew what crisis was happening in his life?

I stepped out and held the door for him.

"Thank you much," he said with a Russian accent.

I nodded and stepped into the street. Just in case, I must retrieve the ransom money. I shoved my way back through the crowds to the streetcar stop.

I rode to the Schöneberg station. First, I had to make certain that I was not being followed. Even though I saw no one when I left the streetcar to call, I had to be careful and not lead them to Anton. After my meeting with Lang, I dared take no more risks.

I paced as I waited for a train. No one seemed familiar or suspicious, and I worried that I wasted time. Perhaps I should hail a taxi instead of trying the dangerous trick I was thinking of doing in the tunnels. Before I changed my mind, the train clattered into the station.

I hopped on, noticing who climbed aboard with me. When the train stopped at the next station, a train going the opposite direction pulled beside us and disgorged passengers on the other platform.

The trains stood side by side. I stepped to the doors closest to the other train. Yanking open the door, I leaned out across the rails. It was hard to keep my balance, and if I fell between the trains, I would be crushed.

I pulled open the door to the other train. Before either train started moving, I jumped onto the other train. Behind me, passengers exclaimed in surprise. If anyone had followed me, they were stuck on my old train, or they had to try the same maneuver I had. And I could catch them at it.

I kept my head stuck out the open door. The doors of my old train slammed shut and it roared away. No one had followed me. And no one would have had time to climb the stairs and run to the platform. If I had pursuers, I had lost them.

I settled into the new seat, heart racing. It had been dangerous, and if I had been followed, they were aware that I knew it, but for the moment I had peace.

I picked up a battered leather valise at the front desk of the Hotel Adlon. It had been left for a Hannah Vogel. The concierge did not remember who had left it, nor did anyone else.

Hidden in a bathroom stall, I opened the valise and counted the money, then wrapped the bills in my peacock-green scarf and tucked the package into my satchel. I brought the empty valise back to the front desk. Perhaps the owner would return to claim it.

I did not allow the friendly doorman to hail a taxi, afraid of being traced from here. It was probably paranoid, but the harder I made it to follow my tracks, the safer I felt.

I walked several blocks, checking behind me for anyone following, before I hailed a taxi. Frau Röhm could have me followed from here.

Where to go? I thought of Anton, held captive by Mouse, perhaps locked in a closet somewhere. Years ago I had promised him that no one would lock him away again as his mother had done. I clenched and unclenched my fists. I could not keep that promise if I could not find him.

16

Today was finally Tuesday. I pulled out my pocket watch. After three. She would be there. I smiled, already looking forward to the encounter. If anyone could put a name to a Berlin pimp named Mouse who broke ribs, Agnes could.

A short taxi ride later I stood in front of an office building on the Kufürstendamm.

Stability and respectability radiated from its bulky Wilhelminian-style curves. I let myself into the lobby and checked the notice board to see if the business I wanted had a listing. It did not, but it never had before, so that did not worry me.

I hurried to a set of Art Nouveau–style bronze elevator doors and my best chance to trap Mouse. As an excuse to study the street behind me, I smoothed my hair in the mirror hanging next to the elevator. No one seemed out of place in the street. Better I worry less about what I ran from and more about what I ran to.

I pressed the elevator button, and it ground into action. A moment later the door opened to reveal a liveried elevator operator. He tipped his hat when I entered. "Fourth floor."

I hoped that Jack Ford still kept his offices here, and that Agnes still answered his telephones. The operator nodded and pulled the door closed behind me, white gloves smudged gray from the metal.

We rode in silence. On the fourth floor I stepped out of the elevator. The operator did not close the door.

"Thank you," I said, in a tone of dismissal.

I waited for him to step back into the elevator before I turned down the hall. Like everyone else in the building, he must be curious about the activities on this floor.

Alone in the hall, I hurried to a single door at the end. The door had no sign on it, and the frosted glass hid its secrets. Only people who knew what went on behind the door came here.

I rapped on the wood. Three taps, a pause, and another tap, Peter Weill's knock. The door lock buzzed.

"Please come in," called a mellifluous voice. Agnes.

I smiled and opened the door.

The room had not changed much in the past three years. Jack loved modern styles and his office showed it. Black tiles lined the walls, oil paintings arranged above them. At a spotless glass desk sat a dwarf, garbed in a tailored black dress. She spent fortunes on her wardrobe. Every time we met, her perfectly tailored clothing was the apex of current fashion.

"Agnes!" I rushed across the room.

She hugged me with her tiny arms and I took care not to disturb her coiffed dark hair. I inhaled the scent of her French perfume.

"If it isn't Peter Weill." Her amber eyes glittered. "We've missed you."

The telephone burred, and she held up one lacquered red fingernail, admonishing me to silence. I fell quiet. Although little more than a meter high, Agnes Johannson commanded respect.

Knowing better than to try to rush her, I examined the paintings. One looked like a Tamara de Lempicka. Jack had not suffered under the Nazis. Behind me, Agnes's sultry voice repeated a customer's details and assured him that all would be well. The customer had ordered one, for delivery at seven that night. He would pay rush fees, but expected the best. She hung up the telephone and beamed at me, teeth bright white.

"What is Peter looking for these days?" She gestured to the leather chair next to the desk. I sat, knowing it was an honor. Most were not allowed to sit in this office.

She had once been one of my best informers. She knew I did not snitch to the police. And she enjoyed the extra money. I had always been as generous to her as my newspaper expense account allowed.

I leaned forward to drop a gold Swiss coin on the desk. It rang against the glass. "An enforcer. Hired muscle."

"You need one?" She dropped her hand on a red book next to the telephone. "I could procure you one. At a discount."

I shook my head and gestured to the coin. She slipped it in her doll-sized purse.

"I am looking for a particular man."

"For a story? You haven't been in here for ages for a story."

I nodded, glad I had not revealed her as a source to anyone who would have told Maria, the woman who had assumed my role as Peter Weill, crime reporter for the *Tageblatt*. "I worked in Switzerland for a while."

"That explains the real money." She tapped her handbag. "Why are you searching for this man?"

I ignored her question. "Early forties, about one hundred eighty centimeters tall. Large man. I would guess that he works at a factory, or the docks. Blond hair with some gray."

"I know a few." She raised a shapely eyebrow.

"He might be a pimp. And he specializes in broken ribs." I tried not to wince and give myself away. "One shot with his elbow. And he has a squeaky voice. His nickname is Mouse."

She jerked her head. "I don't recall having heard of him."

I pulled two more coins out of my pocket. I let each clink onto the glass desk. "Maybe you haven't. Maybe you have."

She tucked the coins away like a magpie. I suppressed a grin, glad to be home. "He doesn't run girls anymore. He works for the SA now. Close to Röhm."

"Tell me about him." I kept my voice neutral. This was supposed to be about a story, not about finding a nine-year-old boy. I could not look too interested. But I was more terrified than ever. If Anton recognized Mouse, then he would try to escape. And I did not dare think what Mouse would do to punish him.

She gave a deep throaty sigh that sounded as if it came from a blond starlet, not a tiny brunette. "Not much use searching for him. I imagine he's dead like all the bigwigs there. That'll cost us. Jack's livid."

I nodded. Jack ran high-class prostitutes out of this office. Agnes took the messages and sent them out with young boys who acted as runners, carrying the notes to the prostitutes.

"Did you work for Röhm?"

Her Cupid's bow mouth turned up only at the corners in a flirtatious smile. "I have no idea what you mean, Herr Weill."

I handed her another coin. "It is worth no more to me. I am just curious."

She palmed it. "We supplied line boys for Röhm's parties. A few girls too. A profitable sideline. And Röhm kept the Nazis at bay."

The telephone rang again. She repeated the order into the polished black telephone. The customer wanted three prostitutes, immediately, as if they were cakes for a party. She shook a brass handbell, and a boy who looked no more than ten dashed into the office, the sound of his footfalls eaten up by thick carpet. He hopped from one foot to the other, torn singlet half untucked and a dirt smudge on his cheek. The part of me that had been Anton's mother for the past three years longed to wipe it off. I did not move. In this room, I was not a mother. As far as Agnes knew, I was Peter Weill, hardened crime reporter chasing another story.

The boy glanced in my direction. His eyes widened when he realized that I sat in the chair. He had probably seen no one but Jack sit there.

"For Josette." Agnes handed him an envelope. "No one else."

He nodded. She dropped a coin in his palm. He closed bone-thin fingers around it and jammed it into the pocket of his dirty trousers.

He looked me up and down. Did he think I was interviewing with Agnes for a prostitute job? Jack did the auditions after she passed them along. Shrugging as if it did not matter why I sat there, the boy turned and darted out the front door, closing it softly behind him. Agnes tolerated no slamming doors. I suspected she would make short work of Frau Inge.

Anton still slammed doors from time to time. And here was a boy, one year older than he, carrying messages to prostitutes, probably to earn money for food. I tightened my lips. If Anton's prostitute mother had not latched on to Ernst Röhm, or if I had not met Anton, he would have been lucky to get such a job.

"Still," she continued our conversation as if we had never been interrupted, "I suppose they'll keep Röhm out of it. He has too much on Hitler."

"Give me back one of those. And I will tell you."

She thought for a long moment before handing me a coin. I held it in my palm. If I knew her, I would be giving it back before long.

"Röhm is dead. Executed at Stadelheim. That is from a reliable source."

Her face darkened. "Is Mouse a political concern?"

I shook my head. "Perhaps you will read about it in the *Tageblatt*. It is not political."

She studied me, coppery eyes calculating. I smiled and waited, as if her answer were unimportant.

"Mouse used to have a wife." She lowered her voice and leaned closer. I smelled her flowery perfume again. "They have a little boy; he must be ten. She and the boy live over the Sing-Sing in Neukölln."

I remembered the place, a common hangout for exconvicts. An entire bar decorated like the famous New York prison. Made the ex-cons feel at home. Or maybe they just liked walking out of the barred room free at the end of the night.

She pursed her lips. "I heard he relocated, but it might be a place to begin."

"Does Mouse have a partner? Someone he works with regularly?" If he was not at Sing-Sing, I did not want to have to come back here for another lead.

"Amsel. Swiss. Speaks like an actor. Wonderful elocution."

I nodded. Sounded like Jannings. "SA?"

"Yes."

"I believe he is dead. Anyone else?"

"Are you certain? He was always so clever."

"Fairly certain." I did not mention that I had seen his body. "But do not pass that along."

She nodded. She would pass it along for the right price, but she would not reveal me as a source, nor would she be expected to.

"Anyone else?" I hoped that she would give me someone besides Santer, who was beyond helping me too.

"He had one partner who wasn't with the SA, so he might still be alive. His name's Gregor Gerber."

"Where could I find him, if I needed him?" I would look him up after I found Mouse, if I still needed to.

She hesitated. The telephone burred, and we both jumped.

I studied her artful face while she talked to the client. Although as well-groomed as always, her hair was the flat black that comes from a bottle, and I wondered when she had started dyeing it. We were all, I hoped, getting older.

She replaced the receiver in its black cradle and looked pointedly at my satchel.

"Here is that last one. Then I am out of funds."

She pocketed the money. "I don't know where Gerber lives, but I will ask around for you. I know he's often at Wittenbergplatz. Low-class trade when he's short of funds."

I filed that away. I did not have time to stake out Wittenbergplatz today. "And when he is flush?"

"He calls here."

"Where do you send the girls?"

"Different hotels. I'd tell you more if I knew it."

"What does he look like?"

"About your size, but strong. Dark hair. Lost his right index finger and thumb during the War. Dresses well, black suits and colorful ties."

I leaned across the desk and kissed her powdered cheek. "I can always count on you, Agnes."

She blushed, but shook her head. "You can't count on anyone anymore. Don't forget that."

17

Hailing a taxi outside Agnes's office building took less than a minute. Jack probably paid one to wait.

"Sing-Sing." I repeated the address twice.

The weathered driver examined my breasts in the rearview mirror. "You don't want to go there, Fräulein." Apparently he had decided I was no prostitute. Or at least one who would not do well at Sing-Sing.

"Oh, but I do. And I will pay the fare to get there."

"Begging your pardon, but it's no place for a lady." I was flattered that he had not assumed I was one of Jack's ladies.

"I appreciate your concern. But I must go there."

"Can't imagine why." He moved into traffic.

We drove a few blocks before he spoke again. "I won't wait. Even if you pay me double fare on the meter."

"I am not asking you to," I said, although I had been planning to ask him that very thing. How would I get out of there? There would be no hailing a taxi. "Is it near Potsdamer Bahnhof?"

He nodded. "A few blocks away. I'll pass it on the way there so you can see how to get back to it, in case you need to get there in a hurry."

It would have to do. I leaned back, sitting upright to spare my rib. I swung my satchel into my lap. The Luger and ransom money weighed heavy against my legs. I hoped to need neither.

Should I have asked Anges for hired muscle to talk to Mouse? A trip

to Sing-Sing would be safer with a large man skilled in physical violence. But a thug would more likely be a friend of Mouse's than a
friend of mine. The Berlin underworld was not as large as one might
think. Whom could I trust? I did not trust the state. I did not trust the
criminals, even formerly reliable ones. I was not certain I could trust
ordinary people anymore either. I trusted only Anton, and Boris, even
if he no longer trusted me.

The sun had angled across the sky by the time we made it to Sing-
Sing. Time slipped by. If Anton was not there, I had no choice but to
take the ransom money, and my hope, to Britz Mill and trust that
Mouse would keep his word and let us live. I did not have that much
trust.

I had barely closed the taxi door when the driver roared off, leaving
me alone on a street that smelled of garbage put out too early on a hot
day.

I stood across the street from the café, studying it. Bars clad the first
floor, like a prison. There would be no climbing through them. A
square man with a bulldog's face stood by the front door. His nose,
broken at least once, zigzagged down his face. His burly frame bulged
against the striped uniform of a convict.

I circled the bar. Two exits on the first floor. The main one for
guests, and one in back that opened into the filthy alley. Crates of
empty beer bottles lined the back wall, the smell of stale beer warring
with the smell of hot garbage.

Soot-streaked curtains fluttered in the open second-floor windows.
A shadow crossed in front of one. Anton?

I went back to the front door. The bouncer stared, astonished. Before he recovered his wits at the sight of a woman dressed in middle-
class clothing and without the heavy makeup of a prostitute, I opened
the dented steel door and walked past.

I stepped into the yeasty smell of beer, spilled so often that a thin
layer of sawdust covered the floor to absorb it. It might have worked,
if they ever swept it out. I tried not to think about the sticky grit under
my shoes.

Afraid to tarry by the door and attract attention, I strode across the sawdust. On a platform against one wall sat what appeared to be an electric chair, complete with thick leather straps. Grease blackened the edges of the straps, as if they saw frequent use. I aimed for the bar. The barman was the one most likely to answer my questions.

"How about a good time?" called a beefy man at a table to my right. His tattoos marked him as an ex-convict. I did not study them long enough to find out more.

"Perhaps later," I said with a smile, closing in on the bar stool. "If you can afford it."

His friends laughed, but he scowled. Lovely. Ten seconds in and already one enemy.

The barman, like the doorman, wore a convict's uniform, complete with numbers and a hat. I wondered if he had worn the same one in prison.

He trained his yellow-rimmed eyes on me before I sat. "That seat's reserved. For paying lady customers."

I edged away from the stool. I wanted no trouble.

"If you're here for customers, we already have two ladies working this patch." He was loyal to the women who worked the bar, and I liked him for that.

"I am not here for that. Just a lager."

He cracked a smile, revealing four missing teeth on the top of his jaw. "We serve lager. Drink fast."

Behind the bar I spotted a tiny framed picture of a little boy on the first day of school. His smile too revealed missing teeth. His tiny hands gripped the candy-filled paper cone that even the poorest parents struggled to give their children on the day they started school. Anton had missed that too, since he had never been to school. And he might never go unless I concentrated on the task at hand and got him away from Mouse. I smiled at the barman. Perhaps he was the proud father of the boy in the picture. Or perhaps he was a pederast.

A waiter in another convict uniform walked by carrying a metal prison tray holding a viscous green substance. It smelled like pea soup after a long, hot day. In his left hand he held a prison-issue spoon. I was far from Hotel Adlon. The barman slammed a beer in front of me.

"Handsome boy." I pointed to the picture and sipped the watery beer. Warm as soup, probably from sitting in the sun out back. No money wasted on glamour at Sing-Sing.

His lumpy face rearranged itself into a smile. "He's mine."

A proud father. That might save me francs. "Boys are a handful. But worth it."

He nodded.

"I am here about my own son, Anton." I let worry slide into my voice. "He had a disagreement with his father and ran away from home."

"That's rough." He swiped the dirty bar with a filthy towel. Prison-issue? If so, it had not been washed since its liberation.

"He is only nine years old. Loves Winnetou the Apache."

"We got some of them books ourselves. The missus is a reader." He paused in his wiping. "How's that go? A brave keeps his wits—"

"And his arrows sharp," I finished for him. "Words to live by."

I took another sip of beer. "One of his friends said that he might have come here, that he plays with a boy who lives upstairs."

He smiled again. "It's your lucky day. I seen two boys going up there, walking side by side like the best of comrades."

"Is one blond? He wore a white singlet when he left. His name—"

"Anton. I heard you. The other kid called him something French like that."

"Thank God." My head spun. I had found him. Anton might be upstairs, meters away. Tears welled up. I sagged against the bar.

"My missus had a time with mine when I was in jail. He's straightened out now. Hard, raising boys."

"I do not know how we get through it." I drank a swallow of beer to steady my head. My heart thumped.

He pointed a thumb toward a door against the back wall. Yellow paint peeled in strips off its surface. "Stairs back there lead upstairs. They keep it locked, but they'll hear if you pound. I bet your boy's there right now."

"Thank you. Thank you."

"Think nothing of it. And don't punish him too hard. Boys will be boys, you know."

"Depends on the boys," I answered, thinking of my brother, Ernst. "But I will be glad to have him home."

I paid and left my unfinished beer with a sizable tip on the bar.

Anton was close. I hurried to the yellow door. My heart raced. Perhaps I could sneak him out before Mouse saw me. I did not want to use the gun. I had never shot anyone, and I dreaded to think how I could get past the men in the bar if I had just shot one of their own.

I turned the warm knob. The door held fast, then finally broke loose with a crack. When I pulled it open all the way, the smell of urine spilled into the warm bar. Grime rounded the corners of the empty stairs. The only door was at the top. No way out except back through the bar or forward into the apartment. If anyone followed me in, I had nowhere to run. But at least I could not be grabbed from the sides.

I stepped through, leaving the door to the bar open in case I came back in a hurry. The railing stuck to my hand. I peeled my hand off, gritted my teeth, and wiped my palm on my dress. I mounted uneven stairs. The farther I climbed, the darker it became. If there was a light at the top, it was off. The satchel banged against my hip.

Without taking the Luger out, I flipped off the safety before knocking. Mouse was fast. I dared not give him a second to react. But could I shoot him, in cold blood, in front of his child, and mine?

No answer from inside.

I pounded on the door. It opened as far as the chain would allow. Gray light filtered through the crack. One bloodshot eye watched me.

"Bar's downstairs," a woman rasped, voice ruined by cigarettes and alcohol. "Piss room in the back."

"I am not here for that—"

"You can't use the room up here for customers. Nor the stairs." She started to close the door.

"I am alone." I stepped aside so that she could see past me down the empty stairs to the sallow light of the bar.

I cast about in my head for a story, something that would make her open that door.

"I need a place to stay for a few hours. There is a man out there. And I cannot go back out the front door until he leaves or passes out." As Mouse's girl, she must know plenty about angry drunkards.

"This ain't no hotel." Her rough voice contained no sympathy.

"I can pay. Gold." I pulled a five-franc coin out of my satchel with my left hand, my right never leaving the gun. "Just a floor to stretch out on until morning."

I moved the coin toward the crack. Her hand snaked out and grabbed it. Her face disappeared from the door. Was she examining the coin, or was that the last I would see of her?

Her eye reappeared. "Let me see both your hands. And turn around."

I lifted both hands over my head. Then I turned in a circle. Where was Mouse? Was he standing behind her? He might hear my voice, and be ready for me.

The woman closed the door. The chain rattled, then tapped against the doorframe.

"Come in, but quick." She opened the door wide enough for me to fit sideways. If Mouse was on the other side and recognized me, I would have no chance to respond. But if Anton was there, I had to risk it. I slipped through the opening.

No one else was in the filthy room. I let out a breath I had not realized I held. With my first breath, I drew in the stench of urine, excrement, and spoiled milk. I breathed through my mouth and tried not to think of Anton living in this room.

I strained my ears for the slightest sound. The apartment was silent. As near as I could tell, we were alone. My heart sank. I would have to check each room. I counted three: the one I stood in, and whatever was behind the two doors set into the far wall. I guessed that one led to a kitchen, the other to a bedroom.

I slid my hand into my satchel, feeling the pistol, keeping it close in case I needed it.

"You want food or tea, it's extra." She gestured toward the doors. One hung askew on its hinges, the other partially open.

I followed her. "I can pay extra for tea." Anything to see one more room.

She kicked open the door, and I followed her into the dirtiest kitchen I had ever seen. Grime and grease coated every surface. I wished I had not asked for tea. I would not consume anything prepared in this room. Who knew what foul diseases lurked here? Had Anton been taking his meals in this room? Be grateful that he ate at all, I chided myself.

I cast about for a conversation opener. A slingshot rested on the windowsill. Her son's? "What is the slingshot for?"

She looked at it and scowled. "Boy likes to shoot cats with it. Or pigeons. For dinner."

I wondered if only the pigeons were for dinner, or also the cats, but I did not ask. I did not want to know the answer. I had to get to that last room.

"You have a bedroom? I will pay extra for that. One with a door."

She turned on a faucet. Rust-colored water bled into a teakettle. She carried it to the stove, but found no match. I smelled gas before she gave up and turned the stove off. "No matches. No tea."

"I can manage," I said, relieved. I stood in the center of the kitchen, clutching my satchel, unwilling to sit down.

"Sit." She pointed to a wooden chair textured with something I charitably hoped was oatmeal. I forced myself not to wipe off the chair before I sat. That was no way to be friendly.

I extended a hand and continued lying. "My name is Maria." I almost smiled. Maria was an old enemy from the newspaper.

She shook it. "Claire. Like the saint."

"What a lovely name," I said, on cue.

She smiled. She had been a beauty in her youth, but now she had only one upper tooth, a handful in her lower jaw. Bad dental hygiene, or Mouse? She sat in a chair next to me. Her threadbare housecoat slipped up, revealing a thigh as white as a haddock, and smudged with bruises. When she caught me looking, she pulled the housecoat down.

"About that bedroom?" I wanted only to view the last room, find Anton, and leave without having to draw my gun. I held up a coin between my thumb and forefinger.

"Might as well. But first I need to roust the boy from his nap." My heart raced. Her boy, or mine?

I peeled myself off the chair and stood. Frau Inge would have fainted dead away at the housekeeping standards.

"Manny!" she screeched. "Company."

A small boy with her curly hair appeared at the kitchen door before she finished yelling. Even though supposedly straight from a nap, he was dressed in short trousers, a dirty vest, and shoes.

"I'm here, Mum." Even with his head bowed I saw his black eye. More evidence of Mouse? Or his mother? Had they hurt Anton too? I clenched my jaw. If they had, they would regret it.

"Show the nice lady the bedroom."

Manny turned and headed toward the bedroom. Red welts on the backs of his legs showed where he had been beaten with a switch. The state of his family made it easier to contemplate shooting Mouse.

I followed Manny, hating to turn my back on Claire, but seeing no alternative. I did not hear her follow, but did not turn to look. I was more worried about finding Mouse ahead of me than her behind.

The door was ajar, and Manny kicked it open all the way, just as his mother had kicked open the one in the kitchen. I guessed that was how they moved between rooms here. Thinking of the chair, I did not blame them for not wanting to touch the doors.

I reached behind him to turn on the light. He blinked.

Mouse was not there. Nor was Anton. I staggered back against the dented doorframe. It could not be. But it was. Anton was gone. If he had ever been here.

A brown SA uniform shirt hung over the door. Without moving my head I recognized Mouse's vinegar sweat smell. Anton had been here.

I drew my pocket watch out of my satchel. My hands trembled so much that it was hard to read the time. Almost five o'clock. Four hours until the ransom. Far too early for Mouse to go to Britz Mill. Where was he?

Manny stared at me curiously. "Whatcha got there?"

"A watch." My mind worked furiously on a good lie that would elicit information about Anton. "I bought it from Buffalo Bill Cody."

"I had a friend who talked about Buffalo Will." He scratched his neck. He probably had lice, as Anton had the night I met him. A line of bruises encircled his pale wrist.

"What was your friend's name?" My heart pounded.

"Anton. French, like my mum's name."

"Where is he now?"

"They left a little while ago." He looked back at my watch.

"Where did they go?" In my mind, I begged Claire to stay away one more minute.

"Don't know. Don't matter anyway. I won't see him no more."

"Why not?" My heart lurched.

"Papi's going to sell him. Just as well. He was trouble."

"What kind of trouble?"

"Tried to run away. Papi had to handcuff us together." He held up his bruised wrist. "But before he did, he beat me. Said he couldn't beat Anton. Told Anton he'd beat me again every time he tried something."

I swallowed. Anton would have been hobbled by his sense of honor, even assuming he could have gotten free of the handcuffs. What else had he been through in the past days? Damn Mouse.

"But it'll turn out fine. The rich lady will pay a lot for him."

Frau Röhm must look like a rich woman to Mouse; I probably did as well. "Do you know her name?"

He shook his head. He lifted his chin to scratch his throat, exposing two rings of gray grime in the folds of his neck. "But we'll get a pile of money."

"How will you spend it?" I hurried out of the bedroom. I must get to the ransom location.

"Papi says he'll buy me a pony." He followed. "And we're going to leave this place and move someplace where there's grass everywhere to feed one."

"That sounds wonderful." I was halfway to the front door.

He slapped greasy hair out of his eyes. "At least that's what he says. He don't always keep his word, but Anton said that part of being a man is always keeping your word."

Anton believed in honesty and honor. And he knew that I would hold to my word to keep him safe, or die trying. Manny had no one to trust. I stopped and handed him a gold coin. "Use it to buy sugar for the pony. Or something for yourself."

He slid it in his vest pocket before Claire stepped out of the kitchen.

"I must go." I thrust coins into her palm and bolted down the stairs. I shot through the bar. Out on the street I ran without stopping until I sat on a streetcar, speeding south toward Britz Mill.

Mouse had left early. I had no time to beat him there and make sure that he could not double-cross me.

18

When I had traveled far enough to hail a taxi, I traded the streetcar for one.

"Where to?" The driver's dark hair was shaved almost to his scalp, and bristles stuck up like a pig's. Round piggy eyes added to the effect.

"Britz Mill."

"The windmill?"

I nodded. He did not ask why I wanted to go to an empty windmill after business hours. Not a curious sort. I hoped that he stayed that way.

Bending forward so that he could not see, I pulled the Luger out of my satchel, to feel it in my hands. If I had to tangle with Mouse, I would want to incapacitate him from as far away as possible. Pistols were inaccurate at great distances, but it would have to do. I closed my eyes and pictured the anguished expression Anton must have worn while Mouse beat Manny in his stead. He would be as angry as I. I dropped the gun back into my satchel, on top.

The driver never once looked into the backseat.

As we drove through lengthening shadows cast by the late evening sun, I worried. Tall buildings full of contented families flashed by. Automobiles heading home at the end of a long workday congested the streets.

I checked and rechecked my pocket watch. Even though I left after

Mouse, I would still arrive at Britz Mill long before the appointed time. Nothing to do but stay calm and be ready when the time came; but still I fretted. Would Mouse keep his end of the bargain and bring Anton? Or would he shoot me, steal the money, and deliver Anton to the Nazis?

We were near the mill when another black taxi heading in the opposite direction appeared. It looked like the taxis would collide head-on. I braced myself against the front seat. At the last moment, my driver spun his wheel hard to the right and we careened off the road.

I whipped my head around to see who sat in the other taxi, but dust obscured the window. We bumped through a field and stopped in a tan cloud. I coughed, taste of dirt strong in my mouth. Why was a taxi heading back from Britz Mill at this hour?

"*Scheisse*. What was that bastard doing?" He steered back to the road, but even on its smooth surface we lurched forward. He stopped.

We both climbed out.

"I just washed the taxi. Now look." The driver shook his head.

Air hissed from the front wheel, fountaining dust onto the fender. He cursed again, and I longed to join him.

"Can you repair it?"

"It'll take a while. Make yourself comfortable in the back."

"I can help." Anything to get the taxi moving.

He opened the trunk. "Begging your pardon, Fräulein, but I'd just as soon do it myself."

Before I could argue further, he pulled the spare tire out of the trunk. Flat as well. I poked the warm rubber.

A string of profanities issued from his mouth.

I interrupted. "What now?"

He ran the back of his hand across his pink forehead. "I'll walk back. I saw a house with lights on a short way away. If they have a telephone, I'll have the taxi company send another tire."

I might be late for the ransom. "I can walk."

"It's about five kilometers."

I checked my watch. Quarter past seven. I could still be early. "Meet me there when the taxi is fixed. For your fare."

He looked about to argue, but stomped off down the hard-packed street instead. I hurried toward the setting sun.

Not a single automobile passed on my way to the mill. I arrived winded, cursing Mouse with each painful breath I drew. My feet and sides ached too, but it was worth it. I was an hour early. My watch read eight o'clock, and late evening sunlight lit the mill.

The mill rose out of the sere field like a scene from a Dutch movie, four sails rotating. The bottom two stories were constructed of burnt-orange brick that looked bright against a spade-shaped door built large enough to admit a wagon. A wooden platform ran around the outside of the structure where the brickwork ended, which made the platform at the base of the third floor. The platform looked empty, but I could not see the back. Wooden shingles overlapped like scales on the third, fourth, and fifth floors. On top rested the cap, with the sails attached to it, dark against the apricot sky.

Each wooden story had two fingernail-shaped windows that stared, black and lonely, at me. Someone might be standing behind one, spying on me.

I turned, looking in each direction. No one. But hiding was simply a matter of dropping into the tall grass out of sight. An entire battalion could be steps away, and I would never know. From the top floor I might see anyone hiding in the grass, just as anyone there could watch me.

I pulled the satchel up on my shoulder and slipped one hand inside to touch the oily surface of the Luger. "Mouse! I am here for Anton."

No answer.

Mouse had probably not arrived. I decided to check inside the mill and secure the high ground.

I marched down the beaten dirt path. The sails groaned in the wind, loud as a train. I had never been to a windmill before, but I had thought them more peaceful.

I circled the mill. It was not round, as it appeared from a distance. Instead it had twelve sides. The large spade-shaped wooden door was the main entrance, a smaller door led out the back.

The thick front door stood open a crack. A chill stole down my spine. Were Mouse and Anton here already, even so early?

I drew the gun from my satchel and pushed the door open. Blackness gaped inside. "Take the risks, Old Bird. Life's too long already," Ernst had counseled me. Of course, he was talking about dating, not leaping into mortal danger. But perhaps he was right. I clenched my jaw and stepped into the darkness. It could be a trap, but I had no choice.

Noise smote my ears. Huge wooden cogs creaked. Stone ground against grain. I sneezed out flour dust and edged forward. Anyone waiting here would see me before they would hear me.

The exits on this floor were the front and back doors. I crouched, straining to see through the gloom. I saw no one, but it was too dark to be certain.

I decided to climb to the top and work my way down. I hurried to a set of rough wooden steps built into the wall and climbed to the second floor, wishing for more light. I crept up the stairs. Anyone above could grab me.

The second floor had windows. Umber light wavered through dusty panes, illuminating a floor grayed by decades of flour ground into its wood. I climbed ladder after ladder until I reached the tiny room at the top where giant wooden cogs turned, pushed by wind on the sails. The top floor had no window. The turning machinery drowned all sound, and dark blanketed the room. I groped along, hoping not to stick my fingers into machinery.

I climbed down to the fifth floor. The windows afforded a good view of the field around the mill. The fifth floor was the most likely place to meet Mouse. It was where I would wait if I were him, where I could see everyone who came and went, and shoot them if I wanted. If he was there, he did not call out, or the ocean of sound produced by the mill swallowed his voice.

I hugged the side wall, hand slippery with sweat on the Luger's stock. I circled the room, feeling with one outstretched hand. The fifth floor was empty. I wiped flour dust from the window with the edge of my dress and peered through the glass. Not a soul stirred. I swept the field, my vision repeatedly obscured by the rotating sails. Near the dirt path, large strips of flattened grass showed where someone had turned off the road to park an automobile or truck behind a stand of trees. Was the automobile still parked there?

Cogs ground above me, relentless as the wind. The miller would not have left them turning, would he? Where was the miller?

I hurried through the fourth and third floors. Both empty. I opened the door to the third-floor platform and stepped into the cool breeze, shutting the door. The closed door blocked much of the sound. Failing light made it difficult to see, but I still felt exposed. I looked left.

Mouse's crumpled form leaned against the wall. My stomach dropped into my feet. Where was Anton? I looked right. No one else was visible, but I could not see behind the mill.

I circled the platform, making certain it was empty before approaching Mouse, gun gripped tight in my hand. He turned his head when I came close. Blood stained his brown shirtfront. I dropped to my knees. His coppery blood smell mingled with the smell of ground grain. I gagged.

His breathing rasped through the air. When was he shot? While I was upstairs?

"Mouse?" I tore off one of his sleeves to make a bandage to staunch the blood, but it looked hopeless. Blood pooled thickly around his legs.

He opened his eyes and watched me.

"Won't help," he choked out through gray lips. His breathing bubbled.

I pressed the bandage against the bloodiest part of his chest. "It might."

Blood drenched my makeshift bandage. Too much blood. I could not drag him to the taxi before he died. I knew the signs, from my days as a nurse.

"Where is Anton?" I peeked through the railings down at the field. Still no one.

"Gone." Blood stained his lips like lipstick.

"Where?"

"You never know." He labored to breathe. "What a person can do."

"Who?" If he did not tell me before he died, I would never know. "Did you give him to the Nazis?"

"You trust someone." He coughed, a wet tearing painful sound. "Always a mistake."

"Where is Anton?"

Then he simply died, staring up at me until his gray eyes lost focus. I closed his eyelids, picturing Claire and Manny, alone. They were better off without him.

I went through his pockets, hoping for a clue. He had a few coins, a subway ticket stamped at Potsdamer Bahnhof, and a crumpled pack of cigarettes. Nothing of use to me. Or to him, anymore.

Where was Anton? I jumped to my feet, shaking. I had to search for him before the twilight failed. He had to be fine. Perhaps he ran away, hid somewhere. Perhaps I could make a torch, then he could find me in the darkness. "Anton!"

I searched the grass again. He was so small. I would never see him from up here.

A pair of headlights tore across the dusky field below me. Then another. Police.

I dropped to my hands and knees to crawl across the splintery boards to the edge of the platform, hoping that the police had not seen me. I scanned the fields around the mill. Only police cars. Anton and whoever had killed Mouse must be gone.

I stood and ran back toward the door to the inside, past Mouse's body, thrusting the gun back into my satchel. I had to get away. If the police caught me, they would arrest me for murder. I would never find Anton.

I nearly fell down the stairs to the second floor, caught myself, and climbed more carefully to the first. I stumbled through darkness to the back door. I rattled the handle. Locked. How could I get out?

My shoe trod on something soft, and I pulled back to examine the object in the weak light from the window. A hand.

I stifled a scream and looked closer. The miller, a blotch of sticky blood on his apron. Gritting my teeth, I crouched next to him, first searching for a pulse on his limp arm. No sign of life.

The miller must have had keys. I groped around on the floor next to his body. Nothing. Where would he keep his keys? I bit my lip and slid my hand into his pocket. Still warm, and so were his keys.

I drew them out and unlocked the back door. With shaking hands I wiped any fingerprints off the keys with my dress and dropped them on the floor. I sprinted across the field, satchel bouncing against my hip, dress wet with blood.

19

When I reached the edge of the field, I scrubbed my bloody hands on grass. Someone arrived before me and killed Mouse and the miller. Perhaps the person in the taxi that forced us off the road. There could be no explaining to the police why I was covered in blood, carrying a gun, but completely innocent. I could not have done it even before the Nazis infiltrated the police force.

Whoever had killed Mouse must know about the ransom, or they would not have been here. Surely someone like that would keep Anton safe for another ransom attempt.

I limped along, knees stinging. Blood trickled down my shins. Warm blood, so it had to be mine. I must have torn them open crawling across the platform. My dress covered the wounds, but if anyone looked closely, they would see bloodstains. I should have worn a darker dress.

I circled through the field back to the road, shielded only by tall grass. I wished that the sun did not linger so long in the middle of summer. I had about a kilometer to go before I reached a civilized place where I might hide. The taxi driver probably supplied the police with a detailed description of me. After all, I had stiffed him on the fare.

Sweat ran down my back. Where was Anton? Had Mouse's killer snatched him? Had Anton been here? I tried in vain to remember details from the taxi that had forced us off the road. I had only glimpsed it. Had he been in that taxi?

What if Mouse had a partner? Perhaps the partner killed him and kidnapped Anton. Gerber. Agnes had mentioned a partner named Gerber. That fit with Mouse talking about betrayed trust. If I had not known that Claire could not have beaten me to the ransom, I would have pegged her as the killer. He might have trusted her. But she would not kill him before I arrived with the money. Why had the killer run before the ransom money arrived? And who notified the police? Unlikely that someone not involved had heard the shots over the mill.

My side ached by the time I reached a street with houses. Dead or not, I cursed Mouse for breaking my rib.

I had to change clothes. I cut behind the row of houses, peeking over each fence. There should be laundry hung out to dry on such a windy night. At the third yard, fabric snapped on the line. I scaled the fence, praying that they had no dog. Keeping laundry between me and the cozy lighted windows of the house, I crept across the lawn. Though I longed to leave money in exchange for the clean dress I pulled down, it might be a clue for the police. I hoped that the owner would think the garment blew away.

I stopped at a rain barrel tucked under the house's eaves. Hoping to be left alone, I slipped out of my bloodstained dress. Wearing only underclothes, I wet the back of my old dress and used it to scrub my knees, hands, and arms clean before putting on the new dress. Soft and threadbare, it smelled of hay and sunlight. I smoothed it over my hips. My size. I balled up my own dress and tucked it into my satchel, having no place to hide it. It would not do for the police to find a bloody dress purchased in South America at the town nearest the murder. They must not suspect that I was ever here.

I walked back down the sidewalk along the empty main street. What should I do? A lighted inn beckoned to my right, but I dared not register. The police might start house-to-house questioning. I must find my way back to Boris's, where I could disappear. Even though we had fought yesterday, I trusted him to take me in. Since I had met him, he had been my haven from danger.

I hurried on, hoping to find a bar, the most likely place for a taxi to park at this hour. Luck favored me, for an ordinary black taxi stood in front of a place called Haus Hubertus. I circled the building. Crates of mostly empty bottles lined the back wall, like behind Sing-Sing. I searched for the newest-looking crate, reached in, and pulled out a bottle. I needed to have beer breath without taking the time or calling the attention on myself to order and drink one. I swished a swallow around my mouth, gagging, then spit it out before creeping around to the front. Walking into a small-town bar, where everyone would know I did not belong, where the gossips would mark the details of my appearance, was too risky. I preferred to take my chances with the taxi driver and the night.

The taxi driver's head lolled against the seat back. I hoped that he was asleep and not dead. I climbed into the backseat and closed the door.

He started and turned surprised dark eyes to me. "I didn't see you come out, Fräulein."

"Quiet as a mouse, I am." Thinking of how quiet Mouse was, I wished I had put it another way. I slipped into a Berlin accent that matched my faded clothing and the patrons of the bar. I gave him the name of a street near Tempelhof Airport. Nearly ten kilometers away, but if anyone followed my trail, he might think I left on an airplane. I could hop onto the streetcar there and ride it almost all the way to Boris's. "How much?"

"Whatever's on the meter. It's a fair price."

I nodded uncertainly, as if I had never been in a taxi before. "That'll do."

I leaned against the seat to hide my face in shadow.

I clenched my hands in my lap and tried not to think of Anton, Mouse, or the police. I counted in my head until we arrived, concentrating on my breathing and the reassuring rumble of the taxi's engine. I could not break down and cry, or I would never find Anton.

I dropped money on the front seat before climbing out, face turned from the driver. I walked to the first house, flattening against the door until he drove away. If he remembered where he brought me, the address was a dead end for the police. After he left I doubled back to Tempelhof, boarded a streetcar to Zehlendorf Mitte, then a taxi down Kronprinzenallee to Boris's house.

In near darkness I limped past the pillars at the gate and down the familiar path to his front door. A light burned in the downstairs parlor. I let myself in with the key he had given me and followed the light.

He did not stand. "That's not what you were wearing when you left the house."

"I got blood on the other," I said, trying to decide how much to tell him. I did not want him considered an accessory for Mouse's murder.

"I'm not surprised."

I lifted my dress to display my bloody knees. "May I clean up?"

He winced at my lacerated knees. "What did you do to yourself?"

"I crawled on some splintery boards. You are better off not knowing details."

"Right." He clenched his jaw and walked to me. "Let me clean that up."

He led me to the upstairs bathroom and ran a hot bath. I let him. I did not have the energy to insist on doing it myself.

The last man to draw me a bath was Ernst Röhm.

He undid my buttons and slipped off the dress. "Are you hurt anywhere else?"

"Not where it shows." I climbed into the tub.

He washed my hair, hands gentle on my scalp. "What happened? Is it Anton?"

I nodded, biting back tears while he rinsed my hair.

"Hannah?"

"I lost him." I sobbed. Boris pulled me out of the tub, wet, onto his knees. He rocked me back and forth, waiting for the rest of the story.

When I stopped crying he wrapped me in one of his thick towels and sat me on the stool in front of the sink. "Do you want to talk yet?"

I shook my head, afraid that I would break down again if I started talking.

He wiped my face with a washcloth, eyes on mine. "I'll take the splinters out of your knees."

He winced more than I as he removed them. He doused my knees with alcohol, and bandaged them with deft fingers, a parent used to binding up skinned knees. I thought of all the times I had bandaged Anton's knobby knees. Would I ever do that again?

"All done." He kissed the bandages covering my knees and I flinched. "I'll fetch you something to wear."

I sat alone in the bathroom. Where was Anton? He must be with a stranger, someone who may have shot Mouse in front of him. He probably feared for his own life, and knew the adventure was over.

Boris touched my shoulder. "Hannah?"

I stood and let him dress me in a nightshirt. He had changed out of his wet clothes into pajamas.

He led me to his bedroom, tucked me under the quilt, and held my hand between his. "Tell me."

A thousand images ran through my head. What could I tell him? Knowing of Mouse's murder made him an accessory. Hearing it would pull him into a web of politics and murder. "It puts you in danger too. Implicates you."

"So, you decide what's in my best interest, as if I were no older than Anton?" He handed me a glass of water. "Let me help you."

"You cannot help me." I cradled the glass in my palms.

"Quite a testimony to my abilities." He ran his thumb across my cheek, where the tears had been earlier.

I lost my train of thought and relaxed under his hands.

"Hannah?" His voice brought me back. If I told him, the court would find him as guilty as I appeared to be. I did not want him landing in jail as an accessory.

"I know something about discretion. And I won't give in. Let's save time."

I looked into his serious gold-flecked eyes. I believed him.

I drank a long draught of water, then told him what I could: a man had kidnapped Anton and the ransom had gone badly, with the ransomer dead and Anton gone when I arrived. The police had reason to suspect me, and the Nazis were after Anton.

He stroked my hands for a moment before speaking. "I know a detective. I've worked with him on insurance cases at the bank. He's an ex-policeman, dogged, and very smart."

"I cannot trust anyone right now."

A muscle twitched in his jaw. "Do you trust me?"

I studied him. I heard my brother's voice saying "You don't have to do every damn thing alone, Old Bird."

"Can't I help you?" He stroked a curl of wet hair off my forehead.

I gave in. "Tomorrow could you check the orphanages around Britz Mill? If Anton . . ." I gulped. "If Anton escaped and got picked up, the police might have brought him there."

"And you?"

"I will try to reach Frau Röhm." I could try Agnes again tomorrow too.

He climbed into bed and held me. I lay awake for a long time. Anton was gone, and I had no idea where he might be. And neither did Frau Röhm. For the first time since he had arrived on my doorstep filthy but proud, Anton was truly lost to me.

We had a quick breakfast and left the house early, still tired from our late night.

I thought of Frau Inge's face in the mirror while wearing the wedding dress. I could leave nothing unattended at the house. I hefted my satchel of ransom money onto my shoulder.

I found a call box and laid out my pfennigs. Boris had given me a pile of German money my first day, refusing to take Swiss money in exchange, insulted that I offered.

I fed in coins and listened to the telephone burr in Frau Röhm's front hall. I pictured her black Bakelite telephone ringing in its special alcove next to a pad of paper and fountain pen. I had seen it during my futile search for Anton.

I hoped that she had already received another ransom note. That would mean there was still a chance that Anton lived.

"Röhm." The burly maid sounded worried. She had likely received only bad news over that telephone for days. In the background dogs barked.

"I must speak to Frau Röhm immediately," I said, reluctant to give my name. "Is she in?"

The maid chirped as she had the day I visited the house. As before, the dogs fell silent. "She's not taking calls. She's ill."

"I must speak to her."

"Are you calling from prison?"

"Why would you think such a thing?" Prison?

Silence stretched out between Berlin and Munich. "Who is this? We're expecting a call from . . . Stadelheim Prison."

"It is I, Hannah," I said, surprised that she did not recognize my voice.

"I will inform her that you called."

She broke the connection. When I placed the call again, the line was engaged.

Had Frau Röhm received another ransom note? What if she had heard nothing? What if someone not intent on a ransom kidnapped Anton? If the Nazis had Anton, he was already dead, so that just could not be. There must be another answer, and I had to find it.

I pressed my forehead against a glass pane, trying not to cry. Why would Nazis go all the way to the windmill to kill Mouse? How would they know he was there? Could Lang have made the connection? He knew Röhm's associates. Perhaps the only one with an *M* name left alive was Mouse. But if they wanted Anton dead, why not kill him there with Mouse? Why take him?

I must assume that someone else had killed Mouse. That possibility left Anton alive. I ran through my options. Visit Claire and see what she knew. Difficult, as she had already seen me. Return to Agnes and find out more about Mouse's partner, Gerber. Impossible, as Agnes would not arrive at work until late afternoon. That left me with difficult or impossible. I chose difficult.

I left the stifling telephone booth and headed for Sing-Sing, all the while checking to see if someone shadowed me. I saw no one, but that did not mean that no one was there.

Just as my taxi pulled to the curb in front of Sing-Sing's dilapidated front door, Claire emerged with a suitcase in one hand, her other clutching Manny's shirtsleeve. He carried a small cardboard suitcase, his chin raised defiantly. They looked like a battered version of Anton and me. Early for her to be up and about. Something was amiss.

I climbed out. "Wait," I told the driver, and hurried off before he had a chance to complain and drive away. If he wanted his fare, he had to wait.

"Claire," I called. She jumped.

"I lost my watch last night. Did you find it?"

She gave Manny a suspicious look before answering. "We didn't steal it, if that's what you mean."

I shook my head. I knew that. It was in my satchel. "Heavens no. I just thought it might have fallen from my pocket."

"We're going," she said. "No time to take you upstairs to look. But I checked pretty close when I packed. Nothing there."

I nodded. "Thank you." The taxi horn beeped.

She hefted her suitcase. Too heavy for her. I smiled.

"Perhaps you might care to share my taxi? We are headed back to Anhalter Bahnhof." I suspected that was her destination—a place to get a train out of Berlin. I waved back toward the taxi. The horn beeped again.

She shook her head.

"I do not expect you to pay part of the fare." I guessed at the reason behind her reluctance. "To return the favor of letting me hide last night."

She tottered two steps with the suitcase and stopped.

I opened the taxi door and climbed into the front seat, leaving her and Manny to load themselves.

"Extra passenger is extra fare," said the driver sourly.

"I will pay."

Claire, who fortunately had heard nothing, climbed into the back with Manny, luggage on the seat next to them.

Where were they going? To a prearranged rendezvous point with Mouse? If so, the man who had killed him might be there, assuming that it was not the Nazis. But if the Nazis wanted her, they would have come to Café Sing-Sing and killed her already.

"Holiday?" I gestured to the suitcases. We both knew it was no holiday. She was not the type of woman who had ever had a holiday.

"Of a sort."

"Going to see your pony?" I asked Manny.

He shook his head. "He didn't come back with the money."

Claire elbowed him. My side twinged in sympathy. "Enough," she said, and he fell silent.

So Mouse had been due back at home. They were not going somewhere to meet him, somewhere that the killer might know about. My heart lightened. "Sometimes money makes people do crazy things."

"Don't it now," she said.

"Are you two in trouble?" I hated to be so direct in questioning, but Anhalter Bahnhof lay only minutes away, and after that I might never see them again.

Manny's eyes filled with tears, but he looked out the window without speaking, hand on his ribs.

"None of your affair," Claire snapped.

"I am in trouble too," I said. "I know how it is."

"Do you now?" She looked at me levelly, beautiful blue eyes shuttered.

"My man cleaned out the house." I hated to keep lying. "Nothing there when I got home last night. Not even furniture. Or my son."

She grimaced. She knew how that was. "Mine took off. Had something that belonged to me too. Or at least half did."

"You going after him?" I hoped not.

"I'm through with him. Either he double-crossed me, or someone double-crossed him. Either way I'm done with Berlin."

Manny shifted on the seat and shot her an angry look. Plainly he was not done with Berlin.

"We're going to stay with my folks. On their farm."

That was a safe place, if they went there.

"You?" she asked.

"I must find where he took our son. Then we will leave Berlin. Away from him."

She nodded. "Men's more trouble than they are worth." She tousled Manny's greasy hair, the first sign of affection I had seen. "Except when they're little."

He pulled his head away. Like Anton, too old for that. Claire and I exchanged wistful glances, both remembering smaller boys.

The taxi stopped next to the russet-colored brick front entrance of Anhalter Bahnhof. Built in the 1870s, the station had the tallest hall in the world and was once known as the Gateway to the South. If she was staying in Germany, she was probably heading for Leipzig or Munich, but trains left Anhalter Bahnhof for as far away as Athens and Rome. I would not know where she went unless I watched her buy a ticket and climb onto a train.

While they struggled with their suitcases, I dug out coins for the taxi driver. He snatched the fare from my fingers and pulled into the busy traffic.

She let Manny run ahead. After he stepped up and through the middle archway, she turned to me. "I know you're not who you say. I talked to the barman at the Sing-Sing. He said you were looking for a boy named Anton."

I nodded, glad to have a chance to tell the truth. "He is my son."

"Last night you lied." A party of Orthodox Jews bustled past, marked by their black clothing and skullcaps. I hoped they boarded a train that would carry them far from Germany.

"I had to search your apartment, to see if he was there."

She walked up and through the archway. "But you didn't want to pay for him." Her voice sounded bitter.

"I went to the spot where I was supposed to pay, but . . ." My voice trailed off.

"He weren't there?" Her voice was hard to hear in the bustle of the station. The huge hall teemed with people.

"Anton was not there. Mouse was." I kept an eye on Manny's messy head, not wanting him to get lost.

"So you knew his name too?"

"Almost a week ago he kidnapped the boy and me for Ernst Röhm."

"You got free?" She whistled and Manny stopped walking, as obedient as Frau Röhm's dogs.

"I did. And came here to find my son."

"What did Mouse do when he saw you?"

"He was dying," I said. "Someone shot him."

Her shoulders sagged. She bit her lower lip. "Best thing for him, I guess. For the boy too. He was a mean man." She sniffed. "You could fry a sausage on his temper."

I could not mourn for Mouse either. Still too far away to hear, Manny settled himself on an empty cart. "I have told you the truth. Who do you think killed him? He said it was someone he trusted."

"Couldn't have been a lot people. He didn't trust no one. Not even me. Didn't trust his own mother."

"Did he have a partner?"

"Don't think so. Not for this."

"What about Gregor Gerber?"

"You do your homework, Maria, if that's your name."

"Gerber?"

"Him and Mouse had a fight. I don't imagine Mouse'd of used him. He didn't need a partner to deal with you and one little boy."

I cleared my throat. "Where could I find Gerber?"

"Some flophouse. He don't have no regular address."

That matched what Agnes had said. "Thank you."

"Don't tell nobody where we went," she said. "But if you do, it's not where we're going anyway. And we won't leave until I see that you're gone."

"I promise not to follow you," I said. "One more thing. What was Mouse's real name?"

"Manfred. Manfred Brandt."

His real name and his nickname started with M. Lang could have made the connection. "Anyone else you can think of who might have wanted to kill him?"

She turned away from me, voice barely audible. "Should have been me, years ago. But it weren't."

She walked away lugging the heavy suitcases, limping on her bruised leg. Her head hung down, as if she had already given up. When she reached Manny, I turned, keeping my promise not to follow.

I sat on a bench outside the station, under the huge shady tree, and thought of what to do next. My worry for Anton could not turn to panic. I must keep moving, keep busy.

I assumed that Mouse killed the miller. But what if Anton had escaped from Mouse? What if he had shot Mouse? After all that Mouse had put him through, he would have been angry and frightened. Could he have shot him? I clenched my hands together to keep them from trembling. I must consider all possibilities. If Anton escaped, where, in all of Berlin, would he go?

20

I boarded the subway to Bettina's apartment. If Anton had escaped, he might head there. Bettina was a childhood friend who had minded Anton a few times. Before we left Berlin three years ago, I made Anton memorize her address. And he forgot nothing. His life had been too dangerous to allow him that luxury.

The apartment block looked the same, although fewer people were on the street, perhaps because of the heat. A respectable neighborhood of clean, classic buildings and broad, well-swept streets, it too had its dark side. It reminded me of Munich. I lifted the familiar polished brass knocker and rapped.

"Come in." Bettina opened the door and dragged me inside, glancing up and down the street. Then she pulled me into a quick embrace. Her vanilla smell enveloped me. A threadbare blue dress hung loose over her frame. It was wonderful to see her again. I'd had no contact with her since I left, not wanting to endanger her.

The house was as clean as always, but no baked goods scented the air.

She held me at arm's length, with a shocked expression. "Oh, Hannah! It's wonderful to see you. Where's Anton?"

"I do not know." My voice threatened to break.

She pulled me down the hall hung with family photographs, lovingly dusted, toward her tiny and always-busy kitchen. "I haven't done any baking today, but I can put on a kettle for tea."

"You have done no baking?" I was so surprised that I stopped walking. "You?"

She laughed in an embarrassed way and tucked a strand of dark hair back into her bun. She wore the same light blue dress as last I saw her.

"Is everything in order?" I asked, concerned.

"Just because I'm not baking?" She laughed a shell of her usual laugh. "Things have changed in the past few years, Hannah. We didn't all go jaunting off to Switzerland, or wherever you've been."

"I had no choice."

"You could have written. Once in three years."

"I was afraid to involve you in my problems."

She gave me an irritated look, then sat me at her kitchen table. She bustled about putting on a gleaming copper teakettle that she had from her mother. My gaze roved around her little kitchen, surfaces polished till they shone, copper pans reflecting morning sun. Still cozy.

"How are things, Bettina?"

She turned to face me, her usually busy hands folded. "Not good. Fritz joined the Party, as I suppose you know. All the policemen are supposed to."

I nodded.

"And now there are all these party events we must attend. My oldest son wants to join the Hitler Youth. They're all encouraged to. I've said that we can't spare him weekends, but that's obviously a lie, so I had to buy a garden plot outside the city to keep him busy on weekends, although we can't afford it. But we do need the extra vegetables."

The kettle shrieked, and she turned. Neither of us said a word as she filled the teapot and tossed in a handful of leaves.

She turned back, pot in hand, and tears in her eyes. "There's no escaping the Nazis now, Hannah. They've taken over everything. You must mind every word you say, even in front of your own children. You hear tales of little children informing on their parents for anti-

Nazi sentiments. And I can't be pro-Nazi, I don't have it in me. So I must prattle on about nothing, even at home."

I stared, aghast. Bettina and Fritz had always been model, loving parents. How had things reached a point where they could not trust their own children? How had the Nazis managed to drive a wedge between parents and children in just a year? That was how they had won: terrifying the old, and separating out the children, like wolves. Would Anton have informed on me had we stayed? I shook my head. No, he would not have. I was sure of him, enough to trust him with my life.

She sat the teapot on the small well-scrubbed table with a clunk and dropped into a chair. "But you didn't come here to listen to my troubles. If I know you, you have enough of your own."

"I do, but I would rather hear about yours. You should leave Germany."

She shook her head. "Fritz would never find work anywhere. And it would be almost impossible to sell the apartment. And the children's friends are here. Where would we go?"

"America?"

"I'm too old to learn another language, even if they'd take us."

"Austria?" We both knew there was no hope of legally emigrating to Switzerland.

"It's little better there than here, from what I can tell." She poured tea. "I keep hoping that Hitler will disappear."

I sipped my tea. Orange pekoe—her favorite. "You should leave."

"And who would take care of Mother?" She tucked in another wayward strand of hair. "She's too ill to move. It's not so simple for me. We can't all drop our responsibilities and head for the hills."

"I did not—" I stopped myself. Why argue? She had enough troubles, but it hurt to think that she had such a low opinion of me. "I am sorry it is so difficult."

She picked up her teacup. "Tell me your troubles." She put down her cup again without taking a sip. "They must be more interesting than mine."

"I am looking for Anton. I do not know who has him, but he might come here if he escaped."

A few years ago she would have peppered me with questions, but today she merely said, "I'd take him in, of course, at least for a while. How can I reach you?"

"You cannot."

Her eyebrows raised in the middle, as they always did when she was conflicted. She probably wanted to invite me to stay, but worried about what the neighbors might think, whom the children might tell. My best childhood friend feared my mere presence in her kitchen. I wondered if she was more afraid of the Nazis, or angry at me for leaving.

"I had to leave, Bettina."

"I know that," she answered, but her eyes were hard. "Lucky for you that you did. Those of us who didn't have to leave stayed."

I touched her arm. "I am sorry it turned out like this."

She gave me a wry smile. "I don't blame you for the Nazis, Hannah."

"But—"

"You'd better run along before someone knows you were here."

I drew my hand back. "Do you have a telephone?"

She wrote a number with the stub of a wooden pencil. "We hardly use it, because Fritz thinks that the Nazis are listening in."

I memorized the number and handed her back the slip of paper. I would carry nothing to link me to someone else, least of all her. "I will call and ask if you have finished my dress. If Anton is here, say yes. Then meet me at noon by the bison at the zoo. If he is not here, say that you are having trouble finding time to work on the dress."

"You're good at this kind of thing." She crumpled the paper in her palm.

"I have always had to come up with codes. My sources have been hiding from police longer than the Nazis have been in power."

She leaned forward. Her doe-brown eyes were serious. "Get out as fast as you can, Hannah."

"If I do, would you join me?" She inhaled sharply, but I forged ahead. "Or send the children?"

She stared into her teacup. "I might. At least the boys. Hitler wants war and it's only a matter of time before he'll send my babies to be cut down."

I did not stay to finish my tea, anxious to be gone before her daughter Sophia or the boys spotted me. If she could not trust her own children, neither could I. I had always trusted Anton with my life, and he had trusted me with his. It seemed simple and matter of fact, but it was nothing to take for granted. Even if I let him down, he would know I did everything possible. But that was not enough. I had to find him.

Agnes would not be at work for hours. Someone had to know about Mouse and his murder. I remembered the lights tearing across the field at Britz Mill. The police.

Terrified but determined, I rode the subway to the Berlin Alexanderplatz police station, now filled with Nazis. Dangerous, but I saw no way around it. The only way to find Anton was to discover who had killed Mouse, assuming the murderer had kidnapped him. Perhaps the police had uncovered something. Whether or not they would divulge that to me was another question.

The imposing police building covered a city block. At each corner a squat tower stuck up, like the castle in a child's playset. At one time, it was the largest building in Berlin, complete with stables. I sniffed the air. The stables were still there, or at least the smell was. My shoes carried me through the building to the Hall of the Unnamed Dead, a route that for years I followed every week. I tried to ignore the black-framed photographs hanging there—death scenes used to identify those who died in Berlin with no one to claim them. From one such photograph I had learned of my brother's murder. I was grateful that his had long since been removed. Mouse's picture would not be hung yet. And perhaps the police would recognize him, although I had found no identification when I searched his pockets.

At the end of the hall was Fritz Waldheim's old office. I had not thought to ask Bettina if he still worked in that part of the building. I could not imagine him anywhere else. He had been my source at the police station for almost a decade before I had fled with Anton. He, Bettina, and I had been friends since I was in my teens. Once I knew his routine as well as I knew my own. But now I did not. Did he still eat his lunch late? If so, I might catch him almost alone there. But so much else had changed in the intervening years, I knew better than to take it for granted.

Hoping that no one recognized me, I pushed open the frosted glass door a crack. I peeped through. If Fritz was not there, I did not want to enter. The room was different from the bustling place I visited so often as crime reporter Peter Weill. The rhythm of typing had changed—the quick staccato sound now slower, unfocused.

I checked each man. It looked like a lot of them ate lunch late these days. In the corner Fritz hunched over a typewriter, pecking at the keys. His eyes widened in surprise when he recognized me, but otherwise he gave no sign that he knew me.

I walked to the counter where I once read so many police files and ran my fingertips over the smooth wood, familiar with each curve in the grain.

Fritz jerked his head toward the door.

"Excuse me," I said. "Is this the passport office?"

"Wrong hall." A clean-shaven young man came to the counter and gave overly complicated directions to the passport office. I thanked him and left.

Minutes later, Fritz joined me in the hall.

"Hannah!" he said. "It's been so long."

When he enveloped me in a bear hug, the familiar stink of his cigar made me cough. My eyes watered.

"Careful. Fragile goods here."

He laughed and let go. "You must stop by the house. Bettina would love to see you."

He walked down the hall, past the death photographs. I kept pace.

"I did. I might come back again, assuming you still want me."

"Why?" He chewed the end of his cigar and dropped his voice. "Does this have to do with Röhm?"

"Indirectly. One of Röhm's men was killed last night. I wish to know about the case."

He laughed bitterly. "Case? We've been ordered by none other than Hermann Göring to burn files related to murders around the time of the Night of the Long Knives."

"But this was no execution. He was—"

"No investigation. In case you hadn't heard, they killed your friend Röhm."

"He was not my friend." I stopped walking. "Really, Fritz—"

He ignored me. "They killed him and many others. We don't have numbers. But we do have orders."

My heart sank. No one investigated Mouse's death. Or anyone else's. "Did you take crime scene photos?"

"Probably, if it didn't look like an SA matter. In case someone changes his mind, and we must investigate after all."

I described the murder location, and he installed me in the office of a colleague out for the day so that no one would see me loitering in the hall. Then he hurried to fetch the folders. He clearly wanted me out of the police station as soon as possible. I had no desire to tarry.

He returned with two gray folders. The miller and Mouse. I opened them. He read upside down, like old times.

I examined the first picture. A chubby man in a long apron sprawled next to a partially open door, lifeless eyes open and surprised. A ring of keys rested near his outstretched right hand where I had dropped them. The miller. I had not seen his face. According to the file, he had a broken rib, Mouse's trademark, and had been stabbed through the heart. Had Mouse killed him? The miller was survived by a wife and three children.

I opened the second folder and looked at Mouse. He looked just as he had when I left him the night before. Eyes that I had closed, palms up by his sides, blood soaking the front of his brown shirt, my makeshift bandage drenched. Seeing the picture brought back the smell of his blood mingled with the overwhelming smell of flour. I swallowed, nauseated. "How close was the shooter?" I said, trying to distance myself.

"Close." Fritz tapped his thick finger against tiny black dots on the edges of Mouse's shirt, near the bullet hole. "See the powder burns on his clothes?"

"Why would he let someone get so close with a gun?" Mouse was more savvy than that.

He shrugged. "Perhaps someone he didn't perceive as a threat."

"Can you tell how tall the shooter was?"

"Now why would you ask that? But no."

Because I wanted to know if it was a child. I looked back at the miller's file. "Different causes of death. Seems odd."

He scanned both reports. "Looks like the miller was killed first, perhaps a half hour before the second one."

I suspected that Mouse had killed the miller, and someone else had killed Mouse. But who? I shuddered. Whoever it was, he had Anton. I stared at the picture, trying to forget Anton's trusting eyes. He had stood somewhere in the frame of this picture, not long before it was taken.

My gaze moved to Mouse. He wore a sheathed SA dagger, one of the commemorative ones Röhm had commissioned earlier this year for SA members who had joined before December 1931, complete with an engraving of Röhm's signature. They would be grinding those signatures off soon, I bet. Loyalty to the SA and Röhm were not the honor they had been last week.

I traced my finger across the picture of the bloody blade. Mouse had been armed with the same kind of weapon that had killed my brother. And he could have killed me with it when I bent over him to work on his wound. A chill ran down my back. "Do you suppose he used that dagger to kill the miller?"

Fritz took a deep breath. "No comment."

I held the photo close to my eyes. Dropped near the body was a bent twig. Anton's Indian sign! My heart leaped. He had been there. I studied the twig. Three bends. So he had been there with two people. Mouse and someone else.

"What do you see?"

I pointed to the twig, furious with myself for having it missed it when I stood near Mouse. "Anton was there. That is his sign."

"Anton? At a murder scene? Where is he?"

"I do not know, Fritz." I fought down a wave of tears. "I think that the man who shot Mouse took him."

"The victim's name was Mouse?" His square hand twitched. The police officer in him wanted to write that down.

"Manfred Brandt," I whispered. "SA."

He skimmed the report. "We have a suspect, if we could investigate, but the SA connection precludes it."

"You have a suspect?" I kept my voice calm.

"A woman. Mid-thirties, short blond hair, cleft chin—" He looked at me in shock. "That's you."

The taxi driver had given them my description, as I had known he would. "He was shot before I found him."

"God damn it, Hannah." It was so incongruous for him to swear that I almost smiled. Almost. "What are you mixed up in this time?"

"Röhm's men caught us. His men kidnapped Anton, and they took me to Hanselbauer. Friday night."

"But the next morning they started the killing there."

"I know. I last saw Anton the night before the killings. . . ."

He came around the desk to my side. His arm went around my shoulder.

"Easy there," he said, as if I were a horse or a dog.

I leaned against him, pulling myself together. When I stepped away, he dropped his arm, revealing his Nazi party badge.

"You are a Nazi too. Devout?"

"I'm as devout as I must be. Like most of us." I nodded. I too had helped the Nazis to save a child's life. Who was I to judge? "So who do you think killed him?"

"We had one other lead." He ran his stubby finger down the report. "Here." His finger tapped a line. "We found an automobile parked near the mill. Registered to a Gregor Gerber."

Mouse's partner. Had he killed him to keep the ransom for himself? Or had he only lent Mouse his automobile?

"If Gerber's a Nazi, then—"

"I heard he is not SA," I said, remembering Agnes telling me so.

He shrugged and fell silent.

I let him think for a while, then cleared my throat.

He came out of his reverie and spoke. "If I had to speculate, and this would be off the record, if you still had a record, I'd guess that if your man was close enough to Röhm, then they've been hunting him since that first night. Don't know why the automobile would still be there. Seems as if the Nazis who shot him would have retrieved it."

"So Mouse is just a latecomer to the executions?" I hoped that was wrong. If not, the Nazis had Anton, and he was already dead.

"The explanation doesn't always have to be complicated, Hannah." He reordered the reports and shuffled them into the folders.

"If he was on their list, then why did they not murder him the first day?"

"They had a list? Have you seen it?"

My mind clicked. "Or perhaps he betrayed Röhm."

"Assuming there was a betrayal."

"Perhaps it was not the Nazi leadership. Perhaps it was an SA man out to get revenge for someone betraying them to the SS."

"Or perhaps he committed suicide," said Fritz with a wry smile. "Speculation will only get you so far."

"He did not commit suicide by shooting himself in the torso. I imagine he would have picked the head."

"Given it some thought, have you?"

I changed the subject. "Do you wish to notify the next of kin? The murder victim's wife and son live over the Sing-Sing in Neukölln." I did not tell him that I already notified the widow, or that he would not find her there in any case.

"We're not allowed to notify next of kin." He looked at the office door.

"So the widows, the sisters, the mothers, wait, never knowing?" I tried to catch his eye, to make him think of the next of kin. How would Bettina feel if she waited for him to come home, never to know if he was alive or dead?

He shifted. "I don't like it any more than you do."

I found that hard to believe. He had not seen the women, chronicled their pain and loss. He saw only files. "Is that so?"

A muscle twitched under his eye. I was being unfair, but my heart was with those women standing in line, never to find out what had happened.

I sighed. "Tell Bettina I send my love."

"I will, Hannah." He smiled, a worn-out version of the smile I had known for more than a decade. "And I'll check around, discreetly, to see if the police picked up Anton last night, a boy on his own. If they did, I'll bring him back to our house."

Tears of gratitude stung my eyes. "Thank you, Fritz. I am sorry for what I said. You are a good friend."

"I do the best I can, and I know it's not enough." He spread his broad hands. "It's all closing in. You don't know."

"I don't. And I wish you didn't either."

We embraced, and he hurried out the office door. I gave him a few minutes' head start, then left.

A travesty that the police were not following up on Mouse's murder. Perhaps it was not political. Why would the Nazis follow him to a windmill in the middle of nowhere? They could have shot him at his house, in front of his wife and child, or dragged him to Lichterfelde for the firing squad. Unless Lang had made the connection with the telegram and followed them to the windmill to see where they might lead him. One more loose end tied up.

Back out on the street with my notes, I resolved to go to the address where Gerber had registered his automobile. If Gerber had killed Mouse and kidnapped Anton, perhaps they were holed up there waiting for another ransom attempt. But if he had, why had he abandoned his automobile for the police to find and fled in a taxi? Perhaps the automobile had engine trouble.

I hiked my satchel up on my shoulder. Anton had to be at Gerber's. Why waste time second-guessing Gerber's motives? The best plan was to go to his address, get him back, and leave the mystery of the automobile unexplained. I could think about it in Switzerland.

I sat on a bench in front of the police station, facing the busy street, and pulled my satchel into my lap. Uniformed policemen trotted in and out of the imposing front doors, once tough and independent thinkers, now registered Nazis. How had Hitler gotten to them so quickly and so thoroughly? As devout as they needed to be, so Fritz had said, but how devout was that? If the police picked Anton up and discovered that he was Anton Röhm, would they try to find his mother, or would they devoutly turn him over to the Nazis for execution?

I pulled Boris's street map out of my satchel and looked up Gerber's address. The street was near the Spree, in the factory district, if I recalled correctly. I sighed. It looked like a business address, not a home. If so, I would have to track him from there.

On the way to Gerber's, I bought a lemonade, too bitter, from a vendor in a stuffy underground shop. That would have to do for lunch.

I arrived at an empty lot, fenced on all sides. I circled until I found a knothole to peep through. Yellowed newspapers and trash blown against the fence formed an unbroken ring. Brown grass grew high and undisturbed. Gerber did not live here. No one did. Nor was there a business. He gave a false address when he registered his automobile. I slumped against the fence. I had no leads, nothing.

I sat in the hard-packed dirt and leaned my back against the fence and thought. Anton was gone, and I had no idea where to find him. I bit back tears. But sitting here would not help me to find him. Perhaps Agnes had found a number for Gerber.

And if not, there was always Wittenbergplatz. Agnes had said he sometimes went there. Tonight I would stake out Wittenbergplatz for a man with no right index finger and thumb. I thought back to the time that I was almost raped there, in 1931, when investigating my brother's death. I did not relish the idea of going back after dark.

I stood and brushed dust from my dress. I could not sit around until tonight or hope that someone would contact Frau Röhm about a ransom, or that Anton would escape on his own and end up at Bettina's. I could not stand still.

21

Who else might know about Mouse's murder? Agnes might, but it was still too early to reach her. Sefton was next, I decided. He had known Röhm, and Mouse and Röhm were close. A slim chance, but I was beyond caring.

I hailed a taxi to the Adlon, hoping that Sefton was in and wondering if the man who had left Frau Röhm's valise of money might also be there and recognize me. I hurried up the grand staircase.

No one took special notice of me, and when I knocked on Sefton's elegant door he answered it himself, wearing his paisley dressing gown. He looked as if he had been awake for a long time, although patchy dark stubble on his jaw showed that he had not yet shaved.

"You know it is almost two?"

He rubbed his eyes, but he did not look tired. "Too early to get up. Come back at tea time."

He started to close the door, but I pushed my way in.

A small self-possessed woman stood in the center of his room, fashionable gown and shoes immaculate and in stark contrast to my shabby shoes and sweaty dress.

I had not seen her in years and never expected to find her in Sefton's bedroom. Her men came from the major aristocracy. Sefton's pedigree was too short, so this was something beside a simple assignation. Or perhaps she was mixing with the lower classes for a thrill.

"Bella." I inclined my head. Bella Fromm was the society reporter for the Ullstein papers. Her family was old aristocracy. She mingled with counts, dukes, and even the kaiser. She was also Jewish. Berlin was no place for her anymore. Still, while my friend Paul, another Jewish reporter, had been replaced, I was certain that her powerful patrons had enabled her to keep her job. "Lovely to see you again."

"Hannah." She held out her gloved hand at such an angle that I could kiss it or shake it. I shook it, rings hard against my palm, even through her glove. "I thought you'd left Berlin."

"I returned."

"Leaving soon?" She glanced at Sefton's polished hotel door.

"Germany?" I said, pretending to misunderstand her. "Are you?"

She shook her head, flashing her jewelled earrings. "Not while I still can do good."

She was braver than I, and I had to respect her for it. She would stay until the SS dragged her off to a camp. "Admirable sentiments. I am grateful there are still Germans working to do good."

"Why are you here?"

"Same as you." I forced a smile on my face. "Working to do good."

Sefton looked from one of us to the other in fascination, as if we played a highly amusing game of tennis.

"I haven't heard from you in years." Her tone was accusatory, as if I had left as a personal affront.

"I do not appear in the society pages. So perhaps you were looking in the wrong place."

"Perhaps not."

I turned to Sefton. "Get dressed. I cannot stare at those pale hairy legs another minute."

"Hear, hear!" She clapped her gloved hands.

"This is where I point out that, all evidence to the contrary, this is in fact my hotel room. And I can dress howsomever I wish, pet." But he padded to the dresser and pulled out a pair of finely creased trousers.

"I was sorry to hear about the von Schleichers," I said to Bella. I was not, much. With his shady backroom deals, ex-Chancellor von Schleicher had done as much to help the Nazis into power as anybody, albeit inadvertently. His new bride, however, was probably innocent, and both had been gunned down by the Nazis even before Röhm. "I know that you were close."

She nodded, little chin set firm. "I lost more than a few dear friends to this purge."

Sefton rummaged in the wardrobe behind her, eventually pulling out a white shirt. I smelled starch across the room. Adlon had wonderful laundry service.

"For goodness' sake, sit down," he said before leaving us alone.

I perched on the desk chair I had sat in while typing the day before yesterday, when the world, already complex, seemed simpler than now. The typewriter was nowhere in evidence. Back under his dancing shoes?

She sat on the wingback chair, her own back straight.

"What is the governmental reaction to the purge?" She would know. She had friends in the highest of places, even amongst aristocratic Nazi sympathizers.

She hesitated. We had disagreed politically for years, she a monarchist, I a socialist. But we both knew that neither of us would ever be a Nazi. "Officially they are delighted."

"What do the diplomats think?" She attended most diplomatic functions and threw the most extravagant diplomatic parties in Berlin. Although I knew of them, I, as Peter Weill or Hannah Vogel, had never been invited to one. Sefton might have been deemed worthy of a few, if he brought someone interesting with him.

"I'll know more tomorrow." She opened a gold cigarette case and extracted a cigarette. "Do you mind if I smoke?"

"I do," I said, more to annoy her than because I minded.

She returned the cigarette to the case and closed it with a snap. "Hitler is due to attend a party the Americans are having at their embassy tonight. I'm certain that the official version of the bloodbath will be trotted out then."

"What are the Americans celebrating?"

"Their independence day, July Fourth."

"Ironic timing. Considering."

She gave a wry chuckle and slipped the cigarette case in her bag.

"So, what do you know now?" I said, not letting my original question go.

She shrugged her tiny shoulders. "Some think it's the beginning of the end for the Nazis. Others think it's the end of the beginning."

"I vote for the second. But I hate it."

"I fear that you are correct." The way that she said *you* let me know how surprised she was that I was correct.

Sefton emerged from the bathroom, fully clothed. "How are you two getting on?"

"Smashing!" Bella said.

I smiled at him.

He looked worried. "Right-o. I'll just go shave. Back in a tick. Order coffee or drinks or something." He disappeared into the bathroom again.

I let her order from room service. She knew more about gourmet dining than I, or even Sefton. If I was the poor country mouse, allowed into the city mouse's larder, I might as well let them trot out the best delicacies.

"What did you bring for Sefton?" Her dark eyes were sharp.

"So suspicious of a social call."

"You are no more on a social call than I." She poured herself a glass of water from a crystal carafe on the table.

"Sefton's bedroom is the nexus of the social scene."

We both laughed at that.

"Perhaps I can help you." Her tone let me know that she expected little help from me in return. Just as well because I could do little for her.

"Can you get information out?"

"It's tricky." She sipped her water. "But I might, if it's valuable enough."

I told her an abbreviated version of what I told Sefton, leaving out the names of the women at Lichterfelde and my connection with Röhm. Then I told her what I had learned from Fritz, without naming him. I trusted her to release the information to her diplomatic connections. The more places the information came from, the less likely it would be traced back to me or to Sefton or to any one source.

When I finished she nodded. "So, no investigations."

"But pictures. Just in case."

Sefton came out of the bathroom wiping stray dabs of shaving cream off his neck with a towel.

"There won't be a just-in-case," she said. "Yesterday the Reichstag passed a law retroactively declaring the murders of the past few days legal."

"Really?" Sefton's hooded eyes were alert. He tossed the towel behind him into the bathroom like a man who had never had to pick up a towel off the floor.

"Yes." She recited it, hands clasped in front of her like a schoolgirl. "The statute reads as follows: 'The measures taken on June thirtieth, July first, and July second, 1934, to thwart attempts at treason and high treason, are considered as essential measures for national defense.'"

"Very efficient," Sefton said. "It's no longer a crime."

"It didn't even happen," she said. "The papers have received notice that they may not print obituaries of those murdered in the last few days."

"That too?" I blinked several times. So they would disappear, and only their immediate families would mourn them. Like my brother, even their deaths would not appear in the newspaper. It would be as if they never existed to all but the tiny few who loved them best. Bella's eyes were wet. Sefton coughed.

We stood so until a rap sounded on the door. This time I did not jump.

"Room service," announced a muffled voice.

Sefton opened the door to a white-jacketed waiter pushing a covered cart. The plates on top held grapes, bread, caviar, and soft French cheese. My stomach rumbled.

"You can put it over here, dear." Bella gestured with her arm, graceful as a ballerina.

The waiter parked the cart where she indicated and turned to Sefton for a tip.

Out of the corner of my eye I caught him give Sefton a rogue's smile. Two proper ladies in his room for lunch, quite a coup. Sefton, the ladies' man. I hid a smile. When I looked at Bella, she giggled.

After the waiter closed the door, I turned to Sefton. "Do either of you know a Manfred Brandt?"

She reached for a roll, a diamond bracelet that cost more than Boris's Mercedes glittering on her arm. I knew, without asking, that it was genuine. Privileges of the aristocracy.

"Should I?" Sefton asked, ever cautious.

She looked interested. "I've not heard the name."

"He was a friend of Röhm's. And he was murdered yesterday."

"How do you know that he was murdered?" Sefton asked, a bit sharply.

"He was shot in the chest. And the gun was missing. Unusual in suicide, yet common for murder."

"A lot of other close friends of Röhm have been murdered in the past few days," Bella put in. "Enemies too."

She poured us each a tall glass of mineral water.

"But this man's murder was not political." I picked up the mother-of-pearl caviar spoon and spooned out sturgeon's roe. The faint fish smell reminded me of the sea.

I spread caviar onto a piece of soft bread. The silky rich taste burst on my tongue. Sefton looked at the black beads and winced, probably calculating the cost and the argument he would have with his editor when he returned to London. I inclined my head toward Bella, to indicate that she ordered. He sighed and helped himself to caviar. Already on his bill, after all.

"His nickname was Mouse. Used to be hired muscle."

He dropped his caviar and caught it deftly with his napkin. "Mouse. Squeaky voice? Big?"

I nodded and sat straighter in my seat, a twinge in my ribs. I had never seen him drop anything before.

"You've been awfully uncomfortable. I noticed last time I saw you," Sefton said.

Trying to act nonchalant, I picked up a handful of purple-black grapes cold and beaded with moisture. Each looked as if it belonged in a painting. Quite the attention to detail here at the Adlon.

"Cracked rib?" he asked, Groucho Marx eyebrows raised.

"Mouse's calling card." I popped a grape in my mouth. Its sweetness complemented the savory taste of caviar. Bella knew her food, and Sefton knew his thug.

She shot me an interested glance. Something new.

"I don't know a great deal." He settled into the other wing chair. "Mouse was one of Röhm's enforcers. Good at thrashing folks to force them to change their political opinions. Liked to break ribs."

"Known associates?" I wanted to take notes, but was also certain that I wanted no written record.

"Mostly Röhm's gang, as far as I know. He didn't serve in the Great War, like most of them, so he had a bit of a hurdle to overcome. That and not liking men." He paused, evidently enjoying his caviar. Bella had yet to taste hers, but I supposed that to her it was no special treat. "If he weren't so good at his job, Röhm would have tossed him. But Röhm always chose efficiency over politics."

"Was he loyal to Röhm?" He knew a good deal about Mouse, more than I had expected. A coincidence, or were he and Mouse connected?

He shrugged, but I found the gesture unconvincing. "He never approached me. Beyond that I can't say."

"Could he have been an SS spy?" I wanted to plant that seed. Who knows what they might discover if alert to that possibility.

"He didn't seem quite clever enough. But then that would be the best way to seem if one were involved in something like that."

Bella looked between us, caviar forgotten.

"What else do you know about him?"

"Married to a prostitute. Had a son, I believe. I believe they were estranged, but he might have gone back there in a pinch."

"Have either of you heard of a Gregor Gerber, associate of Mouse?"

I sipped water, eyes on them. Both shook their heads, bewildered. That made sense. Agnes had said that he was not in the SA.

"Why are you looking for him?" Bella asked.

"I am looking for Mouse's killer. He has something that belongs to me."

"Really?" Her eyebrows arched up toward her perfect hair. She obviously did not think that I had anything I would much miss. "Political?"

"Personal." I worried that she might reveal something to someone who would pass it on to Hitler and that would be the end of Anton. She let nothing slip, but she was not above playing politics with Anton's life to make the Nazis look like fools. And, perhaps, neither was Sefton. "But important."

Seeing that nothing more was forthcoming, she nibbled her bread with even white teeth.

"He belonged to a Ring," Sefton said. "If this Gerber was close to him, perhaps they belonged to the same one."

My heart leaped. That was useful. Before the Nazis came to power, the criminals in Berlin were organized into Rings. The Rings had clever names and posed as legitimate clubs, such as sporting associations or music clubs. Each felony had its own Ring, pickpockets in one, murderers in another. Some were quite large and wealthy. Members spent time at the local clubhouse, and the yearly dues covered legal fees for members should they be arrested. Very practical.

"Nazis broke those up, you know," he said, sensing my excitement. He wiped his fingers on the thick napkin spread on his lap.

"They wanted to be the only criminals in town," Bella said dryly.

"Still. Perhaps there is something there."

"Tough gigs," Sefton said, "even before the Nazis. Be on your guard."

Bella looked shocked at the thought of entering a Ring clubhouse, and I worried about it myself. I would call Agnes. Perhaps she had discovered a number for Gerber. If not, she probably knew which Ring he and Mouse had belonged to. I checked my pocket watch. Nearly three. She would be there soon.

"Indeed." I rose to leave.

Bella gave me a look of grudging respect. I felt flattered and squashed the feeling. What did I care what the helpless aristocracy thought of me? Yet I admired her and cared about her opinion more than I liked to admit. And, I told myself, if anyone knew a safe house and a way to arrange passage out of the country discreetly, it would be Bella. Best to keep her as an ally.

I brought Sefton out into the hall to tell him of my encounter with Lang, without mentioning Anton or the telegram. I told him to be careful. If I needed to reach him, I would leave him a message at the front desk. We would meet one hour later and one block south of whatever I left on the message. As for him reaching me, that was impossible.

I could give him no information until I completed my business. My business was finding Anton, but I dared not tell him that. Who had been in that taxi coming from Britz Mill? What if it was Sefton, dependent as he currently was on our lovely taxi fleet? I remembered our leisurely dinner, when he mentioned how useful Anton would be as a pawn to temper the moral outrage of the Nazis. He was not above using Anton to further his own political goals. I could trust no one.

22

I headed for the bank of beeswax-scented telephone booths in the lobby and put through the call.

Agnes answered at once. "Ford's."

"Peter here." A well-dressed woman stomped around the lobby like an ostrich.

"Peter," Agnes said, rich voice full of recognition. "Haven't heard from you in days and days."

"You offered to find the number for a laborer last time we spoke." I hoped she would know I meant Gerber. "For an odd job."

"Carpentry, wasn't it?" She seemed to know that her line might be tapped too, although she had always been discreet. "How did the last one work out?"

"Not as well as I had hoped." I wondered if she knew that Mouse was dead. She had better sources than the police. Would she think that I had murdered him? I forged ahead. "I wish to build a ring around my vegetables. To keep out the mice. You know how every mouse has a partner and soon you are overrun?"

She inhaled slightly, the same as a gasp from a less experienced person. Investigating the Rings was dangerous for anyone. "Quite. One moment."

Ostrich woman stepped to one side. Behind her stood Hauptsturmführer Lang. I slowly turned my back to him, afraid that a sudden movement might attract his attention. Then I froze, like a hare heading from a hound. What was he doing here? Had he somehow followed me? If he caught me here, would he make the connection to Sefton? Had he made the connection to Mouse?

"Here we go," Agnes said. Paper rustled. I pictured her paging through her red leather book and silently begged her to hurry. She read off a number. "Gregor. He's quite reliable. But be sure not to pay him everything up front. He drinks."

"A pleasure doing business with you." Gregor Gerber.

"I'll send you the bill," she said, a hint of sarcasm in her voice.

I hung the telephone on its elegant cradle. Lang's reflection made its way into the dining room. I would have thought it above his budget, but they obviously paid Hauptsturmführers more than I thought. I had to stay in the telephone booth until he was out of sight. Was he here to eat, or had he somehow followed me?

No reason to waste the time. I decided to call and trust that I would find Gerber there.

The telephone rang. "Café Sing-Sing," said a familiar voice. The barman I had spoken to about Anton. Could he be Gerber? I held my breath and remembered his hands. He had all his fingers. I let out a sigh of relief.

"Hello? No time for the shy here."

"Pardon." I affected a Berlin accent. "Is Herr Gerber there?"

There was a long silence. Had he recognized my voice?

"I'll get him," he said at last.

The receiver crashed against something none too gently. I pictured it lying next to a puddle of amber beer covered with flies. Indistinct conversation rumbled.

Another voice came on the line, deep and gruff. "Gerber."

"I am a friend of Agnes. She recommended I contact you about a carpentry job."

"I can't give estimates on the telephone. Let's meet."

Someplace public and well lit. "The zoo, by the entrance."

He grunted. "A nature lover?"

"Something like that."

"Can't today. Busy. Tomorrow. Ten in the morning."

I stifled a groan. In the morning the zoo would be deserted. Right now, in the midafternoon, it was full. And I did not want to wait another day. But I also knew that I could not seem desperate in front of this man. "See you there."

I hurried behind the telephones and walked into the kitchen. I could not walk across the lobby with Lang in the dining room. The cooks stared at me, openmouthed.

"Excuse me." I walked past them and out the back door, knees shaking.

I went down Unter den Linden, then ducked into a side street to find another telephone booth.

This one smelled of beer. I dialed Agnes again.

"Did he call to check on me?" I assumed that he would. And if he had not, he was not careful enough for my purposes.

"He wanted to make sure that you were aware of the rates for finish carpentry. And that you are a fair employer. I recommended you most heartily. Don't make me regret that."

"Have I ever made you regret anything, my dear?"

"We're still young."

I laughed into the telephone. I did not feel young. "I have missed you."

"And I you. Don't make me regret that either."

I spent the rest of the day bribing taxi services to view their logs for the Britz Mill area. A few taxis had been dispatched to nearby addresses, but only two taxis were on record as going to the mill itself. One entry was for me, one passenger there, zero passengers back. More interesting was one that left with one passenger, but returned with two. Both were dropped at a street near the Leine Strasse subway station, presumably for the same reason I had been dropped at Tempelhof—to keep from laying a trail.

The driver was on vacation in Hamburg, so I could not reach him. According to the dispatcher, it had been a long-planned vacation. Likely he had not been bribed or threatened to leave town.

So, only two. Of course, any number of passengers might have traveled to Britz Mill. All the logs showed was that other trips had never been recorded, and I knew from personal experience how simple it was to pay a taxi driver to forget to record a trip.

The sun set; my feet ached. I checked the time. Nine thirty. Perhaps Gerber would be at Wittenbergplatz tonight, and I could talk to him before the zoo meeting. Then I would not have to wait for tomorrow. I could not rest until I found Anton. No point in going home to worry. Luckily I wore my most comfortable, and oldest, shoes. Wittenbergplatz after dark was a place where one wanted to run and not worry about what one stepped in.

I took the subway to Wittenbergplatz. No one seemed to follow. At least no one whom I could see.

I paid a local resident to spend the night on her balcony, watching the square below with field glasses. She did not seem surprised by the request, and I wondered how many people had paid for the favor before me. There was much to see. In spite of the Nazis, the prostitution business still throve here.

A few extra marks bought me a pot of hot tea and a sugar bowl. The tea helped fight off exhaustion. Where was Anton? I tried not to think of him alone and on the run in the streets around Britz Mill. But was that better than being held by a kidnapper who had murdered Mouse, perhaps in front of him? I paced the balcony until my legs trembled with exhaustion and I longed to curl up under the table and sleep like a cat. But I dared not.

At around three in the morning the sky lightened to gray. The sun would be up in a few hours, and I had not seen Gerber. I stretched my back and trained my eyes on an arriving black taxi. It halted at the subway stop, and an immense fat woman and dark-haired man climbed out under a streetlight. They kissed passionately. He wound his fingers through her hair.

He was missing his right index finger and thumb. Gerber!

I ran through the apartment and down the stairs, but by the time I reached the street the taxi and the man with the missing fingers were gone.

I walked to the woman, trying to figure out how to get information. She watched me approach, made-up eyes dark in the streetlights. Catering to men who preferred overweight women was an expensive proposition. Hard to afford food to stay at that weight on a prostitute's wages. A straight bribe might be best.

"Did you know the man who was just here?"

"Why?" She lit a hand-rolled cigarette, blowing cheap tobacco smoke at me.

"He interests me."

"You're not his sort." She dragged on her cigarette and wheezed out the smoke. "Skinny as a chicken you are."

This would work only if I sounded convincing. I needed a good reason to be here. "I work for his wife."

"Why you need to come here to follow him?"

"Because he has not been home since yesterday morning. She worries."

"Guess she don't give him what he needs." She smiled, displaying rotten teeth.

"Or the other way around."

She shrugged.

I pulled a banknote from my satchel. "Where was he last night?"

She grabbed for it, but I pulled it out of reach. "And convince me that it is true."

"Same as tonight. With me until late."

"When did he pick you up last night?"

"Right after his work, around four, same as always. He had a car then. Some friend borrowed it from the hotel. Interrupted us and all." She shook her head. "The friend brought his kid. We've been using taxis ever since."

My heart lurched. "What did his kid look like?"

"Like a kid." She gave me a withering look. "Blond. Skinny. At least he was quiet."

"What hotel?" I had to keep calm, to get a hotel name out of her, something to double check.

She stared at me. I waved the bill.

"You're not police?" Her eyes narrowed.

"No." So she was no control girl, registered with the police as a prostitute, or she would not have asked. Not surprising, as most prostitutes were unregistered.

"Look." I let exhaustion creep into my voice. I suspected she wanted to go home and go to bed. "I just want to tell the wife that he was with a girlfriend and let her sort it out. I will not tell her where or with whom."

"Then why you need to know the hotel?"

I smiled and answered honestly, something I love to do. "So I can check for myself whether you are lying."

"By then I'll have the money." She took a deep drag off her cigarette, letting it burn down to her fingers before tossing the still-burning butt into the gutter.

"But I know you work Wittenbergplatz. You will be here if I want a refund."

She ground out the cigarette and stood in thought, obviously something she did not like doing this early in the morning. I imagine she'd had a long night.

I pulled out another bill. "I need to get home soon. So let's do this quickly or not at all. And this one is for not telling anyone that we had this conversation."

She named a flophouse a block from where we stood. I gave her the money.

"Where is he now?"

"He's like the wind. Never settles long in one place. Could be anywhere."

I walked straight to the flophouse. Gerber had checked out. For less than I had paid her, the clerk confirmed her story. At around six, a man matching Mouse's description had walked in with a young boy and headed off to Gerber's room. Minutes later he and the boy came back through the lobby, and this time the man carried keys.

Gerber had an alibi. He had been in a cheap hotel with a prostitute and had not left. Unless the prostitute and flophouse clerk lied, a possibility, it meant that my only lead was gone.

I was too tired and empty to cry about it. I had to hope that Gerber would give me more information tomorrow. He was one of the last people to see Mouse alive. And one of the last people who I knew had seen Anton. I clenched my jaw. I tried not to think about where Anton might be as I limped to the subway, tired knees still aching from last night's crawl across the mill platform. The subways had long since stopped running for the night, but the first one of the day would be coming soon.

Sunrise gilded the sky before I finally made it to Boris's, eyes gritty with exhaustion. I watched him sleep, trying to decide whether to climb in or take a spare blanket down to the couch. Before I decided, he opened his eyes.

He stared at me, then looked over to the window where early morning light glowed on the curtains.

"News?" I asked.

He shook his head. "Are you all right?"

I did not know how to answer that question, so I just nodded.

He pulled the quilt up with one hand and drew me in next to him. I fell into an uneasy sleep in the warmth of his embrace.

I slept until eight, a good three hours. A slamming door nearby woke me. I sat up in bed, heart pounding. Panicked, I looked around the room. I was alone, and at Boris's. When the bedroom door opened, I jumped.

"Slept in, did you?" said Frau Inge. "Herr Krause left instructions that I was to prepare you breakfast, and I have done so."

I bet he had also left instructions to let me sleep, and she certainly had not done that. "I will be down shortly."

Even though I hurried, I sat down to a cold breakfast, including cold coffee. Frau Inge was predictable. But why did she dislike me? Was it because I disrupted her household, or did she have feelings for Boris? It seemed as if she did, but she was married to someone else. I sipped cold coffee. As if being married to someone else changed one's feelings.

I walked to the telephone booth I used yesterday, nowhere near as nice as the one at the Adlon, and called Bettina. Perhaps Fritz had found Anton, or he had turned up on his own.

"Waldheim." Her voice sounded strained.

"Good morning. I am calling about my dress."

"I haven't had time to get to it, Fräulein. Please check back tomorrow."

After I hung up I felt lonelier than ever.

I called Frau Röhm again, and this time after I spoke to the maid, Frau Röhm returned my call fairly quickly.

"Do you have him?" she asked, quavery voice brisk.

"No," I answered, just as short. "You?"

"What went wrong?"

"The big mouse was dead in the trap." I did not know if her telephone was secure. "But the little mouse was gone."

Silence stretched out. I wondered if she had any idea what I meant. "I see."

"Have you heard anything else?" I hoped she would tell me of a second ransom attempt.

"No. What do we do?" The bossy overbearing woman was gone; in her place was a scared grandmother. I suddenly wondered if she would give him back to me if she got him.

"We wait." I could not think of a better answer.

I arranged to call the next day and hung up. Where was Anton? If Frau Röhm had not heard of another ransom attempt, then perhaps Mouse's death had not been for the ransom money. What if it had been the Nazis? What if they had Anton?

I clasped my shaking hands together. I would not let myself think that. I could not. I had to assume that whoever had killed Mouse had Anton, and that he would give him back as soon as he received the ransom money.

23

I took the subway from Dahlem Dorf north to the Zoological Gardens, paid my entrance fee, and walked through the Japanese-style entrance, noticing how much friendlier the concrete elephants seemed than the stone sentries at Lichterfelde. But both the elephants and sentries were large enough to crush me should they topple.

A tiger paced in a cage, bright orange-and-black coat out of place in the concrete-and-straw confines of his enclosure. He rubbed against the bars as if against friendly hands, then turned and snarled. I did not know how to escape from my cage either. And I understood the urge to bite.

I walked through the zoo. Gerber was not due to arrive yet, and I had nowhere else to go. I visited the bison, where Anton would certainly come if he visited the zoo. He would talk of stalking them, ready to kill one with an arrow and use the hide for a teepee. A nanny walked a pram in the early morning sunshine, the only person there so early.

I slid Anton's pocketknife out of my satchel. He had given it to me to hold for him on the zeppelin, over a week ago. I still had the knife, if not the owner. I leaned against an oak tree next to the bison and carved a feather into the bark. Anton's symbol. A few months ago he created a lexicon of symbols for coded messages, something he had read that Sioux Indians did. I was a bird, he a feather. I had suggested he use an egg as his symbol and had been treated to an evening of frosty silence.

Apparently, he was much too grown up to be considered an egg, or even a chick, and I should have known better.

I added a full moon and a bird next to the feather. If Anton passed this way, he would see it and know that I had been here near the full moon, looking for him. Ridiculous, I knew. I shot a guilty glance over my shoulder for the zookeeper.

Was the gesture really for him, or for me? Finished, I stepped back and stared at the brave white lines against the gray bark. I felt comforted, even though I knew how futile my actions were. Before I lost heart, I carved a house under the bird. Bettina's symbol. If Anton came here, he would know to go there and look for me.

With a lighter step I walked across the zoo to the entrance.

"Peter Weill?" said a voice behind me.

I recognized it from the telephone. "Herr Gerber?"

He nodded and grabbed my arm. We strolled through the zoo together as if we had known each other all our lives. He was bigger than he had seemed from the balcony last night, and exactly what one expected when hiring muscle. Only a few centimeters taller than I, but twice my weight. His face was broad and unlined. Scars lined his knuckles, and muscles in his forearms bulged out from beneath rolled-up sleeves. A scarlet tie hung down the front of his shirt like a rivulet of blood.

"Miss Agnes speaks highly of you. Not many folks impress her."

"Agnes recommended you as well."

"What will you be needing from me?" He propelled me deeper into the zoo, head swiveling as if taking in the animals and not looking for human followers, as I suspected he must be. A natural predator.

"Protection. And questions answered."

"Answer mine before I answer yours." No expression flickered in his gray eyes.

"Let's see."

"Mouse."

I slowed, but his hand under my arm pushed me forward. "What about Mouse?"

"You kill him?" Who had told him about Mouse's death, or that I looked for him? Agnes knew both men, as did Claire. But, as far as I knew, only Claire knew that he was dead.

"No. Did you?"

He laughed, a quick bark like a seal. "You know who killed him?"

"No. But Mouse had something of mine with him when he died. I want it back."

"What was it?" We stopped next to the monkey house. Monkeys scampered in grass on the other side of a deep empty moat. The monkeys knew better than to try to jump it. A fall that far onto concrete would kill a monkey. Or a woman.

"My son." I braced myself against the warm steel railing. We were alone, and he could easily toss me in the moat. No one would hear.

"Short kid, but scrappy? Blond?"

"You knew him?"

"Met him, once."

"When?"

"Day before yesterday." That tallied with what the prostitute said.

Was he part of the kidnapping scheme? A mother monkey clambered up a frayed gray rope, baby clinging on her back with long brown fingers. "I want him back."

"I want Mouse back." His grip tightened. "He was a good man in a fight."

I drew in a deep breath and winced at the pain. Mouse had a friend after all. What would he do with the truth? "Not in that last fight. The police report says he stood there and let someone standing right next to him put a bullet in him."

"He'd have to trust someone to let them get that close."

"Whom did he trust like that?"

He laughed his seal bark again. "Nobody. Not even me."

I tried to shrug, but he held my arm down. "Then whom?"

"Someone he didn't think could hurt him. Maybe the boy."

I studied his battered face. He thought Anton had killed Mouse? Had Anton? If so, where was he?

"Been checking the orphanages, to make the boy pay if he did it."

"Did you find the boy?" I struggled to keep my voice level. What if he had been there before Boris? "He is worth a great deal of money to me." I knew better than to appeal to his softer side.

"Don't expect to, really."

"What do you expect to find?"

"Not you. A pretty blonde, looking for a lost boy. I'm looking for someone who'd have cause to hate Mouse."

"Many had cause to hate him, from what I have heard." I did not want to implicate Claire.

He leaned his weight against me, loosening his grip on my arm. "But Mouse was always partial to blondes."

I thought of Claire's unkempt blond hair.

"He'd do most anything for one, for a while."

I realized that he thought that Mouse and I had a relationship. I suppressed a smile. "You think we were working together to kidnap my son and collect ransom money from Frau Röhm?"

"Till I saw you. You're not his kind of blonde."

"Oh." I viewed that as a compliment, having met his kind of blonde.

"Don't reckon you know who killed him either." He spat a string of brown juice into the monkeys' moat. Chewing tobacco.

I studied him in silence. I had no idea.

"Don't reckon you did it, either. Or you'd have nabbed the boy and bolted."

"The boy is mine." He was correct about what I would have done. I wondered if I would have had the courage to shoot Mouse, if it had come to that.

"But I can't figure what you'd hire me for." He turned flat gray eyes on me again. "You seem like you can take care of yourself."

"I heard that you and Mouse were in the same Ring. I want to get into the clubhouse, ask around about Mouse. See if someone knows who killed him."

"I did that myself. Nothing. Not many were man enough to take him like that."

The monkeys frolicked. From here, they looked safer in their cage. "Who was man enough? You?"

He did not look insulted. "Not me. Not no one. It had to be someone he never would have suspected."

"Can I hire you?"

He shook his head. "But when you find out who killed Mouse, turn him over to me, and you won't have to worry about him no more."

He released my arm and strode off through the dappled shadows.

So, if he had no leads and had not killed Mouse himself, that left Anton, or something political. Was Mouse a traitor to Röhm, and surviving members of the SA had tracked him down? Or was he loyal to Röhm, and Lang and the SS had come for him? If Mouse was loyal to Röhm, he should be on the purge list Wilhelm had mentioned back in the Hanselbauer. That list had to exist, and I had to see it.

I headed back to Wittenbergplatz to see if Gerber's prostitute was on duty. If so, I planned to slip her money and find out more about him. I climbed the stairs of the subway station, smiling at the lady in the Café Möhring advertisement, auburn hair piled on top of her head and a mole above her knowing smile. She always reminded me of my late brother Ernst; she knew the score and still found it somehow amusing.

The prostitute was gone, probably home sleeping, as anyone who had been up that late should have been. Bedraggled women milled around waiting for the lunch trade, but none would tell me the name of the woman I met last night.

I wandered down Kleist Strasse to Motz Strasse, home of the El Dorado. At the corner I stopped still. Whitewash covered the El Dorado mural. Giant swastikas alternating with Nazi slogans decorated the windows. Wilhelm was right. El Dorado was not in its old form at all.

Peeking out from the corners of a Nazi poster were the words HERE . . . RIGHT. The full sign used to read HERE IT IS RIGHT. It cheered me to see these defiant little vestiges. They had papered them over, but the words were there, and maybe they would be revealed again.

Two black-uniformed SS men conversed on the sidewalk in front. One leaned against the pole that supported the street sign.

I walked to the door and put my hand on the familiar metal handle.

"Excuse me," said the larger SS man. "You can't go in there."

"I am sorry." I sounded as contrite as I could. "I am meeting someone."

The men looked from one to the other. "Who?" said the second man.

The only SS men I knew were Wilhelm, whom I did not want to get into trouble, and Lang, whom I did not want to know where I was. "Robert Schmidt," I lied. A common name.

"Why are you meeting him?" asked the first man.

"Personal reasons."

"I'll go in with her," said the second man.

He opened the door, and I stepped through the looking glass. The inside bore no resemblance to the old El Dorado. The coat-check counter was gone, the red curtains that separated the bar from the coat check removed. Whitewash obscured the Chinese murals, round brass gongs vanished as surely as my brother and the other men who had once played here.

In their place men lounged on rickety chairs. A few poked at ancient typewriters, but most sat on the floor playing cards. No one looked up when we entered.

I scanned the room, as if looking for Robert Schmidt. "I guess he is not—"

"Hannah?" I turned. Wilhelm again.

"You know her?" asked the man who had let me in.

"In every sense." Wilhelm slipped an arm around my waist. The man sniggered.

"Including the biblical?" I hissed under my breath as he led me away. He had cleverly implied that we'd been intimate.

He leaned down and kissed me, a quick stage kiss. When he pulled back I was so shocked, I froze.

"Play along. It's the only way to keep us both out of trouble."

"Aren't I a little old for you?" I gave him a fake intimate smile.

"Better than nothing." He smiled back. "You're well preserved."

Someone whistled from across the room, and I blushed.

I let him lead me into the leftmost dark room. When the El Dorado was a queer club the patrons used these rooms to have intimate relations, and I suppressed a shudder remembering the last time I had been in one.

Although it had no windows, the room had a light, a desk, and a chair. The scene of my terrifying encounter on the sticky floor with Röhm had been transformed into an office much like Frau Doppelgänger's. If anything, it was more menacing than before.

Wilhelm pulled a string hanging from the lightbulb and closed the door. "What are you doing here?"

I shrugged. "I was in the neighborhood and thought to drop in."

"Into the lion's den. Sounds about right."

I sat in the chair behind the desk. It gave me a feeling of control, something I liked, especially in this room.

"Have you found Anton?"

I shook my head. "Have you?"

"I said that I would bring him to your friend." His voice sounded hurt.

"I do not mean to sound rude."

"Apology accepted. Such as it was."

"Am I under investigation by the SS? Have they taken Anton?"

He ran his index finger over his lips. I remembered the gesture from the first time I met him at El Dorado when he was still a teenager. Would he help me? I was the enemy, although if the SS scratched the surface of his life, they would know that he was too. It was dangerous for him to help me, and all I had on my side was hours spent in my kitchen, his love for my brother, his sense of honor, and his reckless nature. I folded my hands in my lap and waited.

Finally, he flashed a devil-may-care grin that reminded me of my brother. "I can try to find that out. If you're under investigation, there would be a file."

I let out a breath I had not known I held. My brother, Ernst, was watching out for me. "Can you check the purge list for a Manfred Brandt?" I opened the desk drawer. Rubber bands and a handkerchief.

"Who was Brandt?" I noted his use of the past tense. If Mouse was on the list, he was expected to be dead. Nazi record keeping was that matter of fact, and that thorough.

"Friend of Röhm's." I closed the drawer with a thud.

"Then he was probably on the list."

"I like to be certain."

"So you want me to check the purge list, and the files for you and Anton?"

"Are they secret?"

"Not from me. I have the highest level of clearance."

He sounded so proud of it. I gritted my teeth. "Could you find out about the existence of the files without telling anyone that you are looking?"

"Of course," he said, sounding surprised that I had asked such a thing. I had to hope that he was correct and would be able to go undetected. I did not want him to endanger himself.

"Have you heard of a Hauptsturmführer Lang?"

"Little guy. Interrogations. They use him before they send people to the more . . . hands-on interrogators. He's known for tricking people into revealing things. Clever."

I felt proud of Lang for getting information without having to beat it out of people. What kind of woman had I become? "Do you know where his office is, or where he lives?"

"Based on the last time you asked me a question like that, you want to break in," he said, referring to how he had helped me to sneak into El Dorado dressed as an SA brownshirt, complete with moustache, three years before.

"You are learning." I hoped to find out what information Lang had about me, and about Anton. If the Nazis had Anton, he would know, as closely as he followed the case. He might be the only one I knew who had that knowledge.

"If it's not one thing, it's another with you." He sighed and stood. "Let's go."

As we neared the door, he unbuttoned his fly, so that when he stepped out he was buttoning it up.

My face burning, I slid my arm through his, and we left the building amid catcalls.

"Was that necessary?" We walked down Motz Strasse in the bright sunlight.

"Would you rather them think we were talking about breaking into SS offices or fucking?"

"We were not in there long. You must not have much stamina."

"Really?" He looked insulted. We both laughed.

We strolled down Potsdamer Strasse, arm in arm. I wondered what Boris would think and looked around guiltily.

He dropped me off a few blocks away at Haus Vaterland, a giant building full of theme restaurants. "Wait for me at the Wild West Bar."

I put my hand on his arm. "Let me go with you."

"It's more dangerous if you're there. You're not SS. I don't want you leaving the building as a prisoner."

I hesitated, but I saw his logic.

I paid my entrance fee of one Reichsmark and walked across the lobby, past the immense fountains to the ugly marble staircases.

I pushed through the swinging saloon doors and took a gander at the Wild West Bar. Anton would have loved it. If we were ever free, and in Berlin, I would bring him here. Tears welled up in my eyes. Would he ever see this room, or any room?

A cowboy in a ten-gallon hat ushered me to a seat beside a round wooden table. The tabletop was painted billiard-green and each place had a *trompe l'oeil* painting of cards and stacks of poker chips. The cowboy handed me a menu with a flourish and touched the brim of his hat. I pictured Anton holding his hand palm-out in an Indian greeting.

"Something to wet your whistle?"

I tried not to laugh at his Western accent. "Something without alcohol. What do you recommend?"

"Lemonade, fresh squeezed."

"One of those and . . ." I hurried through the menu. "Pork and beans."

He pulled an order pad out of his holster.

The only other patrons were a table of tourists, British judging by their tweeds.

The lemonade was, as promised, fresh squeezed. The beans and pork fat were salty, inedible, and authentic. I wished that Anton were here to share some. He would have bolted them down, authenticity being more important than flavor. I hoped he was eating well.

I pulled out my notebook and wrote down what I knew so far. Lang could hang me for the contents of the notebook, but I had to keep the information until I knew that Sefton or Bella had gotten it out. I might as well add to it. It already contained enough to condemn me many times over.

Still, I kept a weather eye on the door. I closed the notebook and put it away when Wilhelm walked in a few hours later.

He sat across from me and ordered a whiskey from the cowboy. They held eye contact a second too long.

"Pardner of yours?" I asked. The cowboy sauntered to the bar.

"Once. Now he's only someone to inform on me."

"Should we go?"

"Doesn't matter."

"What did you find?"

The cowboy headed over to our table with Wilhelm's whiskey. Wilhelm leaned forward and kissed me full on the lips, for the second time that day, a warning to the cowboy.

The cowboy plopped the shot glass on the table so forcibly that whiskey slopped onto the painted poker chips.

I stared straight down at the green table until he was out of earshot. I remembered how years before, Wilhelm had gone into that same left-most dark room with an aging and unattractive transvestite to get even with my brother. "Enough of that, Wilhelm. I will allow you to kiss me to save us both from SS enquiries, but not to get even with some waiter."

He knocked back his whiskey in one gulp, just as he did the night I saw him at El Dorado, when he wore a brown SA uniform instead of a black SS one. "My reasons were the same the second time."

I sighed. No point in arguing. And maybe he was right. He knew far more about the dangers that he confronted than I. "What did you find?"

"No file on you or Anton Vogel or Anton Röhm. Not in the general files or in Lang's office."

I relaxed my shoulders. One less thing to worry about.

"Which is strange." He toyed with his empty glass. "There should be one on Anton Röhm. There was a police file on him when he disappeared. I should have at least found that."

My shoulders tightened again. "What about Manfred Brandt?"

"And that's stranger. Even if he wasn't on the purge list, which I couldn't find either by the way, he'd have a file. Practically everyone has a file. There's even a file on me. Clean. I checked."

"Did you find Lang's address?" If he did not have files in his office, perhaps he had brought them home.

Wilhelm recited a street address not too far from Haus Vaterland. "He left headquarters with some other officers so he's not going to be home for at least a little while."

"Now is the time," I said. "And this time it is my turn. I will do this one alone. Two people will cause more notice than one."

He ducked his head in acknowledgement. We stood. He abruptly pulled me into a real embrace. I clung to him. When we separated, both our eyes were full.

"Be careful," he whispered.

"You too."

The cowboy stormed over and handed Wilhelm the bill.

We walked out of the Wild West Bar together. I hoisted my satchel higher on my shoulder, Luger bumping my hip.

24

I walked to Lang's apartment, sweat running down my back. Berlin had never been so hot in all my memory. Already late afternoon, and I walked in the shadows of the apartment buildings, but heat radiated off the stone sidewalks. We needed rain.

How could I gain access to his apartment? I had no key, and no idea of how to open a locked door without one. I thought of calling Agnes and hiring a lock picker, but that would take too much time, even assuming I trusted her to find someone. And who would be willing to break into the home of a leader of the SS? Only a mother desperate for news of her child.

Perhaps he left his windows open, not an uncommon thing to do in this heat. I circled his apartment, an older building, built in the classical Wilhelminian style, like Lang himself. Large windows faced the street. According to Wilhelm, Lang lived on the bottom floor.

Even in this heat his windows stayed shut. In fact, his was the only apartment in the building with closed windows. I supposed that too was in character.

A Room to Let sign hung in a window on the top floor. I rang the landlady's bell, and she hurried out to look me over before letting me in. Unlike most landladies, she was young, younger than I. Her unfashionably long hair was pulled back in a bun and dark circles shadowed her eyes. On her thin hip she bounced a baby wearing only a diaper.

"May I help you?" Her diction was pure Hanover, high German at its finest. What was she doing in Berlin?

"I noticed the sign." I pointed upward. "May I see the room?"

I had no idea how that would help me break into his apartment, but it would get me closer. I would have to trust to luck and a sharp eye.

"Please follow me." She led me past his apartment door. The baby starfished his limbs out to the side as she bent to unlock her own door.

Instinctively, I reached for him as he tipped back. She hefted him safely back onto her hip and gave me a surprised look, as if trying to catch a falling baby were an unusual act.

"Here." She handed him to me. "Hold this."

The baby smiled. I guessed his age at about six months. He reached one sweaty hand up and grabbed my hair in his fist. I laughed and untangled it. It had been too long since I held a baby. I bent my head and sniffed his soft curls. Nothing smells quite like a baby.

When I raised my head, the landlady gazed at me, astonished.

"I am sorry. It has been a long time since I smelled a baby."

"The room is not for children."

"Mine are grown."

We stepped into her front hall. Along the wall next to the door ran a row of neatly labeled pegs. On each peg hung an apartment key. Lang's key was second from the bottom. I turned my back to the pegboard and handed her the baby. When her eyes moved down to his, I grabbed Lang's key behind my back.

The baby fussed and stretched his arms back toward me.

"He's so hot. Nothing suits him."

"Perhaps a wet cloth. My son used to love to suck on those." True, after a fashion. My brother, Ernst, had loved that and raising him was the closest I had come to having a baby. He had never been a fussy baby except when teething.

"Wait here." She carried the wailing child down the hall.

Lang's house key was standard, not much different from Boris's, which I carried in my satchel. I dug out Boris's key and, not without a pang, switched Lang's key for his. He would be unhappy to learn that

I had switched out his house key with another man's. I dropped Lang's key into my satchel and hung his keyring, now holding Boris's key, back on the peg. Eventually it would be discovered, but perhaps not for days.

I stood fanning myself with my notebook when she returned. The baby sucked mightily on a scrap of blue flannel.

She extolled the virtues of the single room, desperate for a tenant. Not surprising, since the stifling tiny room looked like attic storage. I thanked her, but told her it was too hot.

"Everywhere is too hot." She shifted the baby to her other hip.

"Nevertheless, I am not interested."

She led me downstairs and showed me through the front door. On the outside, I caught it before it closed, waited to give her time to get back inside her own apartment, and sneaked in.

I hurried down the hall to Lang's door. What if he was home? I did not dare to knock and alert his neighbors to my presence. I would have to trust Wilhelm, and hope that I was not about earn myself a free ride to Gestapo headquarters.

With sweat-slick hands I fumbled with the key before jamming it into the lock. I turned it. The door clicked open smoothly. I stepped over the threshold, wincing when a floorboard in the entryway creaked. I pushed the door closed with a soft thud, then relocked it. I did not want anyone stumbling in, and if Lang came home, he would suspect nothing.

The apartment felt as hot as the high plains of the Apache in August, or at least that's what Anton would have said. The smell of lemon polish filled the hall. A stand by the door held a lone umbrella, furled. A hat tree stood to attention next to the umbrella stand, holding a recently brushed gray fedora and an overcoat, both too warm to wear in this weather. I ran my fingers through the silken pockets, shuddering at the sense of intimacy. One pocket yielded a clean, pressed handkerchief, the other nothing.

I tiptoed down the hall into the parlor. His furniture was Spartan, but surprisingly modern: a simple black leather couch and chair grouped around an oval wooden table. Everything gleamed. On the table a young Lang smiled from a framed photograph of a boy on a beach with his mother and father, a terrier now long dead jumped in front of them with a stick of driftwood in his mouth. Lang's eyes were alight with mischief and his left arm was throwing something out of view of the camera, perhaps another stick for the dog. I wondered what had happened to change the mischievous boy into the sinister man.

I drew my eyes from the picture and focused on searching his apartment. He knew a great deal about me when he stopped me at Lichterfelde. If the files were not in the SS office, perhaps he had them here.

It would be easy to search because it was so spare. I did a quick pass through the parlor. Not a scrap of paper, let alone a file. Even the desk in the corner stood empty, as if he had known I was coming and cleared it out. In spite of the punishing heat, goose bumps raised on my arms. I wiped my palms on my dress and searched the desk for hidden compartments, but found none.

The kitchen, also immaculate and containing little food, yielded up no secrets either.

I stepped into the only remaining room: his bedroom. It too smelled of lemon, and I wondered how often his housekeeper came, or if he polished his furniture himself. The curtains were drawn, but light filtered through.

A black wool blanket covered his immaculately made single bed. On a whim, I lifted the blanket and smiled, perfect corners. Atop his night table rested a clock and a pair of folded reading glasses, the only personal touch in the room. I spun around, trying to decide where to search.

I started with his simple dresser, top to bottom. The first drawer contained neatly folded underwear. I gritted my teeth and rifled through them, expecting to find nothing. But in the corner I spotted a square of paper. I pulled it out, surprised, and turned it over. My mouth dropped open in shock. A picture of me.

I practically dropped the photograph. Almost two decades old, taken when I received my Abitur, the last day of school. I wore a light summer dress much like today. My wide and innocent smile said that I had no idea my fiancé would be dead in the War within a week. Where had Lang found the picture?

My apartment. He had entered my apartment with me three years ago. He must have stolen it then. I tried not to think about my picture lying in his underwear drawer for three years as I returned it. As tempted as I was to steal it back, I did not wish to tip him off. The other drawers contained nothing interesting.

I moved to his tall wardrobe, ignoring my reflection in the mirror. I did not want to see myself in his room again. Dark suits hung neatly, hangers perfectly spaced. I slid my hand into the empty pockets. Did he ever come here? Perhaps his real home was elsewhere.

A pair of polished shoes and a pair of boots rested on the bottom of the wardrobe, next to cedar shoe trees and a folded flannel cloth mottled with black shoe polish. A spare SS hat on the top shelf.

I closed the door, about to give up in despair, when I spotted a grain of sawdust on the floor. I tapped on the back. A muffled thud answered my knock. The door sounded hollow.

My heart pounded as I ran sweaty palms across the door, looking for a trigger. Nothing. I pressed on each corner, and finally a panel slid open. Specks of sawdust drifted to the floor. Gray file folders, held in place by elastic bands, nestled in a painstakingly carved out compartment. He had secrets after all.

I slid out the topmost folder. A tingle ran down my spine as I read my own name. *Hannah Vogel.* I flipped it open. My police folder from 1931. I raced through his case notes. He had done a thorough history of me, listing details about my life back to my school times. He knew far more about my everyday life than Boris.

I read on. After my disappearance he suspected that I kidnapped Anton from Röhm. The last page listed my known associates. A penciled circle surrounded Boris's name. Banker was written next to it with a question mark. I flipped back a page. He had penciled in a page of recent notes in his cramped handwriting. They mentioned that I was expected to marry Ernst Röhm and listed the date that Hitler had him arrested. No mention of my meeting with Sefton, so hopefully he had not followed me there. I set the folder on the floor and went to the next one.

The next folder was Anton's. The file listed him as *Anton Röhm*, with a question mark next to the name. Lang was unconvinced that Röhm was his father. The file listed me as his mother, but my name was struck through. *Elise Karlson* was written in and circled. Death by overdose. The woman who had raised Anton, whom he called Sweetie Pie. Anton's location was listed as *Unknown*. My heart lifted. If the Nazis had killed him, surely there would be a note of it here.

Manfred Brandt's file was next. My knees buckled. Lang knew. He had made the connection between Mouse, Anton, and me. If he had read the telegram, he must have known that Mouse had Anton. He could have followed Mouse to Britz Mill and killed him. And I knew what he would do with Anton. I swallowed.

I read Mouse's file to find another reason for his murder. He had been reporting on Röhm's activities to the SS, including treasonous statements Röhm had made about Hitler while drunk. Mouse was a spy. So perhaps he had been killed by Röhm loyalists. If they knew about Anton, they would keep him safe until they could use him against the Nazis. That seemed the safest scenario for Anton. I stood, uncertain what to do.

The door held other files. I had to get through them. I would think about what it meant after I was outside of the apartment and somewhere safe.

I pulled out the next file. *Theodor Eicke*, Röhm's murderer and the head of the camp at Dachau. I hurried through the other files. Most contained information on prominent members of the Nazi party. Röhm's was not among them. These files had been started before the Nazis came to power in 1933, and they contained notes as recently as a few days ago. He was keeping track of his own people. A sheaf of paper between the folders contained the purge list. I ran my finger down the alphabetized names. Manfred Brandt's name was not there, probably spared because he had betrayed Röhm to the SS. Not taking time to

read the other names, but wishing I could, I set the papers on the floor
and pulled out the last folder. I gasped when I read the name. *Boris
Krause.*

Against my better judgement, I opened it. The file listed his address, his telephone number, and the address and telephone number of
the bank. Trudi was down as next of kin, noted as a devoted National
Socialist. That alone would break his heart.

Lang had catalogued every trip Boris made to London to visit me,
although he did not note what he did overseas. I was safe. It chilled me
to think how close the SS had been to finding me during the last three
years. Was I the reason they had started watching Boris?

I read further. He was under suspicion of helping Jewish depositors
transfer their assets to Switzerland. I felt proud of him, until I turned
the page. The informant who had tipped the SS off: Frau Inge.

I skimmed the details. She joined the Nazi party right after they
came to power, a little over a year ago. The report listed her as devout
and reliable. She had needed six months of membership to decide to
inform on Boris. She had delivered her first report days after he returned from visiting me in London. Her husband, also a party member,
was a clerk at the bank. According to Frau Inge, she and Boris were
engaged in an ongoing sexual affair. I read that part twice before continuing. Her behavior toward me made sense. How dare he question
my relationship with Sefton or anyone when he was involved in an
"ongoing sexual affair" with Frau Inge?

I swallowed my anger and forced my attention back to the file. I
was not mentioned by name, so either she had not told Lang about
me, or he had written nothing down.

The file described a plan to arrest Boris when a certain transaction
completed. I checked the date and time: Friday, July 6, 1934 at 1700.
Tomorrow when the bank closed. They had reserved him interrogation
room seven, and a place at Dachau Concentration Camp.

I do not know how long I stood with the files in my hand. I might
have been standing there staring at them when Lang arrived, but the
baby wailed next door.

With shaking hands I replaced the folders in the order I had found them and slid the panel back into the wardrobe. Boris was one day from torture and perhaps death in Dachau. As angry as I was over his affair, I felt guilty too. She would not have informed on him if he had not met me.

I knelt and swept the sawdust that had fallen under the wardrobe, removing all traces that I had ever been here.

As I turned to leave, a key clicked in the front lock. Lang.

25

I looked at the wardrobe. Too small to hold me, and likely one of the first things Lang would do was open it to hang up his clothing.

My eyes darted to the closed windows. Even assuming I had time to open one, the sound might alert him.

Boards by the front door creaked as he stepped over the threshold.

I raced across the rug and slid under his single bed, the only hiding place. My heart thudded so loudly, he must hear it from his entryway.

He wandered around his parlor, opening windows and whistling Beethoven's "Für Elise." He was quite a good whistler.

How could I get past him? Perhaps luck would favor me, and he would leave again, even if only for a moment. I gripped his warm metal key. The gun in the satchel pressed against my hip. I thought of drawing it, but I could not shoot him for the crime of entering his own home.

Shiny black shoes marched into the bedroom. He paused and stopped whistling. I thought he sniffed, and I held my breath. Could he smell me?

He crossed the room in a few strides and opened the windows. The left window opened silently, but the right squeaked. He would have heard if I had tried to escape through it. A light breeze trickled into the room. He stood at the window for a long moment before beginning to whistle again.

Shoes disappeared into the bathroom. He did not close the door, a long-term bachelor. Water turned on. Perhaps he would take a bath? That might give me time to escape out the front door. But the water turned off again quickly. I almost groaned in frustration. I listened to him brush his teeth, use the toilet, and flush. He washed his hands for a long time. His mother would have been proud.

Polished shoes walked to the bed. He sat. The slats drooped centimeters closer to my sweaty nose. He removed each shoe and placed his black stocking feet on the floor. He crossed to his wardrobe. A soft swish and the smell of shoe polish drifted down to me. His hands picked a shoe tree off the bottom of the wardrobe and placed it in his left shoe, then slid the other shoe tree into his right.

He slipped off his jacket and gave it a shake before hanging it in the wardrobe. I lay still under the bed, listening to him undress. He was getting ready for bed. I cast my mind back over the drawers that I searched. No pajamas. He must sleep in the nude. Lovely.

Bare feet padded over to his dresser. He opened a drawer, but I was unsure which until a whisper of paper brushing against the side of the dresser drifted down to me. He had removed my picture.

I held my breath. He closed the drawer again and padded back to bed. I wondered if he had the picture with him as he pulled back the blanket and sheet and climbed in.

The slats on the bottom of the bed almost touched my nose.

I lay under the bed, heart pounding so loudly, I could barely hear anything else. He moved and shifted centimeters above me, breathing restless. He did not fall asleep easily. Should I wait until he left in the morning? If they moved up the timetable, the SS might have Boris by then. And Lang might discover me at any time.

Finally his breathing slowed and deepened. I waited a bit longer to be sure that he was asleep, then eased off my shoes and gripped them in my right hand with the satchel, the key in my left. I eased out from under the bed centimeter by centimeter. He did not stir.

I slunk out of his room, across the parlor, and down the hall. Careful to avoid the squeaky board by the door, I slid the key into the lock.

The tumblers crashed like boulders rolling down a cliff.

I stepped through and silently closed the door. I weighed whether or not to lock it again, but decided not to. Too loud.

I hurried down the hall shoes in hand, sliding out the front door.

I turned in the opposite direction of his window and ran down the sidewalk, stone warm against the soles of my feet even this late at night. I ran a full block before I stopped to put on my shoes. The subway clattered to Boris's house. I knew that I should be wondering why Lang kept the files in his house, especially Mouse's, mine, and Anton's, or why he spied on his own people, but all I thought about was Boris's file, his imminent arrest, and his ongoing sexual relationship with Frau Inge. Hopefully the impeccable Lang had made a mistake.

No wonder she loathed me. I thought she disapproved of my erratic way of popping in and out of Boris's life and having relations with him outside of marriage. But it went well beyond that.

At Boris's house the windows were dark. He had not waited up for me, although he had left the light on near the front door. I stood outside the circle of light. I was exhausted, but I hated to knock and risk waking the neighbors, especially when he knew that I should have a key.

I could not stand there forever. In this posh suburb of Zehlendorf a policeman would run me in for loitering.

I tapped on the door. What if Frau Inge slept inside? I knocked more loudly. He had kept any hint of an affair with her hidden. He certainly would not have her sleeping in his bed on a night when I was due to arrive and slip into the house unannounced with my key. I hoped.

The bolt drew back with a clunk.

"Where's your key?" He stepped aside to let me in. I brushed past his sleep-warmed body and resisted the urge to fit myself against it.

"I do not have it."

"Did you find Anton?"

I shook my head. If he asked that question, then neither had he.

His gaze flicked to the grandfather clock standing in the entryway. "Come to bed."

The little girl part of me wanted to climb the stairs obediently and enjoy one more sweet night's sleep in his arms. The part that had been dwelling on his file for the entire ride home shook her head and marched past. I turned on a reading light instead of the overhead light. I did not want to see clearly.

He sighed and followed. "Please let this be quick. I have work to-morrow."

"Perhaps."

He rubbed his eyes with the back of his hand like a little boy. "Have you eaten? Would you like something to drink?"

Always the host.

I sat on the chair. I did not want to sit on the couch and have him sit next to me.

"I was trapped in the house of an SS officer. Hauptsturmführer Lang."

"Did he hurt you?" He pulled his dressing gown around himself and moved next to me.

"He did not know that I was there."

His shoulders relaxed, and he sat on the couch. "Is he related to the Kommissar who investigated Anton's disappearance?"

"The same. He is holding files on various high-level members of the Nazi party."

He yawned. "I see."

"He also has my file there, Anton's file, and, of most interest to you, yours."

"Mine?" He sat up straight. "The SS has a file on me?"

"They have records of you transferring Jewish assets illegally out of the country."

Even in the dim light I saw him pale. It was enough to send him to a concentration camp. "How did they get them?"

"Frau Inge."

"She would do no such a thing! I've always been good to her."

"Perhaps," I said, and my voice sounded cold. "Perhaps she is angry that you are sleeping with me, considering your history together."

He whistled. "Those SS investigators are thorough."

"That does not ring of a denial." Hot rage flooded my belly. Jealousy? I had never been jealous before. I had never needed to.

He shrugged his broad shoulders carelessly. "Why deny it? You've seen the files. You've met Frau Inge. You'll draw your own conclusions."

For the first time, I doubted the files. Relief washed over me, and I chastised myself. He had denied nothing. And, if he had, could I trust him? What hold did I have over him? We had never discussed the future, never discussed the terms of our relationship. When we could, we met. Beyond that nothing had ever been mentioned, but I knew what I felt.

I stared at his lovely brown hands, imagining them buried in her luxuriant long hair.

"Hannah?"

"Are you having an affair with her? I mean, Boris, a servant?" My mother's rigid upbringing echoed in my words, and I hated myself the moment I uttered them.

Sensing my thoughts, he said, "Shocked to find that your socialist background doesn't run as deep as you thought?"

I gritted my teeth. "Not that a servant is unworthy of you. More that you are in a position of power over her. A position from which you should not exploit her for your own sexual gain."

"Very upright of you." He smiled without warmth and crossed his arms. His dressing gown gaped open, displaying curly chest hair. I longed to reach over and put my palms on his warm skin, but instead I looked at the floor.

"Are you?" I vowed not to ask again.

"As you reminded me the last time we discussed this topic, I don't recall making promises of fidelity. Nor did you."

"And yet I have kept them." I clasped my hands together.

"Have you?" He sounded as if he wanted to believe me as much as I wanted to believe him.

"Yes."

He knelt in front of my chair. "I have no desire to fight." His palms rested lightly on the backs of my hands and, as always, a jolt of electricity shot through my body. Damn him and the effect he had on me. He cleared his throat. "I'll say this one time. I am not currently having an affair with Frau Inge. That part of the file is wrong."

I wanted to believe him. But I did not. I reluctantly pulled my hands from his. "Currently?"

He sighed. "I had an affair with her for a brief time after my wife died."

I twisted my hands in my lap.

"It was over long ago. More than fifteen years. Once I came to my senses, I ended it. We talked about it, and she wanted to continue working here." He looked at the floor. "And she was always so good with Trudi."

The grandfather clock ticked.

"I am not proud of my actions, but it's been over for a long time. It was never a problem. Until you arrived."

He had kept secrets from me just as I had from him. Was that so wrong?

"Hannah?" His voice was pleading.

"They have reserved you an interrogation cell for tomorrow. If you live through that, they are sending you to Dachau."

He swore and glanced around the room, as if expecting the SS to be there already. His shoulders drew up, and I longed to reach out and massage them.

"Now that I've been honest." He covered my hands with his. "What were you doing in Lang's apartment until this late?"

"Snooping. He threatened me a few days ago, and I wanted to see what he had on me."

"How did you get in?" He released my hands.

"I stole his key. I switched it for yours when the landlady was distracted."

"And *you* don't trust *me*?"

We did not have time to talk through this tonight. He had to leave before the SS came. "Are you helping Jews move their money out of Germany? Is that correct?"

"I'm afraid so." He leaned his head against my hip. "And it's more than enough to have me killed."

I told him what had happened in Lang's apartment, except for the part about my picture in his underwear drawer. I did not know if I was embarrassed or avoiding another argument. Or, improbably, perhaps I was protecting Lang's secrets.

"You must flee."

He nodded, but did not move.

We sat in silence in the dark parlor, his head on my lap. I ran my fingers through his warm, thick hair. As always, time with him felt as if it stood apart from all else.

"Do you have a picture of me?"

"You've never given me one." He rubbed his face against my leg and my breath caught in my throat. I had to concentrate to remember what I was saying. Picture. "If you had a picture, where would you keep it?"

"The mantel." He lifted his head and pointed to the marble mantelpiece behind me where his family pictures stood in a long row. "Why?"

"What if you needed to hide it? If you were married?"

"But I'm not."

"If you were."

"In a drawer at the office, I suppose. I imagine my wife would have full run of the house." He looked up at me calculatingly. "But if *you* were my wife I don't suppose any place would be safe."

I smiled.

He stood and held out a strong hand to help me from the chair. I let him pull me into an embrace. I held him fast and dropped my head against his chest to listen to his heartbeat. My muscles relaxed. I spoke without lifting my head. "You must leave Germany, you know."

"Perhaps." His voice sounded deeper than usual because my ear rested against his heart. "Perhaps Lang wants a pile of cash in exchange for silence."

"I do not think so."

"How well do you know him?" He leaned back to look at me.

"I spent hours under his bed. And I went through his house. If he cared for money or possessions, I found no sign of it there."

"What does he care for then?"

I thought of my picture in his drawer, and his polished and pressed SS uniforms. "Only the party," I lied.

"He might be more complicated than you think."

"Where will you go?"

He glanced around his beautiful parlor. His eyes lingered on a large antique globe that his father had purchased for him when he graduated from university. Objects that his family had owned for generations filled the house. He would have to leave them.

"Trudi," I cleared my throat, "is listed in the files as a devout National Socialist."

"That should keep her safe. Until they change their minds and come for her. I'll have to convince her to come with me."

"Will she go?" I asked, surprised.

"No. But I must try."

"If you tell her." I hated what I must say. "She will know what you plan to do. And even if she does not inform on you—"

He dropped his arms and turned away. I was grateful I could not see his expression.

"Even if she does not, she will know, and that will compromise her."

"Are you suggesting I don't even say good-bye?" His voice echoed around the room.

"What is the cost to her of you saying good-bye?" I did not wish to be the one to tell him this, but he must be reminded. Although I could not see his eyes, the set of his shoulders telegraphed anger as he retreated toward the entryway and the steps leading upstairs. I followed.

"I am sorry, Boris." I climbed behind him, trailing my hand over the railing for the last time.

"What's in your file?" he asked, stopping so abruptly, I crashed into him.

I gripped the railing to steady myself. "That I kidnapped Anton. That I was supposed to marry Röhm. That I have been interviewing people about the events during the Night of the Long Knives." If he was leaving, I need not hide it.

"Sometimes you don't have the sense God gave a flea." His voice sounded exasperated.

I stepped up next to him. "In this instance it has proven useful to you."

He laughed. Not quite his old, deep laugh, but something. He sobered. "So they have enough to arrest you too, then."

"If they catch me, yes." He squeezed my hand, and we went up the stairs together.

He stopped on the top step, moonlight illuminating his worried face. "Will you go with me?"

"I cannot." I dropped my eyes from his. "Not without Anton."

He turned and strode into his bedroom. He pulled a suitcase from under his bed and dropped it on his rumpled quilt. "Then I can't either. We must leave this house, of course, but I won't leave Germany without you."

I stared at him, mouth dry. He moved to his wardrobe and pulled out a stack of neatly folded shirts. Frau Inge's handiwork.

I could not let him run such a risk. "If the SS find you—"

"I imagine things won't go any better if they find you." His hands packed swiftly, and his voice was determined.

I put my hands on top of his. "You have to leave. I cannot—"

He turned to me and wrapped both arms around my waist. "You control many things, Hannah, but you don't control me. I will do as I please, and you waste time trying to convince me otherwise."

"Stubborn bastard."

He smiled and returned to packing. "Part of my charm."

"Such as it is," I answered, but I was grateful.

26

Boris wrote Frau Inge a note saying that we would be gone for a few days. Perhaps that would keep her suspicions at bay long enough for us to get clear. We packed the wedding dress and his best suit. Let her think we were getting married.

We drove to Anhalter Bahnhof, where I had left Claire days before. The great hall loomed out of the darkness, lights blazing. People were already on the move. We could find a hotel near here easily. I leaned across the seat and kissed him, inhaling his musky citrus scent. "Are you certain?"

"Enough, Hannah. I am certain."

We found a nearby hotel and paid extra to use false names on the register. Hannah Vogel and Boris Krause needed to disappear.

I stood staring out the tiny hotel window at the street below. Even though few people moved in the darkness, I worried that each was a member of the SS. Not just my life was forfeit. If they caught me, or I led them to Boris, his life was gone as well.

He wrapped his arm around me from behind, fingers resting on my collarbone. My heart pulsed under his palm.

I turned to him and we kissed with an urgency that I had never experienced before, even the first time. There was fear, and an understanding that this might be the last time, ever. In two steps we reached the bed. A button clinked on the wooden floor as I struggled to pull off his shirt.

But once we were in bed, time slowed down almost unbearably. I could drown in his eyes, darker than usual. He brushed a strand of hair off my forehead as gently as if I were made of fragile glass. Never looking away from his eyes, I turned and kissed his palm.

We made love slowly, and without breaking eye contact. I could not stop looking at him, afraid that he would disappear. He held me tightly even after he fell asleep. I could not even turn over in his arms, and I did not want to.

What would tomorrow bring? I did not know where Anton was, or if I would ever find him. I tried to shake off those thoughts, to concentrate on what to do to find him, but panic rose in my chest, smothering me.

The next morning we had a quick breakfast at Anhalter Bahnhof. I choked down a stale snail pastry and a cup of strong tea. I would need my strength today, and every day, until I got Anton back.

Boris ate silently. He was paler than usual, but seemed calmer than I. How did he manage that? It had been difficult for me to leave behind my life in Berlin three years ago, and he had far more to walk away from than I. How long before Trudi realized that her father had gone?

I leaned over and kissed him on the cheek. He smiled and laid a warm arm across my shoulders. "Don't look so worried. We're still free and alive."

"So far."

He chucked me under the chin. "What's next, Optimistic Little Detective?"

"I need you to search the woods around Britz Mill for any trace of Anton."

"I will."

"I would do it, but I am the top suspect in the police file, and the SS linked me to Mouse's murder and—"

"I am happy to help, Hannah. You don't need to explain. What will you do?"

"Try to reach Frau Röhm. Perhaps she has heard something." Desperation colored my words. "After that? I do not know."

He took my hand. "We'll get through this."

I hoped that he was right. "I will be back tonight. Perhaps even in time for lunch."

"I will be here," he said, kissing my hand.

I stroked the top of his head, glad to have him with me.

Then I stood and gathered myself together for the day.

Already the air was hot. I hurried to the nearest telephone booth.

"Röhm," answered the maid in a hushed voice.

"Frau Röhm, please." I did not give my name, trusting her to recognize me.

"She is not here. She has gone to church."

Church on Friday morning. "When do you expect her to return?" If I did not speak to her today, I would travel to Munich and see her in person.

"She said." The maid gulped, as if she were crying. "She said that you should meet her at the church."

"What church? When? How am I to get to Munich?"

"She said to meet her at the Kaiser Wilhelm Memorial Church. Now."

Then, as they say, the other coin dropped. I gripped the telephone receiver while the world spun. Frau Röhm was here, in Berlin. And if she was here, she could have been here at any time. Including the day of Mouse's murder. I had never once reached her directly in Munich.

The maid must have a number where she could be reached. A number in Berlin, somewhere close to the church.

"Hello?" asked the maid. "Can you hear me?"

"Yes," I whispered. Frau Röhm could have been the one in the taxi. One passenger arrived, but two left.

"Do you know where that church is?"

Only a Bavarian would ask that question. The neo-Gothic Kaiser Wilhelm Memorial Church was a Berlin landmark near the zoo, home to weddings of the rich and famous, including Marlene Dietrich. "I do."

The maid cleared her throat. She was crying.

"Is something wrong?"

"Talk to Frau Röhm." She broke the connection.

I stood in the hot telephone booth and listened to static crackle. Why was the maid so upset? I did not recall tears the day I visited and told Frau Röhm of her son's impending execution. Sweat trickled down my back. I hung up the receiver and pushed open the door.

I hopped into the subway. The hot air barely stirred, even with the windows open. It had been hot for so long that the tunnels had heated up, so the underground provided no respite.

At Zoo Station a man in the corridor serenaded me with a guitar. His haunting melody echoed off the concrete walls, and I paused to listen. Other commuters pushed past as if they could not hear the music.

The man's dark eyes were grateful when I dropped coins into his velvet-lined guitar case. He inclined his curly black head in my direction without pausing in his song. He dressed like a Gypsy, in colorful patched pants and a red vest, although that did not mean that he was one. What would become of the Gypsies under Hitler? He had no tolerance for nomads, especially dark-skinned ones. Everyone must be placed and counted. I dropped in an extra coin and hurried on.

I climbed the stairs blindly, mind on Frau Röhm's invitation. What did she want of me? Did she have Anton?

I paused in front of the Gothic spires, glancing at the tall steeple with its gold cross poking the belly of the sky. A stained glass rose window at the front glowed, oval windows surrounding the central circle like exquisite petals of a glass flower. It looked fragile, yet it had survived wars without a single broken pane.

I stepped through the thick front door into the cooler church, inhaling the scent of incense and stone dust. My rib twinged. Gold mosaics drew my eyes upward. An angel held his arms out, blue wing feathers deepening to purple, finally tipped with black. Curlicues swirled behind like jungle plants about to engulf him.

I turned toward the door as it closed behind me. Above the door hung a marble sculpture of a woman holding Jesus' body, a marble sun setting behind them. Underneath words carved in stone read IT IS DONE.

I turned away and stepped into the nave. Dark figures shuffled in the shadows on either side as I walked down the line of wooden pews. An old woman in a black hat knelt in prayer near the altar. She fidgeted from knee to knee.

I moved down the pew and eased to my knees next to her, the wooden kneeler pressing against my bandaged knees. It must be playing havoc with hers too. I glanced over. Frau Röhm, face obscured by a black veil. In mourning for her son.

"Good day," I murmured. Had she killed Mouse?

She finished a whispered prayer. "Fräulein Vogel."

"I am sorry for your loss." The words sounded stiff and formal, although I felt compassion for her. Her son had been taken, and she was alone. I sympathized.

She inclined her head fractionally to indicate that I continue, veil grazing her shoulder.

"I have filled out the paperwork to have your son returned to you." I pressed on through the awkwardness, certain that she would give me no information until I had told her what I knew. "I have been assured that his remains will be released in a few weeks."

"Remains?" Her raspy voice sounded loud in the church.

"It is my understanding that they are cremating his body." I stopped, not knowing what else to say. I did not want to tell her how he had died. I wanted to spare her that.

"Do you know who killed him?" She gripped the pew in front of her so tightly that her clawlike knuckles whitened.

"Theodor Eicke." She deserved to know. "And, I believe, another SS officer, but I do not know his name."

She nodded and turned to the altar, head bowed. I clasped my hands in prayer and offered up a plea that Anton be returned to me. Prayer felt unfamiliar, but I figured it could not hurt.

We knelt in silence. My knees throbbed. Behind and around me the sounds of shuffling feet reverberated through the church. Why were so many people here on a hot summer day?

"Excuse me." I interrupted her prayer. "But I must ask now. Have you news of Anton?"

"Yes." Her quavery voice was barely audible.

"Thank God." Excitement gave me renewed energy. "Where is he? Was there another ransom note?"

She shook her head, veiled face still turned away.

"Do you have him?" I tried to contain my anxiety. I dared not anger her. "Where is he?"

"You love him much."

"Yes. I have cared for him for these past three years as if he were my own son."

"Sons are a precious gift." Tears filled her voice. "I learned that too late, you know."

"I am sorry to hear that." I shifted on my sore knees. I longed to throttle the information out of her. "But please tell me news of mine."

"I shall." She dipped her head. "In my own good time."

I bit my lips and waited.

"You would never leave him? Even if it was best for him?"

"Leaving him in Germany would not be best for him. It is too dangerous. Surely you see that too. We must flee."

We sat in silence for a long time.

"If I had him, I would give him up to you." Her voice had changed. It sounded more decisive, as it had when I stood at the bottom of her stairs in Munich.

"You do not have him?" My heart sank. She had received no further ransom note, and she did not have him herself. Or was she lying?

"He is with God," she whispered.

"What does that mean?" My voice echoed off the walls. She flinched. I stood. "With God?"

"I have seen him."

Had the stress of losing her son affected her mind? "Seen him with God?"

She turned to me impatiently. "I am not an addled old woman, Hannah."

"You have seen him how?" I struggled to maintain my patience.

"At the morgue."

I grabbed her shoulders and drew her to her feet. "Anton? You saw Anton at the morgue?"

I shook her thin frame.

"Yes." She pulled from my grasp. "The Nazis took him at Britz Mill."

Lang. He knew the contents of the telegram. He had followed Mouse to Britz Mill and taken Anton.

"You can leave Germany."

I stared at her, dumbfounded. "Anton is dead?"

27

I collapsed on the pew and wept great howling sobs that would soon bring priests out to shove me from the quiet sanctuary into the harsh sunlight.

Frau Röhm hobbled to the end of the pew. I was past caring what happened to her.

I sobbed into my folded arms. It could not be true. It could not be. Surely they could not murder an innocent boy for an accident of parentage. But I knew that they could.

A gentle hand touched my shoulder, and I turned to face the priest.

Not a priest. Lang. Behind him stood two black-uniformed SS men. I turned the other way; two other men stood between me and the end of the pew. They must have been listening when I called the maid.

"You must come with me," Lang said. He slipped my satchel off my shoulder. Now he had my Hannah Vogel passport and my notebook. Either was enough to send me to the camps. He spoke, but what he said did not matter. He had killed my son.

I stood, and we sidestepped down the pew. Poor Boris would not meet me for lunch, or any other time. I hoped that he had the sense to get clear. Someone I loved should live through this day.

At the end of the church stood Frau Röhm, face invisible under her veil. Had she set a trap for me, or was she merely basking in my arrest? I could not summon up energy to care.

I let them lead me out of the dark church into the heat of the day. Lang put his hand protectively on the crown of my head as he helped me into a waiting automobile. As if it mattered that I might bump my head.

I folded in half in the backseat and wept. When we pulled away, I did not look out the window.

Eventually we stopped, and someone pulled me out.

I squinted against bright sunlight. The street sign read Prinz Albrecht Strasse. Headquarters for the Gestapo, a branch of Himmler's SS. We entered the building. I wondered if I would ever come out through the door alive. It did not matter.

They led me to a cell where I collapsed on the floor. On the warm floor I cried and slept, slept and cried, indifferent to the bed in the corner.

Sometime later I awoke on the warm floor to black boots, in need of a polish, positioned next to my face. Rough hands yanked me to my feet.

"Walk with me," a voice said. I fell back to the floor.

He and another man, one with shinier boots, hauled me to my feet again. Each grabbed my arm below the shoulder and marched me off. My chin bobbed against my chest. If they wanted me to look at something, they could move my head.

They dumped me in a chair and left. The door closed silently. Well-kept hinges, I supposed. I imagined a diligent Nazi janitor oiling them. Amazing what one's mind thinks about when it is on holiday. My mind wanted to be anywhere but in my body, knowing what it knew.

A broad mahogany desk, intended for a larger room, swallowed half the space. Had the owner been demoted but held on to his desk? Or was the desk a symbol of hope for a bigger office? Or just surplus?

I thought of Anton: how he folded those little airplanes, throwing his name out into the world to say hello; or how his hair stuck up in the back, no matter how he wet it down; or how he talked as if he lived in a Karl May novel.

Where was my interrogator? They were supposed to be prompt. Or perhaps they were letting me stew, worry about what I had done. Perhaps they wanted to catch me doing something else.

I stood listlessly and circled the wooden desk. I opened desk drawers. The top one contained pens and ink. The bottom right drawer was locked. The bottom left held confession forms. I supposed I would be writing and signing one before this ended. Like Sefton, I was unconvinced that I would stand up to torture, although I would try.

Atop the confession forms rested a form stamped URGENT. A death warrant for an interred prisoner, a man not much older than I. I read the signature. Hauptsturmführer Lang. In his careful handwriting, with no signs of hesitation. Would he have as little trouble signing mine?

I clambered on the desk and peeked out the tiny open window. Too small to climb through, so I rested my chin on the hard sill. Judging by the light, it was afternoon. People strolled on the sidewalk below. Free. Had Frau Röhm trapped me? Or was she in custody too? After all, she was a known associate of Ernst Röhm. Perhaps as much of a loose end as I.

I pulled out two forms meant for confessions. On the first I wrote *Anton Vogel June 10, 1925–July 6, 1934*. I folded it into a paper airplane, always straight on the creases, as Anton and Señor Santana had admonished. I spared a glance at the door. The SS would have me killed for being a known associate of Röhm, as they had so many others. I did not have much time.

I climbed back on the desk and threw the airplane out the window. It wheeled down like a hawk, into the street of innocent passersby. A young boy reached up and caught it before it landed. He walked away with it in his hand. A child should not be holding information on a murder, but if they murdered children, then children needed to know.

I climbed down and looked at the other form. The door opened as I finished the final crease on my second airplane. Written inside the airplane was my name, and today's date.

"Good day, Fräulein." I recognized Lang's voice, but did not turn to face him.

I cradled the paper airplane in my lap. A wing bent wrong. I straightened it. It should fly like an arrow.

He came around the desk and sat across from me. A broad expanse of gleaming mahogany separated us.

"Why do you think you are here?" he asked, giving me the rope to hang myself.

He did not know that I no longer cared. I redid creases on the airplane.

"Fräulein. I must insist that you answer me."

With an enormous effort I raised my head. An expression flickered across his eyes so quickly that I could not place it. Surprise? Hurt? Sympathy? Anger? Anton's expressions too had been mercurial.

He unlocked the bottom drawer of his desk. I stroked a fingertip down the wing, having lost interest in him.

He came around his desk and pressed a warm glass into my free hand. I stared at it, unsure what to do.

"Drink it," he said, voice soft.

Clear liquid burned its way down the back of my throat. Vodka. I downed the rest in a gulp. Part of me knew that drinking during an SS interrogation was foolish. But I had nothing more to lose. "More?"

He pried the glass from my hand. "No."

His action shocked me enough that I looked at him again. He walked behind the desk, back stiff. He returned the glass to its drawer and locked it. Then he sat again and steepled his fingers. "Why do you think you are here?"

I shrugged.

"It will be worse for you if you refuse to answer my questions."

I laughed. "Worse for me?"

He cocked his head.

I stroked the airplane.

"I would have to pass you along. To men not as circumspect in their methods."

I stared at my fingers. Dirt lodged under my nails. Where had I picked that up? It did not matter. None of it mattered.

"Will you cause trouble for the party?"

"Me? Cause them trouble?" My bitter words shot across the room.

"The party has caused you trouble?"

"For years."

A sharp rap sounded on the door. He opened it. Angry voices squabbled behind me.

I sailed the airplane around the room. It crashed into the window. I retrieved it.

"Why are you out of your chair?" He turned toward me, disbelief in his voice.

"I had to get the airplane."

"Sit down."

I walked back and dropped into the chair. He closed the door and came back.

"In a few minutes others will come for you," he said in a hoarse whisper. "You must cooperate."

I checked the airplane's nose. It had a dent from the wall. It was meant to be flown outdoors.

He slipped the airplane out of my hand and set it on his desk. "You are being held for the murder of Manfred Brandt. If you killed him, there is worry that you are part of a wider SA conspiracy. Brandt was in league with members of the SS, reporting on Röhm's movements."

"Oh."

"They know nothing of your activities as a reporter at Lichterfelde. Do not tell them. And do not admit to being part of an SA conspiracy."

I reached for the airplane again. He grabbed my hand, his fingers cold.

"Hannah?" He cupped my chin and tilted it up so that he saw my face, and I his. His eyes wandered from mine, probably swollen from crying, to my mouth.

I had no strength to pull my chin away.

"What did she say to you?" He sounded worried, not something an SS officer should be.

I closed my eyes, and we sat so for who knows how long, my chin in his palm, neither of us moving. Finally he cleared his throat. "What did she say to you?" he repeated in a whisper.

I opened my eyes and stared into his. "That you killed Anton. She saw . . ." I could not finish the sentence.

"*Verdammt*," he swore.

I flinched.

"I apologize for the language," he said, and I envisioned the mother in the photograph in his apartment nodding approvingly. "But Anton is not dead."

I pulled my chin out of his hand, wanting to believe him. "Then where is he?"

"With his grandmother." I sagged in the chair. He put his hands up as if to catch me. I gripped both arms of the chair to keep upright.

"But—" My mind whirled. I had known that Frau Röhm was scheming and had suspected that she killed Mouse since I talked to her maid this morning, but this went beyond that. "She—"

"We have little time. Your name is Adelheid Zinsli. Do you understand?"

I nodded. That was the name on my Swiss passport. Frau Inge must have found it in my suitcase and given it to him. She had inadvertently helped me. I could get through this. Somehow I would make it through the interrogation and reclaim Anton. I struggled to listen, to understand.

"No one knows of a link between Adelheid and the Röhms." His voice was clipped.

"No one?" I raised my eyebrow. He knew.

He rushed on. "Deny everything. Tell them you were not near the mill. You do not know the Röhms. You are not Hannah Vogel. Frau Röhm is a woman driven mad by grief and has mistaken you for someone else. Above all, do not mention the boy. He is not in any paperwork. He won't be if you say nothing about him."

"When I was arrested, I had a German passport in the name of Hannah Vogel." I fought to think, tried to reason. Anton was alive. I had to get free to find him.

"I substituted that passport for the Zinsli one." He patted my knee. "And the Hannah Vogel files are unavailable."

"In your wardrobe," I said, without thinking.

He swore again, and I suppressed a smile when he apologized. "This complicates matters."

"For whom?"

A sharp rap sounded on the door. He leapt to attention.

"I will keep your secrets as best as I can," I said, my voice cold. "But if I find that you killed Anton, I will deliver you over to them."

And we both knew that I would. I would do things I had never thought possible. I hated to learn it, but there it was.

"I would expect nothing less from you," he said with a crooked smile. Another knock. "Good luck, Adelheid."

He picked the airplane off his desk and stuck it in his pocket before striding to the door.

I stayed in the chair, not trusting my knees to support me. Was Anton really alive? Or was this a trick? If I did not mention Anton and he never went into any paperwork, it would be as if he did not exist. Perfect for the Nazis if they had killed him. Could I trust Lang? Why would he risk his life to help me?

He threw the bolt and opened the door to the interrogation room.

"She knows nothing," he said. I wondered how he could trust me to play along with his plan. What would happen to him if I turned him in? "She was never there. Your informant is wrong."

A giant crowded in. He looked out of place in the tiny room, like a horse in a kitchen.

"I'll need to verify that, Hauptsturmführer Lang." His guttural voice brooked no argument.

Behind him Lang's cheek twitched. Adelheid would not like verification.

"Frau Zinsli is a Swiss citizen," he said. "Certain protocols must be followed."

"The Swiss don't run Germany. The Führer does." The man glared at me. A bully. I straightened in my chair.

While they argued, I concocted Adelheid's story. I stuck to the truth as much as possible. Adelheid had to be a reporter for a Swiss paper, writing under the same pseudonym that I did. Let them check my articles. My Swiss editor did not know my real name. I decided to say that I had traveled to Berlin to do a piece on celebrated National Socialist monuments. That might give them pause.

I had broken down in church because the old woman, whose name I did not know, had accused me of murder and told me that the Gestapo would put me away forever. One heard such dreadful things were happening in Germany these last few days. I mentally practiced my Swiss accent, wondering if it would hold up under torture. It had to.

I had to be released to free Anton from that woman. Whether he knew it or not, Lang's alibi for me had a grain of truth: she had been driven mad by grief. She was evil, and I had to get Anton.

The next hours went better than I had any right to expect. Lang intervened when he could. The idea that I was writing an article about National Socialist monuments and my standing as a Swiss citizen carried weight. Even the Gestapo did not want to anger the Swiss, and my story was more plausible than Frau Röhm's contention that I had followed a German thug to an abandoned mill and murdered him, an odd thing for a Swiss travel reporter to do.

The questioning took hours. Although dizzy and terrified, I sat upright in my chair, ankles crossed like a proper Swiss lady. My stocky interrogator never erupted into violence, although the threat hovered always.

Eventually he left me alone, clearly disappointed that he found no reason to hurt me. I longed to curl up under the massive desk and sleep. When Lang came through the silent door and touched my shoulder, I jumped.

"I apologize for your difficult day, Frau Zinsli," he said in a clipped voice. "We have cleared up the misunderstanding. You are free to go." He tucked my hand in the crook of his elbow and held it, so that I would know I was not free to go.

I gripped the top of the desk with my free hand while the room pitched around me.

"Can you stand?"

"I can." Hopefully.

"I will walk you to the door."

With Lang at my side, I walked down the long halls to the front door. Three years ago I had walked next to him through the Hall of the Unnamed Dead like this. I had not trusted him then, either.

28

We stepped into the dregs of twilight. Two soldiers posted by the front door gave Lang a crisp "Heil Hitler!" and I remembered that he was a Hauptsturmführer, an officer. He could not have attained that position without staining his hands with blood.

The day's heat radiated off the stone sidewalk. Lang stayed in step by my side. "Do you know where you are going next?"

I shook my head. I could not go back to Boris's hotel, not with the SS tailing me. If I headed to his house, Frau Inge might be there, and the SS would be arriving to arrest Boris soon in any case. I could not involve either. I would find a hotel, one suitable for a Swiss reporter. Then I would find a way to call Boris.

"I wish to talk to you a bit more, perhaps over a late dinner?" His voice told me that it was a command, not a request.

I stiffened, longing to refuse. I did not want to be alone with him. "Why?"

"We are being watched." He smiled, as if we were choosing a restaurant. "They will continue to watch. I wish to make you a proposal, then drop you at the train station, where you can take a train to Switzerland."

"I will not leave Germany without Anton."

He sighed and gave me an exasperated look that reminded me of Boris. I forced myself not to recoil at the familiarity. "Let us eat, and find a place for you to spend the night."

I thought about arguing, but decided that I was safest from my watchdogs in the company of a more powerful watchdog. "Dinner sounds delightful."

He patted my hand and escorted me down Prinz Albrecht Strasse, past the lighted windows of Gestapo offices where industrious interrogators still worked.

He must want to know how I knew about the files in his wardrobe, but I sensed that there was more. He had not known that I knew his secrets when he switched my passports. He had a use for me, and I shuddered to think what it might be.

He broke the silence. "I know a restaurant near here. Good German food."

"That would be acceptable." It felt like a date, and I stiffened. But a date suited me better than an official appointment back at Prinz Albrecht Strasse, so I held my peace.

We strolled down the street in the warm evening air. I waited for him to talk, assuming that he would know when it was safe to do so.

"I apologize for what you went through today."

"Was it your fault?" I looked over at him as we walked, but the streetlights illuminated an expressionless face under the brim of his SS hat.

"I would not put you through that." He lowered his voice. "Hannah."

I disliked the tenderness with which he said my name. "Then why?"

"Once the accusation was made," he continued in a normal tone, "you had to be arrested. I delayed as long as I could, but that was only a few days. I hoped that she would change her mind or you would leave Berlin, but you and Frau Röhm were both persistent. When there was nothing else to be done, I arranged to be in charge of the arrest to help you."

"Like switching my passport with the one that Frau Inge procured for you."

"Hannah Vogel would never have made it out of Prinz Albrecht Strasse alive, you must realize that."

My jaw clenched. I did know that, but I did not wish to hear it. "Why are you taking Frau Zinsli to dinner?"

He glanced casually over his shoulder. "As an apology from the SS. I do not wish her to print anything compromising about her visit here." Then, more softly. "And I hope that we may become . . . more closely acquainted."

I gave him a guarded look.

"I know that Fräulein Vogel is involved with the banker. I have always been aware of his trips to London to visit you," he said in a bitter tone. "Have no worries on that score."

We strolled on in silence. He knew where I had been all along and could have turned me over to Röhm at any time during the last three years. But he had not done so. I owed him more and more, and the bill was soon to come due.

A man walking a dachshund started to cross the street when he saw Lang's uniform, but checked himself. Lang bent and scratched the dog behind its floppy ears. The owner looked worried.

"Beautiful animal," Lang said.

"Th-thank you, Hauptsturmführer," the owner stuttered.

"We will be late." I plucked at Lang's sleeve. The man was obviously frightened and wanted us to leave him in peace.

He rose. "Certainly, Frau Zinsli."

We entered a beer garden with round tables arrayed around a massive oak tree and colored lights strung by the dance floor. The band in the corner played a polka. I had not heard one in a long time. I could not suppress a quick laugh at such a cliché.

He turned to me. "Is it acceptable to you?"

I nodded. "Of course."

He pulled out my chair, and I sank into it. Exhausted and ravenous, I scanned the menu. It felt as if we were in Bavaria, not Berlin. I ordered a schnitzel, spätzle noodles, and red cabbage from a chubby waitress wearing a dirndl. I thought of ordering a beer, but instead had mineral water. I needed a clear head for the meeting.

"Frau Zinsli, we must look like two people who barely know each other."

"That should not be too difficult, as it is the truth."

He smiled. "Quite."

"This would be the part where we would be asking each other about our history, but I imagine we can skip that, since I know that you work for the SS and you know every single thing that could be stuffed into a file. You have more experience than I at having dinner with people under interrogation. What does one talk about?"

"I like your Swiss accent. Have you practiced long?"

"All day."

He smiled. It reminded me of his smile in the photograph back at his apartment, the one with his parents and the dog. A real smile.

"What brings you to Germany? Besides your article, that is."

"I hoped that the interrogation part of the day was over." I nodded to the plump waitress as she set my mineral water and an earthen bowl of pretzels in front of me. I bit into a pretzel.

"I suspect that you smuggled information about the Night of the Long Knives to England," he said in an undertone, as casually if we spoke about the weather. He sipped his beer.

I forced the pretzel down my suddenly dry throat with a sip of water. "You are not much for small talk, are you?"

"If I can't ask questions, then I must make statements." We ate pretzels in silence, listening to the band and watching each other. How much could I trust him? Although it might have been a trick, he seemed to have saved my life. And if he had, I had to assume that he had reason to do so. I probably would not like confirmation of that reason.

An unassuming man in a workman's cap sat at a nearby table and unfolded the *Völkische Beobachter*. From the way Lang avoided looking at him, I suspected that he was the man tailing us. Or one of many men tailing us. It would not do to underestimate them.

"Shall we dance?" Lang stood and proffered his arm.

I stared in disbelief, then caught myself and took his arm. "I have not danced the polka for a long time."

"It will come back to you."

Unsure that I wanted it to come back to me, I let him lead me to the dance floor.

He put one arm on my shoulder blade and took my right hand. I put my left atop his black shoulder.

"Why would you put your career in jeopardy to help me?" I winced when he stepped on my toes as he stepped forward too far.

"Perhaps I like you. It could be as simple as that."

I dodged his foot the second time. He had a terrible sense of rhythm. "That would not be simple. And I do not think it is the reason."

"You are a very attractive woman." He pulled me closer than the dance usually dictated. "You don't give yourself enough credit."

"But I give you sufficient credit." I pushed myself away from him and into a turn. When we were face-to-face again, I continued. "Your motives are more complex than that. That is not enough."

He pulled me forward, and his boot-black eyes gazed into mine in an unmistakably flirtatious way. "It would be enough. I assure you."

I counted steps, speechless. One, two, three. Two, two, three.

The song ended, and I returned gratefully to our table. The man with the newspaper at the neighboring table still read the front page.

Lang pulled out my chair and I sat. Before I could figure out how to start another conversation, our waitress appeared with dinner. The spätzle tasted heavenly, but the schnitzel was dry and overcooked. I devoured both.

Over dinner we chatted about the unseasonable heat and worries about a drought. We both hoped that it would not turn into the kind of drought destroying farmlands in the American Midwest and driving families from their homes with dust. I wanted to talk about Anton, but was too afraid of being overheard.

After dinner we danced again, better this time, then talked over coffee. The exhaustion that had been at the edge of my consciousness all day overwhelmed me, and I yawned.

He was solicitous. "I am waiting for our closest watcher to leave, then I have a proposal to make. Soon you may go to bed."

I snapped alert so sharply that my rib twinged.

He glanced at our shadow, who had not yet turned a page. We had not outlasted him.

"Let us go to my apartment," Lang said, under his breath.

"I beg your pardon?" I had not expected him to make such an improper suggestion so easily.

"Be logical." He looked annoyed. "You cannot return to your banker's house without making the connection between you explicit to others in the SS. Correct?"

As usual, he was correct. I nodded.

"If you register at a hotel, you reveal to your SS follower that you have not been registered there before tonight which opens up questions about where you were. I stamped your Swiss passport the day I procured it, not knowing that you'd be wanted for murder so soon after. Your best option is to tarnish your honor by spending the night at my apartment."

I blinked several times. The third choice involved ridding myself of the SS tail, but I was unsure that I could and, in any case, I did not want to alert him yet. "My honor is my own. And perhaps it is more valuable to me than you realize."

He ducked his head, a lock of hair falling across his forehead. "Forgive me. I wish to make clear that nothing beyond conversation will take place in my apartment."

"Make your proposal here. Then I will decide where I go."

He smoothed his hair back. "I count three men in here. I want control of the situation when I tell you what I need to tell you."

"As do I. Move your chair closer to mine. We will discuss it here."

He stared at me. I kept my eyes on his. When he looked away first, I stifled a sigh of relief.

He shifted his chair next to mine, so close that our shoulders touched. I turned toward him, the back of my head toward our watcher. Well choreographed. The watcher would see only Lang's expressions, not mine. He did not trust me not to give him away.

"This is as much control as I will give you."

He bent his head closer to mine, and I feared that he would kiss me. I was unsure what I would do if he did. But he did not.

"As I said earlier, I believe that you smuggled information about the Night of the Long Knives out of Germany into England."

Had Sefton or Bella moved the information out so quickly? Regardless, I started to deny his allegation, but he put his index finger on my lips.

"I want no details. It is enough to know that you did. As you seem to know, I have files in my apartment." He looked at me expectantly.

I peeled his finger off my lips. "Yes. I do."

"I thought you had been there," he said, smiling. "I smelled your scent, but I thought that my mind played tricks on me."

I shifted in my chair, and he slid one arm around the back of it. My instincts screamed to run, but my logic told me to stay.

"I want you to take some of those files to the intelligence community in England. Especially The Reich List of Unwanted Persons, those killed in the purge."

I stared at his obsidian eyes, as mesmerized as a bird before a snake. If he told the truth, those boys who had been shot could be marked somewhere—if I helped him.

"If it works, I propose an ongoing intelligence exchange."

"Why would you do such a thing? You have been a devoted National Socialist for years."

His eyes were so sad that I pitied him. "That is why I must do this. I helped to build this apparatus that controls the state. I believed in them, and I did my part."

"But you would betray it?"

He traced his fingertips down the side of my face, as if we talked about something as frivolous as a sexual relationship. "Things have been done in the name of the party, horrible things. Women tortured. Children killed." His fingers stopped on my jaw. "Some of it is political, yes, but much of it is personal. As you likely know, much killing during the purge was out of revenge."

"I know." But I could not believe that a senior member of the SS confessed it.

"It is not the party I once thought. I am a policeman at heart, and I believe in the rule of law, not the rule of one man."

I stared at him, astonished. "You are an idealist."

He closed his eyes briefly. "I was an idealist. Now I am a realist. And I must follow my conscience. My conscience says that the National Socialists must be stopped. I helped to create them, and I must help to destroy them."

"If they catch you . . ." My voice trailed off.

"I know. I've seen." He cupped my chin as he had in the Gestapo headquarters, the tender gesture at odds with his words. "And I've participated."

Lively polka music played as if we were at a party. I stared into the saddest eyes I had ever seen. I looked away first.

"What if they interrogate me and I tell them about you?"

"Any punishment they give me, I've earned."

My heart raced. I did not know what to do. He had access to high-level intelligence that Sefton could put to good use. If I smuggled out those files, and others he accumulated, it might damage the Nazi party. Perhaps I could undo the harm I had caused by not publishing the sexually explicit letters that Röhm had written my brother all those years ago, when it might have made a difference. And those thousand men executed would be noted somewhere and not disappear into unmarked Nazi graves.

But could I trust him, or was this an elaborate trap to catch Sefton? A skilled interrogator like Lang could construct such a clever trap. He leaned in closer, but I barely noticed. This one action would change my life. If I chose to collaborate with him, the Nazis would kill me if they found out. If I did not collaborate, I must live with the knowledge that perhaps I could have helped, assuming that he let me go. And what would become of Anton?

He kissed me full on the lips, angling his body slightly so that the our watcher at the next table had a proper view. The kiss was passionate,

barely restrained, but also frightened. Either he was a consummate actor, and I could not dismiss that possibility, or the kiss was genuine,
not staged as Wilhelm's had been. I closed my eyes and let him, having
made my decision. I would not pass up another chance to fight the
Nazis, whatever the cost.

When he pulled back, fear shadowed his eyes. Did he fear that I
would reject his proposal, or that I would reject his advances? Either
one gave me power over him, but would it be enough to keep me alive?
I hated thinking in such terms, but the time had come for it.

Finally he spoke. "Choose where you go, and what you wish to reveal to the men following you."

He stood and offered his arm. I hesitated, then took it.

He bent his head close and whispered, "Thank you."

29

Even though I spotted the men following us, I felt safer in the open air. "Tell me about Anton," I said quietly. I had not dared ask before.

Lang strolled next to me. We looked like a couple enjoying the warm night, but my stomach churned.

"Not much to tell. I have a man on Frau Röhm."

"Did she kill Mouse?" I imagined that she had. He would not have seen her as a threat. He would have let her get close.

His shoulder shrugged next to mine, too close, but for the sake of our charade I dared not move away. "We may never know."

"Was she followed that night?"

He shook his head, his voice low. "We didn't pick her up until she called to arrange your arrest at the church."

"Is she being watched?" I dared not trust whatever answer he gave.

He squeezed my hand. "Every minute."

Our tail stopped to look in the window of a closed tobacco shop. Too far away to hear.

"Where is Anton?" My voice broke.

"Safe at Hotel Adlon."

I stopped, dumbfounded. How much simpler it could have been. Our minder looked over at us, probably surprised that we had stopped. I took a step forward, then another. I had been near Anton and had not known it. But the most important thing was that he was safe.

"I can move the man at the Adlon outside tomorrow. But not before lunch."

Whatever the price for Anton's freedom, I would pay it. By tomorrow, I would have him back. "Thank you."

He looked over, his face in shadows. "I know what it means to you."

"Who betrayed us on the zeppelin?"

"A couple from Bolivia, but I don't know their real names."

The smoking Santanas? I thought of how they had pretended to dote on Anton, how I had left him alone with them mere minutes before the zeppelin docked in Friedrichshafen. If they had kept him then, he would have been lost to me forever. I stumbled on the pavement, and he caught my arm.

"Are you ill?"

I shook my head, breathless. Together, we climbed the stairs to his front door. It felt intimate, but unreal, as if I watched a film of myself climbing the stairs with a man in full black SS uniform, double lightning bolts shining silver on his collar.

I stepped into the hall that I had fled through at a run last night. It seemed a hundred years ago.

He fumbled with his key. After he opened the door, proper as always, he gestured that I cross the threshold in front of him. I stepped over the squeaky board and into his entry.

"I see you are familiar with my creaky board."

I simply nodded and walked into his parlor. Everything was as it had been on my previous visit. Unwilling to go to the sofa a moment before I had to, I sat on the chair.

"Would you care for a drink?"

"Please." Perhaps the alcohol would cut through the sense of unreality.

He handed me a traditional schnapps glass—small and with a short, thick stem. He filled it with a clear gold liquid. I sipped. Corn schnapps. Strong, but higher quality than I expected.

He sat on the sofa across from me, pulling on the crease of his trousers, glass in hand.

We discussed how I would rid myself of my SS tails and pick up his files, stored on two rolls of undeveloped film, to deliver to Sefton. I did not name Sefton, and he did not ask. Either he already knew, or he did not want to.

"Who else knows of your plans?"

"I have told no one but you. I do not trust anyone else."

"Yet you trust me. Why?" I sipped my schnapps.

"I have watched you. You are honest. You had something on Röhm."

"Did I?" I'd had the letters to get me out of the sticky room, but I escaped only because Röhm underestimated me.

"You did, or he would never have let you go. I know that you are no Nazi, yet you kept his secrets. If you kept his, I believe that you will keep mine."

"What if you are wrong?" I finished my drink, too fast.

He refilled my glass. "Then I pay for that with my life. But I was a policeman for many years. I can judge character, and you are not so complex as you seem to think."

I laughed. "How flattering."

"It is flattering, whether you believe it or not," he said gently.

Unable to meet his eyes, I picked up the photograph of his parents. Soon I could snap this kind of carefree picture of Anton, if I kept on Lang's good side.

"My parents and I on the North Sea." He ran his index finger along the frame. "A week later they were murdered."

I almost dropped the picture.

"I became a policeman to find their killers." His lips twisted into a bitter smile. "One of my first actions when I had gained enough seniority was to reopen the case. Their killers were never found."

"I am sorry." I returned the photograph to the table.

"I keep the picture to remember them." He positioned the frame parallel to the edge. "And to always remind myself of how I have failed."

I had no answer. "Why are you telling me this?"

"Because I want one person to know me." He paused. When he spoke again, his voice was a whisper. "Then after you leave, I will not be wholly alone."

He tucked a strand of hair behind my ear. I sat still, unable to reach out, although that was what he wanted, and the best way to build a relationship where I could trust him.

I drank my second glass of schnapps in one swallow. "I want to be with those who know secret things or else alone."

"And I want my grasp of things true before you." He smiled. "Rilke."

I was not sure if I was more surprised that I had quoted Rilke to him, or that he had recognized it and quoted it back.

I stood too quickly, eager to escape, and the room spun. I had drunk too much, too fast. "May I use your bathroom?"

He gestured toward the door, as if I did not know its location from my previous visit. I needed to keep a clear head. Getting Anton back was far too serious to let emotion cloud my judgement.

I washed my hands and face. I flattened my palm against the door, trying to slow things down. I should not be drinking so much. But I did not want to face what might happen while sober.

I was being forced into an unwanted intimacy with him because he had told me his secrets. I felt sympathy for him, and I did not want to. I could not forget the signed death warrant in his desk drawer.

I had no intention of opening up, so the imbalance would always be there. And he did not seem a man who dealt well with imbalance. I did not wish to be his secret keeper, but I also knew how it felt to be alone. I had been alone for most of the past three years, afraid to trust anyone.

I owed him. He had saved my life, told me where Anton was, and was the only one who could help me free him from his grandmother. I did not know what she wanted from Anton, and I did not want to know. I just wanted him back. I would have to pay whatever price required.

I remembered my file in his wardrobe. I thought of things that he knew and had not put into my file, such as my activities at Lichterfelde, my connection to Mouse and his murder, and my visits to London to see Boris. He had been protecting me for years.

I opened the door and walked through the bedroom where I had spent uncomfortable hours crammed under the bed the night before. In the darkened parlor, he sat as I had left him, except that he had removed his boots and unbuttoned the top button of his tunic. I sat next to him on the sofa. Knowing that this started a relationship I could not avoid, I touched his arm and asked, "How old were you when your parents died?"

"Nine." The same age as Anton. What must that have been like for him? What would it be like for Anton if I did not reclaim him?

He told me of a childhood spent in boarding schools, vacations at military camps, always alone. He moved on to his experiences in the Great War, his shame at not solving his parents' murder, his belief in the Nazi party, and his disillusion. He never said what one action had proven too much for him, and I did not ask. I did not want to know.

I already knew more than I wanted, but I did not interrupt him, realizing that my one thousand days of silence were insignificant compared to his lifetime of isolation. He was unused to talking about himself, but once started he was difficult to stop. I hoped that he would not punish me later for having seen the wounds that he revealed.

When he finally fell silent, I remained still, exhausted. "Hauptsturmführer," I said, hating the title, but having nothing else to call him. "What is your first name?"

He laughed, loud and long. "You know more about me than anyone, yet you do not know that. My full name is Lars Engelbert Lang."

"Lars Engelbert," I said. *Engelbert* meant "bright angel." I was close to falling asleep.

"You look done in."

"I am, Lars." I stumbled over his first name.

He brushed a strand of hair off my cheek, fingers tracing my jaw-line. "Let's get you to bed."

The next morning we left the building and hailed a taxi together, as be-fit a Swiss reporter and an SS man beginning an affair. Behind us, a man flagged down his own taxi and followed. At Anhalter Bahnhof I retrieved the suitcase that Lars had left there yesterday, while I had waited for my interrogation at Prinz Albrecht Strasse.

He installed me in the first-class compartment of a train bound for Switzerland, much nicer than the sleeper car in which I had arrived in Berlin. After a quick kiss to underline the relationship we would use to meet and smuggle information out of Germany, he left the compart-ment, but not before revealing the location of my two followers, one on the train and one on the platform.

I hurried into the compartment bathroom, carrying his suitcase. The suitcase contained an SS uniform, complete with shoes, and my satchel. I reached inside and ran my fingers over the scarf wrapped around the ransom money, my tattered notebook, and the Luger. He had returned everything.

I changed into his spare SS uniform and placed the satchel in the suit-case. It fit. We were much the same height and build. I swept my hair into the hat and eyed myself in the mirror. I did not look like a man up close, but with the hat brim pulled down, I might be mistaken for one.

I shoved my dress inside the suitcase, then stepped into the com-partment just as a woman with two small children entered. I touched the brim of my hat respectfully and went out into the corridor. The children giggled. I hoped that they had not caught me out playing dress up.

Lars spoke to my SS tail on the train, as planned, and he faced away from me. That left only the man on the platform to deceive. I turned away and hurried to the next compartment.

When the conductor shouted "All aboard!" I stepped onto the plat-form.

I walked toward the main hall, avoiding the man stationed there.

He wore an SS dress uniform and would be required to salute me. My voice as I returned his "Heil Hitler!" would give me away as a woman. Lars and his companion exited the train before it left the station. As far as anyone knew, Adelheid Zinsli was on her way to Switzerland.

I stepped into the ladies' room. If anyone was in there, I would have to apologize and leave, but I thought that would cause less trouble than coming out of the men's room in a dress. Luckily, the bathroom was empty. I hurried into a stall and changed out of the SS uniform. I repacked the suitcase, shoes on the bottom, black wool uniform in the middle, and SS hat on top.

Giving the SS team time to leave the station, I transferred two small film canisters from the suitcase to my satchel and dropped Lars's suitcase at Left Luggage, tucking the claim check into my dress pocket. I slung the satchel over my shoulder.

I could not hope to get Anton before lunch, when Lars pulled his man off surveillance, but I longed to see him now.

Instead I called Boris at the hotel.

"Hello?" His voice was ragged with worry.

"I was detained." I dared not give specifics in case the SS was listening.

Boris knew what that meant. "Are you—" Boris's voice broke. "—well?"

"I am," I answered quickly, to spare him. "Meet me at the dining room where I had wine with my friend."

"I will be there soon." I felt grateful for our argument over Sefton. It had given us a place to meet that we both recognized without explanations.

A quick stop at the chemist, then I hurried to Hotel Adlon. When I walked into the lobby, Lars strode toward me. He caught my eye, then turned and headed for the bank of telephones. I glanced around for Sefton. Not there. I did not want him to associate me with Lars, or Lars to associate him with me.

I walked as slowly as I could force myself to the telephones. Soon I would have Anton.

Lars stepped out of a booth. We were alone in the hall. "She's in her room. I'll pull my man to the outside of the building in an hour. It is too dangerous for me to remove him entirely."

"Thank you." I wondered what the consequences would be for him when Anton slipped through the SS's fingers.

"Be careful." He stepped close, eyes worried. "If you are caught, I cannot free you. Adelheid is supposed to be in Switzerland. And your face is recognized at SS headquarters."

"I know," I said, smiling. "Mother."

He ducked his head. "You need one, with the risks you run."

"The only one who could have filled that role did not. And she is dead. So do not try."

His face grew serious. "It's hard not to. Snatching him is dangerous."

"True, but I have done it before. And taking out your information puts me in as much danger as anything else I do."

"If there were any other way." His tone was pleading.

"I take the risks I take. And that is enough said."

"When will I see you again?"

"I will write you a love letter from Switzerland, with no news, but an address."

He glanced around the hallway. No one. I pressed the claim check for his suitcase into his palm and his hand lingered on mine. "We can set up a time for you to return to Berlin via letters," he said.

"Or you to visit Switzerland." I thought of his life here and the risks he ran. "You can walk away."

He shook his head almost imperceptibly.

"Safe passage." He embraced me quickly. "And for the sake of God, take care."

30

Lars bowed and clicked his heels together softly. After he walked out the splendid front doors, I waited a minute to make certain that he did not return, then hurried to the elevators. He assumed that I came to the Adlon to see Frau Röhm, but instead I took the elevator straight to Sefton. I had an hour before the SS man would be gone, and I needed it.

Sefton answered on the first knock. Did he ever leave his room?

"Hannah, it's only been three days and here you are in front of my door again, catching me barely dressed." He tied the belt of his paisley dressing gown, clearly just out of bed. I smiled. That's what reporters without responsibilities were allowed to do, stay up late interviewing sources and drinking. "Is this a proposition?"

"Something like that. May I come in?"

He stepped aside, shaking his head.

I hurried into his room. His typewriter and a messy stack of paper covered the desk, but everything else was immaculate. Housekeeping standards at the Adlon were impeccable, as always.

"How secure is your room?" I whispered.

He scratched his head. "Not as secure as I'd like."

"Get dressed and meet me behind the building. We need to take a walk."

I circled the Adlon and waited in the back by the entrance to the kitchen.

He appeared more quickly than I expected, and clean-shaven too. "Shall we?"

We ambled down the broad boulevard of Unter den Linden. Traffic was light, and we both checked to see if anyone followed.

Finally he glanced over, amused. "You'd better have something good, Hannah, waking me so early."

"It is almost lunchtime." Once again I envied his schedule. "And I do."

I palmed the two film canisters in my satchel and slipped my hand into his tweed jacket pocket.

"What did you just drop in there?"

"Film." I explained what was on it, keeping Lars's name and rank secret.

Sefton's jaw dropped. I reached over and closed it, my fingers skating over a rough patch of stubble he had missed.

"Can you get them out?"

"Of course. Can you get more?"

"Not yet."

"Who is your source? What's his name? Can I speak to him?" His words tumbled over each other.

"You only assume that my source is a man. And you know I will not tell you."

"How can we get more from the source? Can I meet him or her or the family dog or whatever it is?"

"The source does not know who you are, and does not want to." I suspected he would work directly with Sefton, but I intended to keep them apart until I learned whether I trusted them both. I wanted the blood of neither on my hands.

We stopped in the shade of a linden tree. "Do you trust him?"

"Or her. I do."

"Do you trust me?"

"Strangely enough, I do," I lied. I had not liked his reactions when we talked about Anton or Mouse. I would find out for myself if the information I had given him made it to Britain. Then, perhaps, trust would follow.

"Will you act as a go-between?"

Automobiles drove by. He waited. I wanted to say no, to get Anton, Boris, and myself out of the mess that Germany was becoming, and never come back. But I thought of Lars, risking his life to procure the files, and Sefton, risking his life to get them to England, where they might persuade the world to deal more firmly with Hitler. And I thought of the unpublished Röhm letters I had kept to protect Anton's and my life, even though they might have affected the Nazi rise to power. My conscience knew how much I had to answer for.

"Hannah? Once you start, you cannot go back."

"I know." I had been inside Gestapo headquarters. I knew what would happen if we were caught.

"Will you do it?" He stuck his hands in his jacket pockets. "Don't take it lightly."

"I have something to take care of first. I will be out of contact for a while. Do you have an address where you can be reached, somewhere more secure than the Adlon?"

He handed me a card. "That's my address at the paper in London. Mail is intercepted before it gets there, then forwarded to my real office."

I memorized the information and handed back the card. "I do not want it to be found on me, in case something goes wrong."

"Wise decision. We'll get through this."

I hoped so.

We headed back toward the Adlon.

"Now, what cracking adventure are you having this afternoon? Something I can help with?"

I shook my head. Too dangerous. I could not risk Sefton and Lars seeing me with the other.

We separated a few blocks from the Adlon. I walked the rest of the way alone.

I paused in the doorway to the dining room. Elegant diners talked in low voices, light glinting off silver and crystal. I remembered the well-appointed breakfast room at the Hanselbauer, bodies on the table. Money did not buy safety anymore.

Boris sat alone at a table, napkin spread on his lap. His skin was paler than I'd ever seen it, eyes swollen from lack of sleep. He too had spent a long day and night while I was with the Gestapo and in Lars's apartment.

I hurried to him.

"Hannah!" Even though he kept his voice low, the emotion in it caused diners at nearby tables to turn. The Adlon dining room was no place to express strong emotion.

I clung to him, and his arms were so tight around me, I could barely breathe. Yesterday I had been certain that I would never see him again.

"We are making a spectacle of ourselves." I forced myself to step back.

"I don't care." He pulled out a chair for me to sit and took my hands again. "What happened yesterday?"

I told him of my meeting with Frau Röhm, how she must blame me for her son's death, and the steps she had taken to exact revenge.

"A trap?"

"The church was a trap. The mill was a trap. The telegram was a lie." I swallowed my bitterness and anger. Her day would come. I would see to that. "She set me up as Mouse's murderer, and when the police did not catch me at the mill, as she had intended, she turned her dirty work over to the SS."

He shifted closer to me. "How did you get free?"

A white-gloved waiter presented me with a menu before I could answer. I ordered a pot of tea. Boris ordered something for our lunch, but I was too intent on his face to know what he ordered. The waiter collected the menus and left us alone.

"Now," Boris said, turning to me. "How did you get away?"

I told him of my interrogation and my release. I did not tell him of Lars's involvement, although I think he guessed. Once we were in

Switzerland, I promised to tell him everything. There had been too many secrets between us.

We sat in the Adlon dining room, positioned where we could see the elevator. I barely tasted my food. Lars said that they had eaten here every day. I may have missed them by minutes the day I met Sefton and Bella. I fought to stay calm as I listened to the genteel chink of silver on china and the low laughter of the well heeled. Everyone else was so serene, but I itched to see Anton.

Once again, I told Boris how to slip the sleeping powder I had purchased at the chemist into her tea. I could not do it. She would recognize me.

"Relax." He ran his hand up my arm. "If they don't come for lunch, they'll be down for dinner."

Where were they? If Lars's man was correct, they had not left their rooms all day, and it was almost three. I ordered another tea.

Frau Röhm and Anton exited the elevator. Tears sprang unbidden to my eyes. He was alive.

Anton wore a Bavarian costume: white shirt, lederhosen, and long white socks. I imagined she had tried to make him wear an alpine hat too. He was pale, as if he too had not slept much in the past week. But he looked whole and healthy. I longed to cross the room and sweep him into my arms. We had not been separated for even a few hours for three years, and so much had happened.

Boris followed my gaze. He reached over and patted my hand. "You need to work on your poker face."

I dropped my head so that he could not see my tears, and she could not see my face. Anton was safe, and so close. Once we drugged her, we would be on our way. Anton, at least, would stay in Switzerland for a long, long time.

She made her slow way across the lobby, holding his hand. She looked so old and frail that I almost pitied her. I was about to steal the only remnant she had of her own son, and with him dead only days. Then I remembered the Gestapo cell, where she expected me to die.

I palmed a tiny packet of sleeping powder and slipped it into Boris's hand underneath the table. A quick rip of tearing paper. "The whole packet."

He did not remind me that I had told him this many times.

But they did not sit. Instead they wheeled and headed toward the kitchen. Boris and I rose as one. I grabbed my satchel and ran for the kitchen as they disappeared through the swinging doors.

Boris stayed two steps ahead. We pushed through the door. Halfway across the room she headed for an old-fashioned wooden door with a wrought-iron handle. The wine cellar. And it ended in a tunnel that led to another building.

The cooks paused in their work, staring at us with surprised eyes while Frau Röhm slipped through the door with Anton, Boris and I steps behind. She had disappeared, spryer than she looked.

I pelted down the stairs. The smell of damp earth and old wine struck me. Dusty wine racks formed a maze. The low ceiling was almost invisible in the darkness. Boris ducked to keep from scraping his head and kicked a basket. Corks ran across the floor like rats. I bit back a scream. This was no time to lose my nerve.

At the end of a dark row I spotted her, Anton in tow. I raced forward, Boris still two steps ahead. Anton lunged toward me, one hand reaching to pry off her thin fingers.

She pulled a small pistol out of her handbag and jammed it into his side.

31

I stood close enough to hear Anton's intake of breath, but I dared not reach for him.

I froze, afraid to move. His wide eyes told me that he believed she would shoot him, as did I.

"She said they would kill you if I tried—"

Her hand tightened. He fell silent, his eyes sending an apology to me for not escaping. I swallowed tears.

"I am proud of you." I stepped toward him. "You did the correct thing."

"They killed my son." She dragged him past more racks. His white socks glowed in the darkness. "And it's your fault. If you had married him earlier, he would be alive."

"You cannot know that," I said in my most soothing tone, reaching for my Luger, hidden in the satchel. "Whatever Hitler says, your son was killed because he was too powerful. He was a threat. His . . . marital status had nothing to do with it."

"That's what you say. But you lie."

The tunnel pressed in close. She blamed me for her son's death, as I had blamed Lars when I thought he had killed Anton. What would I have done to exact revenge on him? She would do no less, and probably more. "You cannot hurt your grandson," I pleaded, hoping to remind her where the barrel was pointed.

"I can. It will be no harder than killing a mouse."

I flinched; Boris tensed next to me.

"You are wilier than I expected." She stepped backward. "But then that's the same problem my son had with you."

I kept my voice level and reassuring. I had to keep her calm. "This is not Anton's fault."

"But he is yours." She looked quite mad, and she had Anton at the other end of a gun. Boris cursed under his breath, but I did not listen. I had to hold her attention. Anton looked between us, clearly trying to decide whether to flee. I shook my head. She would kill him.

We crept farther into the labyrinth, a fortune in dusty wine bottles stacked around us. The immense wine cellar held many places to hide, and if she got through the tunnel and out onto the street, we might never catch her.

"He is yours too. Your grandson. He is all you have left of your Ernst." And all I have left of mine.

"Ernst was no more his father than you are his mother." She laughed, a high cackle quickly eaten by the close space.

I followed, mere paces away. Boris stayed in front of me. I knew he wanted to protect me, but I needed him out of my way so I could move closer to Anton.

"If your son was not his father—" I stepped forward "—then why not give him to me?"

"Because you want him." She jammed the barrel harder against his side. He cried out.

I fought a flash of rage. I had no time for it. Later, I promised myself, later I would. I sidestepped Boris and held my hands palms up near my shoulders to show that I was no threat. I wished that Lars's men were still inside, that they could step in and stop her. But I had them sent away.

"I will kill him before I let you have him." She backed down the dark mouth of the tunnel, dragging Anton with her. He pulled away, and she yanked him back. "Or if he fights me."

My stomach roiled with panic. What if she shot him in front of me?

She would revel in my suffering as his body fell. "If you want to hurt me, shoot me. This has nothing to do with him."

"He has everything to do with you. As we both well know."

I closed my eyes, waiting for the shot, afraid a grab for the gun or any other move might set her off. Boris stopped too.

"I will not kill him here unless I have to. It will be worse for you not to know when and where that will happen. I will raise him as a good National Socialist. My Ernst has friends in high places, even now. I know where he will be safe as long as I want him to be."

A sharp pain stabbed my hip. I gasped. Something large bumped past, light glinting at its middle.

My leg went out from under me as if the dirt had turned to ice. Pain lanced from my hip to my foot. My arm scraped the rough wall. The ground rushed toward my face, but I could not get my hands forward in time.

I landed facefirst in dirt. Everything went out of focus. I sensed Boris kneeling next to me, warm against my side. I pulled my head back so I could breathe.

Go after Anton, I wanted to scream, but soil filled my mouth. A gunshot roared. Glass crashed to the floor. I turned my head and bloodred wine gushed onto my face.

Boris ran deft hands up my leg. "You've been stabbed."

I spit out dirt and gulped air. Blood oozed down my hip, and pain knifed from my hip up my back. "Go after them."

Another gunshot boomed. Boris pulled me behind a rack of wine bottles. Glass crunched underfoot. The bottles around us would not stop the bullets, but we had no other shelter.

"I have a gun." I fumbled with my satchel.

He pulled out the Luger and swung the satchel strap over his shoulder. He aimed down the dark passage.

Another gunshot thundered. A bottle shattered near my ear. It smelled like a good year, ruined.

"You might hit Anton!" I screamed, but he had already fired. Someone ahead fell heavily against a wine rack. Bottles thudded to the dirt.

I struggled to my feet and lurched forward. My wounded leg would not obey my will. He put an arm around my waist and pulled me with him. "I shot the bastard who stabbed you. He won't be taking any more potshots."

I hoped that he was right, and that Anton did not lie bleeding on the ground ahead.

Finally we were close enough to see. Frau Röhm's maid stared with wide eyes. She held a kitchen knife in one hand, a gun in the other. I should have been grateful that she had stabbed me instead of shooting.

"A woman?" Boris's voice shook. His shot had hit her in the neck. He lowered me to the floor and checked her pulse. He need not bother. No blood pumped from her wound. Her heart had stopped.

"I killed an innocent woman." He closed her cobblestone-gray eyes with trembling fingers.

"She was not innocent." I pressed my palm harder against my wounded hip.

He remained kneeling. I wished I could stay to comfort him, but I dragged myself deeper in the passage after Anton. Blood saturated the side of my dress and dripped onto the floor.

Another gunshot cracked. I jumped to the side. My bloody leg buckled. I slammed against a wine rack. My head struck the end of a bottle.

Boris lifted me to my feet. "Upsadaisy," he said as if I were a small child. "Are you hurt?"

"No more than before," I lied through gritted teeth.

He supported my weight.

We stumbled down the tunnel, hugging the sides in case she kept shooting. But she had vanished. How would I find them?

The clatter of feet on wood resounded in the tunnel. They were climbing the steps on the other end. What if she bolted the door from the top? We would never make it in time. I limped faster.

Gritting my teeth against the pain in my leg, I pulled myself up the ladder and hefted my shoulder against the hatch. It burst open. I climbed up into the light, a mixture of wine and blood spattering on the floor. We were in an office building across the street from the Adlon. A janitor pointed to the door with his mop. Boris stuck my Luger in his trouser pocket.

We careened by and onto the street.

Sunlight blinded me. I squinted and shaded my eyes with one bloody hand. I did not see them. She had won. We had lost him. My eyes watered.

Boris yanked me into the doorwell. "There!"

Their car pulled into traffic. Two men who made Mouse look small sat in the front seat. Anton's pale face looked at me through the back window.

My heart rose. "Where is your automobile?"

Boris pointed to the street. I staggered toward it, Boris holding me up with one arm. We were too slow. He helped me into the passenger seat and climbed behind the wheel.

I pressed my hands against my hip to staunch the bleeding while he manuevered onto Unter den Linden. We shot down the street, horn blaring. I searched frantically for their car.

"Someone's behind us," he said.

I turned. A man in an SS uniform followed less than a car length behind. Lars's man.

"Do not get too close to her car," I said. "If he does not know where she is, I am not helping him find her."

"But we might lose Anton."

"Better to lose him than to turn him over to the SS." Tears ran down my cheeks. My hands were too dirty to wipe them off.

We slowed. As the SS automobile closed in, I hoped that she would keep him safe, safer than I could. Lars could never get us out of this.

The SS automobile closed to within inches of our bumper. Boris's hands twitched on the wheel. I knew he longed to outrun the SS car, but we did not dare to lead them past Frau Röhm. Instead I watched her lead lengthen until I was no longer sure which automobile was hers.

I glanced at the SS car. Blue smoke billowed from under the hood. It veered right and hit a lorry.

"Engine trouble?" Boris was already accelerating.

I smiled, heart light. "Thank you, Lars," I muttered.

"Where could they be going?"

"Clean up," Boris said. "Wherever it is, they won't let you in looking like that."

When I leaned into the backseat, my rib twinged in protest. I opened my suitcase, pulling out a fresh dress. I used the old one as a rag to clean myself. Boris had a jug of water in the backseat. I scrubbed blood off my hands and legs and combed pieces of glass from my hair with clean wet fingers. I tore my old dress into lengths and fashioned a bandage for my hip.

Boris winced when I tied it.

"It is not so bad. Deep, but short. I can stitch it later."

His face took on a greenish cast. "Lovely."

Having made myself presentable, I looked beyond the dash at the hood ornament at the end of the long black bonnet. The ornament doubled and lurched back together. I closed my eyes, nauseated. "I do not see them."

"After that crack on the head, I doubt you can see beyond the hood. They accrued too sizable of a lead while we were ditching your SS friend."

"Where are we?"

"Mehringdamm. Bearing south. Where do you think they're headed?"

"I do not know." I shook my head. Lights popped at the corner of my vision, and I resolved never to shake my head again. I swallowed.

He glanced at me. "There's a flask of brandy in the glove box. Help yourself."

I pulled out a silver flask with a *BK* engraved on the front in filigree. The brandy slid down smoky and warm. Only the best for Boris. "She must be going somewhere Röhm still has friends."

"I don't imagine he has many living friends left."

I sipped more brandy. "Bolivia." A warmth flooded through me that had nothing to do with Boris's brandy. "Röhm lived there, training their army."

"That's just a guess." He stowed the flask back in the glove box.

"All we have are guesses."

He looked unconvinced. "You think they are headed to Tempelhof?"

"It is the correct direction. And the zeppelin is there. The *Graf Zeppelin* leaves today for South America."

Boris turned hard right on Friedrichstrasse. "How do you know that?"

"Anton and I were going to take it back to South America. It stops in Switzerland after it leaves here. After that it flies straight to Pernambuco, Brazil."

"What if she's taking a train, or a boat?"

My stomach tightened. He could be right.

We turned left into the airport. A parade ground under the kaiser, its open fields had plenty of space for a zeppelin. I sighed with relief at the familiar silver cigar shape, even with its swastika on the tail.

I spotted their car.

Anton, Frau Röhm, and one of her thugs jumped out and disappeared into the long brick terminal building. The other thug stayed with the automobile.

Someone was expected back.

Boris touched his trouser pocket, probably feeling for the Luger.

I opened the door almost before we stopped. When I stepped onto the hot pavement, the ground heaved and lurched. Boris grabbed my arm to keep me from falling.

"I will be fine," I said, doubting it.

His lips twisted into a smile, but he knew better than to argue. "Your head looks bad. Put on a hat."

"Font of sympathy, you are." But I followed his advice.

The thug who had gone in with Frau Röhm exploded out the front door and hopped into the automobile. They idled, not leaving. Boris pulled my suitcase out of the backseat. "She's alone."

"I hope Anton does not bolt." I bent to pick up my bag.

"Let me take that." He reached for it.

I shook my head, remembering too late my resolution to never shake my head again. I held the car door until the ground stopped swaying. "Do you have papers for Switzerland?" I hoped that he did, but did not see how he could have procured them so quickly.

"I've had an escape route planned for months, just in case," he said, one hand still on my arm. "Through Poland."

"You cannot enter Switzerland legally without papers. And it is almost impossible to sneak in." I stepped close. "They watch the Swiss border closely, especially for escaping bankers."

He chuckled. "Where else would an escaping banker go?"

"Be careful in Poland." I slid my hands around his waist. "And meet me in Zürich."

"I won't let you go again." He wrapped his arms around my shoulders and I relaxed into his chest. I inhaled his familiar scent. "I'll get on that zeppelin somehow, Hannah."

"I need you here in case we come out of there in a hurry."

"They'll never know I'm there. I'll get a mechanic's uniform. I can—"

I reached up and traced my index finger across his warm lips. "If I have to get on the zeppelin, any commotion puts Anton and me in danger."

"But—"

"If I can grab him before the zeppelin leaves, I need you here. You cannot help me there." Hurt flashed in his brown-gold eyes.

"But you are wounded. And Frau Röhm is armed." Muscles worked in his jaw.

"I can handle myself. She is only an old woman."

He kissed the knot on my head through my hat. "She's a tough old woman."

"Last time," I said grimly, "she had the element of surprise. This time, I do."

He shook his head stubbornly. I stepped away.

"Do not make us pay the price for your heroism. If I get him in the hangar, I need you on the outside, motor running."

He stared at me for a long minute. I held his gaze. He knew I was right.

"Very well." I heard how much he hated saying it. He placed the Luger into my satchel and handed me the paper packet of sleeping powder I'd given him at the Adlon, the top carefully folded so that none had spilled out.

I smiled at the care he had taken with it, even under dire circumstances, and slipped it into my clean dress pocket.

He drew me into a long sad kiss. I wished that I did not have to leave the shelter of his arms. He pulled back reluctantly and wiped tears from the corners of my eyes with his thumbs. "Take care, Hannah."

"You too." Missing him already, I told him where I would wait in Zürich.

I slipped my satchel over my shoulder and hefted my suitcase, biting my lips against the pain. He draped the wedding dress, still surprisingly pristine, across my free arm, then touched his hat like a chauffeur. I walked toward the Flughafen Berlin sign, wondering if I would ever see him again.

Poland was hours away. Much could happen before he got clear. And I too faced dangers. I shook myself. I would not succumb to melancholy and exhaustion. I would see him soon. We would meet in Switzerland and enjoy our scheduled weekend. And whatever came after.

With a rising sense of dread I limped up the three steps and pushed open the tall glass terminal doors.

My rib twinged as I set my suitcase and the wedding dress in front of the zeppelin ticket counter and handed the smartly dressed woman my ticket. I had only moments before departure.

She glanced at my ticket and passport, then my face. "Hello, Frau Zinsli. You and your little boy disappeared so mysteriously last week."

"When the boy's grandmother heard that the zeppelin was docking here, she insisted on a visit."

"How lovely." She ticked my name off her list. "Was it enjoyable?"

"Exhausting, but rewarding. She said they would meet me here. Have they arrived?" I hoped that they had. If they boarded an airplane instead of a zeppelin, I might never find them.

She handed me my ticket and passport. "They're already on board."

My knees buckled. I clutched the counter. My guess was correct. I would not think what would have happened if I had guessed wrong. "Will the Santanas be on this flight?"

Papers rustled as she paged through her roster. "No, I'm afraid not. You must hurry. The zeppelin leaves soon. You should see a glorious sunset from up there tonight. And have a wonderful flight back to South America."

"I shall."

She gestured toward my suitcase and a boy ran forward to grab it. She gave him a scrap of paper. "Here's the lady's cabin number. Leave her bag there, but go quickly."

I pulled my hat farther down on my head and marched across the dry grass. Only a week before, three men, now dead, had kidnapped me from this very zeppelin. It felt like another lifetime.

I stayed behind the boy who carried my suitcase. I wondered if Frau Röhm watched as I climbed the ladder. What was her cabin number? How would I find her?

It was a needless concern. Frau Röhm faced away from me by the viewing window, Anton beside her. His back was tense, one fist thrust deep into the pocket of his lederhosen. Her veined hand clutched his other wrist. She whispered in his ear, but he shook his head, face set.

He glanced toward the door and shifted on the balls of his feet, poised to run. I positioned myself in his line of sight and waited. When he looked again, I held up my hand palm out, like an Indian greeting. He grinned.

I shook my head when he leaned toward me, but flashed him a quick smile. I bent my fingers forward, our sign to wait. He turned back to her.

I walked to the other side of the viewing area and paced. We had hours before Switzerland. I pulled my wide-brimmed hat lower on my face. I ached to cross the viewing area and hold Anton in my arms, but I had to be patient.

Frau Röhm must be neutralized first. Our false identities might not stand up to the scrutiny she could bring to bear. Anton fidgeted and squirmed next to her. The zeppelin rose into the sky.

"Come, Anton," she finally said in her quavery voice.

He followed her obediently. If she knew him, that should have made her suspicious.

My heart pounded. I followed them to their cabin, feet silent on the carpet. Their cabin adjoined mine. They would have to pass my door to leave. They could not get by without my knowing.

I paced my cabin, the folded-up beds and striped stool achingly familiar. Even the daily Argentinian roses rested in their vase. Red tipped the fragrant white petals, as if the blooms had been dipped in blood.

I cleaned myself up thoroughly. Were they in for the night? I could knock on the door and hope that Anton heard and she did not, but she was a light sleeper. And she was armed, with no compunctions against shooting me.

When the steward came to fold down the lower bunk I asked him to have someone bring me a late dinner.

The jingle of a food cart sounded outside my open door. I had to do something soon. Switzerland was close.

I stepped into the corridor and ran into Dieter, the waiter who had been enamoured of Señora Santana. He pushed a cart with three covered plates.

"Frau Zinsli!" he said in a delighted voice. "I did not know you were returning on this flight. Are Herr and Frau Santana with you?"

"Regrettably, they are not."

His face fell. "This plate is yours." He carried it into my cabin and set it next to the roses, carefully aligning the silver on the linen napkin. I longed to tell him to hurry, but kept silent.

"There you go!" he said.

I handed him a tip, and stepped out into the corridor. When he pushed the cart away, I stopped it with one hand. It was heavier than it looked.

"I have a strange request." I gave him an uncertain smile. "My son Anton is in the next cabin with his grandmother. Is that where you are taking this food?"

He nodded. They too had ordered dinner. Perfect. I had an idea.

"May I perhaps borrow your uniform to serve it? It would be a funny surprise." I injected warmth and humor into my voice, trying to play it as light as the hydrogen that held us aloft. And as dangerous.

"That is irregular." Dieter was not a man who liked irregular things.

"But Señora Santana taught him so many practical jokes. I would like to show him one myself." My heart pounded, but I forced out a giggle.

"Did she?" A smile lit his face. "I didn't know that about her."

"She is quite a whimsical woman." My lie gained strength. "I cannot wait to tell her about this prank in my next letter."

"You have her address?" he asked, eyes open wide in surprise.

I lied again. "Of course."

"Would you . . ." His voice trailed off. It was improper to finish the sentence.

"If you gave me something to write her about, I would be happy to mention your part. I am sure she would find it amusing."

He shifted from foot to foot.

I smiled again, conspiratorial. "Or perhaps I could give you her address so you could tell Inez yourself."

Dieter grinned. I tried not to picture the unrequited letters he would write.

"Inez is a poor correspondent," I warned.

We stepped into my cabin. He undressed standing next to the folded-down bed. I tried not to imagine what Boris would think. Dieter handed me his stiff jacket, shirt, and pants, looking awkward in only his shorts and undershirt.

I changed in the bathroom, palms slick from nerves. I rolled the trouser cuffs up on the inside and pinned them in place. The jacket sleeves extended a centimeter over my hands. A close-enough fit. I slipped my Luger into the right pants pocket.

When I came out, I handed Dieter one of the zeppelin's robes. "In case you get cold."

He shrugged into the robe gratefully, more modest than chilled.

With trembling hands I pulled his cap on my head and walked out to the hall. I slipped sleeping powder into the coffee, sure that Anton would not drink it. I stirred thoroughly and rapped on the door.

"Steward here with your dinner." I deepened my voice, hoping the door would muffle the sound further.

"Come in. It's unlocked," called Frau Röhm, as her son had done only days before. A chill chased down my spine.

I opened the door more gently than Hitler and bumped the laden cart over the threshhold. I kept my head down. Just as I had for her son, I poured Frau Röhm coffee. She too did not bother to look beyond my uniform. The rich scent of Bolivian coffee filled the room.

A slow smile spread across Anton's face when he recognized me. I touched my left eyebrow, our secret farewell gesture, then turned to go before he gave us away.

"Wait," she said, voice full of command. I steeled myself and turned, eyes still downcast. I could overpower her, but keeping her quiet would be another matter, especially with Dieter next door. "Your tip."

I held out my hand, palm up. She dropped a coin in it. I bowed, already on my way out. I did not trust my voice to thank her.

I closed her door behind me, then took three giant steps to my own.

"And?" Dieter asked when I stepped inside. He held the robe tightly closed. "What did they say?"

"They did not even know it was me." I struggled to control my breathing. It would not do to make him suspicious. "She even tipped me." I gave him the coin she had handed me, plus a few of my own. I hoped that he would not get into too much trouble tomorrow.

"I will tell them in the morning. What a lovely surprise it will be!" I twirled his hat in my hands with forced energy. "I wish Inez were here to see it."

I changed into my own clothes, transferred the Luger to my pocket, and relinquished the bathroom.

When he emerged, he held out a callused hand. I handed him a sheet of paper with a false address in Bolivia. I did not want to deceive him, but saw no other way.

He folded it carefully in half and stuck it in the inner pocket of his uniform jacket. "Thank you."

I nodded without meeting his eyes and ushered him out of my room.

I sat on my canvas stool and waited. I had to give her time to drink the coffee and let the drug take effect. She must be tired already. It was growing late. Orange and red streaked across the sky, eventually fading to purple and indigo, the glorious sunset promised by the woman at the ticket counter. Was Frau Röhm watching it too?

The sky darkened. I could wait no longer, one way or the other. When the zeppelin docked in Switzerland, Anton and I must disembark. If we did not, we would be playing cat and mouse all the way to South America. It was only a matter of time before the staff from the previous voyage gave me away.

I put my hand in my pocket and touched the cold gun. Would a gunshot ignite the entire zeppelin? I pictured its silver surface turning into a fireball, the nose tipping toward the ground. Everyone on board would die. Nonsense, I told myself sternly. How much harm could a single gunshot really do?

I stepped into the empty hall and crept the three steps to her door. Slowly, I turned the silver knob. If she slept, I did not want to wake her. Gathering my courage, I opened the door and stepped inside.

Electric light illuminated a room like my own, stools pushed to the side, beds folded down, suitcases neatly closed. I stepped past the food cart and peered at the bunks.

Anton slept curled up on the upper bunk like a puppy. From the lower bunk Frau Röhm stared at me in astonishment. I looked back just as astonished. She probably expected our SS tail had picked me up and expected me to be in a Gestapo interrogation center. For my part, I had expected her to be asleep. As usual, we were both disappointed.

She opened her mouth to scream and I raised the Luger. She froze. Anton sat and rubbed his eyes sleepily.

"Stay quiet." Her cold blue eyes took my measure, trying to decide if I would shoot her. I could not see the coffeepot from where I stood. Was it empty, or full?

"You will bring out the entire crew if you fire that." She sat and straightened her nightcap. Her hand smoothed an old-fashioned cotton nightshirt edged in lace. She looked like the grandmother from Little Red Riding Hood. But she was the wolf.

"I do not need it."

She cocked her head to the side, interested. The upper bunk creaked when Anton moved forward.

"Stay back, Anton," I said, louder than I had intended. I did not want her to take him hostage. He yelped and crawled to the back corner of his bunk.

"You are indeed resourceful," she said. "You and Ernst would have made a good match."

I almost laughed. "The time for that is long since past."

"That is your fault. If you had only married him, he would be alive and we would all be safe in Munich." She shifted in her bunk. I knew she measured the space between us, trying to find an advantage. I kept my distance.

"Did you like your coffee?" She looked puzzled.

Her eyes widened and her veined left hand fluttered to her throat. Then she smiled. "I never drink coffee in the evening."

Truth or lie? I kept up my bluff.

"Thank you for the excellent tip." I held the barrel steady, though the gun grew heavier with each passing second. I could not hold it forever. "Most unexpected."

"I believe you thrive on the unexpected." She blinked. Her eyelids fought to open again. The drug? Or did she try to fool me?

Her right hand emerged from under her pillow holding a pistol. The barrel pointed right at my chest. "Checkmate."

"Not quite." I struggled to keep my voice as level as her barrel. "I slipped something into your food."

She raised an eyebrow skeptically, but her eyes looked glassy. Or did I imagine it?

"I think you can feel it." At least I hoped so.

She shook her head, but fear crept into her eyes. Good.

"You have to wonder," I continued, as the gun wavered in her hand. "If you will ever wake up from it."

Anton gasped from the top bunk. "Mother?" His voice sounded shocked and hurt. Even after all she had put him through, she was still his grandmother. If there is a later, I will explain it to you, I promised silently.

"Then I had best shoot you now."

"Unless the poison requires an antidote," I lied grimly. "Then you will need me."

She stared at me. She raised the pistol shakily.

I stepped forward and snatched the gun from her grip. Her hands clawed for my throat. I dropped both weapons and grabbed her thin wrists. I pinned her tiny form on the bunk with my weight.

"When you wake." I leaned harder on her struggling form. "Thank your lucky stars that I am a better woman than you."

"Lucky," she slurred. She gave a small laugh and fought until her eyes rolled back.

I did not move for several long minutes. Then I slid to one side and checked her pulse. Steady, but slow. She slept.

"Come, Anton."

I stood and he leaped into my arms, knocking us backward against the wall. "I knew you'd come. I knew it."

My eyes were wet when I tousled his smooth blond hair. "Always."

While he dressed, I pushed the cart outside for Dieter to collect. We gathered our belongings. I insisted that he bring the suitcase of clothing she had purchased him. Leaving it might arouse suspicion.

I arranged her ivory wedding dress next to the bed so it would be the first thing she saw when she awoke. She would know instantly what she had lost. And what I had won.

On top of the bodice I placed the receipt for the forms I filed with Frau Doppelgänger. She would need it to claim her son's body. I had Anton, and I had given her everything I had promised. Unlike her, I kept my word. We would step off the zeppelin in Switzerland, a little

over a week late. By the time she woke, she would be far over the At-
lantic Ocean, and alone.

The zeppelin's motors changed pitch and we raced down the corridor, hopefully for the last time.

We positioned ourselves at the end of the small line of passengers
leaving in Switzerland. We were free again. Soon we would be reunited with Boris. I hoped. I tousled his hair, and he did not move my
hand. Instead he tapped my arm and I ducked my head down to his.

"Will she be all right?" he whispered.

"In a few hours she will wake up, as well as ever," I whispered back.

"But as angry as a wolverine stung by a bee." His eyes smiled up at
mine, and my stomach relaxed. I pulled him into a hug and kissed the
top of his head.

He hugged me back. "We are in Switzerland?"

I knew what he wanted. I opened my satchel and pulled out a sheet
of paper and my jade-green fountain pen. He carefully printed his first
name, then drew a feather. He folded an airplane, straight on the
creases.

We stepped onto the well-lit Swiss airfield hand in hand.

Halfway between the zeppelin and the terminal, he dropped my
hand and launched his white airplane into the night. His wrist snapped
forward. The ring of bruises from the handcuffs had already begun to
fade.

Abitur. German equivalent of a high school diploma.

Alexanderplatz. Central police station for Berlin through World War II. Also called "The Alex."

Bahnhof. Train station or subway station.

El Dorado. Gay bar in Berlin that was popular during the 1920s and early 1930s, closed by the Nazis, and reopened in the 1990s.

Ernst Röhm. Early member of the National Socialist Party and close friend to Adolf Hitler, often credited with being the man most responsible for bringing Hitler to power in the early days. Openly gay.

Der Führer. The leader. Term used to refer to Adolf Hitler, leader of the National Socialist Party.

Hall of the Unnamed Dead. Hall in the Alexanderplatz police station that showed framed photographs of unidentified bodies found by the police.

Heinrich Himmler. Head of the Schutzstaffel. He eventually oversaw all police and security forces, including the Gestapo, concentration camps, and extermination camps. He was named the greatest mass murderer of all time by *Der Spiegel* magazine.

Hotel Adlon. Expensive hotel in Berlin, built in 1907. It quickly became known for its vast wine cellars and well-heeled clientele. On May 2, 1945, the main building was burned to the ground, either accidentally or on purpose, by Russian soldiers. The East German government opened a surviving wing as a hotel, but it was demolished in 1961 to create the no-man's-land around the Berlin Wall. A new Hotel Adlon was rebuilt on the original location and opened on August 23, 1997.

Il Duce. The leader. Term used to refer to Benito Mussolini, leader of the Italian fascist party and later prime minister of fascist Italy.

Kaiser. Leader of Germany before the founding of the Weimar Republic. After World War I, the last kaiser, Wilhelm II, abdicated his throne and fled to the Netherlands.

Kinder, Küche, Kirche (children, kitchen, church). Policy of the Nazi party on where women belonged.

Kommissar. Rank in the police department similar to a lieutenant.

Munich Post (*Münchener Post*). Newspaper in Bavaria that was very critical of the National Socialist Party until it was taken over in 1933.

National Political Institute for Education (Potsdam). Boarding schools set up by the Nazis. Many students were used as child soldiers and died during the last months of the war.

National Socialist German Workers Party (Nazi party). Party led by Adolf Hitler that eventually assumed control of Germany.

Night of the Long Knives. The Nazi purge that took place between June 30 and July 2, 1934. Although most victims, including Ernst Röhm, were members of the Sturmabteilung, many other political enemies of Hitler were also executed. The exact death toll is unknown.

Paragraph 175. Paragraph of the German penal code that made homosexuality a crime. Paragraph 175 was in place from 1871 to 1994. Under the Nazis, people convicted of Paragraph 175 offenses, which did not need to include physical contact, were sent to concentration camps, where many died.

Pfennigs. Similar to pennies. There were one hundred pfennigs in a Reichsmark.

Reich List of Unwanted Persons. The precompiled list of political enemies to be executed during the purge.

Reichsmark. Currency used by Germany from 1924 to 1948. The previous currency, the Papiermark, became worthless in 1923 due to hyperinflation. On January 1, 1923, one American dollar was worth nine thousand Papiermarks. By November 1923 one American dollar was worth 4.2 trillion Papiermarks. Fortunes were wiped out overnight. In 1924 the currency was revalued and remained fairly stable until the Wall Street crash in the United States in 1929. When the novel takes place, one American dollar was worth 2.54 Reichsmarks.

Reichstag. Elected legislative assembly representing the people of Germany.

Schultheiss pilsner. Pale lager brewed at the Schultheiss factory in Berlin.

Schutzstaffel (SS or Blackshirts). Nazi paramilitary organization founded as an elite force to be used as Hitler's personal bodyguards. Led by Heinrich Himmler.

Stadelheim Prison. Prison in Munich. Hitler, Röhm, and others were held there after their arrest for the Beer Hall Putsch in 1923. Röhm was executed there on July 2, 1934. In 1943, Sophie Scholl, Hans Scholl, and Christoph Probst were guillotined there for distributing anti-Nazi leaflets. The prison still exists today.

Sturmabteilung (SA, Brownshirts, or storm troopers). Nazi paramilitary organization that helped intimidate Hitler's opponents. Led by Ernst Röhm.

Tempelhof Airport. Famous airport in Berlin, remodeled under the Nazis, used in World War II, and the central airport for the Berlin Airlift of 1948. It was shut down in 2008.

Theodor Eicke. Commander of the Death's Head Division in the Waffen SS. He helped establish concentration camps in Nazi Germany. He either executed Röhm or witnessed the execution.

Zehlendorf. Wealthy borough in Berlin. Boris's house is on Kronprinzen Avenue in this borough, later renamed to Clayallee to honor General Clay, the American general who ordered the Berlin Airlift in 1948.

Author's Note

A Night of Long Knives is set in Germany in 1934, around the time of the Night of the Long Knives purge, when Hitler killed the leadership of the SA, including his old friend Ernst Röhm, and a long list of political enemies. Most characters in the book are fictional, and I took great liberties with those who weren't.

Although I carefully researched the events leading up to Ernst Röhm's death, I took artistic liberties to further the plot. As far as I know, he never fathered (or pretended to father) any children. Nor was he planning a wedding that weekend. Historical sources say that Röhm was murdered by Theodor Eicke and another SS officer as I described. Hans Frank did visit him in Stadelheim, where Röhm told him, "All revolutions devour their own children."

Little is known about his mother, Emilie Röhm, and nothing that she does in *A Night of Long Knives* actually occurred.

The executions at Stadelheim Prison and Lichterfelde Barracks are historically documented, although no one knows how many people were killed in those forty-eight hours. Estimates range from Hitler's claim of sixty-one to seven thousand (Winston Churchill, in *The Gathering Storm*). At the trials in Munich in 1957 the number was set at more than one thousand. It's unlikely that we will ever know the exact death toll, as all records were destroyed shortly after the purge under the orders of Göring and Himmler. The edict legalizing the purge I mention in the book was, of course, real.

Bella Fromm existed and wrote a detailed diary chronicling her time as a journalist in Berlin under the Nazis, *Blood & Banquets: A Berlin Social Diary 1930–1938*. I suspect Hannah will meet her again in a future book.

Sefton Delmer, likewise, was a real British journalist who befriended Ernst Röhm, who believed Delmer was a spy. Delmer was acquainted with Hitler, Goebbels, Göring, and other top Nazis, as documented in his witty autobiography, *Trail Sinister*. Later in the war, Sefton Delmer approached Ian Fleming (who worked for British Intelligence, but is more famous for creating James Bond and *Chitty Chitty Bang Bang*) and was hired to create black propaganda radio broadcasts into Germany, and later to German submarine crews, to damage morale. He had no known involvement with smuggling out information about the Night of the Long Knives, although he did publish a "purge list" of some of those executed and was given forty-eight hours to leave Germany on July 6, 1934 (mere days after Hannah sees him for the last time). Also, his friends called him "Tom" instead of "Sefton," but I thought the name Sefton was more evocative so I used it instead.

For plot reasons, I changed the time line of the executions, and I could never determine where Hannah would have had to go to claim Röhm's remains. I chose Lichterfelde because it seemed plausible and got her to Berlin. Also, I scheduled the *Graf Zeppelin* to stop in Zürich and Berlin, although that week it was scheduled to stop in Friedrichshafen, Germany.

For more information on this period of German history, I consulted *The Night of the Long Knives* by Paul Maracin for a quick summary, *The Gathering Storm* by Winston Churchill, and *The Rise and Fall of the Third Reich* by William Shirer. For specific, heartbreaking details of life under the Nazis, I highly recommend Victor Klemperer's diary *I Will Bear Witness: A Diary of the Nazi Years, 1933–1941*. Mel Gordon's *Voluptuous Panic: The Erotic World of Weimar Berlin* exhaustively documents the bars and nightclubs of the era.

Turn the page for a sneak peek at Rebecca Cantrell's new novel

A Game of Lies

Available Summer 2011

1

The crowd pushed the three of us between the Marathon Towers toward the Berlin Olympic Stadium. The left tower displayed a simple clock. On the right, both politically and geographically, hung a twisted iron cross—the swastika. I understood the message: it was 1936, and the time of the Nazis had come.

Inside the stadium I shied away from the enclosed white cabins that signaled press boxes. The journalists inside knew me as German crime reporter Hannah Vogel, wanted by the Gestapo for kidnapping the young son of the now-deceased Ernst Röhm. I nervously tilted my wide-brimmed hat to conceal my face and moved with the crowd down the stairs. Surely I would be difficult to notice among so many faces.

My current identity was Adelheid Zinsli, neutral Swiss reporter and hopefully incognito part-time spy for the British. I looked over at my contact, SS Hauptsturmführer Lars Lang, as we moved toward our seats in the stadium. Years of our deadly game made most trips feel routine, but this time I was frightened.

Lars and I pretended to be lovers, a fiction he enjoyed, and every few months we switched off weekends in our home cities of Berlin and Zürich. But instead of a few days, my editor had insisted that this time I stay in Berlin for a full two weeks to cover the Olympic Games. To keep my job, I had agreed to attend events clogged with my old colleagues.

The crowd stopped and I bumped against Lars's friend, chemistry professor Andreas Huber. When he caught my arm, his sweaty hand lingered there.

I pulled my arm free. He let go reluctantly and I shot him an inquisitive glance. Lars did not seem to notice. "Forgive me for running into you," I said.

"Of course." Andreas looked down at me with a crooked smile. "Quite a crowd."

"I believe that the German government expects one hundred thousand people for the opening ceremony." I quoted the statistic just to make conversation. I did not add that what the Nazis expected, they too often made happen.

"I hope it doesn't rain on them all." Andreas looked at the overcast sky.

"We will have to hope for sunlight," I said. "Even the Führer cannot control the weather—"

"There's a bar nearby," Lars interrupted. He pushed his black hair back. Longer now than he usually kept it, the new length made him look less militaristic. "We have time for another belt."

"I must stay in the stadium. For the paper." I hiked my leather satchel up on my shoulder. A drink sounded like just the thing to calm my nerves, but Lars did not need another one.

"So dedicated." Lars glared at me. "To your job."

"Not such a bad quality, dedication." Andreas took Lars's arm and led us down the nearest row to a seat at the end. A staunch party man, he understood the possible consequences of Lars's indiscretions. And his own responsibility to report them.

Lars sat, peeled off his dark brown suit jacket, clumsily folded it in half, and rolled up his wrinkled shirtsleeves. He caught me watching and blew me a sloppy kiss. If my life did not depend on the world thinking we were lovers, I would have left without a backward glance. Instead I put a warning hand on his bare arm.

Although he was not, he looked harmless in civilian garb. Ordinarily, he cleaved to his black SS uniform, but an order had come down requesting all SS and SA members to refrain from wearing uniforms to the Games.

The German government had issued the order in response to criticism from the Winter Olympics in Garmisch-Partenkirchen the previous winter. Reporters had commented on the number of uniformed Germans in the crowds. This time we would have to guess how many men were trained for warfare.

Although I noted the new order, I would not write about it. If I did, I would not be able to move freely into Germany. Instead of exposing Nazi politics, any story I wrote would have to extol Nazi pageantry.

Indeed, it felt like a royal court with the peasants awaiting a thundering and massive coronation. I spotted a complete orchestra, several military bands with gleaming brass instruments, and a choir dressed in white that must have numbered a thousand. All calculated to impress German and international spectators. Nazis staged spectacles as cleverly as ancient Greeks.

My eleven-year-old adopted son, Anton, was far fonder than I of such events. He would have adored it. I wished I could take photographs for him, but foreign journalists were forbidden from taking pictures at the Games. I would tell Anton details when I got back home and retrieved him from Boris, my one-time lover, but for now I tried not to think of him. Superstitious, I knew, but I did not like to bring even thoughts of Anton into Germany these days.

When I searched for a pen, my fingers rolled over my perfume atomizer, a costly French gift from Boris. The tiny mother-of-pearl creation was called a Le Kid and evoked memories of the Charlie Chaplin movie and happy times together.

When this assignment came up, Boris had begged me to stay safe in Switzerland. When I refused, he ended our five-year relationship. It had been more than a month, and I felt unmoored. I woke every night with my hand searching for him across empty sheets.

I dropped the atomizer and rooted around until I found my pen. I sketched the arc of the stadium first, then the crowd, the bands, the special booths, and the far-off oval of the field. I had often drawn pictures of courtroom scenes in my days as a crime reporter and I enjoyed using the skills again. A shadow fell across the page and I looked up.

Overhead the *Hindenburg* ponderously circled the stadium. A white Olympic flag, bigger than a house, flapped under her gondola. The familiar black swastika stood out on her tail. The Nazis owned even the skies.

Although Anton and I had traveled by zeppelin from South America to Germany a few years before, the giant silver shape made me nervous. One spark in the wrong location and explosive hydrogen would ignite and shower a stadium of eager spectators, including me, with flaming debris.

Andreas followed my gaze. "They are very safe. All precautions have been taken to ensure it."

"Yet hydrogen is quite flammable, is it not?" I countered.

"Under the correct conditions, everything is explosive." Lars draped a heavy arm across my shoulders and I gave him an annoyed look. "And don't I always protect you?"

"So far, we have escaped fiery death," I said. "But that is no reason to let our guard down."

Andreas laughed.

"Must you always keep your guard up?" Lars leaned in close and mouthed the word "Hannah."

If he said my real name aloud, fiery death might look like a good option, and he knew it. I turned the worry in my voice to anger. "It has served me well so far."

In the past, I had relied on his natural reserve and the caution he had cultivated during his years as a policeman to maintain enough discretion to keep us both out of trouble. But, as with everything else, those rules had changed. I had to figure out a strategy to deal with him before he got us both killed.

To spite me, he kissed me on the nose. I smelled Korn schnapps. "Back in a flash, Spatz."

I wanted to tell him that I was not his sparrow. Instead I smiled so unconvincingly that he snorted out a laugh. He forced his way down the row and hastened up the stairs. I hoped his destination was the men's room and not the bar. I longed to abandon everything and head back to Switzerland, but I worried about how I could support Anton without the newspaper job. We did not have Boris to rely on anymore.

I moved to the seat next to Andreas, leaving my satchel to hold Lars's seat for him from the crowds that thronged into the stadium. The smell of the antiseptic tar soap Andreas favored drifted to me. He and Lars seemed like an odd match. They had met back when Lars was still a policeman and Andreas often testified as an expert witness about the presence of poison in corpses. I wondered what they had in common, save an early interest in National Socialism. Perhaps they had grown close during those long and fevered meetings.

"How long has he been like this?" I asked in a low voice to prevent those nearby from overhearing. The noise of so many excited voices chattering made it unlikely, but you always had to be careful in Germany these days.

"Off and on for about two months. Worse in the past month."

My stomach sank. "Do you know why?"

"Do you?" His brown eyes were curious and perhaps accusatory. What had Lars told him about our relationship? Did he know it was a sham?

"Should I?" I met his challenge with one of my own.

He spread his thin hands wide in a gesture of peace. "I am not trying to make problems. I fear you have enough of your own."

"Have I?" I struggled to appear calm while I wondered what he thought my problems were. Had Lars told him the true reason for my trips to Berlin?

"I apologize." Andreas kept his voice low. "I did not intend to imply anything."

"What would there be to imply?"

"Indeed," he answered.

We sat in awkward silence until Lars slid in next to me, face shades paler. He gave me an apologetic look. "I believe I have a touch of stomach flu."

"I hope you feel better soon," I said, as if I believed that his trip to the men's room had more to do with flu than it did with alcohol. At least now he seemed fairly sober.

When the orchestra curtailed our conversation, I closed my eyes in relief, concentrating on the music and the weak sun on my arms. With my eyes shut, I did not see the swastikas, and I pretended that Germany was as free as it had been when I first escaped with Anton five years before.

But it was not and that was why I was here. I had to do everything I could to keep the Nazis from taking over Europe as they had taken over Germany. The Nazi regime had killed many already, and I feared that many more would die before they were removed from power. Anything I could do to save those lives, I had to do, and not just because it was morally right, but also because I bore some blame. To save my adopted son, Anton, I had traded my chance to discredit Nazi leader Ernst Röhm by publishing his sexually explicit letters. Perhaps their publication would have made no difference, but perhaps my decision had helped the Nazis more than I dared to contemplate.

The music faded. Fanfare trumpeted from the fortress-like Marathon Towers. Hitler must have arrived. I opened my eyes and sighed. No more pretending.

Instead I pulled battered field glasses from my satchel and trained them on Hitler as he descended the stairs in a khaki suit and knee-high boots in front of two men in dark frock coats and top hats. Both wore the heavy gold chains of the International Olympic Committee around their necks. A larger group trailed behind.

Everyone rose to scream and clap. I stood too. Tens of thousands of arms shot up in the Hitler salute, mine, regrettably, among them. I dared not stand out. I wished I knew how many in this forest of arms saluted out of fear, and how many out of patriotism. I quickly dropped my arm and picked up my field glasses with both hands. Surely demonstrating a desire to see the Führer up close would excuse me from continuing the vile salute.

Hitler marched along the crimson cinder track while strains of

Wagner, his favorite composer, rose above adoring screams. A girl in a cornflower blue sundress, blond braids pinned up in a wreath, ran to Hitler. She looked about five, the same age Anton had been when he showed up dirty and alone on my doorstep. I hated the way the little girl lent the proceedings an air of gentleness and innocence.

She dropped into a curtsy, bare knee pressed onto red cinders. Her upraised hands offered a bouquet of posies. Smiling indulgently, Hitler took the flowers and pulled her to her feet. He patted her head once before trotting to his loge of honor. The child scampered off the field and I lost sight of her in the crowd. Her sweet and simple gesture would be reported across the globe tomorrow. Another shrewd Nazi propaganda victory.

I glanced at Lars's wristwatch. I needed to sneak away soon to meet my one-time mentor, Peter Weill. Peter claimed to have uncovered something that would change the course of the war we were both certain would come. Thousands of lives were at stake, he had said.

I had a few minutes before my meeting with Peter, but I decided to leave while the men were distracted so I would not have to invent an excuse. I had not told Lars about my meeting with Peter and hoped to keep it from him. The less he knew about anything beyond our work together, the better, especially now that he seemed to be falling apart.

I stepped through standing crowds and lifted voices, hoping that Lars would not follow. I suspected that he trusted me no more than I trusted him, and he kept very close to me when I visited Berlin, but perhaps he was drunk and distracted enough by the spectacle to let me alone.

I hurried up the stone stairs. At the top I turned and ducked behind one of the wide square pillars that lined the corridor that ran along the upper rim of the stadium. Spectators filled even the topmost row of seats, but the pillar hid me from their view. With all eyes on the spectacle, I felt blessedly alone. I breathed in the dusty smell of limestone.

Silence descended as the last notes of the German national anthem died away. The "Horst Wessel Song" followed. Written by a Nazi killed by a Communist in 1930, it had served as the accompaniment for more Nazi events than I cared to think about. A hundred voices sang it when a Nazi mob attacked Anton and me in front of Wertheim, a Jewish-owned department store, in 1931.

A hand grabbed my shoulder. I gasped.

"Shush," said a familiar rasping voice.

"Peter!" Rumpled navy suit, fedora tilted too far back on his head, grin as wide as ever. Peter Weill had mentored me at the *Berliner Tage-blatt* and insisted that I take over his crime beat when he moved to Dresden to retire. I had not seen him in years, since before I fled, but it had been his urgent message, more than anything else, that made me brave coming to the Games. Seeing him, I was glad I had.

His faded blue eyes sparkled with excitement when he pulled me into an embrace. Never large, now he felt like a bundle of sticks. I hugged him back with care, conscious of every one of his seventy-four years.

"Hannah!" I winced at the sound of my name. He gave me an appraising look. "It is good to see you again."

I stepped back and glanced up and down the empty corridor. "Like-wise. But we are supposed to meet farther down. How did you find me here, and early?"

"Always so suspicious." He chuckled. "Made you the best Peter Weill."

"After you, of course." I had taken over his name when I took over his beat at the newspaper; someone else used it now. "So, how did you find me?"

"I've been watching you for over an hour."

I imagined him dividing the stadium into sections and methodically sweeping each with binoculars, patient and thorough. And, like so many things he did, it had worked despite the odds. "Have you?"

"You and your SS consort. With your blond hair and blue eyes, you are quite the Aryan prize, I see."

"Why do you think he is SS?" I knew better than to lie to Peter directly.

Military music and applause swelled. Below athletes marched in, starting with Greece.

"Did I teach you nothing? It's how they walk. How they stand. Their sense of entitlement." He ticked items off on his thumb and twiglike fingers. "They don't need uniforms anymore. It's under their skins."

Correct and dangerously astute, as always. I kept quiet.

"I could also see, even from across the stadium, that you are not pleased with the one who is pawing at you. Although he fancies you. I think Huber does too."

"It is a very long, very private story." I paused. "How do you know Andreas's name?"

"Chemist. Used him as a source once." His blue eyes shifted left, away from mine.

I would follow up on how he knew Andreas later. For now I hugged him again, smelling pipe tobacco and whiskey. "It has been far too long."

"Hasn't it though? But I did not skulk around here to question your dubious taste in men. I'm here because I have news." His voice rose on the last word, like a thousand times before.

I smiled. News. Peter always had news.

He studied the empty hall. Then he stepped closer and lowered his voice as if to keep unseen watchers from hearing. "I've found out something horrible. Something that will show the world definitively that the Nazis are not peace seekers or peace keepers, or whatever they call themselves these days."

Two huge Olympic bells, cast for the occasion, tolled homage to Hitler and the Games; softly at first, but steadily increasing in volume. "And you would tell me this, though you just saw me with the SS? Seems like bad judgment."

He grinned. "You're not one of them. Whatever you're doing over there, it has more to do with Bella than them."

"Bella?" I cocked a curious eyebrow, knowing I would not fool him. My head throbbed with the peals of the bell.

"She gets things out, doesn't she? And I guess you work for her."

"Interesting guess." I did not work for the well-connected socialite reporter Bella Fromm, but he was close enough. When Lars delivered me canisters of film containing pictures of top secret SS documents, I couriered them not to Bella, but to a British espionage contact provided by an old friend and journalist, Sefton Delmer.

"I want you to get information out. Information and something else." His faded eyes sharpened as he studied me.

He pulled a silver flask from his hip pocket. Peter's Famous Flask. He carried it everywhere and started drinking from it when events got well underway. He offered it to me and I knew that the news was sure to come soon.

I took a small sip of whiskey to be polite. Although Peter's expensive whiskey tasted smooth as always, watching Lars today had soured any taste for alcohol. "And if I say I have no idea what you are talking about?"

Peter took the proffered flask and raised it in a mock toast. "Then I'd be proud of you."

"If you think Bella can get your information out, why not go to her directly?" As curious as I was to know Peter's news, something did not make sense.

His gnarled fingers lined up with geometric patterns engraved in his flask. "We don't move in the same circles."

A lie. But why? I knew that he and Bella were acquainted. The lie appeared pointless, and he did not believe in pointless lies. "When does the pfennig drop?"

His face crinkled in a smile. "There is a certain package that she can't deliver. But you can."

"Package?" Bella's network of sources and helpers was far more extensive than mine. I would have thought that she could deliver anything. A wave of heat ran through my body. I brought my hand to my forehead. I could not have a sudden fever. That made no sense.

Peter took a swig of whiskey and coughed. He sniffed the flask. "Peter?"

He wiped his trembling chin. "I don't feel well."

Tears coursed down his cheeks. Sweat broke out on his brow. Saliva dripped from both sides of his mouth. He reached up to wipe it off, knocking his fedora to the ground. I thought of picking it up, but took his arm instead.

"Are you in any pain? Chest pain?" His pulse raced under my fingertips. My own heartbeat sped up.

"No." His voice rasped.

"Perhaps you should sit?" We took a step toward a nearby bench.

"Hannah—" His face darkened to brick-red. Not a sign of a heart attack. I listed conditions in my head, but none seemed to match his symptoms.

I wrapped my arm around his thin shoulders and dragged his trembling body another step toward the bench. Should I leave him and fetch a doctor? Did I dare leave him alone? Could I find one even if I did?

Before I decided what to do, Peter collapsed against my side, convulsing. Together we fell heavily to the concrete. My hip took the brunt of our weight and the flask clattered to the floor.

"Peter!" I rolled off his too-light body. His pupils shrank to pinpoints.

His bowels let go. He twitched once, then lay quite still. I knew what to expect before I lay my cheek against his wet lips. "Please. Oh, please."

No breath.

No need to check his pulse.